was born in 1873. T...
gentleman, from the ...
living, which she did ...
then in north Londo...
mother committed suicide, the family broke up and Dorothy
Richardson began a new life in London as secretary assistant to a
Harley Street dentist. During her years in London her friends were
the socialist and avant garde intellectuals of the day. She became an
intimate of H. G. Wells, who, among others, encouraged her to
write. She began in journalism and for the rest of her life she lived
as a writer, earning very little. In 1917 she married the young
painter, Alan Odle, who died in 1948. For the whole of their married
life they lived their winters in Cornwall and their summers in
London. Dorothy Richardson's journalism includes scores of essays,
reviews, stories, poems and sketches written and published between
1902 and 1949. Her journalism was her livelihood but the writing of
PILGRIMAGE was her vocation; this long novel absorbed her
artistic energy between 1914 and her death in 1957.

PUBLISHING HISTORY

FIRST EDITIONS:
Pointed Roofs (1915), *Backwater* (1916), *Honeycomb* (1917), *The
Tunnel* (Feb 1919), *Interim* (Dec 1919), *Deadlock* (1921), *Revolving
Lights* (1923), *The Trap* (1925), *Oberland* (1927), *Dawn's Left Hand*
(1931) — all published by Duckworth: *Clear Horizon* (1935) —
published by J. M. Dent & Cresset Press

COLLECTED EDITIONS:
Pilgrimage (including *Dimple Hill*), 4 vols, 1938 — J. M. Dent &
Cresset Press, London: A. Knopf, New York

Pilgrimage (including *March Moonlight*), 4 vols, 1967 — J. M. Dent,
London: A. Knopf, New York

Pilgrimage, 4 vols, 1976 — Popular Library, New York

Pilgrimage, 4 vols, 1979 — Virago, London
   Volume 1: *Pointed Roofs, Backwater, Honeycomb*
   Volume 2: *The Tunnel, Interim*
   Volume 3: *Deadlock, Revolving Lights, The Trap*
   Volume 4: *Oberland, Dawn's Left Hand, Clear Horizon, Dimple
         Hill, March Moonlight*

DOROTHY M. RICHARDSON

PILGRIMAGE

with an introduction by Gill Hanscombe

I

Pointed Roofs
Backwater
Honeycomb

Virago
London

TO
WINIFRED RAY

Published by VIRAGO Limited,
5 Wardour Street, London W1V 3HE,
1979, in association with
Mrs Sheena Odle and Mark Paterson & Associates

Copyright under the Berne Convention

Introduction copyright © 1979 by Gill Hanscombe

ISBN 0 86068 100 9

Reproduced Photolitho in Great Britain by
J. W. Arrowsmith Limited Bristol

CONTENTS

INTRODUCTION

OF THE early twentieth-century English modernists, there is no one who has been more neglected than Dorothy Miller Richardson. There are several reasons for this. First, the style she forged in the writing of *Pointed Roofs*, the first volume of the *Pilgrimage* sequence, was new and difficult, later earning the nomination 'stream-of-consciousness'. *Pointed Roofs* was published in 1915 and was, therefore, the first example of this technique in English, predating both Joyce and Woolf, its more famous exponents. Secondly, the thoughts and feelings of its protagonist, Miriam Henderson, are explicitly feminist, not in the sense of arguing for equal rights and votes for women, but in the more radical sense of insisting on the authority of a woman's experience and world view. Thirdly, *Pointed Roofs* explores Miriam's sympathetic response to German culture and in 1915, when it was first published, this was an unpopular subject which contributed to the establishing of adverse critical reaction. Undaunted, however, by ambivalent response to her work, Richardson persisted in her task of completing the *Pilgrimage* sequence, a task which occupied her, intermittently, for the rest of her life.

Richardson regarded *Pilgrimage* as one novel and its constituent thirteen volumes as chapters. She regarded it, also, as fiction, even though the life of Miriam Henderson so closely resembles her own. The reason for this was that Richardson, after many attempts to write a more conventional novel, resolved finally that she must write about the subject she knew best, which was, she maintained, her own life. This is not to claim that every incident and every character in the novel add up to a photographic reproduction of Richardson's early life; but it is to claim that the genuine impulse of her work derives from the tension between her own life and that of Miriam, her fictional *alter ego*. The whole world of *Pilgrimage* is filtered through Miriam's mind alone; the reader sees what she sees and is never told what any of the other characters sees. Fiction usually means that the author invents or imagines his or her material. Richardson used the real material of her own life for her writing, and she used herself as her central character. The fictional process in *Pilgrimage* consists in how she shaped and organised and interpreted that material. There is, therefore, much in her life and personality to lend interest to her work.

She was born in Abingdon, Berkshire, on 17 May 1873, the third of four daughters. Her father, Charles Richardson, came from a family who had achieved financial success through a grocery business, but Charles longed to give up 'trade' and to become a gentleman. He sold the business and lived off the proceeds for some years. His wife, Mary Taylor, came from East Coker in Somerset, from a family whose name was listed among the gentry in local registers. When she was five years old, Dorothy Richardson was sent for a year to a small private school where she learned to read and spell and where nothing else interested her. When she was six, the family moved to the south coast, near Worthing, owing to her mother's ill health and her father's financial straits. Her school made no impression on her. In Dorothy's eleventh year, her father's investments improved and he moved his family up to London. Her life at this stage included croquet, tennis, boating, skating, dances and music; apart from musical evenings at home, she was introduced to the classics, to Wagner and Chopin and to Gilbert and Sullivan. She was taught by a governess, of whom she later wrote: 'if she could, [she] would have formed us to the almost outmoded pattern of female education: the minimum of knowledge and a smattering of various "accomplishments" . . . for me . . . she was torment unmitigated.' After this, she was sent to Southborough House, whose headmistress was a disciple of Ruskin, where the pupils were encouraged to think for themselves. Here Richardson studied French, German, literature, logic and psychology. At this point, her father, through disastrous speculation, lost the greater part of his resources, which forced Richardson at the age of seventeen, to seek employment as a teacher. Her first appointment, in a German school, later provided the material for *Pointed Roofs*.

After six months Richardson returned to England; two sisters were engaged to be married, the third had a position as a governess and her mother was near to a nervous collapse. In order to be near her mother, she took a post at the Misses Ayre's school in Finsbury Park, North London. Her impressions and experiences here provided the material for her second volume, *Backwater*. In 1893,

Charles Richardson was finally made a bankrupt; his house and possessions were sold and the family moved to a house in Chiswick, generously provided by John Arthur Batchelor, who became the husband of Dorothy's eldest sister Kate. By 1895, Richardson had moved from Finsbury Park to a post in the country as governess to two children, her experience of which is recorded in *Honeycomb*, her third volume. On 29 November 1895, while on holiday at Hastings with Dorothy, Mary Richardson committed suicide by cutting her throat with a kitchen knife.

After this, Richardson wanted a complete break: '. . . longing to escape from the world of women, I gladly accepted a post . . . a secretarial job, offering me the freedom I so desired.' She lived in a Bloomsbury attic on a salary of one pound per week. London became her great adventure. During these years she explored the world lying outside the enclosures of social life, which included writers, religious groups from Catholic to Unitarian and Quaker, political groups from the Conservative Primrose League to the Independent Labour Party and the Russian anarchists, and, through books and lectures, science and philosophy. At this time she found the philosophers 'more deeply exciting than the novelists'. These interests and activities provided the contextual material for her subsequent volumes. From working as a secretary, she gradually branched out into translations and freelance journalism which 'had promised release from routine work that could not engage the essential forces of my being. The small writing-table in my attic became the centre of my life'.

As a result of a series of sketches contributed to *The Saturday Review*, a reviewer urged her to try writing a novel. She later wrote that the suggestion 'both shocked and puzzled me. The material that moved me to write would not fit the framework of any novel I had experienced. I believed myself to be . . . intolerant of the romantic and the realist novel alike. Each . . . left out certain essentials and dramatized life misleadingly. Horizontally . . . Always . . . one was aware of the author and applauding, or deploring, his manipulations.' In 1917, at the age of forty-four, she married Alan Odle, an artist many years younger than herself. The marriage, in spite of misgivings, was a happy one, providing her with 'a new world, the missing link between those already explored'. She died in 1957 at the age of eighty-four.

A niece of Alan Odle's, who knew Dorothy Richardson and Alan Odle can add some human detail to this picture. In middle age, Richardson still had a golden heap of very long hair, piled on the top of her head; she had a 'massive' face, dark brown eyes, a clear skin, and pince-nez balanced on her nose, because she was 'always reading'. She created the impression of being tall, because she was 'so stately'. Alan Odle, in fact over six feet tall, was very thin, with waist-length hair wound around the outside of his head. He never cut his hair and rarely his fingernails, but since he had 'beautifully long elegant fingers', the image he presented was not an unattractive one. He, like Dorothy, had dark brown eyes and an ascetic face. They were very controlled together, extremely calm, always sitting side by side. Dorothy talked the most and late into the night; she seemed never to do 'anything ordinary' and had a voice 'like dark brown velvet'. She spoke very slowly indeed and was 'immensely impressive as a person'. Her life seemed to be arranged 'very very carefully' and she was 'not at all spontaneous in her actions'. She could 'only work on a certain image of herself' which was 'very cerebral'. It was hard for her to deal with ordinary people. Although she and Alan were affectionate with each other, they 'didn't touch'. Dorothy always called him 'sergeant', a joke arising from the fact that after only one day's service in the army, he had been discharged on medical grounds. Dorothy, in contrast to Alan, was 'very plump, with white creamy arms and very beautiful hands'; 'as she spoke she would screw up her eyes and slightly purse her mouth and everyone would listen'.

Charles Richardson often called Dorothy his 'son', as a compensation, it seems, for his lack of a male child. Indeed there is the evidence of Richardson's own recollections, as well as the portrayal in *Pilgrimage* of Miriam's relationship with her father, to reinforce the view that much of the original stimulus of the novel was owed to Dorothy's failure to adjust to the feminine role expected of her by late nineteenth-century middle-class society. But was it a failure? Or might it be seen as a triumph? Miriam's pilgrimage is partly the journey towards the resolution of that question. Because Richardson's father used all the family resources, it was necessary for the four daughters to make their own ways and accordingly, at the age of seventeen, Richardson answered an advertisement for an English student-teacher in a German academy for girls. *Pilgrimage* begins at this point, a point at which, for Miriam, the beginning of economic autonomy corresponds with the beginning of autonomous self-consciousness. From this point until her meeting with Alan Odle, Richardson's life is paralleled by that of her protagonist Miriam. The parallels are numerous and strictly consistent, as Richardson's letters and papers confirm.

Consistent with ordinary reality, also, are the descriptions of London life at the turn of the century. And equally convincing are the detailed accounts of households, lectures, activities and even conversations. The precision of Richardson's memory at some twenty to forty years distance is itself remarkable. It should not be assumed, nevertheless, that she saw her function as a writer in traditional autobiographical terms. On the contrary, she always insisted that her task was truly appropriate to fiction and that *Pilgrimage* should be judged as fiction. The mastery with which the author is able to transform the haphazard impressions of subjective experience into a thematically organised psychological narrative is the extent to which this work of fiction achieves artistic integrity.

Miriam's consciousness is the subject matter of this novel. And it seems to her that the experiences and perceptions of women have been brutally and unreasonably discounted by men. Nor has she any mercy for the majority of women who have, in her judgment, colluded with men in the suborning of their female gifts and attributes. Such women are satirised, caricatured and eventually dismissed. On the other hand, her stance is not topical. She does not become a Suffragette. She does not argue for a recognition of the equality of the sexes. She counts it a disadvantage to be a woman only in the sense that the men who govern society refuse to recognise and to allow women's contributions. In all other respects, she affirms, implicitly and explicitly, the value of her own perceptions and judgments, which by inference Richardson would have us generalise to include an equivalent valuation of all women's experiences. The particular virtues concomitant to such a feminism are the deliberate rejection of female role-playing, an insistence on personal honesty, a passionate independence and a pilgrimage towards self-awareness. Its particular vices are correspondingly stark: an inability to compromise adequately in relationship, a tendency to categorise alternative views as ignorance or obstinacy, a not always healthy flight from confrontation and a constant temptation to egocentricity.

These failings, however, Richardson allows Miriam to demonstrate; she is not content, in her authorial role, to idealise either Miriam's moral powers or her intellectual expertise. The qualities of intelligence Richardson most prized were not abstract rationalism and analytic empiricism, but the ability to perceive relationships between phenomena and the effort to synthesize feeling and reflection. This valuation has important consequences for her fiction, since it leads to a breaking down of the structural divisions we normally impose on experience, for example, the assumption that the external world has a finite integrity which is not influenced by subjective states and the further assumption that the division of time into past, present and future is necessary and meaningful. These major structures are, for her, simply categorisations of space and of time which our culture has developed in order to define for the individual his place in nature and in society. The subjective experience of time becomes the framework within which reality exists and the corresponding task of fiction becomes the conscious bringing into relationship of meaningful moments.

The impact on her style of this effort to delineate a female consciousness was radical. She stretched the unit of the sentence sometimes to the length of a long paragraph; she dispensed with the usual rules of punctuation, often substituting a series of full stops in place of explanation or other detail; she changed from one tense to another within a single paragraph; and she changed from the first person 'I' to the third person 'she' within a single reflection. She omitted details about people and places which readers could justifiably demand to know. Yet her feminist stance is not only evident in her uncompromising adherence to the unfolding of Miriam's consciousness and the forging of a new style. Together with her rejection of the technical conventions of the realist novel went a rejection of the values which the tradition of the English novel had attested. This rejection, however, was not formulated either from the principles of aesthetics or from a general philosophical orientation. It issued primarily from her conviction that the novel was an expression of the vision, fantasies, experiences and goals of men and that only rarely in the history of the novel could a genuine account of the female half of the human condition be found.

In *Pilgrimage*, Miriam often argues with Hypo Wilson about the male bias of the novel and in most of these exchanges the main burden of her argument is that authors seek to aggrandise themselves by constructing elaborate edifices which promise to reveal truths about life but which really reveal truths about the author. Nevertheless, like all radicals, Richardson is ambivalent at heart, recognising that a work of fiction must take its place among its predecessors. Therefore, in her own terms, she is forced to make an assessment of the tradition and to take a theoretical stand on the question of the structure and function of the novel. And because of her conviction that the traditional conventions express an overwhelmingly masculine world view, she must transform those conventions to accommodate Miriam's world view. For Richardson, therefore, words themselves become highly charged with ambivalence. The higher insights are above and beyond language.

There is in *Pilgrimage* a direct connection between Miriam's alienation from male consciousness and her distrust of language. Since style is necessary to a structured use of language, it must be acquired. However, she argues in *Deadlock*, style, because of its 'knowingness', is the property of men and of male writers in particular; men who feel 'the need for phrases'. For Miriam, the trouble with language is that it sets things 'in a mould that was apt to come up again'. The fear of things 'coming up again' can be seen as a fear of commitment, which later prompts the extravagance 'silence is reality'. That may, indeed, be true, but it is an impossible position for a writer to hold. Miriam is compelled, therefore, to rationalise her ambivalence by trying to understand how men use language.

Clearly in a work of such length, which owes less than is usual to previous models, there is bound to be some unevenness in technical control, an inevitability Richardson was fully aware of. In fact she often singled out particular sections of her text as failing to fulfil her intentions; such passages she marked 'I.R.', which stood for 'imperfectly realised'. Even so, *Pilgrimage* is a major contribution to our literature. Richardson's very original vision of female experience, together with her uncompromising experimental style, make the novel an extraordinary testament to the validity of female individuality. It is to be hoped that this first paperback edition of *Pilgrimage* to be published in England points to a new, rich and perceptive understanding of Richardson's achievement.

Gillian E Hanscombe, St Hugh's College, Oxford, 1979

FOREWORD

Although the translation of the impulse behind his youthful plan for a tremendous essay on Les Forces humaines *makes for the population of his great cluster of novels with types rather than with individuals, the power of a sympathetic imagination, uniting him with each character in turn, gives to every portrait the quality of a faithful self-portrait, and his treatment of backgrounds, contemplated with an equally passionate interest and themselves, indeed, individual and unique, would alone qualify Balzac to be called the father of realism.*

Less deeply concerned with the interplay of human forces, his first English follower portrays with complete fidelity the lives and adventures of inconspicuous people, and for a while, when in the English literary world it began its career as a useful label, realism was synonymous with Arnold Bennett.

But whereas both Balzac and Bennett, while representing, the one in regard to a relatively concrete and coherent social system, the other in regard to a society already showing signs of disintegration, the turning of the human spirit upon itself, may be called realists by nature and unawares, their immediate successors possess an articulate creed. They believe themselves to be substituting, for the telescopes of the writers of romance whose lenses they condemn as both rose-coloured and distorting, mirrors of plain glass.

By 1911, *though not yet quite a direct supply of documentary material for the dossiers of the* cause célèbre, *Man versus conditions impeached as the authors of his discontent, realist novels are largely explicit satire and protest, and every form of conventionalized human association is being arraigned by biographical and autobiographical novelists.*

Since all these novelists happened to be men, the present writer, proposing at this moment to write a novel and looking round for a contemporary pattern, was faced with the choice between following one of her regiments and attempting to produce a feminine equivalent of the current masculine realism. Choosing the latter alternative, she presently set aside, at the bidding of a dissatisfaction that revealed its nature without supplying any suggestion as to the removal of its cause, a considerable mass of manuscript. Aware, as she wrote, of the gradual falling away of the preoccupations that for a while had dictated the briskly moving script, and of the substitution, for these inspiring preoccupations, of a stranger in the form of contemplated reality having for the first time in her experience its own say, and apparently justifying those who acclaim writing as the surest means of discovering the truth about one's own thoughts and beliefs, she had been at the same time increasingly tormented, not only by the failure, of this now so independently assertive reality, adequately to appear within the text, but by its revelation, whencesoever focused, of a hundred faces, any one of which, the moment it was entrapped within the close mesh of direct statement, summoned its fellows to disqualify it.

In 1913, the opening pages of the attempted chronicle became the first chapter of 'Pilgrimage,' written to the accompaniment of a sense of being upon a fresh pathway, an adventure so searching and, sometimes, so joyous as to produce a longing for participation; not quite the same as a longing for publication, whose possibility, indeed, as the book grew, receded to vanishing point.

To a publisher, nevertheless, at the bidding of Mr J. D. Beresford, the book was ultimately sent. By the time it returned, the second chapter was partly written and the condemned volume, put away and forgotten, would have remained in seclusion but for the persistence of the same kind friend, who acquired and sent it to Edward Garnett, then reading for Messrs Duckworth. In 1915, the covering title being at the moment in use elsewhere, it was published as 'Pointed Roofs.'

The lonely track, meanwhile, had turned out to be a populous highway. Amongst those who had simultaneously entered it, two figures stood out. One a woman mounted upon a magnificently caparisoned charger, the other a man walking, with eyes devoutly closed, weaving as he went a rich garment of new words wherewith to clothe the antique dark material of his engrossment.

News came from France of one Marcel Proust, said to be producing an unprecedentedly profound and opulent reconstruction of experience focused from within the mind of a single individual, and, since Proust's first volume had been published and several others written by 1913, *the France of Balzac now appeared to have produced the earliest adventurer.*

Finally, however, the role of pathfinder was declared to have been played by a venerable gentleman, a charmed and charming high priest of nearly all the orthodoxies, inhabiting a softly lit enclosure he mistook, until 1914, *for the universe, and celebrated by evolving, for the accommodation of his vast tracts of urbane commentary, a prose style demanding, upon the first reading, a perfection of sustained concentration akin to that which brought it forth, and bestowing, again upon the first reading, the recreative delights peculiar to this form of spiritual exercise.*

And while, indeed, it is possible to claim for Henry James, keeping the reader incessantly watching the conflict of human forces through the eye of a single observer, rather than taking him, before the drama begins, upon a tour amongst the properties, or breaking in with descriptive introductions of the players as one by one they enter his enclosed resounding chamber where no plant grows and no mystery pours in from the unheeded stars, a far from inconsiderable technical influence, it was nevertheless not without a sense of relief that the present writer recently discovered, in 'Wilhelm Meister,' the following manifesto :

In the novel, reflections and incidents should be featured; in drama, character and action. The novel must proceed slowly, and the thought-processes of the principal figure must, by one device or another, hold up the development of the whole. . . . The hero of the novel must be acted upon, or, at any rate, not himself the principal operator. . . . Grandison, Clarissa, Pamela, the Vicar of Wakefield, and Tom Jones himself, even where they are not acted upon, are still retarding personalities and all the incidents are, in a certain measure, modelled according to their thoughts.

Phrases began to appear, formulae devised to meet the exigencies of literary criticism. 'The Stream of Consciousness' lyrically led the way, to be gladly welcomed by all who could persuade themselves of the possibility of comparing consciousness to a stream. Its transatlantic successors, 'Interior Monologue' and 'Slow-motion Photography,' may each be granted a certain technical applicability leaving them, to this extent, unhampered by the defects of their qualities.

I—* B

Lives in plenty have been devoted to the critic's exacting art and a lifetime might be spent in engrossed contemplation of the movements of its continuous ballet. When the dancers tread living boards, the boards will sometimes be heard to groan. The present writer groans, gently and resignedly, beneath the reiterated tap-tap accusing her of feminism, of failure to perceive the value of the distinctively masculine intelligence, of pre-War sentimentality, of post-War Freudianity. But when her work is danced upon for being unpunctuated and therefore unreadable, she is moved to cry aloud. For here is truth.

Feminine prose, as Charles Dickens and James Joyce have delightfully shown themselves to be aware, should properly be unpunctuated, moving from point to point without formal obstructions. And the author of 'Pilgrimage' must confess to an early habit of ignoring, while writing, the lesser of the stereotyped system of signs, and, further, when finally sprinkling in what appeared to be necessary, to a small unconscious departure from current usage. While meeting approval, first from the friend who discovered and pointed it out to her, then from an editor who welcomed the article she wrote to elucidate and justify it, and, recently, by the inclusion of this article in a text-book for students of journalism and its translation into French, the small innovation, in further complicating the already otherwise sufficiently complicated task of the official reader, helped to produce the chaos for which she is justly reproached.

For the opportunity, afforded by the present publishers, of eliminating this source of a reputation for creating avoidable difficulties, and of assembling the scattered chapters of 'Pilgrimage' in their proper relationship, the author desires here to express her gratitude and, further, to offer to all those readers who have persisted in spite of every obstacle, a heart-felt apology.

D. M. R.

TREVONE, 1938.

POINTED ROOFS

CHAPTER I

MIRIAM left the gaslit hall and went slowly upstairs. The March twilight lay upon the landings, but the staircase was almost dark. The top landing was quite dark and silent. There was no one about. It would be quiet in her room. She could sit by the fire and be quiet and think things over until Eve and Harriett came back with the parcels. She would have time to think about the journey and decide what she was going to say to the Fräulein.

Her new Saratoga trunk stood solid and gleaming in the firelight. To-morrow it would be taken away and she would be gone. The room would be altogether Harriett's. It would never have its old look again. She evaded the thought and moved to the nearest window. The outline of the round bed and the shapes of the may-trees on either side of the bend of the drive were just visible. There was no escape for her thoughts in this direction. The sense of all she was leaving stirred uncontrollably as she stood looking down into the well-known garden.

Out in the road beyond the invisible lime-trees came the rumble of wheels. The gate creaked and the wheels crunched up the drive, slurring and stopping under the dining - room window.

It was the Thursday afternoon piano-organ, the one that was always in tune. It was early to-day.

She drew back from the window as the bass chords began thumping gently in the darkness. It was better that it should come now than later on, at dinner-time. She could get over it alone up here.

She went down the length of the room and knelt by the fireside with one hand on the mantelshelf so that she could get up noiselessly and be lighting the gas if any one came in.

The organ was playing *The Wearin' o' the Green*.

It had begun that tune during the last term at school, in the summer. It made her think of rounders in the hot school garden, singing-classes in the large green room, all the class shouting 'Gather *ro*ses while ye may,' hot afternoons in the shady north room, the sound of turning pages, the hum of the garden beyond the sun-blinds, meetings in the sixth form study. . . . Lilla, with her black hair and the specks of bright amber in the brown of her eyes, talking about free-will.

She stirred the fire. The windows were quite dark. The flames shot up and shadows darted.

That summer, which still seemed near to her, was going to fade and desert her, leaving nothing behind. To-morrow it would belong to a world which would go on without her, taking no heed. There would still be blissful days. But she would not be in them.

There would be no more silent sunny mornings with all the day ahead and nothing to do and no end anywhere to anything; no more sitting at the open window in the dining-room, reading Lecky and Darwin and bound *Contemporary Reviews* with roses waiting in the garden to be worn in the afternoon, and Eve and Harriett somewhere about, washing blouses or copying waltzes from the library packet . . . no more Harriett looking in at the end of the morning, rushing her off to the new grand piano to play the *Mikado* and the *Holy Family* duets. The tennis-club would go on, but she would not be there. It would begin in May. Again there would be a white twinkling figure coming quickly along the pathway between the rows of hollyhocks every Saturday afternoon.

Why had he come to tea every Sunday—never missing a single Sunday—all the winter? Why did he say: 'Play *Abide with me*,' 'Play *Abide with me*,' yesterday, if he didn't care? What was the good of being so quiet and saying nothing? Why didn't he say: 'Don't go,' or: 'When are you coming back?'? Eve said he looked perfectly miserable.

There was nothing to look forward to now but governessing and old age. Perhaps Miss Gilkes was right. . . . Get rid of men and muddles and have things just ordinary and be happy. 'Make up your mind to be happy. You can be *perfectly* happy

without any one to think about. . . .' Wearing that large
cameo brooch—long, white, flat-fingered hands and that quiet
little laugh. . . . The piano-organ had reached its last tune.
In the midst of the final flourish of notes the door flew open.
Miriam got quickly to her feet and felt for matches.

Harriett came in waggling a thin brown-paper parcel.
'Did you hear the Intermezzo? What a dim religious!
We got your old collars.'

Miriam took the parcel and subsided on to the hearthrug,
looking with a new curiosity at Harriett's little, round, firelit
face, smiling tightly between the rim of her hard felt hat and
the bright silk bow beneath her chin.

A footstep sounded on the landing and there was a gentle
tap on the open door.

'Oh, come in, Eve—bring some matches. Are the collars
piqué, Harry?'

'No, they hadn't got *piqué*, but they're the plain shape you
like. You may thank us they didn't send you things with
little rujabiba frills.'

Eve came slenderly down the room and Miriam saw with
relief that her outdoor things were off. As the gas flared up
she drew comfort from her scarlet serge dress, and the soft
crimson cheek and white brow of the profile raised towards
the flaring jet.

'What are things like downstairs?' she said, staring into
the fire.

'I don't know,' said Eve. She sighed thoughtfully and
sank into a carpet chair under the gas bracket. Miriam
glanced at her troubled eyes.

'Pater's only just come in. I think things are pretty rotten,'
declared Harriett from the hearthrug.

'Isn't it ghastly—for all of us?' Miriam felt treacherously
outspoken. It was a relief to be going away. She knew that
this sense of relief made her able to speak. 'It's never knowing
that's so awful. Perhaps he'll get some more money presently

and things 'll go on again. Fancy mother having it always, ever since we were babies.'

'Don't, Mim.'

'All right. I won't tell you the words he said, how he put it about the difficulty of getting the money for my things.'

'*Don't*, Mim.'

Miriam's mind went back to the phrase and her mother's agonized face. She felt utterly desolate in the warm room.

'I wish *I* 'd got brains,' chirped Harriett, poking the fire with the toe of her boot.

'So you have—more than me.'

'Oh—reely.'

'You know, I *know*, girls, that things are as absolutely ghastly this time as they can possibly be and that something must be done. . . . But you know it 's perfectly fearful to face that old school when it comes to the point.'

'Oh, my dear, it 'll be lovely,' said Eve; 'all new and jolly, and think how you will enjoy those lectures, you 'll simply love them.'

'It 's all very well to say that. You know you 'd feel ill with fright.'

'It 'll be all right—for *you*—once you 're there.'

Miriam stared into the fire and began to murmur shame-facedly.

'No more all day bézique. . . . No more days in the West End. . . . No more matinées . . . no more exhibitions . . . no more A.B.C. teas . . . no more insane times . . . no more anything.'

'What about holidays? You 'll enjoy them all the more.'

'I shall be staid and governessy.'

'You mustn't. You must be frivolous.'

Two deeply burrowing dimples drew the skin tightly over the bulge of Miriam's smile.

'And marry a German professor,' she intoned blithely.

'Don't—don't for *goodney* say that before mother, Miriam.'

'D' you mean she minds me going?'

'My *dear!*'

Why did Eve use her cross voice?—stupid . . . 'for good-ness' sake,' not 'for goodney.' Silly of Eve to talk slang. . . .

'All right. I won't.'

'Won't marry a German professor, or won't tell mother, do you mean? . . . Oo—Crumbs! My old cake in the oven!' Harriett hopped to the door.

'Funny Harriett taking to cookery. It doesn't seem a bit like her.'

'She 'll have to do something—so shall I, I s'pose.'

'It seems awful.'

'We shall simply have to.'

'It 's awful,' said Miriam, shivering.

'Poor old girl. I expect you feel horrid because you 're tired with all the packing and excitement.'

'Oh, well, anyhow, it 's simply ghastly.'

'You 'll feel better to-morrow.'

'D' you think I shall?'

'Yes—you 're so strong,' said Eve, flushing and examining her nails.

'How d' you mean?'

'Oh—all sorts of ways.'

'What way?'

'Oh—well—you arranging all this—I mean answering the advertisement and settling it all.'

'Oh, well, you know you backed me up.'

'Oh, yes, but other things. . . .'

'What?'

'Oh, I was thinking about you having no religion.'

'Oh.'

'You must have such splendid principles to keep you straight,' said Eve, and cleared her throat, 'I mean, you must have such a lot in you.'

'Me?'

'Yes, of course.'

'I don't know where it comes in. What have I done?'

'Oh, well, it isn't so much what you 've done—you have such a good time. . . . Everybody admires you and all that . . . you know what I mean—you 're so clever. . . . You 're always in the right.'

'That 's just what everybody hates!'

'Well, my dear, I wish I had your mind.'

'You needn't,' said Miriam.

'You're all right—you'll come out all right. You're one of those strong-minded people who have to go through a period of doubt.'

'But, my *dear*,' said Miriam, grateful and proud, 'I feel such a humbug. You know when I wrote that letter to the Fräulein I said I was a member of the Church. I know what it will be, I shall have to take the English girls to church.'

'Oh, well, you won't mind that.'

'It will make me simply ill—I could *never* describe to you,' said Miriam, with her face aglow, 'what it is to me to hear some silly man drone away with an undistributed middle term.'

'They're not all like that.'

'Oh, well, then it will be *ignoratio elenchi* or *argumentum ad hominem*——'

'Oh, yes, but they're not the *service*.'

'The service I can't make head or tail of—think of the Athanasian.'

'Yes.' Eve stirred uneasily and began to execute a gentle scale with her tiny tightly-knit blue and white hand upon her knee.

'It'll be ghastly,' continued Miriam, 'not having any one to pour out to—I've told you such a lot these last few days.'

'Yes, hasn't it been funny? I seem to know you all at once so much better.'

'Well—don't you think I'm perfectly hateful?'

'No. I admire you more than ever. I think you're simply splendid.'

'Then you simply don't know me.'

'Yes I do. And you'll be able to write to me.'

Eve, easily weeping, hugged her and whispered: 'You mustn't. I can't see you break down—don't—don't—don't. We can't be blue your last night. . . . Think of nice things. . . . There *will* be nice things again . . . there will, will, will, *will*.'

Miriam pursed her lips to a tight bunch and sat twisting her fingers. Eve stood up in her tears. Her smile and the curves of her mouth were unchanged by her weeping, and the crimson had spread and deepened a little in the long oval of her face. Miriam watched the changing crimson. Her eyes went to and fro between it and the neatly pinned masses of brown hair.

'I 'm going to get some hot water,' said Eve, 'and we 'll make ourselves glorious.'

Miriam watched her as she went down the long room—the great oval of dark hair, the narrow neck, the narrow back, tight, plump little hands hanging in profile, white, with a blue pad near the wrist.

When Miriam woke the next morning she lay still with closed eyes. She had dreamed that she had been standing in a room in the German school and the staff had crowded round her, looking at her. They had dreadful eyes—eyes like the eyes of hostesses she remembered, eyes she had seen in trains and buses, eyes from the old school. They came and stood and looked at her, and saw her as she was, without courage, without funds or good clothes or beauty, without charm or interest, without even the skill to play a part. They looked at her with loathing. 'Board and lodging—privilege to attend Masters' lectures and laundry (body-linen only).' That was all she had thought of and clutched at—all along, since first she read the Fräulein's letter. Her keep and the chance of learning . . . and Germany — Germany, das deutsche Vaterland — Germany, all woods and mountains and tenderness—Hermann and Dorothea in the dusk of a happy village.

And it would really be those women, expecting things of her. They would be so affable at first. She had been through it a million times—all her life—all eternity. They would smile those hateful women's smiles — smirks — self - satisfied smiles as if everybody were agreed about everything. She loathed women. They always smiled. All the teachers had at school, all the girls, but Lilla. Eve did . . . maddeningly sometimes . . . mother . . . it was the only funny horrid thing about her. Harriett didn't. . . . Harriett laughed. She was strong and hard somehow. . . .

Pater knew how hateful all the world of women were and despised them.

He never included her with them; or only sometimes when she pretended, or he didn't understand. . . .

Someone was saying 'Hi!' a gurgling, muffled shout, a long way off.

She opened her eyes. It was bright morning. She saw the twist of Harriett's body lying across the edge of the bed. With a gasp she flung herself over her own side. Harry, old Harry, jolly old Harry had remembered the Grand Ceremonial. In a moment her own head hung, her long hair flinging back on to the floor, her eyes gazing across under the bed at the reversed snub of Harriett's face. It was flushed in the midst of the wiry hair which stuck out all round it but did not reach the floor. 'Hi!' they gurgled solemnly, 'Hi! . . . Hi!' shaking their heads from side to side. Then their four frilled hands came down and they flumped out of the high bed.

They performed an uproarious toilet. It seemed so safe up there in the bright bare room. Miriam's luggage had been removed. It was away somewhere in the house; far away and unreal and unfelt as her parents somewhere downstairs, and the servants away in the basement getting breakfast, and Sarah and Eve, always incredible, getting quietly up in the next room. Nothing was real but getting up with old Harriett in this old room.

She revelled in Harriett's delicate buffoonery ('voluntary incongruity' she quoted to herself as she watched her)—the titles of some of the books on Harriett's shelf, *Ungava; a Tale of the North*, *Grimm's Fairy Tales*, *Wings and Stings*, *Swiss Family Robinson*, made her laugh. The curtained recesses of the long room stretched away into space.

She went about dimpling and responding, singing and masquerading as her hands did their work.

She intoned the titles on her own shelf—as a response to the quiet swearing and jesting accompanying Harriett's occupations. '*The Voyage of the Beeeeeeagle*,' she sang, 'Scott's

Poetical *Works*. *Villette* — Longfellow — Holy Bible *with* Apocrypha—*Egmont*——'

'Binks!' squealed Harriett daintily. 'Yink grink binks.'

'Books!' she responded in a low tone, and flushed as if she had given Harriett an affectionate hug. 'My rotten books. . . .' She would come back, and read all her books more carefully. She had packed some. She could not remember which and why.

'Binks,' she said, and it was quite easy for them to crowd together at the little dressing-table. Harriett was standing in her little faded red moirette petticoat and a blue flannelette dressing-jacket brushing her wiry hair. Miriam reflected that she need no longer hate her for the set of her clothes round her hips. She caught sight of her own faded jersey and stiff, shapeless black petticoat in the mirror. Harriett's 'Hinde's' lay on the dressing-table, her own still lifted the skin of her forehead in suffused puckerings against the shank of each pin.

Unperceived, she eyed the tiny stiff plait of hair which stuck out almost horizontally from the nape of Harriett's neck, and watched her combing out the tightly curled fringe standing stubbily out along her forehead and extending like a thickset hedge midway across the crown of her head, where it stopped abruptly against the sleekly - brushed longer strands which strained over her poll and disappeared into the plait.

'Your old wool 'll be just right in Germany,' remarked Harriett.

'Mm.'

'You ought to do it in basket plaits like Sarah.'

'I wish I could. I can't think how she does it.'

'Ike spect it 's easy enough.'

'Mm.'

'But you 're all right, anyhow.'

'Anyhow, it 's no good bothering when you 're plain.'

'You 're *not* plain.'

Miriam looked sharply round.

'Go on, Gooby.'

'You 're not. You don't know. Granny said you 'll be a bonny woman, and Sarah thinks you 've got the best shape face and the best complexion of any of us, and cook was simply crying her eyes out last night and said you were the light of the house with your happy, pretty face, and mother said you 're much too attractive to go about alone, and that 's partly why pater 's going with you to Hanover, silly. . . . You 're not plain,' she gasped.

Miriam's amazement silenced her. She stood back from the mirror. She could not look into it until Harriett had gone. The phrases she had just heard rang in her head without meaning. But she knew she would remember all of them. She went on doing her hair with downcast eyes. She had seen Harriett vividly, and had longed to crush her in her arms and kiss her little round cheeks and the snub of her nose. Then she wanted her to be gone.

Presently Harriett took up a brooch and skated down the room. 'Ta-ra-ra-la-eee-tee!' she carolled, 'don't be long,' and disappeared.

'I 'm pretty,' murmured Miriam, planting herself in front of the dressing-table. 'I 'm pretty—they like me—they *like* me. Why didn't I know?' She did not look into the mirror. 'They all like me, *me*.'

The sound of the breakfast-bell came clanging up through the house. She hurried to her side of the curtained recess. Hanging there were her old red stockinette jersey and her blue skirt . . . never again . . . just once more . . . she could change afterwards. Her brown, heavy best dress with puffed and gauged sleeves and thick gauged and gathered boned bodice was in her hand. She hung it once more on its peg and quickly put on her old things. The jersey was shiny with wear. 'You darling old things,' she muttered as her arms slipped down the sleeves.

The door of the next room opened quietly and she heard Sarah and Eve go decorously downstairs. She waited until their footsteps had died away and then went very slowly down the first flight, fastening her belt. She stopped at the landing window, tucking the frayed end of the petersham under the frame of the buckle . . . they were all downstairs, liking her. She could not face them. She was too excited and too shy.

. . . She had never once thought of their 'feeling' her going away . . . saying good-bye to each one . . . all minding and sorry—even the servants. She glanced fearfully out into the garden, seeing nothing. Someone called up from the breakfast-room doorway, 'Mim—my!' How surprised Mr Bart had been when he discovered that they themselves never knew whose voice it was of all four of them unless you saw the person, 'but yours is really richer' . . . it was cheek to say that.

'Mim—my!'

Suddenly she longed to be gone—to have it all over and be gone.

She heard the *kak-kak* of Harriett's wooden heeled slippers across the tiled hall. She glanced down the well of the stair-case. Harriett was mightily swinging the bell, scattering a little spray of notes at each end of her swing.

With a frightened face Miriam crept back up the stairs. Violently slamming the bedroom door, 'I'm a-comin'—I'm a-comin',' she shouted and ran downstairs.

CHAPTER II

THE crossing was over. They were arriving. The movement of the little steamer that had collected the passengers from the packet-boat drove the raw air against Miriam's face. In her tired brain the grey river and the flat misty shores slid constantly into a vision of the gaslit dining-room at home . . . the large clear glowing fire, the sounds of the family voices. Every effort to obliterate the picture brought back again the moment that had come at the dinner-table as they all sat silent for an instant with downcast eyes and she had suddenly longed to go on for ever just sitting there with them all.

Now, in the boat, she wanted to be free for the strange grey river and the grey shores. But the home scenes recurred relentlessly. Again and again she went through the last moments . . . the good-byes, the unexpected convulsive force of her mother's arms, her own dreadful inability to give any answering embrace. She could not remember saying a single word. There had been a feeling that came like a tide, carrying her away. Eager and dumb and remorseful she had gone out of the house and into the cab with Sarah, and then had come the long sitting in the loopline train . . . 'talk about something' . . . Sarah sitting opposite and her unchanged voice saying 'What shall we talk about?'. And then a long waiting, and the brown leather strap swinging against the yellow grained door, the smell of dust and the dirty wooden flooring, with the noise of the wheels underneath going to the swinging tune of one of Heller's 'Sleepless Nights.' The train had made her sway with its movements. How still Sarah seemed to sit, fixed in the old life. Nothing had come but strange cruel emotions.

After the suburban train nothing was distinct until the warm snowflakes were drifting against her face through the cold

darkness on Harwich quay. Then, after what seemed like a
great loop of time spent going helplessly up a gangway towards
'the world' she had stood, face to face with the pale polite
stewardess in her cabin. 'I had better have a lemon, cut in
two,' she had said, feeling suddenly stifled with fear. For
hours she had lain despairing, watching the slowly swaying
walls of her cabin or sinking with closed eyes through inverte-
brate dipping spaces. Before each releasing paroxysm she told
herself 'this is like death; one day I shall die, it will be like
this.'

She supposed there would be breakfast soon on shore, a firm
room and a teapot and cups and saucers. Cold and exhaustion would come to an end. She would be talking to her
father.

He was standing near her with the Dutchman who had
helped her off the boat and looked after her luggage. The
Dutchman was listening, deferentially. Miriam saw the strong
dark blue beam of his eyes.

'Very good, very good,' she heard him say, 'fine education
in German schools.'

Both men were smoking cigars.

She wanted to draw herself upright and shake out her
clothes.

'Select,' she heard, 'excellent staff of masters . . . daughters
of gentlemen.'

Pater is trying to make the Dutchman think I am being taken
as a pupil to a finishing school in Germany. She thought of
her lonely pilgrimage to the West End agency, of her humiliating interview, of her heart-sinking acceptance of the post, the
excitements and misgivings she had had, of her sudden challenge of them all that evening after dinner, and their dismay
and remonstrance and reproaches—of her fear and determination in insisting and carrying her point and making them begin
to be interested in her plan.

But she shared her father's satisfaction in impressing the

Dutchman. She knew that she was at one with him in that.
She glanced at him. There could be no doubt that he was
playing the role of the English gentleman. Poor dear. It was
what he had always wanted to be. He had sacrificed everything to the idea of being a 'person of leisure and cultivation.'
Well, after all, it was true in a way. He was—and he had, she
knew, always wanted her to be the same and she *was* going
to finish her education abroad . . . in Germany. . . . They
were nearing a little low quay backed by a tremendous saffron-
coloured hoarding announcing in black letters 'Sunlight
Zeep.'

'Did you see, pater; did you *see*?'

They were walking rapidly along the quay.

'Did you see? Sunlight *Zeep*!'

She listened to his slightly scuffling stride at her side.

Glancing up she saw his face excited and important. He
was not listening. He was being an English gentleman,
'emerging' from the Dutch railway station.

'Sunlight *Zeep*,' she shouted. '*Zeep*, pater!'

He glanced down at her and smiled condescendingly.

'Ah, yes,' he admitted with a laugh.

There were Dutch faces for Miriam — men, women, and
children coming towards her with sturdy gait.

'They 're talking Dutch! They 're all talking *Dutch*!'

The foreign voices, the echoes in the little narrow street, the
flat waterside effect of the sounds, the bright clearness she had
read of, brought tears to her eyes.

'The others *must* come here,' she told herself, pitying them
all.

They had an English breakfast at the Victoria Hotel and
went out and hurried about the little streets. They bought
cigars and rode through the town on a little tramway. Presently
they were in a train watching the Dutch landscape go by. One
level stretch succeeded another. Miriam wanted to go out
alone under the grey sky and walk over the flat fields shut in
by poplars.

She looked at the dykes and the windmills with indifferent
eyes, but her desire for the flat meadows grew.

Late at night, seated wide awake opposite her sleeping companion, rushing towards the German city, she began to think.

It was a fool's errand. . . . To undertake to go to the German school and teach . . . to be going there . . . with nothing to give. The moment would come when there would be a class sitting round a table waiting for her to speak. She imagined one of the rooms at the old school, full of scornful girls. . . . How was English taught? How did you begin? English grammar . . . in German? Her heart beat in her throat. She had never thought of that . . . the rules of English grammar? Parsing and analysis. . . . Anglo-Saxon prefixes and suffixes . . . gerundial infinitive. . . . It was too late to look anything up. Perhaps there would be a class to-morrow. . . . The German lessons at school had been dreadfully good. . . . Fräulein's grave face . . . her perfect knowledge of every rule . . . her clear explanations in English . . . her examples. . . . All these things were there, in English grammar. . . . And she had undertaken to teach them and could not even speak German.

Monsieur . . . had talked French all the time . . . *dictées* . . . lectures . . . Le Conscrit . . . Waterloo . . . La Maison Déserte . . . his careful voice reading on and on . . . until the room disappeared. . . . She must do that for her German girls. Read English to them and make them happy. . . . But first there must be verbs . . . there had been *cahiers* of them . . . first, second, third conjugation. . . . It was impudence, an impudent invasion . . . the dreadful, clever, foreign school. . . . They would laugh at her. . . . She began to repeat the English alphabet. . . . She doubted whether, faced with a class, she could reach the end without a mistake. . . . She reached Z and went on to the parts of speech.

There would be a moment when she must have an explanation with the Fräulein. Perhaps she could tell her that she found the teaching was beyond her scope and then find a place somewhere as a servant. She remembered things she had heard about German servants—that whenever they even dusted a room they cleaned the windows and on Sundays they waited at lunch in muslin dresses and afterwards went to balls. She feared even the German servants would despise her. They had never been allowed into the kitchen at home except when there was jam-making . . . she had never made a bed in her life. . . . A shop? But that would mean knowing German and being quick at giving change. Impossible. Perhaps she could find some English people in Hanover who would help her. There was an English colony, she knew, and an English church. But that would be like going back. That must not happen. She would rather stay abroad on any terms—away from England—English people. She had scented something, a sort of confidence, everywhere, in her hours in Holland, the brisk manner of the German railway officials and the serene assurance of the travelling Germans she had seen, confirmed her impression. Away out here, the sense of imminent catastrophe that had shadowed all her life so far had disappeared. Even here in this dim carriage, with disgrace ahead, she felt that there was freedom somewhere at hand. Whatever happened she would hold to that.

She glanced up at her small leather handbag lying in the rack and thought of the solid money in her purse. Twenty-five shillings. It was a large sum and she was to have more as she needed.

She glanced across at the pale face with its point of reddish beard, the long white hands laid one upon the other on the crossed knees. He had given her twenty-five shillings and there was her fare and his, and his return fare and her new trunk and all the things she had needed. It must be the end of taking money from him. She was grown up. She was the strong-minded one. She must manage. With a false posi-

tion ahead and, after a short space, disaster, she must get
along.

The peaceful Dutch fields came to her mind. They looked
so secure. They had passed by too soon. We have always
been in a false position, she pondered. Always lying and
pretending and keeping up a show—never daring to tell anybody. . . . Did she want to tell anybody? To come out into
the open and be helped and have things arranged for her and
do things like other people? No. . . . No. . . . 'Miriam
always likes to be different'—'Society is no boon to those not
sociable.' Dreadful things . . . and the girls laughing together
about them. What did they really mean?

'Society is no boon to those not sociable'—on her birthday-
page in Ellen Sharpe's birthday-book. Ellen handed it to her
going upstairs and had chanted the words out to the others and
smiled her smile . . . she had not asked her to write her
name . . . was it unsocial to dislike so many of the girls?
. . . Ellen's people were in the Indian . . . her thoughts
hesitated . . . Sivvle . . . something grand—all the grand
girls were horrid . . . somehow mean and sly. . . . Sivvle . . .
Sivvle . . . Civil! Of course! Civil *what?*

Miriam groaned. She was a governess now. Someone
would ask her that question. She would ask pater before he
went. . . . No, she would not. . . . If only he would answer
a question simply, and not with a superior air as if he had
invented the thing he was telling about. She felt she had a
right to all the knowledge there was, without fuss . . . oh,
without fuss—without fuss and—emotion. . . . I *am* unsociable,
I suppose—she mused. She could not think of any one who
did not offend her. I don't like men and I loathe women.
I am a misanthrope. So's pater. He despises women and
can't get on with men. We are different—it's us, him and
me. He's failed us because he's different and if he weren't
we should be like other people. Everything in the railway
responded and agreed. Like other people . . . horrible. . . .
She thought of the fathers of girls she knew—the Poole girls,
for instance, they were to be 'independent,' trained and certificated—she envied that—but her envy vanished when she

remembered how heartily she had agreed when Sarah called them 'sharp' and 'knowing.'

Mr Poole was a business man . . . common . . . trade. . . . If pater had kept to grandpa's business they would be trade, too—well-off, now—all married. Perhaps as it was he had thought they would marry.

She thought sleepily of her Wesleyan grandparents, gravely reading the *Wesleyan Methodist Recorder*, the shop at Babington, her father's discontent, his solitary fishing and reading, his discovery of music . . . science . . . classical music in the first Novello editions . . . Faraday . . . speaking to Faraday after lectures. Marriage . . . the new house . . . the red brick wall at the end of the garden where young peach-trees were planted . . . running up and downstairs and sing-ing . . . both of them singing in the rooms and the garden . . . she sometimes with her hair down and then when visitors were expected pinned in coils under a little cap and wearing a small hoop . . . the garden and lawns and shrubbery and the long kitchen-garden and the summer-house under the oaks beyond, and the pretty old gabled 'town' on the river and the woods all along the river valley and the hills shining up out of the mist. The snow man they both made in the winter—the birth of Sarah, and then Eve . . . his studies and book-buying —and after five years her own disappointing birth as the third girl, and the coming of Harriett just over a year later . . . her mother's illness, money troubles—their two years at the sea to retrieve . . . the disappearance of the sunlit red-walled garden always in full summer sunshine with the sound of bees in it, or dark from windows . . . the narrowing of the house-life down to the Marine Villa—with the sea creeping in—wading out through the green shallows, out and out till you were more than waist deep—shrimping and prawning hour after hour for weeks together . . . poking in the rock pools, watching the sun and the colours in the strange afternoons . . . then the sudden large house at Barnes with the 'drive' winding to the door. . . . He used to come home from the City and the Constitutional Club and sometimes instead of reading *The Times* or the *Globe* or the *Proceedings of the British Association* or Herbert Spencer, play Pope Joan or Jacoby with them all, or table billiards and laugh and be 'silly' and take his turn at being 'bumped' by Timmy going the round of the long dining-room table, tail in the air; he had taken Sarah and Eve to see *Don Giovanni* and *Winter's Tale* and the new piece, *Lohengrin*. No one at the tennis-club had seen that. He had good taste. No one else had been to Madame Schumann's Farewell . . . sitting at the piano with her curtains of hair and her dreamy smile . . . and the Philharmonic Concerts. No one else knew about the lectures at the Royal Institution, beginning at nine on Fridays. . . . No one else's father went with a party of scientific men 'for the advancement of science' to Norway or America, seeing the Falls and the Yosemite Valley. No one else took his children as far as Dawlish for the holidays, travelling all day, from eight until seven . . . no esplanade, the old stone jetty and coves and cowrie shells. . . .

CHAPTER III

MIRIAM was practising on the piano in the larger of the two English bedrooms. Two other pianos were sounding in the house, one across the landing and the other in the *saal* where Herr Kapellmeister Bossenberger was giving a music-lesson. The rest of the girls were gathered in the large schoolroom under the care of Mademoiselle for Saturday's *raccommodage*. It was the last hour of the week's work. Presently there would be a great gonging, the pianos would cease, Fräulein's voice would sound up through the house 'Anziehen zum Aus—geh —hen!'

There would be the walk, dinner, the Saturday afternoon home-letters to be written and then, until Monday, holiday, freedom to read and to talk English and idle. And there was a new arrival in the house. Ulrica Hesse had come. Miriam had seen her. There had been three large leather trunks in the hall and a girl with a smooth pure oval of pale face standing wrapped in dark furs, gazing about her with eyes for which Miriam had no word, liquid—limpid—great-saucers, no— pools . . . great round deeps. . . . She had felt about for something to express them as she went upstairs with her roll of music. Fräulein Pfaff who had seemed to hover and smile about the girl as if half afraid to speak to her, had put out a hand for Miriam and said almost deprecatingly, 'Ach, mm, dies' ist unser Ulrica.'

The girl's thin fingers had come out of her furs and fastened convulsively—like cold, throbbing claws, on to the breadth of Miriam's hand.

'Unsere englische Lehrerin—our teacher from England,' smiled Fräulein.

'Lehrerin!' breathed the girl. Something flinched behind her great eyes. The fingers relaxed, and Miriam, feeling within her a beginning of response, had gone upstairs.

34

As she reached the upper landing she began to distinguish, against the clangour of chromatic passages assailing the house from the echoing *saal*, the gentle tones of the nearer piano, the one in the larger German bedroom opposite the front room for which she was bound. She paused for a moment at the top of the stairs and listened. A little swaying melody came out to her, muted by the closed door. Her grasp on the roll of music slackened. A radiance came for a moment behind the gravity of her face. Then the careful unstumbling repetition of a difficult passage drew her attention to the performer, her arms dropped to her sides and she passed on. It was little Bergmann, the youngest girl in the school. Her playing, on the bad old piano in the dark dressing-room in the basement, had prepared Miriam for the difference between the performance of these German girls and nearly all the piano-playing she had heard. It was the morning after her arrival. She had been unpacking and had taken, on the advice of Mademoiselle, her heavy boots and outdoor things down to the basement room. She had opened the door on Emma sitting at the piano in her blue and buff check ribbon-knotted stuff dress. Miriam had expected her to turn her head and stop playing. But as, arms full, she closed the door with her shoulders, the child's profile remained unconcerned. She noticed the firmly-pcised head, the thick creamy neck that seemed bare with its absence of collar-band and the soft frill of tucker stitched right on to the dress, the thick cable of string-coloured hair reaching just beyond the rim of the leather-covered music stool, the steel-beaded points of the little slippers gleaming as they worked the pedals, the serene eyes steadily following the music. She played on and Miriam recognized a quality she had only heard occasionally at concerts, and in the playing of one of the music teachers at school.

She had stood amazed, pretending to be fumbling for empty pegs, as this round-faced child of fourteen went her way to the end of her page. Then Miriam had ventured to interrupt and to ask her about the hanging arrangements, and the child had risen and, speaking soft South German, had suggested and poked tip-toeing about amongst the thickly hung garments, and shown a motherly solicitude over the disposal of Miriam's things. Miriam noted the easy range of the child's voice, how smoothly it slid from bird-like queries and chirpings to the consoling tones of the lower register. It seemed to leave undisturbed the softly-rounded, faintly-mottled chin and cheeks and the full unpouting lips that lay quietly one upon the other before she spoke, and opened flexibly but somehow hardly moved to her speech, and afterwards closed again gradually until they lay softly blossoming as before.

Emma had gathered up her music when the clothes were arranged, sighing and lamenting gently, 'Wäre ich nur zu Hause' —how happy one was at home—her little voice filled with tears and her cheeks flushed, 'haypie, haypie to home,' she complained as she slid her music into its case, 'where all so good, so nice, so beautiful,' and they had gone, side by side, up the dark, uncarpeted stone stairs leading from the basement to the hall. Half-way up, Emma had given Miriam a shy, firm hug and then gone decorously up the remainder of the flight.

The sense of that sudden little embrace recurred often to Miriam during the course of the first day.

It was unlike any contact she had known—more motherly than her mother's. Neither of her sisters could have embraced her like that. She did not know that a human form could bring such a sense of warm nearness, that human contours could be eloquent—or any one so sweetly daring.

That first evening at Waldstrasse there had been a performance that had completed the transformation of Miriam's English ideas of 'music.' She had caught the word *Vorspielen* being bandied about the long tea-table, and had gathered that there was to be an informal playing of 'pieces' before Fräulein Pfaff. She welcomed the event. It relieved her from the burden of being in high focus—the relief had come as soon as she took her place at the gaslit table. No eye seemed to notice her. The English girls, having sat out two meal-times with her, had ceased the hard-eyed observation which had made the long

silence of the earlier repasts only less embarrassing than
Fräulein's questions about England. The four Germans, who
had neither stared nor even appeared aware of her existence,
talked cheerfully across the table in a general exchange that
included tall Fräulein Pfaff smiling her horse-smile—Miriam
provisionally called it—behind the tea-urn, as chairman. The
six English-speaking girls, grouped as it were towards their
chief, a dark-skinned, athletic-looking Australian with hot,
brown, slightly bloodshot eyes sitting as vice-president opposite
Fräulein, joined occasionally, in solo and chorus, and Miriam
noted with relief a unanimous atrocity of accent in their enviable
fluency. Rapid *sotto voce* commentary and half-suppressed
wordless by-play located still more clearly the English quarter.
Animation flowed and flowed. Miriam, safely ignored, scarcely
heeding, but warmed and almost happy, basked. She munched
her black bread and butter, liberally smeared with the rich
savoury paste of liver sausage, and drank her sweet weak tea
and knew that she was very tired, sleepy and tired. She
glanced, from her place next to Emma Bergmann and on
Fräulein's left hand, down the table to where Mademoiselle
sat next the Martins in similar relation to the vice-president.
Mademoiselle, preceding her up through the quiet house carrying the jugs of hot water, had been her first impression on her
arrival the previous night. She had turned when they reached
the candle-lit attic with its high uncurtained windows and
red-covered box beds and, standing on the one strip of matting
in her full-skirted grey wincey dress with its neat triple row of
black ribbon velvet near the hem, had shown Miriam steel-blue
eyes smiling from a little triangular sprite-like face under a
high-standing pouf of soft, dark hair, and said: 'Voilà!' Miriam
had never imagined anything in the least like her. She had
said: 'Oh, thank you,' and taken the jug and had hurriedly and
silently got to bed, weighed down by wonders. They had
begun to talk in the dark. Miriam had reaped sweet comfort
in learning that this seemingly unreal creature who was, she
soon perceived, not educated—as she understood education—
was the resident French governess, was seventeen years old
and a Protestant. Such close quarters with a French girl was

bewildering enough—had she been a Roman Catholic, Miriam
felt she could not have endured her proximity. She was
evidently a special kind of French girl—a Protestant from East
France—Besançon—Besançon—Miriam had tried the pretty
word over until unexpectedly she had fallen asleep.

They had risen hurriedly in the cold March gloom and
Miriam had not spoken to her since. There she sat, dainty
and quiet and fresh. White frillings shone now at the neck
and sleeves of her little grey dress. She looked a clean and
clear miniature against the general dauby effect of the English
girls—poor though, Miriam was sure; perhaps as poor as she.
She felt glad as she watched her gentle sprite-like wistfulness
that she would be upstairs in that great bare attic again to-night.
In repose, her face looked pinched. There was something
about the nose and mouth—Miriam mused . . . *frugal*—John
Gilpin's wife—how sleepy she was.

The conversation was growing boisterous. She took courage
to raise her head towards the range of girls sitting opposite.
Those quite near she could not scrutinize. Some influence
coming to her from these German girls prevented her risking
with them any meeting of the eyes that was not brought about
by direct speech. But she felt them. She felt Emma Bergmann's warm plump presence close at her side and liked to take
food handed by her. She was conscious of the pink bulb of
Minna Blum's nose shining just opposite to her, and of the
way the light caught the blond sheen of her exquisitely coiled
hair as she turned her always smiling face and responded to the
louder remarks with: 'Oh, thou *dear* God!' or 'Is it possible!'
'How charming, *charming*,'or 'What in life dost thou say, rascal!'

Next to her was the faint glare of Elsa Speier's silent sallow-
ness. Her clear-threaded nimbus of pallid hair was the lowest
point in the range of figures across the table. She darted
quick glances at one and another without moving her head,
and Miriam felt that her pale eyes fully met would be cunning
and malicious.

After Elsa the 'English' began with Judy. Miriam guessed
when she heard her ask for *Brödchen* that she was Scotch. She
sat slightly askew and ate eagerly, stooping over her plate with
smiling mouth and downcast heavily freckled face. Unless
spoken to she did not speak, but she laughed often, a harsh,
involuntary laugh immediately followed by a drowning flush.
When she was not flushed her eyelashes shone bright black
against the unstained white above her cheek-bones. She had
coarse, fuzzy, red-brown hair.

Miriam decided that she was negligible.

Next to Judy were the Martins. They were as English as
they could be. She felt she must have noticed them a good
deal at breakfast and dinner-time without knowing it. Her
eyes, after one glance at the claret-coloured merino dresses
with hard white collars and cuffs, came back to her plate as
from a familiar picture. She still saw them sitting very upright, side by side, with the front strands of their hair strained
smoothly back, tied just on the crest of the head with brown
ribbon and going down in 'rats'-tails' to join the rest of their
hair, which hung straight and flat half-way down their backs.
The elder was dark with thick shoulders and heavy features.
Her large, expressionless, rich brown eyes flashed slowly and
reflected the light. They gave Miriam a slight feeling of
nausea. She felt she knew what her hands were like without
looking at them. The younger was thin and pale and slightly
hollow-cheeked. She had pale eyes, cold, like a fish, thought
Miriam. They both had deep hollow voices.

When she glanced again they were watching the Australian
with their four strange eyes and laughing German phrases at
her: 'Go on, Gertrude!' 'Are you *sure*, Gertrude?' 'How do
you *know*, Gertrude?'

Miriam had not yet dared to glance in the direction of the
Australian. Her eyes at dinner-time had cut like sharp steel.
Turning, however, towards the danger zone, without risking
the coming of its presiding genius within the focus of her
glasses she caught a glimpse of 'Jimmie' sitting back in her
chair tall and plump and neat, and shaking with wide-mouthed
giggles. Miriam wondered at the high neat peak of hair on

the top of her head and stared at her pearly little teeth. There
was something funny about her mouth. Even when she
strained it wide it was narrow and tiny—rabbity. She raised
a short arm and began patting her peak of hair with a tiny hand
which showed a small onyx seal ring on the little finger. 'Ask
Judy!' she giggled, in a fruity squeak.

'Ask Judy!' they all chorused, laughing.

Judy cast an appealing flash of her eyes sideways at nothing,
flushed furiously, and mumbled: 'Ik weiss nik—I don't know.'

In the outcries and laughter which followed, Miriam noticed
only the hoarse hacking laugh of the Australian. Her eyes flew
up the table and fixed her as she sat laughing, her chair tilted
back, her knees crossed—tea was drawing to an end. The
detail of her terrifyingly stylish ruddy-brown frieze dress, with
its Norfolk jacket bodice and its shiny black leather belt, was
hardly distinguishable from the dark background made by the
folding doors. But the dreadful outline of her shoulders was
visible, the squarish oval of her face shone out—the wide forehead from which the wiry black hair was combed to a high puff,
the red eyes, black now, the long, straight nose, the wide,
laughing mouth with the enormous teeth.

Her voice conquered easily.

'Nein,' she tromboned, through the din.

Mademoiselle's little finger stuck up sharply like a steeple,
her mouth said: 'Oh—Oh——'

Fräulein's smile was at its widest, waiting the issue.

'Nein,' triumphed the Australian, causing a lull.

'Leise, Kinder, leise, doucement, gentlay,' chided Fräulein,
still smiling.

'Hermann, *yes*,' proceeded the Australian, 'aber Hugo—*né*!'

Miriam heard it agreed in the end that whereas someone
named Hugo did not wear a moustache, someone named
Hermann did. She was vaguely shocked and interested.

After tea the great doors were thrown open and the girls filed
into the *saal*. It was a large, high room furnished like a
drawing-room—enough settees and easy chairs to accommodate

more than all the girls. The polished floor was uncarpeted save for an archipelago of mats and rugs in the wide circle of light thrown by the four-armed chandelier. A grand piano was pushed against the wall in the far corner of the room, between the farthest of the three high french windows and the shining pillar of porcelain stove.

The high room, the bright light, the plentiful mirrors, the long sweep of lace curtains, the many faces—the girls seemed so much more numerous scattered here than they had when collected in the schoolroom—brought Miriam the sense of the misery of social occasions. She wondered whether the girls were nervous. She was glad that music lessons were no part of her remuneration. She thought of dreadful experiences of playing before people. The very first time, at home, when she had played a duet with Eve—Eve playing a little running melody in the treble—her own part a page of minims. The minims had swollen until she could not see whether they were lines or spaces, and her fingers had been so weak after the first unexpectedly loud note that she could hardly make any sound. Eve had said 'louder' and her fingers had suddenly stiffened and she had worked them from her elbows like sticks at the end of her trembling wrists and hands. Eve had noticed her dreadful movements and resented being elbowed. She had heard nothing then but her hard, loud minims till the end, and then as she stood dizzily up someone had said she had a nice firm touch, and she had pushed her angry way from the piano across the hearthrug. She should always remember the clear red-hot mass of the fire and the bottle of green Chartreuse warming on the blue and cream tiles. There were probably only two or three guests, but the room had seemed full of people, stupid people who had made her play. How angry she had been with Eve for noticing her discomfiture and with the forgotten guest for her silly remark. She knew she had simply poked the piano. Then there had been the annual school concerts, all the girls almost unrecognizable with fear. She had learnt her pieces by heart for those occasions and played them through with trembling limbs and burning eyes—alternately thumping with stiff fingers and feeling her whole hand faint from the wrist on to the notes which fumbled and slurred into each other almost soundlessly until the thumping began again. At the musical evenings, organized by Eve as a winter set-off to the tennis-club, she had both played and sung, hoping each time afresh to be able to reproduce the effects which came so easily when she was alone or only with Eve. But she could not discover the secret of getting rid of her nervousness. Only twice had she succeeded—at the last school concert when she had been too miserable to be nervous and Mr Strood had told her she did him credit and, once, she had sung *Chanson de Florian* in a way that had astonished her own listening ear—the notes had laughed and thrilled out into the air and come back to her from the wall behind the piano. . . . The day before the tennis tournament.

The girls were all settling down to fancy work, the white-cuffed hands of the Martins were already jerking crochet needles, faces were bending over fine embroideries and Minna Blum had trundled a mounted lace-pillow into the brighter light.

Miriam went to the schoolroom and fetched from her work-basket the piece of canvas partly covered with red and black wool in diamond pattern that was her utmost experience of fancy work.

As she returned she half saw Fräulein Pfaff, sitting as if enthroned on a high-backed chair in front of the centremost of the mirrors filling the wall spaces between the long french windows, signal to her, to come to that side of the room.

Timorously ignoring the signal she got herself into a little low chair in the shadow of the half-closed swing door and was spreading out her woolwork on her knee when the *Vorspielen* began.

Emma Bergmann was playing. The single notes of the opening *motif* of Chopin's Fifteenth Nocturne fell pensively into the waiting room. Miriam, her fatigue forgotten, slid to a featureless freedom. It seemed to her that the light with which the room was filled grew brighter and clearer. She felt that she was looking at nothing and yet was aware of the whole room like a picture in a dream. Fear left her. The human forms all round her lost their power. They grew suffused and dim. . . . The pensive swing of the music changed to urgency and emphasis. . . . It came nearer and nearer. It did not come from the candle-lit corner where the piano was. . . . It came from everywhere. It carried her out of the house, out of the world.

It hastened with her, on and on towards great brightness. . . . Everything was growing brighter and brighter. . . .

Gertrude Goldring, the Australian, was making noises with her hands like inflated paper bags being popped. Miriam clutched her wool-needle and threaded it. She drew the wool through her canvas, one, three, five, three, one and longed for the piano to begin again.

Clara Bergmann followed. Miriam watched her as she took her place at the piano—how square and stout she looked and old, careworn, like a woman of forty. She had high square shoulders and high square hips—her brow was low and her face thin, broad and flat. Her eyes were like the eyes of a dog and her thin-lipped mouth long and straight until it went steadily down at the corners. She wore a large fringe like Harriett's—and a thin coil of hair filled the nape of her neck. She played, without music, her face lifted boldly. The notes rang out in a prelude of unfinished phrases—the kind, Miriam noted, that had so annoyed her father in what he called new-fangled music—she felt it was going to be a brilliant piece—fireworks—execution—style—and sat up self-consciously and fixed her eyes on Clara's hands. 'Can you see the hands?' she remembered having heard someone say at a concert. How easily they moved. Clara still sat back, her face raised to the light. The notes rang out like trumpet-calls as her hands

dropped with an easy fling and sprang back and dropped again.
What loose wrists she must have, thought Miriam. The
clarion notes ceased. There was a pause. Clara threw back
her head, a faint smile flickered over her face, her hands fell
gently and the music came again, *pianissimo*, swinging in an
even rhythm. It flowed from those clever hands, a half-
indicated theme with a gentle, steady, throbbing undertow.
Miriam dropped her eyes—she seemed to have been listening
long—that wonderful light was coming again—she had forgotten her sewing—when presently she saw, slowly circling,
fading and clearing, first its edge, and then, for a moment the
whole thing, dripping, dripping as it circled, a weed-grown
mill-wheel. . . . She recognized it instantly. She had seen
it somewhere as a child—in Devonshire—and never thought
of it since—and there it was. She heard the soft swish and
drip of the water and the low humming of the wheel. How
beautiful . . . it was fading. . . . She held it—it returned—
clearer this time and she could feel the cool breeze it made, and
sniff the fresh earthy scent of it, the scent of the moss and the
weeds shining and dripping on its huge rim. Her heart filled.
She felt a little tremor in her throat. All at once she knew
that if she went on listening to that humming wheel and feeling
the freshness of the air, she would cry. She pulled herself
together, and for a while saw only a vague radiance in the
room and the dim forms grouped about. She could not
remember which was which. All seemed good and dear to her.
The trumpet notes had come back, and in a few moments the
music ceased. . . . Someone was closing the great doors from
inside the schoolroom. As the side behind which she was
sitting swung slowly to, she caught a glimpse, through the crack,
of four boys with close-cropped heads, sitting at the long
table. The gas was out and the room was dim, but a reading-
lamp in the centre of the table cast its light on their bowed
heads.

The playing of the two Martins brought back the familiar
feeling of English self-consciousness. Solomon, the elder one,

sat at her Beethoven sonata, an *adagio* movement, with a patch
of dull crimson on the pallor of the cheek she presented to the
room, but she played with a heavy fervour, preserving throughout the characteristic marching staccato of the bass, and gave
unstinted value to the shading of each phrase. She made
Miriam feel nervous at first and then—as she went triumphantly
forward and let herself go so tremendously—traction-engine,
thought Miriam—in the heavy *fortissimos*—a little ashamed of
such expression coming from English hands. The feeling of
shame lingered as the younger sister followed with a spirited
vivace. Her hollow-cheeked pallor remained unstained, but
her thin lips were set and her hard eyes were harder. She
played with determined nonchalance and an extraordinarily
facile rapidity, and Miriam's uneasiness changed insensibly
to the conviction that these girls were learning in Germany
not to be ashamed of 'playing with expression.' All the
things she had heard Mr Strood—who had, as the school
prospectus declared, been 'educated in Leipzig'—preach and
implore, 'style,' 'expression,' 'phrasing,' 'light and shade,'
these girls were learning, picking up from these wonderful
Germans. They did not do it quite like them though. They
did not think only about the music, they thought about themselves too. Miriam believed she could do it as the Germans
did. She wanted to get her own music and play it as she had
always dimly known it ought to be played and hardly ever
dared. Perhaps that was how it was with the English. They
knew, but they did not dare. No. The two she had just
heard playing were, she felt sure, imitating something—but
hers would be no imitation. She would play as she wanted to
one day in this German atmosphere. She wished now she were
going to have lessons. She had in fact had a lesson. But she
wanted to be alone and to play—or perhaps with someone in
the next room listening. Perhaps she would not have even
the chance of practising.

Minna rippled through a Chopin valse that made Miriam
think of an apple orchard in bloom against a blue sky, and was

followed by Jimmie who played the *Spring Song* with slightly
swaying body and little hands that rose and fell one against the
other, and reminded Miriam of the finger game of her childhood: 'Fly away Jack, fly away Jill.' She played very sweetly
and surely except that now and again it was as if the music
caught its breath.

Jimmie's *Lied* brought the piano solos to an end, and Fräulein Pfaff after a little speech of criticism and general encouragement asked, to Miriam's intense delight, for the singing.
'Millie' was called for. Millie came out of a corner. She
was out of Miriam's range at meal-times and appeared to her
now for the first time as a tall child-girl in a high-waisted, blue
serge frock, plainly made with long plain sleeves, at the end
of which appeared two large hands shining red and shapeless
with chilblains. She attracted Miriam at once with the shell-
white and shell-pink of her complexion, her firm chubby
baby-mouth, and her wide gaze. Her face shone in the room,
even her hair—done just like the Martins', but fluffy where
theirs was flat and shiny—seemed to give out light, shadowy-
dark though it was. Her figure was straight and flat, and she
moved, thought Miriam, as though she had no feet.

She sang, with careful precision as to the accents of her
German, in a high breathy effortless soprano, a little song about
a child and a bouquet of garden flowers.

The younger Martin, in a strong hard jolting voice, sang of
a love-sick linden tree, her pale thin cheeks pink-flushed.

'Herr Kapellmeister chooses well,' smiled Fräulein at the
end of this performance.

The *Vorspielen* was brought to an end by Gertrude Goldring's song. Clara Bergmann sat down to accompany her, and
Miriam roused herself for a double listening. There would be
Clara's opening and Clara's accompaniment and some wonderful
song. The Australian stood well away from the piano, her
shoulders thrown back and her eyes upon the wall opposite
her. There was no prelude. Piano and voice rang out
together—single notes which the voice took and sustained with
an expressive power which was beyond anything in Miriam's
experience. Not a note was quite true. . . . The unerring

falseness of pitch was as startling as the quality of the voice. The great wavering shouts, slurring now above, now below the mark, amazed Miriam out of all shyness. She sat up, frankly gazing—'How dare she? She hasn't an atom of ear —how ghastly'—her thoughts exclaimed as the shouts went on. The longer sustained notes presently reminded her of something she had heard. In the interval between the verses, while the sounds echoed in her mind, she remembered the cry, hand to mouth, of a London coal-man.

Then she lost everything in the story of the Sultan's daughter and the young Asra, and when the fullest applause of the evening was going to Gertrude's song, she did not withhold her share.

Anna, the only servant Miriam had seen so far—an enormous woman whose face, apart from the small eyes, seemed all 'bony structure,' Miriam noted, in a phrase borrowed from some unremembered reading—brought in a tray filled with cups of milk, a basket of white rolls, and a pile of little plates. Gertrude took the tray and handed it about the room. As Miriam took her cup, chose a roll, deposited it on a plate and succeeded in abstracting the plate from the pile neatly, without fumbling, she felt that for the moment Gertrude was preparing to tolerate her. She did not desire this in the least, but when the deep harsh voice fell against her from the bending Australian, she responded to the 'Wie gefällt's Ihnen?' with an upturned smile and a warm 'sehr gut!' It gratified her to discover that she could, at the end of this one day, understand or at the worst gather the drift of, all she heard, both of German and French. Mademoiselle had exclaimed at her French—les mots si bien choisis—un accent sans faute—it must be ear. She must have a very good ear. And her English was all right—at least, if she chose. . . . Pater had always been worrying about slang and careless pronunciation. None of them ever said 'cut in half' or 'very unique' or 'ho'sale' or 'phodygraff.' She was awfully slangy herself—she and Harriett were, in their thoughts as well as their words—but she had no provincialisms, no Londonisms—she could be the purest Oxford English. There was something at any rate to give her German girls. . . . She could say: 'There are no rules for English pronunciation, but what is usual at the University of Oxford is decisive for cultured people'—'decisive for cultured people.' She must remember that for the class.

'Na, was sticken Sie da, Miss Henderson?'

It was Fräulein Pfaff.

Miriam, who had as yet hardly spoken to her, did not know whether to stand or to remain seated. She half rose and then Fräulein Pfaff took the chair near her and she sat down, stiff with fear. She could not remember the name of the thing she was making. She flushed and fumbled—thought of dressing-tables and the little objects of which she had made so many hanging to the mirror by ribbons; 'toilet-tidies' haunted her—but that was not it—she smoothed out her work as if to show it to Fräulein—'Na, na,' came the delicate caustic voice. 'Was wird das wohl sein?' Then she remembered. 'It's for a pin-cushion,' she said. Surely she need not venture on German with Fräulein yet.

'Ein Nadelkissen,' corrected Fräulein, 'das wird niedlich aussehen,' she remarked quietly, and then in English: 'You like music, Miss Henderson?'

'Oh, *yes*,' said Miriam, with a pounce in her voice.

'You play the piano?'

'A little.'

'You must keep up your practice then, while you are with us—you must have time for practice.'

Fräulein Pfaff rose and moved away. The girls were arranging the chairs in two rows—plates and cups were collected and carried away. It dawned on Miriam that they were going to have prayers. What a wet-blanket on her evening. Everything had been so bright and exciting so far. Obviously they had prayers every night. She felt exceedingly uncomfortable. She had never seen prayers in a sitting-room. It had been nothing at school—all the girls standing in the drill-room, rows of voices saying 'adsum,' then a Collect and the Lord's Prayer.

A huge Bible appeared on a table in front of Fräulein's high-backed chair. Miriam found herself ranged with the girls, sitting in an attentive hush. There was a quiet, slow turning of pages, and then a long indrawn sigh and Fräulein's clear, low, even voice, very gentle, not caustic now but with something child-like about it: 'Und da kamen die Apostel zu Ihm. . . .' Miriam had a moment of revolt. She would not sit there and let a woman read the Bible at her . . . and in that 'smarmy' way. . . . In spirit she rose and marched out of the room. As the English pupil-teacher bound to suffer all things or go home, she sat on. Presently her ear was charmed by Fräulein's slow clear enunciation, her pure un-aspirated North German. It seemed to suit the narrative— and the narrative was new, vivid and real in this new tongue. She saw presently the little group of figures talking by the lake and was sorry when Fräulein's voice ceased.

Solomon Martin was at the piano. Someone handed Miriam a shabby little paper-backed hymn-book. She fluttered the leaves. All the hymns appeared to have a little short-lined verse, under each ordinary verse, in small print. It was in English—she read. She fumbled for the title-page and then her cheeks flamed with shame, *Moody and Sankey*. She was incredulous, but there it was, clearly enough. What was such a thing doing here? . . . Finishing school for the daughters of gentlemen. . . . She had never had such a thing in her hands before. . . . Fräulein could not know. . . . She glanced at her, but Fräulein's cavernous mouth was serenely open and the voices of the girls sang heartily: 'Whenhy—*com*eth. Whenhy—*com*eth, to *make*-up his *jew*els——' These girls, Germany, that piano. . . . What did the English girls think? Had any one said anything? Were they chapel? Fearfully, she told them over. No. Judy might be, and the Martins perhaps, but not Gertrude, nor Jimmie, nor Millie. How did it happen? What was the German Church? Luther— Lutheran.

She longed for the end.

She glanced through the book—frightful, frightful words and choruses.

The girls were getting on to their knees.

Oh dear, every night. Her elbows sank into soft red plush.

She was to have time for practising—and that English lesson —the first—Oxford, decisive for—cultured people. . . .

Fräulein's calm voice came almost in a whisper: 'Vater unser . . . der Du bist im Himmel,' and the murmuring voices of the girls followed her.

Miriam went to bed content, wrapped in music. The theme of Clara's solo recurred again and again; and every time it brought something of the wonderful light—the sense of going forward and forward through space. She fell asleep somewhere outside the world. No sooner was she asleep than a voice was saying: 'Bonjour, Meece,' and her eyes opened on daylight and Mademoiselle's little night-gowned form minuetting towards her down the single strip of matting. Her hair, hanging in short ringlets when released, fell forward round her neck as she bowed—the slightest dainty inclination, from side to side against the swaying of her dance. She was smiling her down-glancing, little sprite smile. Miriam loved her. . . .

CHAPTER IV

A GREAT plaque of sunlight lay across the breakfast-table. Miriam was too happy to trouble about her imminent trial. She reflected that it was quite possible to-day and to-morrow would be free. None of the visiting masters came, except, sometimes, Herr Bossenberger for music-lessons—that much she had learned from Mademoiselle. And, after all, the class she had so dreaded had dwindled to just these four girls, little Emma and the three grown-up girls. They probably knew all the rules and beginnings. It would be just reading and so on. It would not be so terrible—four sensible girls; and, besides, they had accepted her. It did not seem anything extraordinary to them that she should teach them; and they did not dislike her. Of that she felt sure. She could not say this for even one of the English girls. But the German girls did not dislike her. She felt at ease sitting amongst them and was glad she was there and not at the English end of the table. Down here, hemmed in by the Bergmanns with Emma's little form, her sounds, movements and warmth, her little quiet friendliness planted between herself and the English, with the apparently unobservant Minna and Elsa across the way, she felt safe. She felt fairly sure those German eyes did not criticize her. Perhaps, she suggested to herself, they thought a good deal of English people in general; and then they were in the minority, only four of them; it was evidently a school for English girls as much as anything . . . strange—what an adventure for all those English girls—to be just boarders— Miriam wondered how she would feel sitting there as an English boarder among the Martins and Gertrude, Millie, Jimmie and Judy? It would mean being friendly with them. Finally she ensconced herself amongst her Germans, feeling additionally secure. . . . Fräulein had spent many years in England. Perhaps that explained the breakfast of oatmeal porridge—piled plates of thick stirabout thickly sprinkled with

51

pale, very sweet powdery brown sugar—and the eggs to follow with rolls and butter.

Miriam wondered how Fräulein felt towards the English girls.

She wondered whether Fräulein liked the English girls best. . . . She paid no attention to the little spurts of conversation that came at intervals as the table grew more and more dismantled. She was there, safely there—what a perfectly stupendous thing—'weird and stupendous' she told herself. The sunlight poured over her and her companions from the great windows behind Fräulein Pfaff. . . .

When breakfast was over and the girls were clearing the table, Fräulein went to one of the great windows and stood for a moment with her hands on the hasp of the innermost of the double frames. 'Balde, balde,' Miriam heard her murmur, 'werden wir öffnen können.' Soon, soon we may open. Obviously then they had had the windows shut all the winter. Miriam, standing in the corner near the companion window, wondering what she was supposed to do and watching the girls with an air—as nearly as she could manage—of indulgent condescension—saw, without turning, the figure at the window, gracefully tall, with a curious dignified pannier-like effect about the skirt that swept from the small tightly-fitting pointed bodice, reminding her of illustrations of heroines of serials in old numbers of the *Girls' Own Paper*. The dress was of dark blue velvet—very much rubbed and faded. Miriam liked the effect, liked something about the clear profile, the sallow, hollow cheeks, the same heavy bonyness that Anna the servant had, but finer and redeemed by the wide eye that was so strange. She glanced fearfully, at its unconsciousness, and tried to find words for the quick youthfulness of those steady eyes.

Fräulein moved away into the little room opening from the schoolroom, and some of the girls joined her there. Miriam turned to the window. She looked down into a little square of high-walled garden. It was gravelled nearly all over. Not a blade of grass was to be seen. A narrow little border of bare brown mould joined the gravel to the high walls. In the centre was a little domed patch of earth and there a chestnut tree stood. Great bulging brown-varnished buds were shining whitely from each twig. The girls seemed to be gathering in the room behind her—settling down round the table—Mademoiselle's voice sounded from the head of the table where Fräulein had lately been. It must be *raccommodage* thought Miriam—the weekly mending Mademoiselle had told her of. Mademoiselle was superintending. Miriam listened. This was a sort of French lesson. They all sat round and did their mending together—in French—darning must be quite different done like that, she reflected.

Jimmie's voice came, rounded and giggling, 'Oh, Mademoiselle! j'ai une *potato*, pardong, pum de terre, je mean.' She poked three fingers through the toe of her stocking. 'Veux dire, veux dire—Qu'est-ce-que vous me racontez là?' scolded Mademoiselle. Miriam envied her air of authority.

'Ah-ho! Là-là—Boum—Bong!' came Gertrude's great voice from the door.

'Taisez-vous, taisez-vous, Jair-trude,' rebuked Mademoiselle.

'How dare she?' thought Miriam, with a picture before her eyes of the little grey-gowned thing with the wistful, frugal mouth and nose.

'Na—Miss Henderson?'

It was Fräulein's voice from within the little room. Minna was holding the door open.

At the end of twenty minutes, dismissed by Fräulein with a smiling recommendation to go and practise in the *saal*, Miriam had run upstairs for her music.

'It's all right. I'm all right. I shall be able to do it,' she said to herself as she ran. The ordeal was past. She was, she had learned, to talk English with the German girls, at table, during walks, whenever she found herself with them, excepting on Saturdays and Sundays, and she was to read with the four,

for an hour, three times a week. There had been no mention
of grammar or study in any sense she understood.

She had had a moment of tremor when Fräulein had said in
her slow clear English, 'I leave you to your pupils, Miss
Henderson,' and with that had gone out and shut the door.
The moment she had dreaded had come. This was Germany.
There was no escape. Her desperate eyes caught sight of a
solid-looking volume on the table, bound in brilliant blue
cloth. She got it into her shaking hands. It was *Misunderstood*. She felt she could have shouted in her relief. A
treatise on the Morse code would not have surprised her. She
had heard that such things were studied at school abroad and
that German children knew the names and, worse than that,
the meaning of the names of the streets in the city of London.
But this book that she and Harriett had banished and wanted to
burn in their early teens together with *Sandford and Merton*. . . .

'You are reading *Misunderstood*?' she faltered, glancing
at the four politely waiting girls.

It was Minna who answered her in her husky, eager voice.

'D'ja, d'ja,' she responded, 'na, ich meine, *yace, yace* we
read . . so sweet and beautiful book—not?'

'Oh,' said Miriam, 'yes . . .' and then eagerly, 'you all
like it, do you?'

Clara and Elsa agreed unenthusiastically. Emma, at her
elbow, made a little despairing gesture, 'I can't English,' she
moaned gently, 'too deeficult.'

Miriam tested their reading. The class had begun. Nothing
had happened. It was all right. They each, dutifully and
with extreme carefulness, read a short passage. Miriam sat
blissfully back. It was incredible. The class was going on.
The chestnut tree budded approval from the garden. She
gravely corrected their accents. The girls were respectful.
They appeared to be interested. They vied with each other
to get exact sounds; and they presently delighted Miriam by
telling her they could understand her English much better
than that of her predecessor. 'So cleare, so cleare,' they
chimed, 'Voonderfoll.' And then they all five seemed to be
talking at once. The little room was full of broken English,

of Miriam's interpolated corrections. It was going—succeeding. This was her class. She hoped Fräulein was listening outside. She probably was. Heads of foreign schools did. She remembered Madame Beck in *Villette*. But if she was not, she hoped they would tell her about being able to understand the new English teacher so well. 'Oh, I am haypie,' Emma was saying, with adoring eyes on Miriam and her two arms outflung on the table., Miriam recoiled. This would not do—they must not all talk at once and go on like this. Minna's whole face was aflame. Miriam sat up stiffly—adjusted her pince-nez—and desperately ordered the reading to begin again—at Minna. They all subsided and Minna's careful husky voice came from her still blissfully-smiling face. The others sat back and attended. Miriam watched Minna judicially, and hoped she looked like a teacher. She knew her pince-nez disguised her and none of these girls knew she was only seventeen and a half. 'Sorrowg,' Minna was saying, hesitating. Miriam had not heard the preceding word. 'Once more the whole sentence,' she said, with quiet gravity, and then as Minna reached the word '*thorough*' she corrected and spent five minutes showing her how to get over the redoubtable 'th.' They all experimented and exclaimed. They had never been shown that it was just a matter of getting the tongue between the teeth. Miriam herself had only just discovered it. She speculated as to how long it would take for her to deliver them up to Fräulein Pfaff with this notorious stumbling-block removed. She was astonished herself at the mechanical simplicity of the cure. How stupid people must be not to discover these things. Minna's voice went on. She would let her read a page. She began to wonder rather blankly what she was to do to fill up the hour after they had all read a page. She had just reached the conclusion that they must do some sort of writing when Fräulein Pfaff came and, still affable and smiling, had ushered the girls to their mending and sent Miriam off to the *saal*.

As she flew upstairs for her music, saying, 'I'm all right,

I can do it all right,' she was half-conscious that her provisional success with her class had very little to do with her bounding joy. That success had not so much given her anything to be glad about—it had rather removed an obstacle to gladness which was waiting to break forth. She was going to stay on. That was the point. She would stay in this wonderful place. . . . She came singing down through the quiet house—the sunlight poured from bedroom windows through open doors. She reached the quiet *saal*. Here stood the great piano, its keyboard open under the light of the french window opposite the door through which she came. Behind the great closed swing doors the girls were talking over their *raccommodage*. Miriam paid no attention to them. She would ignore them all. She did not even need to try to ignore them. She felt strong and independent. She would play, to herself. She would play something she knew perfectly, a Grieg lyric or a movement from a Beethoven sonata . . . on this gorgeous piano . . . and let herself go, and listen. That was music . . . not playing things, but listening to Beethoven. . . . It must be Beethoven . . . Grieg was different . . . acquired . . . like those strange green figs pater had brought from Tarring . . . Beethoven had always been real.

It was all growing clearer and clearer. . . . She chose the first part of the first movement of the *Sonata Pathétique*. That she knew she could play faultlessly. It was the last thing she had learned, and she had never grown weary of practising slowly through its long bars of chords. She had played it at her last music-lesson . . . dear old Stroodie walking up and down the long drilling-room. . . . 'Steady the bass'; 'grip the chords,' then standing at her side and saying in the thin light sneery part of his voice, 'You can . . . you 've got hands like umbrellas' . . . and showing her how easily she could stretch two notes beyond his own span. And then marching away as she played, and crying out to her, standing under the high windows at the far end of the room, 'Let it go! Let it go!'

And she had almost forgotten her wretched self, almost heard the music. . . .

She felt for the pedals, lifted her hands a span above the

piano, as Clara had done, and came down, true and clean, on
to the opening chord.   The full rich tones of the piano echoed
from all over the room; and some metal object far away from
her hummed the dominant.   She held the chord for its full
term. . . . Should she play any more ? . . . She had confessed
herself . . . just that minor chord . . . any one hearing it
would know more than she could ever tell them . . . her
whole being beat out the rhythm as she waited for the end of
the phrase to insist on what already had been said.   As it
came, she found herself sitting back, slackening the muscles of
her arms and of her whole body, and ready to swing forward
into the rising storm of her page.   She did not need to follow
the notes on the music stand.   Her fingers knew them.   Grave
and happy she sat with unseeing eyes, listening, for the
first time.

At the end of the page she was sitting with her eyes full of
tears, aware of Fräulein standing between the open swing doors
with Gertrude's face showing over her shoulder—its amazement changing to a large-toothed smile as Fräulein's quietly
repeated 'Prachtvoll, prachtvoll' came across the room.   Miriam,
after a hasty smile, sat straining her eyes as widely as possible,
so that the tears should not fall.   She glared at the volume in
front of her, turning the pages.   She was glad that the heavy
sun-blinds cast a deep shadow over the room.   She blinked.
She thought they would not notice.   Only one tear fell and
that was from the left eye, towards the wall.   'You are a real
musician, Miss Henderson,' said Fräulein, advancing.

Every other day or so Miriam found she could get an hour
on a bedroom piano; and always on a Saturday morning during
raccommodage.   She rediscovered all the pieces she had already
learned.   She went through them one by one, eagerly, slurring
over difficulties, pressing on, getting their effect, listening and
discovering.   'It's *technique* I want,' she told herself, when she
had reached the end of her collection, beginning to attach a
meaning to the familiar word.   Then she set to work.   She

restricted herself to the *Pathétique*, always omitting the first page, which she knew so well and practised mechanically, slowly, meaninglessly, with neither pedalling nor expression, page by page until a movement was perfect. Then when the mood came, she played . . . and listened. She soon discovered she could not always 'play'—even the things she knew perfectly—and she began to understand the fury that had seized her when her mother and a woman here and there had taken for granted one should 'play when asked,' and coldly treated her refusal as showing lack of courtesy. 'Ah!' she said aloud, as this realization came, 'Women.'

'Of course you can only "play when you *can*,"' said she to herself, 'like a bird singing.'

She sang once or twice, very quietly, in those early weeks. But she gave that up. She had a whole sheaf of songs with her. But after that first *Vorspielen* they seemed to have lost their meaning. One by one she looked them through. Her dear old *Venetian Song*, *Beauty's Eyes*, *An Old Garden*—she hesitated over that, and hummed it through—*Best of All*—*In Old Madrid* —the vocal score of the *Mikado*—her little *Chanson de Florian*, and a score of others. She blushed at her collection. The *Chanson de Florian* might perhaps hold its own at a *Vorspielen* —sung by Bertha Martin—perhaps. . . . The remainder of her songs, excepting a little bound volume of Sterndale Bennett, she put away at the bottom of her Saratoga trunk. Meanwhile, there were songs being learned by Herr Bossenberger's pupils for which she listened hungrily; Schubert, Grieg, Brahms. She would always, during those early weeks, sacrifice her practising to listen from the schoolroom to a pupil singing in the *saal*.

The morning of Ulrica Hesse's arrival was one of the mornings when she could 'play.' She was sitting, happy, in the large English bedroom, listening. It was late. She was beginning to wonder why the gonging did not come when the door opened. It was Millie in her dressing-gown, with her hair loose and a towel over her arm.

'Oh, *bitte*, Miss Henderson, will you please go down to
Frau Krause, Fräulein Pfaff says,' she said, her baby face full
of responsibility.

Miriam rose uneasily. What might this be? 'Frau
Krause?' she asked.

'Oh yes, it's *Haarwaschen*,' said Millie anxiously, evidently
determined to wait until Miriam recognized her duty.

'Where?' said Miriam aghast.

'Oh, in the basement. I *must* go. Frau Krause's waiting.
Will you come?'

'Oh well, I suppose so,' mumbled Miriam, coming to the
door as the child turned to go.

'All right,' said Millie, 'I'm going down. Do make haste,
Miss Henderson, will you?'

'All right,' said Miriam, going back into the room.

Collecting her music she went incredulously upstairs. This
was school with a vengeance. This was boarding-school.
It was abominable. Fräulein Pfaff indeed! Ordering her,
Miriam, to go downstairs and have her hair washed . . . by
Frau Krause . . . off-hand, without any warning . . . someone should have told her—and let her choose. Her hair was
clean. Sarah had always done it. Miriam's throat contracted. She would not go down. Frau Krause should not
touch her. She reached the attics. Their door was open and
there was Mademoiselle in her little alpaca dressing-jacket,
towelling her head.

Her face came up, flushed and gay. Miriam was too angry
to note till afterwards how pretty she had looked with her hair
like that.

'Ah! . . . c'est le grand lavage!' sang Mademoiselle.

'Oui,' said Miriam surlily.

What could she do? She imagined the whole school waiting
downstairs to see her come down to be done. Should she go
down and decline, explain to Fräulein Pfaff. She hated
her vindictively — her 'calm' message — 'treating me like
a child.' She saw the horse smile and heard the caustic
voice.

'It's sickening,' she muttered, whisking her dressing-gown

from its nail and seizing a towel. Mademoiselle was piling up her damp hair before the little mirror.

Slowly Miriam made her journey to the basement.

Minna and Elsa were brushing out their long hair with their door open. A strong sweet perfume came from the room.

The basement hall was dark save for the patch of light coming from the open kitchen door. In the patch stood a low table and a kitchen chair. On the table which was shining wet and smeary with soap, stood a huge basin. Out over the basin flew a long tail of hair and Miriam's anxious eyes found Millie standing in the further gloom, twisting and wringing.

No one else was to be seen. Perhaps it was all over. She was too late. Then a second basin held in coarse red hands appeared round the kitchen door and in a moment a woman, large and coarse, with the sleeves of her large-checked blue and white cotton dress rolled back and a great 'teapot' of pale nasturtium-coloured hair shining above the third of Miriam's 'bony' German faces, had emerged and plumped her steaming basin down upon the table.

Soap? and horrid pudding basins of steaming water. In full horror, 'Oh,' she said, in a low vague voice, 'it doesn't matter about me.'

'Gun' Tak' Fr'n,' snapped the woman briskly.

Miriam gave herself up.

'Gooten Mawgen, Frau Krause,' said Millie's polite, departing voice.

Miriam's outraged head hung over the steaming basin—her hair spread round it like a tent frilling out over the table.

For a moment she thought that the nausea which had seized her as she surrendered would, the next instant, make flight imperative. Then her amazed ears caught the sharp bump-crack of an eggshell against the rim of the basin, followed by a further brisk crackling just above her. She shuddered from head to foot as the egg descended with a cold slither upon her incredulous skull. Tears came to her eyes as she gave beneath the onslaught of two hugely enveloping, vigorously drubbing hands—'sh—ham—poo' gasped her mind.

The drubbing went relentlessly on. Miriam steadied her head against it and gradually warmth and ease began to return to her shivering, clenched body. Her hair was gathered into the steaming basin—dipped and rinsed and spread, a comforting compress, warm with the water, over her egg-sodden head. There was more drubbing, more dipping and rinsing. The second basin was re-filled from the kitchen, and after a final rinse in its fresh warm water, Miriam found herself standing up—with a twisted tail of wet hair hanging down over her cape of damp towel—glowing and hungry.

'Thank you,' she said timidly to Frau Krause's bustling presence.

'Gun' Tak' Fr'n,' said Frau Krause, disappearing into the kitchen.

Miriam gave her hair a preliminary drying, gathered her dressing-gown together and went upstairs. From the school-room came unmistakable sounds. They were evidently at dinner. She hurried to her attic. What *was* she to do with her hair? She rubbed it desperately—fancy being landed with hair like that, in the middle of the day! She could not possibly go down. . . . She must. Fräulein Pfaff would expect her to—and would be disgusted if she were not quick—she towelled frantically at the short strands round her forehead, despairingly screwed them into Hinde's and towelled at the rest. What had the other girls done? If only she could look into the schoolroom before going down—it was awful—what should she do? . . . She caught sight of a sodden-looking brush on Mademoiselle's bed. Mademoiselle had put hers up—she had seen her . . . of course . . . easy enough for her little fluffy clouds—she could do nothing with her straight, wet lumps—she began to brush it out—it separated into thin tails which flipped tiny drops of moisture against her hands as she brushed. Her arms ached; her face flared with her exertions. She was ravenous—she must manage somehow and go down. She braided the long strands and fastened their cold mass with extra hairpins. Then she unfastened the Hinde's—two

tendrils flopped limply against her forehead. She combed
them out. They fell in a curtain of streaks to her nose.
Feverishly she divided them, draped them somehow back into
the rest of her hair and fastened them.

'Oh,' she breathed, 'my *ghastly* forehead.'

It was all she could do—short of gas and curling tongs.
Even the candle was taken away in the daytime.

It was cold and bleak upstairs. Her wet hair lay in a heavy
mass against her burning head. She was painfully hungry.
She went down.

The snarling rattle of the coffee mill sounded out into the
hall. Several voices were speaking together as she entered.
Fräulein Pfaff was not there. Gertrude Goldring was grinding
the coffee. The girls were sitting round the table in easy
attitudes and had the effect of holding a council. Emma, her
elbows on the table, her little face bunched with scorn, put out
a motherly arm and set a chair for Miriam. Jimmie had flung
some friendly remark as she came in. Miriam did not hear
what she said, but smiled responsively. She wanted to get
quietly to her place and look round. There was evidently
something in the air. They all seemed preoccupied. Perhaps
no one would notice how awful she looked. 'You're not the
only one, my dear,' she said to herself in her mother's voice.
'No,' she replied in person, 'but no one will be looking so
perfectly frightful as me.'

'I say, do they know you're down?' said Gertrude hospit-
ably, as the boiling water snored on to the coffee.

Emma rushed to the lift and rattled the panel.

'Anna!' she ordered, 'Meece Hendshon! Suppe!'

'Oh, thanks,' said Miriam, in general. She could not meet
any one's eye. The coffee cups were being slid up to Gertrude's end of the table and rapidly filled by her. Gertrude,
of course, she noticed, had contrived to look dashing and
smart. Her hair, with the exception of some wild ends that
hung round her face, was screwed loosely on the top of her

head and transfixed with a dagger-like tortoise-shell hair ornament—like a Japanese—Indian—no, Maori—that was it, she
looked like a New Zealander. Clara and Minna had fastened
up theirs with combs and ribbons and looked decent—frauish
though, thought Miriam. Judy wore a plait. Without her
fuzzy cloud she looked exactly like a country servant, a farm-
house servant. She drank her coffee noisily and furtively—
she looked extraordinary, thought Miriam, and took comfort.
The Martins' brown bows appeared on their necks instead of
cresting their heads—it improved them, Miriam thought.
What regular features they had. Bertha looked like a youth
—like a musician. Her hair was loosened a little at the sides,
shading the corners of her forehead and adding to its height.
It shone like marble, high and straight. Emma's hair hung
round her like a shawl. 'Lisbeth, Gretchen . . . what was
that lovely German name . . . hild . . . Brunhilde. . . .

Talk had begun again. Miriam hoped they had not noticed
her. Her 'Braten' shot up the lift.

'Lauter Unsinn!' announced Clara.

'We've all got to do our hair in clash . . . clashishsher
Knoten, Hendy, all of us,' said Jimmie judicially, sitting forward with her plump hands clasped on the table. Her
pinnacle of hair looked exactly as usual.

'Oh, really.' Miriam tried to make a picture of a classic
knot in her mind.

'If one have classic head one can have classic knot,' scolded
Clara.

'Who have classic head?'

'How many classic head in the school of Waldstrasse?'

Elsa gave a little neighing laugh. 'Classisch head, classisch
Knote.'

'That is true what you say, Clarah.'

The table paused.

'Dîtes-moi—qu'est-ce-que ce terrible classique notte?
Dîtes!'

No one seemed prepared to answer Mademoiselle's challenge.
Miriam's mind groped . . . classic—Greece and Rome—
Greek knot. . . . Grecian key . . . a Grecian key pattern

on the dresses for the sixth form tableau—reading Ruskin . . .
the strip of glass all along the window space on the floor in the
large room—edged with mosses and grass—the mirror of
Venus. . . .

'Eh bien? Eh bien!'

. . . Only the eldest pretty girls . . . all on their hands and
knees looking into the mirror. . . .

'Classische Form—Griechisch,' explained Clara.

'Like a statue, Mademoiselle.'

'Comment! Une statue! Je dois arranger mes cheveux
comme une statue? Oh, ciel!' mocked Mademoiselle, collapsing into tinkles of her sprite laughter. . . . 'Oh-là-là!
Et quelle statue par exemple?' she trilled, with ironic eyebrows, 'la statue de votre Kaisère Wilhelm der Grosse, peut-
être?'

The Martins' guffaws led the laughter.

'Mademoisellekin with her hair done like the Kaiser Wilhelm,' pealed Jimmie.

Only Clara remained grave in wrath.

'Einfach,' she quoted bitterly, 'Simple—says Lily, so
simple!'

'Simple—simpler—simplicissimusko!'

'I make no change; not at all,' smiled Minna from behind
her nose. 'For this Ulrica it is quite something other. . . .
She has yes truly so charming a little head.'

She spoke quietly and unenviously.

'I too, indeed. Lily may go and play the flute.'

'Brave girls,' said Gertrude, getting up. 'Come on, Kinder,
clearing time. You'll excuse us, Miss Henderson? There's
your pudding in the lift. Do you mind having your coffee *mit*?'

The girls began to clear up.

'*Leely, Leely*, Leely Pfaff,' muttered Clara as she helped,
'so einfach und niedlich,' she mimicked, 'ach *was* ! Schwär-
merei—das find' ich abscheulich! I find it disgusting!'

So that was it. It was the new girl. Lily was Fräulein
Pfaff. So the new girl wore her hair in a classic knot. How
lovely. Without her hat she had 'a charming little head,'
Minna had said. And that face. Minna had seen how lovely

she was, and had not minded. Clara was jealous. Her head
with a classic knot and no fringe, her worn-looking sallow face.
. . . She would look like a 'prisoner at the bar' in some newspaper. How they hated Fräulein Pfaff. The Germans at
least. Fancy calling her Lily—Miriam did not like it, she had
known at once. None of the teachers at school had been
called by their Christian names—there had been old Quag-
mire, the Elfkin, and dear Donnikin, Stroodie, and good old
Kingie and all of them—but no Christian names. Oh yes—
Sally—so there had—Sally—but then Sally *was*—couldn't
have been anything else—never could have held a position of
any sort. They ought not to call Fräulein Pfaff that. It
was, somehow, nasty. Did the English girls do it? Ought
she to have said anything? Mademoiselle did not seem at all
shocked. Where was Fräulein Pfaff all this time? Perhaps
somewhere hidden away, in her rooms, being 'done' by Frau
Krause. Fancy telling them all to alter the way they did their
hair.

Every one was writing Saturday letters—Mademoiselle and
the Germans with compressed lips and fine, careful, evenly-
moving pen-points; the English scrawling and scraping and
dashing, their pens at all angles, and careless, eager faces. An
almost unbroken silence seemed the order of the earlier part
of a Saturday afternoon. To-day the room was very still, save
for the slight movements of the writers. At intervals nothing
was to be heard but the little chorus of pens. Clara, still
smouldering, sitting at the window end of the room, looked
now and again gloomily out into the garden. Miriam did not
want to write letters. She sat, pen in hand, and note-paper
in front of her, feeling that she loved the atmosphere of these
Saturday afternoons. This was her second. She had been
in the school a fortnight—the first Saturday she had spent
writing to her mother—a long letter for every one to read, full
of first impressions and enclosing a slangy almost affectionate
little note for Harriett. In her general letter she had said,

'If you want to think of something jolly, think of me, here.'
She had hesitated over that sentence when she considered
meal-times, especially the midday meal, but on the whole she
had decided to let it stand—this afternoon she felt it was truer.
She was beginning to belong to the house—she did not want
to write letters—but just to sit revelling in the sense of this
room full of quietly occupied girls—in the first hours of the
weekly holiday. She thought of strange Ulrica somewhere
upstairs and felt quite one of the old gang. 'Ages' she had
known all these girls. She was not afraid of them at all. She
would not be afraid of them any more. Emma Bergmann
across the table raised a careworn face from her two lines of
large neat lettering and caught her eye. She put up her hands
on either side of her mouth as if for shouting.

'*Hendchen*,' she articulated silently, in her curious lipless
way, 'mein liebes, liebes Hendchen.'

Miriam smiled timidly and sternly began fumbling at her
week's letters—one from Eve, full of congratulations and re-
commendations—'Keep up your music, my dear,' said the
conclusion, 'and don't mind that little German girl being fond
of you: It is impossible to be too fond of people if you keep
it all on a high level,' and a scrawl from Harriett, pure slang
from beginning to end. Both these letters and an earlier one
from her mother had moved her to tears and longing when
they came. She re-read them now unmoved and felt aloof
from the things they suggested. It did not seem imperative
to respond to them at once. She folded them together. If
only she could bring them all for a minute into this room, the
wonderful Germany that she had achieved. If they could
even come to the door and look in. She did not in the least
want to go back. She wanted them to come to her and taste
Germany—to see all that went on in this wonderful house, to
see pretty, German Emma, adoring her—to hear the music
that was everywhere all the week, that went, like a garland, in
and out of everything, to hear her play, by accident, and
acknowledge the difference in her playing. Oh yes, besides
seeing them all she wanted them to hear her play. . . . She
must stay . . . she glanced round the room. It was here,

somehow, somewhere, in this roomful of girls, centring in the
Germans at her end of the table, reflected on to the English
group, something of that influence that had made her play.
It was in the sheen on Minna's hair, in Emma's long-plaited
schoolgirlishness, somehow in Clara's anger. It was here,
here, and she was in it. . . . She must pretend to be writing
letters or someone might speak to her. She would hate any
one who challenged her at this moment. Jimmie might. It
was just the kind of thing Jimmie would do. Her eyes were
always roving round. . . . There were a lot of people like
that. . . . It was all right when you wanted anything or to—
to—'create a diversion' when everybody was quarrelling. But
at the wrong times it was awful. . . . The Radnors and Pooles
were like that. She could have killed them, often. 'Hullo,
Mim,' they would say, 'Wake up!' or 'What 's the row!' and
if you asked why, they would laugh and tell you you looked
like a dying duck in a thunderstorm. . . . It was all right. No
one had noticed her—or if either of the Germans had they
would not think like that—they would understand—she
believed, in a way, they would understand. At the worst they
would look at you as if they were somehow with you, and say
something sentimental. 'Sie hat Heimweh' or something like
that. Minna would. Minna's forget-me-not blue eyes behind her pink nose would be quite real and alive. . . . Ein
Blatt—she dipped her pen and wrote Ein Blatt . . . aus . . .
Ein Blatt aus sommerlichen Tagen . . . that thing they had
begun last Saturday afternoon and gone on and on with until
she had hated the sound of the words. How did it go on?
'Ein Blatt aus sommerlichen Tagen,' she breathed in a half
whisper. Minna heard—and without looking up from her
writing quietly repeated the verse. Her voice rose and
trembled slightly on the last line.

'Oh, chuck it, Minna,' groaned Bertha Martin.

'Tchookitt,' repeated Minna absently, and went on with
her writing.

Miriam was scribbling down the words as quickly as she
could:

Ein Blatt aus sommerlichen Tagen
Ich nahm es so im Wandern mit
Auf dass es einst mir möge sagen
Wie laut die Nachtigall geschlagen
Wie grün der Wald den ich—durchtritt—

durchtritt—durchschritt—she was not sure. It was perfectly lovely—she read it through translating stumblingly:

A leaf from summery days
I took it with me on my way,
So that it might remind me
How loud the nightingale had sung,
How green the wood I had passed through.

With a pang she felt it was true that summer ended in dead leaves.

But she had no leaf, nothing to remind her of her summer days. They were all past and she had nothing—not the smallest thing. The two little bunches of flowers she had put away in her desk had all crumbled together, and she could not tell which was which. . . . There was nothing else—but the things she had told Eve—and perhaps Eve had forgotten . . . there was nothing. There were the names in her birthday book! She had forgotten them. She would look at them. She flushed. She would look at them to-morrow, sometime when Mademoiselle was not there. . . . The room was waking up from its letter-writing. People were moving about. She would not write to-day. It was not worth while beginning. She took a fresh sheet of note-paper and copied her verse, spacing it carefully with a wide margin all round so that it came exactly in the middle of the page. It would soon be teatime. 'Wie grün der Wald.' She remembered one wood—the only one she could remember—there were no woods at Barnes or at the seaside—only that wood, at the very beginning, someone carrying Harriett—and green green, the brightest she had ever seen, and anemones everywhere, she could see them distinctly at this moment—she wanted to put her face down into the green among the anemones. She could not remember how she got there or the going home, but just standing there—the green and the flowers and something in

her ear buzzing and frightening her and making her cry, and
somebody poking a large finger into the buzzing ear and
making it very hot and sore.

The afternoon sitting had broken up. The table was
empty.

Emma, in raptures—near the window, was calling to the
other Germans. Minna came and chirruped too—there was
a sound of dull scratching on the window—then a little burst
of admiration from Emma and Minna together. Miriam
looked round—in Emma's hand shone a small antique watch
encrusted with jewels; at her side was the new girl. Miriam
saw a filmy black dress, and above it a pallid face. What was
it like? It was like—like—like jasmine—that was it—jasmine
—and out of the jasmine face the great gaze she had met in
the morning turned half-puzzled, half-disappointed upon the
growing group of girls examining the watch.

CHAPTER V

MIRIAM paid her first visit to a German church the next day, her third Sunday. Of the first Sunday, now so far off, she could remember nothing but sitting in a low-backed chair in the *saal* trying to read *Les Travailleurs de la Mer* . . . seas . . . and a sunburnt youth striding down a desolate lane in a storm . . . and the beginning of tea-time. They had been kept indoors all day by the rain.

The second Sunday they had all gone in the evening to the English church with Fräulein Pfaff . . . rush-seated chairs with a ledge for books, placed very close together and scrooping on the stone floor with the movements of the congregation . . . a little gathering of English people. They seemed very dear for a moment . . . what was it about them that was so attractive . . . that gave them their air of 'refinement'? . . .

Then as she watched their faces as they sang she felt that she knew all these women, the way, with little personal differences, they would talk, the way they would smile and take things for granted.

And the men, standing there in their overcoats. . . . Why were they there? What were they doing? What were their thoughts?

She pressed as against a barrier. Nothing came to her from these unconscious forms.

They seemed so untroubled. . . . Probably they were all Conservatives. . . . That was part of their 'refinement.' They would all disapprove of Mr Gladstone. . . . Get up into the pulpit and say 'Gladstone' very loud . . . and watch the result. Gladstone was a Radical . . . 'pull everything up by the roots.' . . . Pater was always angry and sneery about him. . . . Where were the Radicals? Somewhere very far away . . . tub-thumping . . . the Conservatives made them thump tubs . . . no wonder.

She decided she must be a Radical. Certainly she did not belong to these 'refined' English—women or men. She was quite sure of that, seeing them gathered together, English Church-people in this foreign town.

But then Radicals were probably chapel?

It would be best to stay with the Germans. Yes . . . she would stay. There was a woman sitting in the endmost chair just across the aisle in line with them. She had a pale face and looked worn and middle-aged. The effect of 'refinement' made on Miriam by the congregation seemed to radiate from her. There was a large ostrich feather fastened by a gleaming buckle against the side of her silky beaver hat. It swept, Miriam found the word during the Psalms, back over her hair. Miriam glancing at her again and again felt that she would like to be near her, watch her and touch her and find out the secret of her effect. But not talk to her, never talk to her.

She, too, sad and alone though Miriam knew her to be, would have her way of smiling and taking things for granted. The sermon came. Miriam sat, chafing, through it. One angry glance towards the pulpit had shown her a pale, black-moustached face. She checked her thoughts. She felt they would be too savage; would rend her unendurably. She tried not to listen. She felt the preacher was dealing out 'pastoral platitudes.' She tried to give her mind elsewhere; but the sound of the voice, unconvinced and unconvincing, threatened her again and again with a tide of furious resentment. She fidgeted and felt for thoughts and tried to compose her face to a semblance of serenity. It would not do to sit scowling here amongst her pupils with Fräulein Pfaff's eye commanding her profile from the end of the pew just behind. . . . The air was gassy and close, her feet were cold. The gentle figure across the aisle was sitting very still, with folded hands and grave eyes fixed in the direction of the pulpit. Of course. Miriam had known it. She would 'think over' the sermon afterwards. . . . The voice in the pulpit had dropped. Miriam glanced up. The figure faced about and intoned rapidly, the congregation rose for a moment rustling, and rustling subsided again. A hymn was given out. They rose again and sang. It was

Lead, Kindly Light. Chilly and feverish and weary Miriam
listened . . . 'the encircling glooo—om' . . . Cardinal Newman coming back from Italy in a ship . . . in the end he had
gone over to Rome . . . high altars . . . candles . . . incense
. . . safety and warmth. . . . From far away a radiance
seemed to approach and to send out a breath that touched and
stirred the stuffy air . . . the imploring voices sang on . . .
poor dears . . . poor cold English things . . . Miriam suddenly became aware of Emma Bergmann standing at her side
with open hymn-book, shaking with laughter. She glanced
sternly at her, mastering a sympathetic convulsion.

Emma looked so sweet standing there shaking and suffused.
Her blue eyes were full of tears. Miriam wanted to giggle too.
She longed to know what had amused her . . . just the fact
of their all standing suddenly there together. She dared not
join her . . . no more giggling as she and Harriett had giggled.
She would not even be able afterwards to ask her what it was.

Sitting on this third Sunday morning in the dim Schloss
Kirche—the Waldstrasse pew was in one of its darkest spaces
and immediately under the shadow of a deeply overhanging
gallery—Miriam understood poor Emma's confessed hysteria
over the abruptly alternating kneelings and standings, risings
and sittings of an Anglican congregation. Here, there was no
need to be on the watch for the next move. The service
droned quietly and slowly on. Miriam paid no heed to it.
She sat in the comforting darkness. The unobserving
Germans were all round her, the English girls tailed away
invisibly into the distant obscurity. Fräulein Pfaff was not
there, nor Mademoiselle. She was alone with the school.
She felt safe for a while and derived solace from the reflection
that there would always be church. If she were a governess
all her life there would be church. There was a little sting of
guilt in the thought. It would be practising deception. . . .
To despise it all, to hate the minister and the choir and the
congregation and yet to come—running—she could imagine
herself all her life running, at least in her mind, weekly to some
church—working her fingers into their gloves and pretending
to take everything for granted and to be just like everybody else,

and really thinking only of getting into a quiet pew and ceasing to pretend. It was wrong to use church like that. She was wrong—all wrong. It couldn't be helped. Who was there who could help her? She imagined herself going to a clergyman and saying she was bad and wanted to be good—even crying. He would be kind and would pray and smile—and she would be told to listen to sermons in the right spirit. She could never do that. . . . There she felt she was on solid ground. Listening to sermons was wrong . . . people ought to refuse to be preached at by these men. Trying to listen to them made her more furious than anything she could think of, more base in submitting . . . those men's sermons were worse than women's smiles . . . just as insincere at any rate . . . and you could get away from the smiles, make it plain you did not agree and that things were not simple and settled . . . but you could not stop a sermon. It was so unfair. The services might be lovely, if you did not listen to the words; and then the man got up and went on and on from unsound premises until your brain was sick . . . droning on and on, and getting more and more pleased with himself and emphatic . . . and nothing behind it. As often as not you could pick out the logical fallacy if you took the trouble. . . . Preachers knew no more than any one else . . . you could see by their faces . . . sheeps' faces. . . . What a terrible life . . . and wives and children in the homes taking them for granted. . . .

Certainly it was wrong to listen to sermons . . . stultifying . . . unless they were intellectual . . . lectures like Mr Brough's . . . that was as bad, because they were not sermons. . . . Either kind was bad and ought not to be allowed . . . a homily . . . sermons . . . homilies . . . a quiet homily might be something rather nice . . . and have not *Charity*—sounding brass and tinkling cymbal. . . . Caritas . . . I have *none* I am sure. . . . Fräulein Pfaff would listen. She would smile afterwards and talk about a 'schöne Predigt'—certainly. . . . If she should ask about the sermon? Everything would come out then.

What would be the good? Fräulein would not understand. It would be better to pretend. She could not think of any woman who would understand. And she would be obliged to live somewhere. She must pretend, to somebody. She wanted to go on, to see the spring. But must she always be pretending? Would it always be that . . . living with exasperating women who did not understand . . . pretending . . . grimacing? . . . Were German women the same? She wished she could tell Eve the things she was beginning to feel about women. These English girls were just the same. Millie . . . sweet lovely Millie. . . . How she wished she had never spoken to her. Never said, 'Are you fond of crochet?' . . . Millie saying, 'You must know all my people,' and then telling her a list of names and describing all her family. She had been so pleased for the first moment. It had made her feel suddenly happy to hear an English voice talking familiarly to her in the *saal*. And then at the end of a few moments she had known she never wanted to hear anything more of Millie and her people. It seemed strange that this girl talking about her brothers' hobbies and the colour of her sister's hair was the Millie she had first seen the night of the *Vorspielen* with the 'Madonna' face and no feet. Millie was smug. Millie would smile when she was a little older—and she would go respectfully to church all her life—Miriam had felt a horror even of the work-basket Millie had been tidying during their conversation—and Millie had gone upstairs, she knew, feeling that they had 'begun to be friends' and would be different the next time they met. It was her own fault. What had made her speak to her? She was like that. . . . Eve had told her. She got excited and interested in people and then wanted to throw them up. It was not true. She did not want to throw them up. She wanted them to leave her alone. . . . She had not been excited about Millie. It was Ulrica, Ulrica . . . Ulrica . . . Ulrica . . . sitting up at breakfast with her lovely head and her great eyes—her thin fingers peeling an egg. . . . She had made them all look so 'common.' Ulrica was different. Was she? Yes, Ulrica was different. . . . Ulrica peeling an egg and she, afterwards, like a mad thing had gone into the *saal* and talked to Millie in a vulgar, familiar way, no doubt.

And that had led to that dreadful talk with Gertrude. Gertrude's voice sounding suddenly behind her as she stood looking out of the *saal* window, and their talk. She wished Gertrude had not told her about Hugo Wieland and the skating. She was sure she would not have liked Erica Wieland. She was glad she had left. 'She was my chum,' Gertrude had said, 'and he taught us all the outside edge and taught me figure-skating.'

It was funny—improper—that these schoolgirls should go skating with other girls' brothers. She had been so afraid of Gertrude that she had pretended to be interested and had joked with her—she, Miss Henderson, the governess had said—knowlingly, 'Let 's see, he 's the cleanshaven one, isn't he?'

'Rather,' Gertrude had said with a sort of winking grimace. . . .

They were singing a hymn. The people near her had not moved. Nobody had moved. The whole church was sitting down, singing a hymn. What wonderful people. . . . Like a sort of tea-party . . . everybody sitting about—not sitting up to the table . . . happy and comfortable.

Emma had found her place and handed her a big hymn-book with the score.

There was time for Miriam to read the first line and recognize the original of 'Now thank we all our God' before the singing had reached the third syllable. She hung over the book. 'Nun—dank—et—al—le—Gott.' Now—thank—all—God. She read that first line again and felt how much better the thing was without the 'we' and the 'our.' What a perfect phrase. . . . The hymn rolled on and she recognized that it was the tune she knew—the hard square tune she and Eve had called it—and Harriett used to mark time to it in jerks, a jerk to each syllable, with a twisted glove-finger tip just under the book ledge with her left hand, towards Miriam. But sung as these Germans sang it, it did not jerk at all. It did not sound like a 'proclamation' or an order. It was . . . somehow . . . everyday. The notes seemed to hold her up. This was— Luther—Germany—the Reformation—solid and quiet. She glanced up and then hung more closely over her book. It was the stained-glass windows that made the Schloss Kirche so dark. One movement of her head showed her that all the windows within sight were dark with rich colour, and there was oak everywhere—great shelves and galleries and juttings of dark wood, great carved masses and a high dim roof and strange spaces of light; twilight, and light like moonlight and people, not many people, a troop, a little army under the high roof, with the great shadows all about them. 'Nun danket alle Gott.' There was nothing to object to in that. Everybody could say that. Everybody—Fräulein, Gertrude, all these little figures in the church, the whole world. 'Now thank, all, God.' . . . Emma and Clara were chanting on either side of her. Immediately behind her sounded the quavering voice of an old woman. They all felt it. She must remember that. . . . Think of it every day.

CHAPTER VI

DURING those early days Miriam realized that school-routine, as she knew it—the planned days—the regular unvarying succession of lessons and preparations, had no place in this new world. Even the masters' lessons, coming in from outside and making a kind of framework of appointments over the otherwise fortuitously occupied days, were, she soon found, not always securely calculable. Herr Kapellmeister Bossenberger would be heard booming and intoning in the hall unexpectedly at all hours. He could be heard all over the house. Miriam had never seen him, but she noticed that great haste was always made to get a pupil to the *saal*, and that he taught impatiently. He shouted and corrected and mimicked. Only Millie's singing, apparently, he left untouched. You could hear her lilting away through her little high songs as serenely as she did at *Vorspielen*.

Miriam was at once sure that he found his task of teaching these girls an extremely tiresome one.

Probably most teachers found teaching tiresome. But there was something peculiar and new to her in Herr Bossenberger's attitude. She tried to account for it. . . . German men despised women. Why did they teach them anything at all?

The same impression, the sense of a half-impatient, half-exasperated tuition came to her from the lectures of Herr Winter and Herr Schraub.

Herr Winter, a thin tall withered-looking man with shabby hair and bony hands whose veins stood up in knots, drummed on the table as he taught botany and geography. The girls sat round bookless and politely attentive and seemed, the Germans at least, to remember all the facts for which he appealed during the last few minutes of his hour. Miriam could never recall anything but his weary withered face.

Herr Schraub, the teacher of history, was, she felt, almost

77

openly contemptuous of his class. He would begin lecturing, almost before he was inside the door. He taught from a book, sitting with downcast eyes, his round red mass of face—expressionless save for the bristling spikes of his tiny straw-coloured moustache and the rapid movements of his tight rounded little lips—persistently averted from his pupils. For the last few minutes of his time he would, ironically, his eyes fixed ahead of him at a point on the table, snap questions—indicating his aim with a tapping finger, going round the table like a dealer at cards. Surely the girls must detest him. . . . The Germans made no modification of their polite attentiveness. Amongst the English only Gertrude and the Martins found any answers for him. Miriam, proud of sixth-form history essays and the full marks she had generally claimed for them, had no memory for facts and dates; but she made up her mind that were she ever so prepared with a correct reply, nothing should drag from her any response to these military tappings. Fräulein presided over these lectures from the corner of the sofa, out of range of the eye of the teacher, and horrified Miriam by voicelessly prompting the girls whenever she could. There was no kind of preparation for these lessons.

Miriam mused over the difference between the bearing of these men and that of the masters she remembered, and tried to find words. What was it? Had her masters been more—respectful than these Germans were? She felt they had. But it was not only that. She recalled the men she remembered teaching week by week through all the years she had known them . . . the little bolster-like literature master, an albino, a friend of Browning, reading, reading to them as if it were worth while, as if they were equals . . . interested friends—that had never struck her at the time. . . . But it was true—she could not remember ever having felt a schoolgirl . . . or being 'talked down' to . . . dear Stroodie, the music-master, and Monsieur—old white-haired Monsieur, dearest of all, she could hear his gentle voice pleading with them on behalf of his treasures . . . the drilling-master with his keen, friendly blue

eye . . . the briefless barrister who had taught them arithmetic in a baritone voice, laughing all the time but really
wanting them to get on.

What was it she missed? Was it that her old teachers were
'gentlemen' and these Germans were not? She pondered
over this and came to the conclusion that the whole attitude of
the Englishman and of Monsieur, her one Frenchman, towards
her sex was different from that of these Germans. It occurred
to her once in a flash, during these puzzled musings, that the
lessons she had had at school would not have been given more
zestfully, more as if it were worth while, had she and her
schoolfellows been boys. Here she could not feel that. The
teaching was grave enough. The masters felt the importance
of what they taught . . . she felt that they were formal,
reverently formal, 'pompous' she called it, towards the facts
that they flung out down the long schoolroom table, but that
the relationship of their pupils to these facts seemed a matter
of less than indifference to them.

She began to recognize now with a glow of gratitude that her
own teachers, those who were enthusiastic about their subjects
—the albino, her dear Monsieur with his classic French prose,
a young woman who had taught them logic and the beginning
of psychology—that strange, new subject—were at least as
enthusiastic about getting her and her mates awake and into
relationship with something. They cared somehow.

She recalled the albino, his face and voice generally separated
from his class by a book held vertically, close to his left eye,
while he blocked the right eye with his free hand—his faintly
wheezy tones bleating triumphantly out at the end of a passage
from *The Ring and the Book*, as he lowered his volume and
bent beaming towards them all, his right eye still blocked, for
response. Miss Donne, her skimpy skirt powdered with
chalk, explaining a syllogism from the blackboard, turning
quietly to them, her face all aglow, her chalky hands gently
pressed together, 'Do you *see*? Does any one *see*?' Monsieur,

spoiling them, sharpening their pencils, letting them cheat over their pages of rules, knowing quite well that each learned only one and directing his questioning accordingly, Monsieur dreaming over the things he read to them, repeating passages, wandering from his subject, making allusions here and there—and all of them, she, at any rate, and Lilla—she knew, often—in paradise. How rich and friendly and helpful they all seemed.

She began to wonder whether hers had been in some way a specially good school. Things *had* mattered there. Somehow the girls had been made to feel they mattered. She remembered even old Stroodie—the least attached member of the staff—asking her suddenly, once, in the middle of a music-lesson, what she was going to do with her life and a day when the artistic vice-principal—who was a connection by marriage of Holman Hunt's and had met Ruskin, Miriam knew, several times—had gone from girl to girl round the collected fifth and sixth forms asking them each what they would best like to do in life. Miriam had answered at once with a conviction born that moment that she wanted to 'write a book.' It irritated her when she remembered during these reflections that she had not been able to give to Fräulein Pfaff's public questioning any intelligible account of the school. She might at least have told her of the connection with Ruskin and Browning and Holman Hunt, whereas her muddled replies had led Fräulein to decide that her school had been 'a kind of high school.' She knew it had not been this. She felt there was something questionable about a high school. She was beginning to think that her school had been very good. Pater had seen to that—that was one of the things he had steered and seen to. There had been a school they might have gone to higher up the hill where one learned needlework even in the 'first class' as they called it instead of the sixth form as at her school, and 'Calisthenics' instead of drilling—and something called elocu-tion—where the girls were 'finished.' It was an expensive school. Had the teachers there taught the girls . . . as if they had no minds? Perhaps that school was more like the one she found herself in now? She wondered and wondered. What was she going to do with her life after all these years at the good school? She began bit by bit to understand her agony on the day of leaving. It was there she belonged. She ought to go back and go on.

One day she lay twisted and convulsed, face downwards on her bed at the thought that she could never go back and begin. If only she could really begin now, knowing what she wanted. . . . She would talk now with those teachers. . . . Isn't it all wonderful! Aren't things wonderful! Tell me some more. . . . She felt sure that if she could go back, things would get clear. She would talk and think and understand. . . . She did not linger over that. It threatened a storm whose results would be visible. She wondered what the other girls were doing—Lilla? She had heard nothing of her since that last term. She would write to her one day, perhaps. Perhaps not. . . . She would have to tell her that she was a governess. Lilla would think that very funny and would not care for her now that she was so old and worried. . . .

Woven through her retrospective appreciations came a doubt. She wondered whether, after all, her school had been right. Whether it ought to have treated them all so seriously. If she had gone to the other school she was sure she would never have heard of the Aesthetic Movement or felt troubled about the state of Ireland and India. Perhaps she would have grown up a Churchwoman . . . and 'lady-like.' Never.

She could only think that somehow she must be 'different'; that a sprinkling of the girls collected in that school was different, too. The school she decided was new—modern—Ruskin. Most of the girls perhaps had not been affected by it. But some had. She had. The thought stirred her. She had. It was mysterious. Was it the school or herself? Herself to begin with. If she had been brought up differently, it could not, she felt sure, have made her very different—for long —nor taught her to be affable—to smile that smile she hated so. The school had done something to her. It had not gone against the things she found in herself. She wondered once or twice during these early weeks what she would have been like if she had been brought up with these German girls. What they were going to do with their lives was only too plain. All but Emma, she had been astounded to discover, had already a complete outfit of house-linen to which they were now adding fine embroideries and laces. All could cook. Minna had startled her one day by exclaiming with lit face, 'Ach, ich Koche so *schrecklich* gern!' . . . Oh, I am so frightfully fond of cooking. . . . And they were placid and serene, secure in a kind of security Miriam had never met before. They did not seem to be in the least afraid of the future. She envied that. Their eyes and their hands were serene. . . . They would have houses and things they could do and understand, always. . . . How they must want to begin, she mused. . . . What a prison school must seem.

She thought of their comfortable German homes, of ruling and shopping and directing and being looked up to. . . . German husbands.

That thought she shirked. Emma in particular she could not contemplate in relation to a German husband.

In any case one day these girls would be middle-aged . . . as Clara looked now . . . they would look like the German women on the boulevards and in the shops.

In the end she ceased to wonder that the German masters dealt out their wares to these girls so superciliously.

And yet . . . German music, a line of German poetry, a sudden light on Clara's face. . . .

There was one other teacher, a Swiss and some sort of minister, she supposed, as every one called him the Herr Pastor. She wondered whether he was in any sense the spiritual adviser of the school and regarded him with provisional suspicion. She had seen him once, sitting short and very black and white at the head of the schoolroom table. His black beard and dark eyes as he sat with his back to the window made his face gleam like a mask. He had spoken very rapidly as he told the girls the life-story of some poet.

The time that was not taken up by the masters and the regular succession of rich and savoury meals—wastefully plentiful they seemed to Miriam—was filled in by Fräulein Pfaff with occupations devised apparently from hour to hour. On a master's morning the girls collected in the schoolroom one by one as they finished their bed-making and dusting. On other days the time immediately after breakfast was full of uncertainty and surmise. Judging from the interchange between the four first-floor bedrooms whose doors were always open during this bustling interval, Miriam, listening apprehensively as she did her share of work on the top floor, gathered that the lack of any planned programme was a standing annoyance to the English girls. Millie, still imperfectly acclimatized, carrying out her duties in a large bibbed apron, was plaintive about it in her conscientious German nearly every morning. The Martins, when the sense of Fräulein as providence was strong upon them made their beds vindictively, rapping out sarcasms to be alternately mocked and giggled at by Jimmie who was generally heard, as the gusts subsided, dispensing the comforting assurance that it wouldn't last for ever. Miriam once heard even Judy grumbling to herself in a mumbling undertone as she carried the lower landing's collective *Wäsche* upstairs to the back attic to await the quarterly *Waschfrau*.

The German side of the landing was uncritical. On free mornings the Germans had one preoccupation. It was generally betrayed by Emma in a loud excited whisper, aimed across the landing: 'Gehen wir zu Kreipe? Do we go to Kreipe's?' 'Kreipe, Kreipe,' Minna and Clara would chorus devoutly from their respective rooms. Gertrude on these occasions always had an air of knowledge and would sometimes prophesy.

To what extent Fräulein did confide in the girl and how much was due to her experience of the elder woman's habit of mind Miriam could never determine. But her prophecies were always fulfilled.

Fräulein, who generally went to the basement kitchen from the breakfast-table, would be heard on the landing towards the end of the busy half-hour, rallying and criticizing the housemaids in her gentle caustic voice. She never came to the top floor. Miriam and Mademoiselle, who agreed in accomplishing their duties with great dispatch and spending any spare time sitting in their jackets on their respective beds reading or talking, would listen for her departure. There was always a moment when they knew that the excitement was over and the landing stricken into certainty. Then Mademoiselle would flit to the top of the stairs and demand, leaning over the balustrade, 'Eh bien! Eh bien!' and someone would retail directions.

Sometimes Anna would appear in her short, chequered cotton dress, shawled and with her market basket on her arm, and would summon Gertrude, alone or with Solomon Martin, to Fräulein's room opposite the *saal* on the ground floor. The appearance of Anna was the signal for bounding anticipations. It nearly always meant a holiday and an expedition.

During the cold weeks after Miriam's arrival there were no expeditions; and very commonly uncertainty was prolonged by a provisional distribution of the ten girls between the kitchen and the five pianos. In this case neither she nor Mademoiselle received any instructions. Mademoiselle would go to the *saal* with needlework, generally the lighter household mending. The *saal* piano at practising time was allotted to the pupil to whom the next music lesson was due, and Mademoiselle spent the greater part of her time installed, either awaiting the possible arrival of Herr Bossenberger or presiding over his lessons when he came. Miriam, unprovided for, sitting in the schoolroom with a book, awaiting events, would watch her disappear unconcernedly through the folding doors, every time with fresh wonder. She did not want to take her place, though it would have meant listening to Herr Bossenberger's teaching and a quiet alcove of freedom from the apprehensive uncertainty that hung over so many of her hours. It seemed to her odd, not quite the thing, to have a third person in the room at a music lesson. She tried to imagine a lesson being given to herself under these conditions. The thought was abhorrent. And Mademoiselle, of all people. Miriam could see her sitting in the *saal*, wrapped in all the coolness of her complete insensibility to music, her eyes bent on her work, the quick movements of her small, thin hands, the darting gleam of her thimble, the dry way she had of clearing her throat, an accentuation of the slightly metallic quality of her voice, expressing, for Miriam, in sound, that curious circumspect frugality she was growing to realize as characteristic of Mademoiselle's face in repose.

The *saal* doors closed, the little door leading into the hall became the centre of Miriam's attention. Before long, sometimes at the end of ten minutes, this door would open and the day become eventful. She had already taken Clara, with Emma to make a third, three times to her masseuse, sitting for half an hour in a room above a chemist's shop, so stuffy beyond anything in her experience that she had carried away nothing but the sense of its closely-interwoven odours, a dim picture of Clara in a saffron-coloured wrapper and the shocked impression of the resounding thwackings undergone by her. Emma was paying a series of visits to the dentist and might appear at the schoolroom door with frightened eyes, holding it open—'Hendchen! Ich muss zum Zahnarzt.' Miriam dreaded these excursions. The first time Miriam had accompanied her, Emma had had 'gas.' Assailed by a loud scream, followed by the peremptory voices of two white-coated, fiercely moustached operators, one of whom seemed to be holding Emma in the chair, Miriam had started from her sofa in the background. 'Brutes!' she had declared and reached the chair-side voluble in unintelligible German to find Emma serenely emerging from unconsciousness. Once she had taken Gertrude to the dentist—another dentist, an elderly man, practising in a frock-coat in a heavily-furnished room with high sash windows, the lower sashes filled with stained glass. There had been a driving March wind and Gertrude with a shawl round her face had battled gallantly along, shouting through her shawl. Miriam had made out nothing clearly, but the fact that the dentist's wife had a title in her own right. Gertrude had gone through her trial, prolonged by some slight complication, without an anaesthetic, in alternations of tense silence and great gusts of her hacking laughter. Miriam, sitting strained in the far background near a screen covered with a mass of strange embroideries, wondered how she really felt. That, she realized, with a vision of Gertrude going on through life in smart costumes, one would never know.

The thing Miriam dreaded most acutely was a visit with Minna to her aurist. She learned with horror that Minna was obliged every few months to submit to a series of small operations at the hands of the tall, scholarly-looking man, with large, clear, impersonal eyes, who carried on his practice high up in a great block of buildings in a small faded room with coarse coffee-coloured curtains at its smudgy windows. The character of his surroundings added a great deal to her abhorrence of his attentions to Minna.

The room was densely saturated with an odour which she guessed to be that of stale cigar-smoke. It seemed so tangible in the room that she looked about at first for visible signs of its presence. It was like an invisible dry fog and seemed to affect her breathing.

Coming and going upon the dense staleness of the room and pervading the immediate premises was a strange savoury pungency. Miriam could not at first identify it. But as the visits multiplied and she noticed the same odour standing in faint patches here and there about the stairways and corridors of the block, it dawned upon her that it must be onions—onions freshly frying but with a quality of accumulated richness that she could not explain. But the fact of the dominating kitchen side by side with the consulting-room made her speculative. She imagined the doctor's wife, probably in that kitchen, a hard-browed bony North German woman. She saw the clear-eyed man at his meals; and imagined his slippers. There were dingy books in the room where Minna started and moaned.

She compared this entourage with her recollection of her one visit to an oculist in Harley Street. His stately house, the exquisite freshness of his appointments and his person stood out now. The English, she assured herself, were more refined than the Germans. Even the local doctor at Barnes, whose effect upon her mother's perpetual ill-health, upon Eve's nerves and Sarah's mysterious indigestion was so impermanent that the very sound of his name exasperated her, had something about him that she failed entirely to find in this German —something she could respect. She wondered whether the professional classes in Germany were all like this specialist and living in this way. Minna's parents, she knew, were paying large fees.

These dreaded expeditions brought a compensation.

Her liking for Minna grew with each visit. She wondered at her. Here she was with her nose and her ear—she was subject to rheumatism too—it would always, Miriam reflected, be doctor's treatment for her. She wondered at her perpetual cheerfulness. She saw her with a pang of pity, going through life with her illnesses, preceded in defiance of all the care she bestowed on her person, by her disconcerting nose, a nose she reflected, that would do splendidly for charades.

On several occasions a little contingent selected from the pianos and kitchen had appeared in the schoolroom and settled down to read German with Fräulein. Miriam had been dispatched to a piano. After these readings, the mid-morning lunches of sweet custard-like soup or chocolate soup or perhaps glasses of sweet syrup and biscuits—were, if Fräulein were safely out of earshot, voluble indignation meetings. If she were known to be in the room beyond the little schoolroom, lunch was taken in silence except for Gertrude's sallies, cheerful generalizations from Minna or Jimmie, and grudging murmurs of response.

On the mornings of Fräulein's German readings the school never went to Kreipe's. Going to Kreipe's, Miriam perceived, was a sign of fair weather.

They had been twice since her coming. Sitting at a little marble-topped table with the Bergmanns, near the window and overlooking the full flood of Georgstrasse, Miriam felt a keen renewal of the sense of being abroad. Here she sat, in the little enclosure of this upper room above a shopful of strange Delikatessen, securely adrift. Behind her she felt, not home but the German school where she belonged. Here they all sat, free. Germany was all around them. They were in the midst of it. Fräulein Pfaff seemed far away. . . . How strange of her to send them there. . . . She glanced towards the two tables of English girls in the centre of the room, wondering whether they felt as she did. . . . They had come to Germany. They were sharing it with her. It must be changing them. They must be different for having come. They would all go back, she supposed. But they would not be the same as those who had never come. She was sure they felt something of this. They were sitting about in easy attitudes. How English they all looked . . . for a moment she wanted to go and sit with them—just sit with them, rejoice in being abroad; in having got away. She imagined all their people looking in and seeing them so thoroughly at home in this little German restaurant, free from home influences, in a little world of their own. She felt a pang of response as she heard their confidently raised voices. She could see they were all, even Judy, a little excited. They chaffed each other.

Gertrude had taken every one's choice between coffee and chocolate and given an order.

Orders for *Schokolade* were heard from all over the room.

There were only women there—wonderful German women in twos and threes—ladies out shopping, Miriam supposed. She managed intermittently to watch three or four of them and wondered what kind of conversation made them so emphatic—whether it was because they held themselves so well and 'spoke out' that everything they said seemed so important. She had never seen women with so much decision in their bearing. She found herself drawing herself up.

She heard German laughter about the room. The sounds excited her and she watched eagerly for laughing faces. . . . They were different. . . . The laughter sounded differently and the laughing faces were different. The eyes were expressionless as they laughed—or evil . . . they had that same knowing way of laughing as though everything were settled—but they did not pretend to be refined as Englishwomen did . . . they had the same horridness . . . but they were . . . jolly. . . . They could shout if they liked.

Three cups of thick-looking chocolate, each supporting a little hillock of solid cream arrived at her table. Clara ordered cakes.

At the first sip, taken with lips that slid helplessly on the surprisingly thick rim of her cup, Miriam renounced all the beverages she had ever known as unworthy.

She chose a familiar-looking *éclair*—Clara and Emma ate cakes that seemed to be alternate slices of cream and very spongy coffee-coloured cake and then followed Emma's lead with an open tartlet on which plump green gooseberries stood in a thick brown syrup.

During dinner Fräulein Pfaff went the round of the table with questions as to what had been consumed at Kreipe's. The whole of the table on her right confessed to one Kuchen with their chocolate. In each case she smiled gravely and required the cake to be described. The meaning of the pilgrimage of inquiry came to Miriam when Fräulein reached Gertrude and beamed affectionately in response to her careless 'Schokolade und ein Biskuit.' Miriam and the Bergmanns were alone in their excesses.

Even walks were incalculable excepting on Saturdays, when at noon Anna turned out the schoolrooms. Then—unless to Miriam's great satisfaction it rained and they had a little festival shut in in holiday mood in the *saal*, the girls playing and singing, Anna loudly obliterating the week-days next door and the secure harbour of Sunday ahead—they went methodically out and promenaded the streets of Hanover for an hour. These Saturday walks were a recurring humiliation. If they had occurred daily, some crisis, she felt sure, would have arisen for her.

The little party would file out under the leadership of Gertrude—Fräulein Pfaff smiling parting directions adjuring them to come back safe and happy to the beehive and stabbing at them all the while, Miriam felt, with her keen eye—through the high doorway that pierced the high wall and then—charge down the street. Gertrude alone, having been in Hanover and under Fräulein Pfaff's care since her ninth year, was instructed as to the detail of their tour and she swung striding on ahead, the ends of her long fur boa flying out in the March wind, making a flourishing scroll-work round her bounding tailor-clad form—the Martins, short-skirted and thick-booted, with hard cloth jackets and hard felt hats, and short thick pelerines, almost running on either side, Jimmie, Millie and Judy hard behind. Miriam's ever-recurring joyous sense of emergence and her longing to go leisurely and alone along these wonderful streets, to go on and on at first and presently to look, had to give way to the necessity of keeping Gertrude and her companions in sight. On they went relentlessly through the Saturday throng along the great Georgstrasse—a foreign paradise, with its great bright cafés and the strange promising detail of its shops—tantalisingly half seen.

She hated, too, the discomfort of walking thus at this pace

through streets along pavements in her winter clothes. They
hampered her horribly. Her heavy three-quarter length cloth
coat made her too warm and bumped against her as she hurried
along—the little fur pelerine which redeemed its plainness
tickled her neck and she felt the outline of her stiff hat like a
board against her uneasy forehead. Her inflexible boots soon
tired her. . . . But these things she could have endured.
They were not the main source of her troubles. She could
have renounced the delights all round her, made terms with the
discomforts and looked for alleviations. But it was during
these walks that she began to perceive that she was making, in
a way she had not at all anticipated, a complete failure of her
role of English teacher. The three weeks' haphazard curricu-
lum had brought only one repetition of her English lesson in
the smaller schoolroom; and excepting at meals, when whatever
conversation there was was general and polyglot, she was never,
in the house, alone with her German pupils. The cessation
of the fixed readings arranged with her that first day by
Fräulein Pfaff did not, in face of the general absence of method,
at all disturb her. Mademoiselle's classes had, she discovered,
except for the weekly mending, long since lapsed altogether.
These walks, she soon realized, were supposed to be her and
her pupils' opportunity. No doubt Fräulein Pfaff believed
that they represented so many hours of English conversation—
and they did not. It was cheating, pure and simple. She
thought of fee-paying parents, of the probable prospectus.
'French and English governesses.'

Her growing conviction and the distress of it were confirmed
each week by a spectacle she could not escape and was rapidly
growing to hate. Just in front of her and considerably behind
the flying van, her full wincey skirt billowing out beneath what
seemed to Miriam a dreadfully thin little close-fitting stockinette jacket, trotted Mademoiselle—one hand to the plain brim
of her large French hat, and obviously conversational, with
either Minna and Elsa, or Clara and Emma, on either side
of her. Generally it was Minna and Elsa, Minna brisk and

trim and decorous as to her neat plaid skirt, however hurried, and Elsa showing her distress by the frequent twisting of one or other of her ankles which looked, to Miriam, like sticks above her high-heeled shoes. Mademoiselle's broad hat-brim flapped as her head turned from one companion to the other. Sometimes Miriam caught the mocking tinkle of her laughter. That all three were interested, too, Miriam gathered from the fact that they could not always be relied upon to follow Gertrude. The little party had returned one day in two separate groups, fortunately meeting before the Waldstrasse gate was reached, owing to Mademoiselle's failure to keep Gertrude in sight. There was no doubt, too, that the medium of their intercourse was French, for Mademoiselle's knowledge of German had not, for all her six months at the school, got beyond a few simple and badly managed words and phrases. Miriam felt that this French girl was perfectly carrying out Fräulein Pfaff's design. She talked to her pupils, made them talk; the girls were amused and happy and were picking up French. It was admirable, and it was wonderful to Miriam because she felt quite sure that Mademoiselle had no clear idea in her own mind that she was carrying out any design at all. That irritated Miriam. Mademoiselle liked talking to her girls. Miriam was beginning to know that she did not want to talk to her girls. Almost from the first she had begun to know it. She felt sure that if Fräulein Pfaff had been invisibly present at any one of her solitary conversational encounters with these German girls, she would have been judged and condemned. Elsa Speier had been the worst. Miriam could see, as she thought of her, the angle of the high garden wall of a corner house in Waldstrasse and above it a blossoming almond tree. 'How lovely that tree is,' she had said. She remembered trying hard·to talk and to make her talk, and making no impression upon the girl. She remembered monosyllables and the pallid averted face and Elsa's dreadful ankles. She had walked along intent and indifferent and presently she had felt a sort of irritation rise through her struggling. And then farther on in the walk, she could not remember how it had arisen, there was a moment when Elsa had said with unmoved, averted face hurriedly, 'My fazzer is offitser'—as if this were the answer to everything Miriam had tried to say, to her remark about the almond tree and everything else; and then she felt that there was nothing more to be said between them. They were both quite silent. Everything seemed settled. Miriam's mind called up a picture of a middle-aged man in a Saxon blue uniform—all voice and no brains—and going to take to gardening in his old age—and longed to tell Elsa of her contempt for all military men. Clearly she felt Elsa's and Elsa's mother's feeling towards herself. Elsa's mother had thin ankles, too, and was like Elsa intent and cold and dead. She could imagine Elsa in society now—hard and thin and glittery—she would be stylish— military men's women always were. The girl had avoided being with her during walks since then, and they never voluntarily addressed one another. Minna and the Bergmanns had talked to her. Minna responded to everything she said in her eager husky voice—not because she was interested Miriam felt, but because she was polite, and it had tired her once or twice dreadfully to go on 'making conversation' with Minna. She had wanted to like being with these three. She felt she could give them something. It made her full of solicitude to glance at either of them at her side. She had longed to feel at home with them and to teach them things worth teaching; they seemed pitiful in some way, like children in her hands. She did not know how to begin. All her efforts and their efforts left them just as pitiful.

Each occasion left her more puzzled and helpless. Now and again she thought there was going to be a change. She would feel a stirring of animation in her companions. Then she would discover that someone was being discussed, generally one of the girls; or perhaps they were beginning to tell her something about Fräulein Pfaff, or talking about food. These topics made her feel ill at ease at once. Things were going wrong. It was not to discuss such things that they were together out in the air in the wonderful streets and boulevards of Hanover. She would grow cold and constrained, and the conversation would drop.

And then, suddenly, within a day or so of each other, dreadful things had happened.

The first had come on the second occasion of her going with Minna to see Dr Dieckel. Minna, as they were walking quietly along together had suddenly begun in broken English which soon turned to shy, fluent, animated German, to tell about a friend, an *Apotheker*, a man, Miriam gathered—missing many links in her amazement—in a shop, the chemist's shop where her parents dealt, in the little country town in Pomerania which was her home. Minna was so altered, looked so radiantly happy whilst she talked about this man that Miriam had wanted to put out a hand and touch her. Afterwards she could recall the sound of her voice as it was at that moment with its yearning and its promise and its absolute confidence, Minna was so certain of her happiness—at the end of each hurried little phrase her voice sounded like a chord, like three strings sounding at once on some strange instrument.

And soon afterwards Emma had told her very gravely, with Clara walking a little aloof, her dog-like eyes shining as she gazed into the distance, of a 'most beautiful man' with a brown moustache, with whom Clara was in love. He was there in the town, in Hanover, a hair-specialist, treating Clara's thin short hair.

Even Emma had a *Jüngling*. He had a very vulgar surname, too vulgar to be spoken; it was breathed against Miriam's shoulder in the half-light. Miriam was begged to forget it at once and to remember only the beautiful little name that preceded it.

At the time she had timidly responded to all these stories and had felt glad that the confidences had come to her.

Mademoiselle, she knew, had never received them.

But after these confidences there were no more serious attempts at general conversation.

Miriam felt ashamed of her share in the hair-dresser and the chemist. Emma's *Jüngling* might possibly be a student. . . . She grieved over the things that she felt were lying neglected, 'things in general' she felt sure she ought to discuss with the girls . . . improving the world . . . leaving it better than you found it . . . the importance of life . . . sleeping and dreaming that life was beauty and waking and finding it was duty . . . making things better, reforming . . . being a reformer. . . . Pater always said young people always wanted to reform the universe . . . perhaps it was so . . . and nothing could be done. Clearly she was not the one to do anything. She could do nothing even with these girls, and she was nearly eighteen.

Once or twice she wondered whether they ever had thoughts about things . . . she felt they must; if only she were not shy, if she had a different manner, she would find out. She knew she despised them as they were. She could do nothing. Her fine ideas were no good. She did less than silly little Mademoiselle. And all the time Fräulein, thinking she was talking and influencing them, was keeping her . . . in Germany.

CHAPTER VII

FRÄULEIN PFAFF came to the breakfast-table a little late in
a grey stuff dress with a cream-coloured ruching about the
collar-band and ruchings against her long brown wrists. The
girls were already in their places, and as soon as grace was said
she began talking in a gentle decisive voice.

'Martins' sponge-bags'—her face creased for her cavernous
smile — 'are both large and strong — beautiful *gummi*-bags,
each large enough to contain a family of sponges.'

The table listened intently. Miriam tried to remember the
condition of her side of the garret. She saw Judy's scarlet
flush across the table.

'Millie,' went on Fräulein, 'is the owner of a damp-proof
hold-all for the bath which is a veritable monument.'

'Monument?' laughed a German voice apprehensively.

'Fancy a monument on your washstand,' tittered Jimmie.

Fräulein raised her voice slightly, still smiling. Miriam
heard her own name and stiffened. 'Miss Henderson is an
Englishwoman too—and our little Ulrica joins the English
party.' Fräulein's voice had thickened and grown caressing.
Perhaps no one was in trouble. Ulrica bowed. Her wide-
open startled eyes and the outline of her pale face remained
unchanged. Still gentle and tender-voiced, Fräulein reached
Judy and the Germans. All was well. Soaps and sponges
could go in the English bags. Judy's downcast crimson face
began to recover its normal clear flush, and the Germans joined
in the general rejoicing. They were to go, Miriam gathered,
in the afternoon to the baths. . . . She had never been to a
public baths. . . . She wished Fräulein could know there
were two bathrooms in the house at Barnes, and then wondered whether in German baths one was left to oneself or
whether there, too, there would be some woman superintending.

Fräulein jested softly on about her children and their bath.

96

Gertrude and Jimmie recalled incidents of former bathings—
the stories went on until breakfast had prolonged itself into a
sitting of happy adventurers. The room was very warm, and
coffee-scented. Clara at her corner sat with an outstretched
arm nearly touching Fräulein Pfaff who was sitting forward
glowing and shedding the light of her dark young eyes on each
in turn. There were many elbows on the table. Judy's head
was raised and easy. Miriam noticed that the whiteness of her
neck was whiter than those strange bright patches where her
eyelashes shone. Ulrica's eyes went from face to face as she
listened and Miriam fed upon the outlines of her head.

She wished she could place her hands on either side of its
slenderness and feel the delicate skull and gaze undisturbed
into the eyes.

Fräulein Pfaff rose at last from the table.

'Na, Kinder,' she smiled, holding her arms out to them all.
She turned to the nearest window.

'Die Fenster auf!' she cried, in quivering tones, 'Die
Herzen auf!' 'Up with windows! Up with hearts!'

Her hands struggled with the hasp of the long-closed outer
frame. The girls crowded round as the lattices swung wide.
The air poured in.

Miriam stood in a vague crowd seeing nothing. She felt
the movement of her own breathing and the cool streaming
of the air through her nostrils. She felt comely and strong.

'That's a thrush,' she heard Bertha Martin say as a chattering flew across a distant garden—and Fräulein's half-singing
reply, 'Know you, children, what the thrush says? Know
you?' and Minna's eager voice sounding out into the open,
'D'ja, d'ja, ich weiss—Ritzifizier, sagt sie, Ritzifizier, das
vierundzwanzigste Jahr!' and voices imitating.

'Spring! Spring! Spring!' breathed Clara, in a low sing-song.
Miriam found herself with her hands on the doors leading
into the *saal*, pushing them gently. Why not? Everything
had changed. Everything was good. The great doors gave,

the sunlight streamed from behind her into the quiet *saal*. She went along the pathway it made and stood in the middle of the room. The voices from the schoolroom came softly, far away. She went to the centre window and, pushing aside its heavy curtains, saw for the first time that it had no second pane like the others, but led directly into a sort of summer-house, open in front and leading by a wooden stairway down to the garden plot. Up the railing of the stairway and over the entrance of the summer-house a creeping plant was putting out tiny leaves. It was in shadow, but the sun caught the sharply peaked gable of the summer-house and on the left the tops of the high shrubs lining the pathway leading to the wooden door, and the great balls finishing the high stone gateway shone yellow with sunlit lichen. She heard the schoolroom windows close and the girls clearing away the breakfast things, and escaped upstairs singing.

Before she had finished her duties a summons came. Jimmie brought the message, panting as she reached the top of the stairs. 'Hurry up, Hendy!' she gasped. 'You 're one of the distinguished ones, my dear!'

'What do you mean?' Miriam began apprehensively as she turned to go. 'Oh, Jimmie——' she tried to laugh ingratiatingly. '*Do* tell me what you mean?' Jimmie turned and raised a plump hand with a sharply-quirked little finger and a dangle of lace-edged handkerchief.

'You 're a *swell*, my dear. You 're in with the specials and the classic knot.'

'What do you mean?'

'You 're going to read—Gerty, or something—no idiots admitted. You 're going it, Hendy. Ta-ta. Fly! Don't stick in the mud, old slow-coach.'

'I 'll come in a second,' said Miriam, adjusting hairpins.

She was to read Goethe . . . with Fräulein Pfaff. . . . Fräulein knew she would be one of the few who would do for a Goethe reading. She reached the little room smiling with happiness.

'Here she is,' was Fräulein's greeting. The little group— Ulrica, Minna and Solomon Martin were sitting about informally in the sunlit window space, Minna and Solomon had needlework—Ulrica was gazing out into the garden. Miriam sank into the remaining low-seated wicker chair and gave herself up. Fräulein began to read, as she did at prayers, slowly, almost below her breath, but so clearly that Miriam could distinguish each word and Fräulein's face shone as she bent over her book. It was a poem in blank verse with long undulating lines. Miriam paid no heed to the sense. She heard nothing but the even swing, the slight rising and falling of the clear low tones. She felt once more the opening of the school-room window—she saw the little brown summer-house and the sun shining on the woodwork of its porch. Summer coming. Summer coming in Germany. She drew a long breath. The poem was telling of someone getting away out of a room, out of 'narrow conversation' to a meadow-covered plain—of a white pathway winding through the green.

Minna put down her sewing and turned her kind blue eyes to Fräulein Pfaff's face.

Ulrica sat drooping, her head bent, her great eyes veiled, her hands entwined on her lap. . . . The little pathway led to a wood. The wide landscape disappeared. Fräulein's voice ceased.

She handed the book to Ulrica, indicating the place and Ulrica read. Her voice sounded a higher pitch than Fräulein's. It sounded out rich and full and liquid, and seemed to shake her slight body and echo against the walls of her face. It filled the room with a despairing ululation. Fräulein seemed by contrast to have been whispering piously in a corner. Listening to the beseeching tones, hearing no words, Miriam wished that the eyes could be raised, when the reading ceased, to hers and that she could go and put her hands about the beautiful head, scarcely touching it and say, 'It is all right. I will stay with you always.'

She watched the little hand that was not engaged with the book and lay abandoned, outstretched, listless and shining on her knee. Solomon's needle snapped. She frowned and roused herself heavily to secure another from the basket on the floor at her side. Miriam, flashing hatred at her, caught Fräulein's fascinated gaze fixed on Ulrica; and saw it hastily turn to an indulgent smile as the eyes became conscious, moving for a moment without reaching her in the direction of her own low chair. A tap came at the door and Anna's flat tones, like a voluble mechanical doll, announced a postal official waiting in the hall for Ulrica—with a package. 'Ein Packet . . . a-a-ach,' wailed Ulrica, rising, her hands trembling, her great eyes radiant. Fräulein sent her off with Solomon to superintend the signing and payments and give help with the unpacking.

'The little heiress,' she said devoutly, with her wide smile, as she returned from the door.

'Oh . . .' said Miriam politely.

'Sie, nun, Miss Henderson,' concluded Fräulein, handing her the book and indicating the passage Ulrica had just read. 'Nun *Sie*,' she repeated brightly, and Minna drew her chair a little nearer, making a small group.

'Schiller' she saw at the top of the page and the title of the poem *Der Spaziergang*. She laid the book on the end of her knee, and leaning over it, read nervously. Her tones reassured her. She noticed that she read very slowly, breaking up the rhythm into sentences—and authoritatively as if she were recounting an experience of her own. She knew at first that she was reading like a cultured person and that Fräulein would recognize this at once, she knew that the perfect assurance of her pronunciation would make it seem that she understood every word, but soon these feelings gave way to the sense half grasped of the serpentine path winding and mounting through a wood, of a glimpse of a distant valley, of flocks and villages, and of her unity with Fräulein and Minna seeing and feeling all these things together. She finished the passage—Fräulein quietly commended her reading and Minna said something about her earnestness.

'Miss Henderson is always a little earnest,' said Fräulein affectionately.

'Are you dressed, Hendy?'

Miriam, who had sat up in her bath when the drumming came at the door, answered sleepily, 'No, I shan't be a minute.'

'Don't you want to see the diving?'

All Jimmie's fingers seemed to be playing exercises against the panels. Miriam wished she would restrain them and leave her alone. She did not in the least wish to see the diving.

'I shan't be a minute,' she shouted crossly, and let her shoulders sink once more under the comforting water. It was the first warm water she had encountered since that night when Mademoiselle had carried the jugs upstairs. Her soap, so characterless in the chilly morning basin lathered freely in the warmth and was fragrant in the steamy air. When Jimmie's knocking came she was dreaming blissfully of baths with Harriett—the dissipated baths of the last six months between tea and dinner with a theatre or a dance ahead. Harriett, her hair strained tightly into a white crocheted net, her snub face shining through the thick steam, tubbing and jesting at the wide end of the huge porcelain bath, herself at the narrow end commanding the taps under the steam-dimmed beams of the red-globed gas-jets . . . sponge-fights . . . and those wonderful summer bathings when they had come in from long tennis-playing in the sun, filled the bath with cold water and sat in the silence of broad daylight immersed to the neck, confronting each other.

Seeing no sign of anything she could recognize as a towel, she pulled at a huge drapery hanging like a counterpane in front of a coil of pipes extending half-way to the ceiling. The pipes were too hot to touch and the heavy drapery was more than warm and obviously meant for drying purposes. Sitting wrapped in its folds, dizzy and oppressed, she longed for the flourish of a rough towel and a window open at the top. She could see no ventilation of any kind in her white cell. By the time her heavy outdoor things were on she was faint with exhaustion, and hurried down the corridor towards the shouts and splashings echoing in the great, open, glass-roofed swimming-bath. She was just in time to see a figure in scarlet and white, standing out on the high gallery at the end of a projecting board which broke the little white balustrade, throw up its arms and leap out and flash—its joined hands pointed down-wards towards the water, its white feet sweeping up like the tail of a swooping bird—cleave the green water and disappear. The huge bath was empty of bathers and smoothly rippling save where the flying body had cleaved it and left wavelets and bubbles. The girls—most of them in their outdoor things—were gathered in a little group near the marble steps leading down into the water farthest from where the diver had dropped, stirring and exclaiming. As Miriam was approaching them a red-capped head came cleanly up out of the water near the steps and she recognized the strong jaw and gleaming teeth of Gertrude. She neither spluttered nor shook her head. Her eyes were wide and smiling, and her raucous laugh rang out above the applause of the group of girls.

Miriam paused under the overhanging gallery. Her eyes went, incredulously, up to the spring-board. It seemed impossible . . . and all that distance above the water. . . . Her gaze was drawn to the flicking of the curtain of one of the little compartments lining the gallery.

'Hullo, Hendy, let me get into my cubicle.' Gertrude stood before her dripping and smiling.

'However on earth did you do it?' said Miriam, gazing incredulously at the ruddy wet face.

Gertrude's smile broadened. 'Go on,' she said, shaking the drops from her chin, 'it's all in the day's work.'

In the hard clear light Miriam saw that the teeth that looked so gleaming and strong in the distance were slightly ribbed and fluted and had serrated edges. Large stoppings showed like shadows behind the thin shells of the upper front ones. Even Gertrude might be ill one day; but she would never be ill and sad and helpless. That was clear from the neat way she plunged in through her curtains. . . .

Miriam's eyes went back to the row of little curtained recesses in the gallery. The drapery that had flapped was now half withdrawn, the light from the glass roof fell upon the top of a head flung back and shaking its mane of hair. The profile was invisible, but the sheeny hair rippled in thick gilded waves almost to the floor. . . . How hateful of her, thought Miriam. . . . How beautiful. I should be just the same if I had hair like that . . . that's Germany. . . . Lohengrin. . . . She stood adoring. 'Stay and talk while I get on my togs,' came Gertrude's voice from behind her curtains.

Miriam glanced towards the marble steps. The little group had disappeared. She turned helplessly towards Gertrude's curtains. She could not think of anything to say to her. She was filled with apprehension. 'I wonder what we shall do to-morrow,' she presently murmured.

'I don't,' gasped Gertrude, towelling.

Miriam waited for the prophecy.

'Old Lahmann's back from Geneva,' came the harsh panting voice.

'Pastor Lahmann?' repeated Miriam.

'None other, madame.'

'Have you seen him?' went on Miriam dimly, wishing that she might be released.

'Scots wha hae, no! But I saw Lily's frills.'

The billows of gold hair in the gallery were being piled up by two little hands—white and plump like Eve's, but with quick clever irritating movements, and a thin sweet self-conscious voice began singing 'Du, meine *Seele*.' Miriam lost interest in the vision. . . . They were all the same. Men liked creatures like that. She could imagine that girl married.

'Lily and his wife were great friends,' Gertrude was saying. 'She's dead, you know.'

'*Is* she,' said Miriam emphatically.

'She used to be always coming when I first came over, Scots wha—blow—got a pin, Hendy? . . . We shan't have his . . . thanks, you're a saint . . . his boys in the schoolroom any more now.'

'Are those Pastor Lahmann's boys?' said Miriam, noticing that Gertrude's hair was coarse, each hair a separate thread. 'She's the wiry plucky kind. How she must despise me,' said her mind.

'Well,' said Gertrude, switching back her curtain to lace her boots. 'Long may Lily beam. I like summer weather myself.'

Miriam turned away. Gertrude half-dressed behind the curtains was too clever for her. She could not face her unveiled with vacant eyes.

'The summer is jolly, isn't it?' she said uneasily.

'You're right, my friend. Hullo! There's Emmchen looking for you. I expect the Germans have just finished their annual. They never come into the Schwimmbad, they're always too late. I should think you'd better toddle them home, Hendy—the darlings might catch cold.'

'Don't we all go together?'

'We go as we are ready, from this establishment, just anyhow as long as we're not in ones or twos—Lily won't have twos, as I dare say you've observed. Be good, my che-hild,' she said heartily, drawing on her second boot, 'and you'll be happy—sehr sehr happy, I hope, Hendy.'

'Thank you,' laughed Miriam. Emma's hands were on her muff, stroking it eagerly. 'Hendchen, Hendchen,' she cooed in her consoling tones, 'to house, to house, I am so angry—hangry.'

'Hungry.'

'Hungry, yes, and Minna and Clara is ready. Kom!'

The child linked arms with her and pulled Miriam towards the corridor. Once out of sight under the gallery she slipped her arm round Miriam's waist. 'Oh, Hendchen, my darling beautiful, you have so lovely teint after your badth—oh, I am zo hangry, oh Hendchen, I luff you zo, I am zo haypie, kiss me one small, small kiss.'

'What a baby you are,' said Miriam, half turning as the girl's warm lips brushed the angle of her jaw. 'Yes, we'll go home, come along.'

The corridor was almost airless. She longed to get out into the open. They found Minna at a table in the entrance hall her head propped on her hand, snoring gently. Clara sat near her with closed eyes.

As the little party of four making its way home, cleansed and hungry, united and happy, stood for a moment on a tree-planted island half-way across a wide open space, Minna with her eager smile said, gazing, 'Oh, I would like a glass Bier.' Miriam saw very distinctly the clear sunlight on the boles of the trees showing every ridge and shade of colour as it had done on the peaked summer-house porch in the morning. The girls closed in on her during the moment of disgust which postponed her response.

'Dear Hendchen! We are alone! Just we nice four! Just only one most little small glass! Just one! Kind, best Hend-chen!' she heard. She pushed her way through the little group pretending to ignore their pleadings and to look for obstacles to their passage to the opposite kerb. She felt her disgust was absurd and was asking herself why the girls should not have their beer. She would like to watch them, she knew; these little German Fraus-to-be serenely happy at their Bier table on this bright afternoon. They closed in on her again. Emma in the gutter in front of her. She felt arms and hands, and the pleading voices besieged her again. Emma's upturned tragic face, her usually motionless lips a beseeching tunnel, her chin and throat, moving to her ardent words, made Miriam laugh. It *was* disgusting. 'No, no,' she said hastily, backing away from them to the end of the island. 'Of course not. Come along. Don't be silly.' The elder girls gave in. Emma kept up a little solo of reproach hanging on Miriam's arm. 'Very strict. Cold English. No Bier. I want to home. I have Bier to home,' until they were in sight of the high walls of Waldstrasse.

CHAPTER VIII

'Sur l'eau, si beau!'

This refrain threatening for the third time, three or four of the girls led by Bertha Martin, supplied it in a subdued sing-song without waiting for Pastor Lahmann's slow voice. Miriam had scarcely attended to his discourse. He had begun in flat easy tones, describing his visit to Geneva, the snowclad mountains, the quiet lake, the spring flowers. His words brought her no vision and her mind wandered, half tethered. But when he began reading the poem she sank into the rhythm and turned towards him and fixed expectant eyes upon his face. His expression disturbed her. Why did he read with that half-smile? She felt sure that he felt they were 'young ladies,' 'demoiselles,' 'jeunes filles.' She wanted to tell him she was nothing of the kind and take the book from him and show him how to read. His eyes, soft and brown, were the eyes of a child. She noticed that the lower portion of his flat white cheeks looked broader than the upper, without giving an effect of squareness of jaw. Then the rhythm took her again and, with the second 'sur l'eau, si beau,' she saw a very blue lake and a little boat with lateen sails, and during the third verse began to forget the lifeless voice. As the murmured refrain came from the girls there was a slight movement in Fräulein's sofa-corner. Miriam did not turn her eyes from Pastor Lahmann's face to look at her, but half expected that at the end of the next verse her low clear devout tones would be heard joining in. Part way through the verse, with a startling sweep of draperies against the leather covering of the sofa, Fräulein stood up and towered extraordinarily tall at Pastor Lahmann's right hand. Her eyes were wide. Miriam thought she had never seen any one look so pale. She was speaking very quickly in German. Pastor Lahmann rose and faced her. Miriam had just grasped the fact that she was

106

taking the French master to task for reading poetry to his pupils and heard Pastor Lahmann slowly and politely inquire of her whether she or he were conducting the lesson, when the two voices broke out together. Fräulein's fiercely voluble and the Herr Pastor's voluble and mocking and polite. The two voices continued as he made his way, bowing gravely, down the far side of the table to the *saal* doors. Here he turned for a moment and his face shone black and white against the dark panelling. 'Na, Kinder,' crooned Fräulein gently, when he had disappeared, 'a walk—a walk in the beautiful sunshine. Make ready quickly.'

'My sainted uncle,' laughed Bertha as they trooped down the basement stairs. 'Oh—my stars!'

'*Did* you see her eyes?'

'Ja! Wüthend!'

'I wonder the poor little man wasn't burnt up.'

'Hurry up, Mädshuns, we'll have a ripping walk. We'll see if we can go Tiergartenstrasse.'

'Does this sort of thing often happen?' asked Miriam, finding herself bending over a boot-box at Gertrude's side.

Gertrude turned and winked at her. 'Only sometimes.'

'What an awful temper she must have,' pursued Miriam. Gertrude laughed.

Breakfast the next morning was a gay feast. The mood which had seized the girls at the lavishly decked tea-table awaiting them on their return from their momentous walk the day before, still held them. They all had come in feeling a little apprehensive, and Fräulein behind her tea-urn had met them with the fullest expansion of smiling indulgence Miriam had yet seen. After tea she had suggested an evening's entertainment and had permitted the English girls to act charades.

For Miriam it was an evening of pure delight. At the end of the first charade, when the girls were standing at a loss in the dimly-lit hall, she made a timid suggestion. It was enthusiastically welcomed and for the rest of the evening she was

allowed to take the lead. She found herself making up scene
after scene surrounded by eager faces. She wondered whether
her raised voice, as she disposed of proffered suggestions—
'no, that wouldn't be clear, *this* is the thing we 've got to bring
out'—could be heard by Fräulein sitting waiting with the
Germans under the lowered lights in the *saal*, and she felt
Fräulein's eye on her as she plunged from the hall into the dim
schoolroom rapidly arranging effects in the open space in front
of the long table which had been turned round and pushed
alongside the windows.

Towards the end of the evening, dreaming alone in the
schoolroom near the closed door of the little room whence the
scenes were lit, she felt herself in a vast space. The ceilings
and walls seemed to disappear. She wanted a big scene, something quiet and serious—quite different from the fussy little
absurdities they had been rushing through all the evening. A
statue . . . one of the Germans. 'You think of something
this time,' she said, pushing the group of girls out into the hall.

Ulrica. She must manage to bring in Ulrica without giving
her anything to do. Just to have her to look at. The height
of darkened room above her rose to a sky. An animated discussion, led by Bertha Martin, was going on in the hall.

They had chosen 'beehive.' It would be a catch. Fräulein
was always calling them her Bienenkorb and the girls would
guess Bienenkorb and not discover that they were meant to
say the English word.

'The old things can't possibly get it. It 'll be a lark, just
for the end,' said Jimmie.

'No.' Miriam announced radiantly. 'They 'd hate a sell.
We 'll have Romeo.'

'That 'll be awfully long. Four bits altogether, if they
don't guess from the syllables,' objected Solomon wearily.

Rapidly planning farcical scenes for the syllables, she carried
her tired troupe to a vague appreciation of the final tableau for
Ulrica. Shrouding the last syllable beyond recognition, she
sent a messenger to the audience through the hall door of the
saal to beg for Ulrica.

Ulrica came, serenely wondering, her great eyes alight with

her evening's enjoyment and was induced by Miriam—
'You 've only to stand and look down, nothing else'—to mount
the schoolroom table in the dimness and, standing with her
hands on the back of a draped chair, to gaze down at Romeo's
upturned face.

Bertha Martin's pale profile, with her fair hair drawn back
and tied at the nape of her neck and a loose cloak round her
shoulders would, it was agreed, make the best presentation of
a youth they could contrive, and Miriam arranged her, turning
her upturned face so that the audience would catch its clear
outline. But at the last minute, urged by Solomon's disapproval of the scene, Bertha withdrew. Miriam put on the
cloak, lifted its collar to hide her hair and, standing with her
back to the audience flung up her hands towards Ulrica as the
gas behind the little schoolroom door was turned slowly up.
Standing motionless, gazing at the pale oval face bending
gravely towards her from the gloom, she felt for a moment the
radiance of stars above her and heard the rustle of leaves. Then
the guessing voices broke from the *saal*. 'Ach! ach! Wie
schön! Romeo! That is beautifoll. Romeo! Who is our
Romeo?' and Fräulein's smiling, singing, affectionate voice,
'Who is Romeo! The rascal!'

Taking the top flight three stairs at a time, Miriam reached
the garret first and began running about the room at a quick
trot with her fists closed, arms doubled and elbows back. The
high garret looked wonderfully friendly and warm in the light
of her single candle. It seemed full of approving voices. Perhaps one day she would go on the stage. Eve always said so.

People always liked her, if she let herself go. She would let
herself go more in future at Waldstrasse.

It was so jolly being at Waldstrasse.

'Qu'est-ce que vous avez?' appealed Mademoiselle, laughing,
at the door, with open face. Miriam continued her trot. Mademoiselle put her candle down on the dressing-table and began
to run, too, in little quick dancing steps, her wincey skirt billowing out all round her. Their shadows bobbed and darted,

swelling and shrinking on the plaster walls. Soon breathless, Mademoiselle sank down on the side of her bed, panting and volleying raillery and broken tinkles of laughter at Miriam standing goose-stepping on the strip of matting with an open umbrella held high over her head. Recovering breath, she began to lament. . . . Miriam had not during the whole evening of dressing up seen the Martins' summer hats. . . . They were wonderful. Shutting her umbrella Miriam went to her dressing-table drawer. . . . It would be impossible, absolutely impossible . . . to imagine hats more beautiful. . . . Miriam sat on her own bed punctuating through a paper-covered comb. . . . Mademoiselle persisted . . . non, écoutez —figurez-vous—the hats were of a pale straw . . . the colour of pepper . . . 'Bee . . .' responded the comb on a short low wheeze. 'And the trimming—oh, of a charm that no one could describe.' . . . 'Beem!' squeaked the comb . . . 'stalks of barley' . . . 'beem-beem' . . . 'of a perfect naturalness' . . . 'and the flowers, poppies, of a beauty'—'bee-eeem—beeem' . . . 'oh, oh, vraiment'—Mademoiselle buried her face in her pillow and put her fingers to her ears.

Miriam began playing very softly *The March of the Men of Harlech*, and got to her feet and went marching gently round the room near the walls. Sitting up, Mademoiselle listened. Presently she rounded her eyes and pointed with one finger to the dim roof of the attic.

'Les toiles d'araignées auront peur!' she whispered.

Miriam ceased playing and her eyes went up to the little window-frames high in the wall, farthest away from the island made by their two little beds and the matting and toilet chests, and scarcely visible in the flickering candle-light, and came back to Mademoiselle's face.

'Les toiles d'araignées,' she breathed, straining her eyes to their utmost size. They gazed at each other. 'Les toiles . . .'

Mademoiselle's laughter came first. They sat holding each other's eyes, shaken with laughter, until Mademoiselle said, sighing brokenly, 'Et c'est la cloche qui va sonner immédiate-ment.' As they undressed, she went on talking—'the night comes . . . the black night . . . we must sleep . . . we must

sleep in peace . . . we are safe . . . we are protected . . .
nous craignons Dieu, n'est ce pas?' Miriam was shocked to
find her at her elbow, in her nightgown, speaking very gravely.
She looked for a moment into the serious eyes challenging her
own. The mouth was frugally compressed. 'Oh yes,' said
Miriam stiffly.

They blew out the candle when the bell sounded and got into
bed. Miriam imagined the Martins' regular features under
their barley and poppy trimmed hats. She knew exactly the
kind of English hat it would be. They were certainly not pretty
hats—she wondered at Mademoiselle's French eyes being so
impressed. She knew they must be hats with very narrow
brims, the trimming coming nearly to the edge and Solomon's,
she felt sure, inclined to be boat-shaped. Mademoiselle was
talking about translated English books she had read. Miriam
was glad of her thin voice piercing the darkness—she did not
want to sleep. She loved the day that had gone; and the one
that was coming. She saw the room again as it had been when
Mademoiselle had looked up towards the *toiles d'araignées*. She
had never thought of there being cobwebs up there. Now she
saw them dangling in corners, high up near those mysterious
windows unnoticed, looking down on her and Mademoiselle
. . . Fräulein Pfaff's cobwebs. They were hers now, had been
hers through cold dark nights. . . . Mademoiselle was asking
her if she knew a most charming English book . . . *La
Première Prière de Jessica?*

'Oh yes.'

'Oh, the most beautiful book it would be possible to read.'
An indrawn breath, *Le Secret de Lady Audley?*

'Yes,' responded Miriam sleepily.

After the gay breakfast Miriam found herself alone in the
schoolroom listening inadvertently to a conversation going on
apparently in Fräulein Pfaff's room beyond the smaller schoolroom. The voices were low, but she knew neither of them,
nor could she distinguish words. The sound of the voices,
boxed in, filling a little space shut off from the great empty

hall, made the house seem very still.   The *saal* was empty, the
girls were upstairs at their housework. Miriam, restlessly
rising early, had done her share before breakfast.   She took
Harriett's last letter from her pocket and fumbled the dis-
arranged leaves for the conclusion.

'We are sending you out two blouses.   Don't you think
you're lucky?' Miriam glanced out at the young chestnut
leaves drooping in tight pleats from black twigs . . . 'real
grand proper blouses the first you've ever had, and a skirt to
wear them with . . . won't you be within an inch of your
life! Mother got them at Grigg's—one is squashed strawberry with a sort of little catherine-wheely design in black going
over it but not too much, awfully smart; and the other is a sort
of buffy; one zephyr, the other cotton, and the skirt is a sort of
mixey pepper and salt with lumps in the weaving—you know
how I mean, something like our prawn dresses only lighter and
much more refined. The duffer is going to join the tennis-
club—he was at the Pooles' dance. I was simply flabber-
gasted. He's a duffer.'

The little German garden was disappearing from Miriam's
eyes. . . . It was cruel, cruel that she was not going to wear
her blouses at home, at the tennis-club . . . with Harriett.
. . . It was all beginning again, after all—the spring and
tennis and presently boating—things were going on . . . the
smash had not come . . . why had she not stayed . . . just
one more spring? . . . how silly and hurried she had been,
and there at home in the garden lilac was quietly coming out
and syringa and guelder roses and May and laburnum and . . .
everything . . . and she had run away, proud of herself, despising them all, and had turned herself into Miss Henderson,
. . . and no one would ever know who she was. . . . Perhaps
the blouses would make a difference—it must be extraordinary
to have blouses. . . . Slommucky . . . untidy and slommucky, Lilla's mother had called them . . . and perhaps they
would not fit her. . . .

One of the voices rose to a sawing like the shrill whirr of
wood being cut by machinery. . . . A derisive laugh broke
into the strange sound. It was Fräulein Pfaff's laughter and

was followed by her voice, thinner and shriller and higher than
the other. Miriam listened. What could be going on? . . .
both voices were almost screaming . . . together . . . one
against the other . . . it was like mad women. . . . A door
broke open on a shriek. Miriam bounded to the schoolroom
door and opened it in time to see Anna lurch, shouting and
screaming, part way down the basement stairs. She turned,
leaning with her back against the wall, her eyes half-closed,
sawing with fists in the direction of Fräulein, who stood laughing in her doorway. After one glance Miriam recoiled. They
had not seen her.

'Ja,' screamed Fräulein—'Sie können ihre paar Groschen
haben!—Ihre paar Groschen! Ihre paar Groschen!' and then
the two voices shrieked incoherently together until Fräulein's
door slammed to and Anna's voice, shouting and swearing, died
away towards the basement.

Miriam crept back to the schoolroom window. She stood
shivering, trying to forget the taunting words, and the cruel
laughter. 'You can have your ha'pence!' Poor Anna. Her
poor wages. Her bony face. . . .

Gertrude looked in.

'I say, Henderson, come on down and help me pack up
lunch. We're all going to Hoddenheim for the day, the whole
family, come on.'

'For the day?'

'The day, ja. Lily's restless.'

Miriam stood looking at her laughing face and listening
to her hoarse, whispering voice. Gertrude turned and went
downstairs.

Miriam followed her, cold and sick and shivering, and
presently glad to be her assistant as she bustled about the
empty kitchen.

Upstairs the other girls were getting ready for the outing.

Starting out along the dusty field-girt roadway leading from
the railway station to the little town of Hoddenheim through
the hot sunshine, Miriam was already weary and fearful of the

hours that lay ahead. They would bring tests; and opportunities for Fräulein to see all her incapability. Fräulein had thrown her thick gauze veil back over her large hat and was walking, with short footsteps, quickly along the centre of the roadway, throwing out exclamations of delight, calling to the girls in a singing voice to cast away the winter, to fill their lungs, fill their hearts with spring.

She rallied them to observation.

Miriam could not remember having seen men working in fields. They troubled her. They looked up with strange eyes. She wished they were not there. She wanted the fields to be still—and smaller. Still green fields and orchards . . . woods. . . .

They passed a farmyard and stopped in a cluster at the gate.

There was a moment of relief for her here. She could look easily at the scatter of poultry and the little pigs trotting and grunting about the yard. She talked to the nearest German girl, of these and of the calves standing in the shelter of a rick, carefully repeating the English names. As her eyes reached the rick she found that she did not know what to say. Was it hay or straw? What was the difference? She dreaded the day more and more.

Fräulein passed on leading the way, down the road hand-in-hand with Emma. The girls straggled after her.

Making some remark to Minna, Miriam secured her companionship and dropped a little behind the group. Minna gave her one eager beam from behind her nose, which was shining rosily in the clear air, and they walked silently along side by side bringing up the rear.

Voices and the scrabble of feet along the roadway sounded ahead.

Miriam noticed large rounded puffs of white cloud standing up sharp and still upon the horizon. Cottages began to appear at the roadside.

Standing and moving in the soft air was the strong sour smell of baking Schwarzbrot. A big bony-browed woman came from a dark cottage and stood motionless in the low doorway,

watching them with kindly body. Miriam glanced at her face
—her eyes were small and expressionless, like Anna's . . .
evil-looking.

Presently they were in a narrow street. Miriam's footsteps
hurried. She almost cried aloud. The façades of the dwel-
lings passing slowly on either hand were higher, here and there
one rose to a high peak, pierced geometrically with tiny windows. The street widening out ahead showed an open cobbled
space and cross-roads. At every angle stood high quiet peaked
houses, their faces shining warm cream and milk-white,
patterned with windows.

They overtook the others drawn up in the roadway before a
long low wooden house. Miriam had time to see little gilded
figures standing in niches, in rows all along the façade and rows
of scrollwork dimly painted, as she stood still a moment with
beating heart behind the group. She heard Fräulein talking
in English of councillors and centuries and assumed for a
moment, as Fräulein's eye passed her, a look of intelligence;
then they had all moved on together deeper into the town.
She clung to Minna, talking at random . . . did she like
Hoddenheim . . . and Minna responded to the full, helping
her, talking earnestly and emphatically about food and the sunshine, isolating the two of them; and they all reached the
cobbled open space and stood still and the peaked houses stood
all round them.

'You like old-time Germany, Miss Henderson?'

Miriam turned a radiant face to Fräulein Pfaff's table and
made some movement with her lips.

'I think you have something of the German in you.'

'She has, she has,' said Minna from the little arbour where
she sat with Millie. 'She is not English.'

They had eaten their lunch at a little group of arboured
tables at the back of an old wooden inn. Fräulein had talked
history to those nearest to her, and sat back at last with her
gauze veil in place, tall and still in her arbour, sighing happily
now and again and making her little sounds of affectionate

raillery as the girls finished their coffee and jested and giggled together across their worm-eaten, green-painted tables.

'You have beautiful old towns and villages in England,' said Fräulein, yawning slightly.

'Yes—but not anything like this.'

'Oh, Gertrude, that isn't true. We *have*.'

'Then they 're hidden from view, my dear Mill, not visible to the naked eye,' laughed Gertrude.

'Tell us, my Millie,' encouraged Fräulein, 'say what you have in mind. Perhaps Gairtrud does not know the English towns and villages as well as you do.'

The German girls attended eagerly.

'I can't tell you the names of the places,' said Millie, 'but I have seen pictures.'

There was a pause. Gertrude smiled, but made no further response.

'Peectures,' murmured Minna. 'Peectures always are beautiful. All towns are beautiful, perhaps. Not?'

'There may be bits, perhaps,' blurted Miriam, 'but not whole towns and nothing anywhere a bit like Hoddenheim, I 'm perfectly certain.'

'Oh, well, not the *same*,' complained Millie, 'but just as beautiful—more beautiful.'

'Oh-ho, Millississimo.'

'Of course there are, Bertha, there must be.'

'Well, Millicent,' pressed Fräulein, '"more beautiful" and why? Beauty is what you see and is not for every one the same. It is an *affaire de goût*. So you must tell us why to you the old towns of England are more beautiful than the old towns of Germany. It is because you prefair them? They are your towns, it is quite natural you should prefair them.'

'It isn't only that, Fräulein.'

'Well?'

'Our country is older than Germany, besides——'

'It *isn't*, my blessed child.'

'It is, Gertrude—our civilization.'

'Oh, civilization.'

'Engländerin, Engländerin,' mocked Bertha.

'Englishwooman, very Englishwooman,' echoed Elsa Speier.

'Well, I *am* Engländerin,' said Millie, blushing crimson.

'Would you rather the street-boys called Engländerin after you or they didn't?'

'Oh, Jimmie,' said Solomon impatiently.

'I wasn't asking you, Solomon.'

'What means Solomon, with her "Oh, Djimmee," "oh, Djim*mee*"?'

Solomon stirred heavily and looked up, flushing, her eyes avoiding the German arbours.

'Na, Solemn,' laughed Fräulein Pfaff.

'Oh well, of course, Fräulein.' Solomon sat in a crimson tide, bridling.

'Solomon likes not Germans.'

'Go on, Elsa,' rattled Bertha. 'Germans are all right, me dear. I think it's rather a lark when they sing out Engländerin. I always want to yell "Ya!"'

'Likewise "Boo!" Come on, Mill, we're all waiting.'

'Well, you *know* I don't like it, Jimmie.'

'*Why?*'

'Because it makes me forget I'm in Germany and only remember I've got to go back.'

'My hat, Mill, you're a queer mixture!'

'But, Millie, best child, it's just the very thing that makes you know you're here.'

'It doesn't me, Gertrude.'

'What is English towns looking like,' said Elsa Speier.

No one seemed ready to take up this challenge.

'Like other towns I suppose,' laughed Jimmie.

'Our Millie is glad to be in Germany,' ruled Fräulein, rising. 'She and I agree—I go most gladly to England. Gairtrud is neither English nor German. Perhaps she looks down upon us all.'

'Of course I do,' roared Gertrude, crossing her knees and tilting her chair. 'What do you think. Was denkt ihr? I am a barbarian.'

'A stranger.'

'Still we of the wild are the better men.'

'Ah. We end then with a quotation from our dear Schiller.
Come, children.'

'What's that from?' Miriam asked of Gertrude as they
wandered up the garden.

'*The Räuber*. Magnificent thing. Play. We saw it
last winter.'

'I don't believe she really cares for it a bit,' was Miriam's
mental comment. Her heart was warm towards Millie, looking
so outlandish with her English vicarage air in this little German
beer-garden, with her strange love of Germany. Of course
there wasn't anything a bit like Germany in England. . . . So
silly to make comparisons. 'Comparisons are odious.' Perfectly true.

They made their way back to the street through a long low
roomful of men drinking at little tables. Heavy clouds of
smoke hung and moved in the air and mingled with the steady
odour of German food, braten, onion and butter-sodden, beer
and rich sour bread. A tinkling melody supported by rhythmic
time-marking bass notes that seemed to thump the wooden
floor came from a large glass-framed musical-box. The dark
rafters ran low, just above them. Faces glanced towards them
as they all filed avertedly through the room. There were two
or three guttural greetings—'N' Morgen, meine Damen. . . .'
A large limber woman met them in the front room with their
bill and stood talking to Fräulein as the girls straggled out into
the sunshine. She was wearing a neat short-skirted crimson-
and-brown check dress and large blue apron and her haggard
face was lit with radiantly kind strong dark eyes. Miriam
envied her. She would like to pour out beer for those simple
men and dispense their food . . . quietly and busily. . . .
No need to speak to them, or be clever. They would like her
care, and would understand. 'Meine Damen' hurt her. She
was not Dame—Was Fräulein? Elsa? Millie was. Millie
would condescend to these men without feeling uncomfortable.
She could see Millie at village teas. . . . The girls looked very

small as they stood in groups about the roadway. . . . Their
clothes . . . their funny confidence . . . being so sure of
themselves . . . what was it . . . what were they so sure of?
There was nothing . . . and she was afraid of them all, even
of Minna and Emma sometimes.

They trailed, Minna once more safely at her side, slowly on
through the streets of the close-built peaked and gabled,
carved and cobbled town. It came nearer to her than Barnes,
nearer even than the old first house she had kissed the morning they came away—the flower - filled garden, the river,
the woods.

They turned aside and up a little mounting street and filed
into a churchyard. Fräulein tried and opened the great carved
doorway of the church . . . incense. . . . They were going
into a Roman Catholic church. How easy it was; just to walk
in. Why had one never done it before? There was one at
Roehampton. But it would be different in England.

'Pas convenable,' she heard Mademoiselle say just behind
her, 'non, je connais ces gens-là, je vous promets . . . vraiment j'en ai peur. . . .' Elsa responded with excited inquiries.
They all trooped quietly in and the great doors closed behind
them.

'Vraiment j'ai peur,' whispered Mademoiselle.

Miriam saw a point of red light shining like a ruby far ahead
in the gloom. She went round the church with Fräulein Pfaff
and Minna, and was shown stations and chapels, altars hung
with offerings, a dusty tinsel-decked, gaily-painted Madonna,
an alcove railed off and fitted with an iron chandelier furnished
with spikes—filled half-way up its height by a solid mass of
waxen drippings, banners and paintings and artificial flowers,
rich dark carvings. She looked at everything and spoke once
or twice.

'This is the first time I have seen a Roman Catholic church,'
she said, and 'how superstitious' when they came upon
crutches and staves hanging behind a reredos—and all the time
she breathed the incense and felt the dimness around her and
going up and up and brooding, high up.

Presently they were joined by a priest. He took them into

a little room, unlocking a heavy door which clanged to after them, opening out behind one of the chapels. One side of the room was lined with an oaken cupboard.

'Je frissonne.'

Miriam escaped Mademoiselle's neighbourhood and got into an angle between the frosted window and the plaster wall. The air was still and musty—the floor was of stone, the ceiling low and white. There was nothing in the room but the oaken cupboard. The priest was showing a cross so crusted with jewels that the mounting was invisible. Miriam saw it as he lifted it from its wrappings in the cupboard. It seemed familiar to her. She did not wish to see it more closely, to touch it. She stood as thing after thing was taken from the cupboard, waiting in her corner for the moment when they must leave. Now and again she stepped forward and appeared to look, smiled and murmured. Faint sounds from the town came up now and again.

The minutes were passing; soon they must go. She wanted to stay . . . more than she had ever wanted anything in her life she wanted to stay in this little musty room behind the quiet dim church in this little town.

At sunset they stood on a hill outside the town and looked across at it lying up its own hillside, its buildings peaking against the sky. They counted the rich green copper cupolas and sighed and exulted over the whole picture, the coloured sky, the coloured town, the shimmering of the trees.

Making their way along the outskirts of the town towards the station in the fading light, they met a little troop of men and women coming quietly along the roadway. They were all dressed in black. They looked at the girls with strange mild eyes and filled Miriam with fear.

Presently the girls crossed a little high bridge over a stream and, from the crest of the bridge beyond a high-walled garden, a terraced building came into sight. It was dotted with women dressed in black. One of the figures rose and waved a handkerchief. 'Wave, children,' said Fräulein's trembling voice, 'wave'—and the girls collected in a little group on the crest of the bridge and waved with raised arms.

'Ghastly, isn't it?' said Gertrude, glancing at Miriam as they moved on. Miriam was cold with apprehension. 'Are they mad?' she whispered.

CHAPTER IX

FOR a week the whole of the housework and cooking was done by the girls under the superintendence of Gertrude, who seemed to be all over the house acting as forewoman to little gangs of workers. Miriam took but a small part in the work—Minna was paying long visits to the aurist every day—but she shared the depleted table and knew that the whole school was taking part in weathering the storm of Fräulein's ill-humour that had broken first upon Anna. She once caught a glimpse of Gertrude flushed and downcast, confronting Fräulein's reproachful voice upon the stairs; and one day in the basement she heard Ulrica tearfully refuse to clean her own boots and saw Fräulein stand before her bowing and smiling, and with the girls gathered round, herself brush and polish the slender boots.

She was glad to get away with Minna.

Her blouses came at the beginning of the week. She carried them upstairs. Her hands took them incredulously from their wrappages. The 'squashed strawberry' lay at the top, soft warm clear madder-rose, covered with a black arabesque of tiny leaves and tendrils. It was compactly folded, showing only its turned-down collar, shoulders and breast. She laid it on her bed side by side with its buff companion and shook out the underlying skirt. . . . How sweet of them to send her the things . . . she felt tears in her eyes as she stood at her small looking-glass with the skirt against her body and the blouses held in turn above it . . . they both went perfectly with the light skirt. . . . She unfolded them and shook them out and held them up at arms' length by the shoulder seams. Her heart sank. They were not in the least like anything she had ever worn. They had no shape. They were square and the sleeves were like bags. She turned them about and remembered the shapeliness of the stockinette jerseys, smocked and small and clinging, that she had worn at school. If these were blouses then she would never be able to wear blouses. . . . 'They 're so flountery!' she said, frowning at them. She tried on the rose-coloured one. It startled her with its brightness. . . . 'It 's no good, it 's no good,' she said, as her hands fumbled for the fastenings. There was a hook at the neck; that was all. Frightful . . . she fastened it, and the collar set in a soft roll but came down in front to the base of her neck. The rest of the blouse stuck out all round her . . . 'it 's got no cut . . . they couldn't have looked at it.' . . . She turned helplessly about, using her hand-glass, frowning and despairing. Presently she saw Harriett's quizzical eyes and laughed woefully, tweaking at the outstanding margin of the material. 'It 's all very well,' she murmured angrily, 'but it 's all I 've *got*.' . . . She wished Sarah were there. Sarah would do something, alter it or something. She heard her encouraging voice saying, 'You haven't half got it on yet. It 'll be all right.' She unfastened her black skirt, crammed the flapping margin within its band and put on the beaded black stuff belt.

The blouse bulged back and front shapelessly and seemed to be one with the shapeless sleeves which ended in hard loose bands riding untrimmed about her wrists with the movements of her hands. . . . 'It 's like a nightdress,' she said wrathfully and dragged the fulnesses down all round under her skirt. It looked better so in front; but as she turned with raised hand-glass it came riding up at the side and back with the movement of her arm.

Minna was calling to her from the stairs. She went on to the landing to answer her and found her on the top flight dressed to go out.

'Ach!' she whispered as Miriam drew back. 'Jetzt mag' ich Sie leiden. *Now* I like you.'

She ran back to her room. There was no time to change. She fixed a brooch in the collar to make it come a little higher at the join.

Going downstairs she saw Pastor Lahmann hanging up his

hat in the hall. His childlike eyes came up as her step sounded
on the lower flight.

Miriam was amazed to see him standing there as though
nothing had happened. She did not know that she was smiling
at him until his face lit up with an answering smile.

'Bonjour, mademoiselle.'

Miriam did not answer and he disappeared into the *saal*.

She went on downstairs listening to his voice, repeating his
words over and over in her mind.

Jimmie was sweeping the basement floor with a duster tied
round her hair.

'Hullo, Mother Bunch,' she laughed.

'It *is* weird, isn't it? Not a bit the kind I meant to have.'

'The blouse is all right, my dear, but it's all round your ears
and you've got all the fulness in the wrong place. There. . . .
Bless the woman, you've got no drawstring! And you must
pin it at the back! And haven't you got a proper leather belt?'

Minna and Miriam ambled gently along together. Miriam
had discarded her little fur pelerine and her double-breasted
jacket bulged loosely over the thin fabric of her blouse. She
breathed in the leaf-scented air and felt it playing over her
breast and neck. She drew deep breaths as they went slowly
along under the Waldstrasse lime-trees and looked up again
and again at the leaves, brilliant opaque green against white
plaster with sharp black shadows behind them, or brilliant
transparent green on the hard blue sky. She felt that the
scent of them must be visible. Every breath she drew was
like a long yawning sigh. She felt the easy expansion of her
body under her heavy jacket. . . . 'Perhaps I won't have any
more fitted bodices,' she mused and was back for a moment in
the stale little sitting-room of the Barnes dressmaker. She
remembered deeply breathing in the odour of fabrics and dust
and dankness and cracking her newly fitted lining at the pin-
holes and saying, 'It is too tight there'—crack-crack. 'I can't
go like that' . . .

'But you never want to go like that, my dear child,' old Miss Ottridge had laughed, readjusting the pins; 'just breathe in your ordinary way—there, see? That's right.'

Perhaps Lilla's mother was right about blouses . . . perhaps they were 'slommucky.' She remembered phrases she had heard about people's figures . . . 'falling abroad' . . . 'the middle-aged sprawl' . . . that would come early to her as she was so old and worried . . . perhaps that was why one had to wear boned bodices . . . and never breathe in gulps of air like this? . . . It was as if all the worry were being taken out of her temples. She felt her eyes grow strong and clear; a coolness flowed through her—obstructed only where she felt the heavy pad of hair pinned to the back of her head, the line of her hat, the hot line of compression round her waist and the confinement of her inflexible boots.

They were approaching the Georgstrasse with its long-vistaed width and its shops and cafés and pedestrians. An officer in pale blue Prussian uniform passed by flashing a single hard pre-occupied glance at each of them in turn. His eyes seemed to Miriam like opaque blue glass. She could not remember such eyes in England. They began to walk more quickly. Miriam listened abstractedly to Minna's anticipations of three days at a friend's house when she would visit her parents at the end of the week. Minna's parents, her far-away home on the outskirts of a little town, its garden, their little carriage, the spring, the beautiful country, seemed unreal, and her efforts to respond and be interested felt like a sort of treachery to her present bliss. . . . Everybody, even docile Minna, always seemed to want to talk about something else. . . .

Suddenly she was aware that Minna was asking her whether, if it was decided that she should leave school at the end of the term, she, Miriam, would come and live with her.

Miriam beamed incredulously. Minna, crimson-faced, with her eyes on the pavement and hurrying along explained that she was alone at home, that she had never made friends—her mother always wanted her to make friends—but she could not—that her parents would be so delighted—that she, she wanted Miriam, 'You, you are so different, so reasonable—I could live with you.'

Minna's garden, her secure country house, her rich parents, no worries, nothing particular to do, seemed for a moment to Miriam the solution and continuation of all the gay day. There would be the rest of the term—increasing spring and summer—Fräulein divested of all mystery and fear, and then freedom—with Minna.

She glanced at Minna—the cheerful pink face and the pink bulb of nose came round to her and in an excited undertone she murmured something about the Apotheker.

'I should love to come—simply love it,' said Miriam enthusiastically, feeling that she would not entirely give up the idea yet. She would not shut off the offered refuge. It would be a plan to have in reserve. She had been daunted, as Minna murmured, by a picture of Minna and herself in that remote garden—she receiving confidences about the Apotheker—no one else there—the Waldstrasse household blotted out—herself and Minna finding pretexts day after day to visit the chemist's in the little town.

Miriam almost ran home from seeing Minna into the three o'clock train . . . dear beautiful, beautiful Hanover . . . the sunlight blazed from the rain-sprinkled streets. Everything shone. Bright confident shops, happy German cafés moved quickly by as she fled along. Sympathetic eyes answered hers. She almost laughed once or twice when she met an eye and thought how funny she must look 'tearing along' with her long thick, black jacket bumping against her. . . . She would leave it off to-morrow and go out in a blouse and her long black lace scarf. . . . She imagined Harriett at her side—Harriett's long scarf and longed to do the 'crab walk' for a moment or the halfpenny dip, hippety-hop. She did them in her mind.

She heard the sound of her boot soles tapping the shining pavement as she hurried along . . . she would write a short note to her mother 'a girl about my own age with very wealthy parents who wants a companion' and enclose a note for Eve or Harriett . . . Eve, 'Imagine me in Pomerania, my dear' . . .

and tell her about the coffee parties and the skating and the
sleighing and Minna's German Christmasses. . . .

She saw Minna's departing face leaning from the carriage
window, its new gay boldness: 'I shall no more when we are at
home call you Miss Henderson.'

When she got back to Waldstrasse she found Anna's suc-
cessor, newly arrived, cleaning the neglected front doorstep.
Her lean yellow face looked a vacant response to Miriam's
inquiry for Fräulein Pfaff.

'Ist Fräulein zu Hause,' she repeated. The girl shook her
head vaguely.

How quiet the house seemed. The girls, after a morning
spent in turning out the kitchen for the reception of the new
Magd were out for a long ramble, including *Schokolade mit
Schlagsahne*, until tea-time.

The empty house spread round her and towered above her
as she took off her things in the basement, and the schoolroom
yawned bright and empty as she reached the upper hall. She
hesitated by the door. There was no sound anywhere. . . .
She would play . . . on the *saal* piano.

'I 'm not a Lehrerin—I 'm not—I 'm—not,' she hummed
as she collected her music . . . she would bring her songs
too. . . . 'I 'm going to Pom—pom—pom—Pom-erain—eeya.'

'Pom—erain—eeya,' she hummed, swinging herself round
the great door into the *saal*. Pastor Lahmann was standing
near one of the windows. The rush of her entry carried her to
the middle of the room and he met her there, smiling quietly.
She stared easily and comfortably up into his great mild eyes,
went into them as they remained quietly and gently there,
receiving her. Presently he said in a soft low tone, 'You are
vairy happy, mademoiselle.'

Miriam moved her eyes from his face and gazed out of the
window into the little sunlit summer-house. The sense of the
outline of his shoulders and his comforting black mannishness
so near to her brought her almost to tears. Fiercely she fixed
the sunlit summer-house, 'Oh, I 'm *not*,' she said.

'Not? Is it possible?'

'I think life is perfectly appalling.'

She moved awkwardly to a little chiffonier and put down her music on its marble top.

He came safely following her and stood near again.

'You do not like the life of the school?'

'Oh, I don't know.'

'You are from the country, mademoiselle.'

Miriam fumbled with her music. . . . Was she?

'One sees that at once. You come from the land.'

Miriam glanced at his solid white profile as he stood with hands clasped, near her music, on the chiffonier. She noticed again that strange, flatness of the lower part of the face.

'I, too, am from the land. I grew up on a farm. I love the land and think to return to it—to have my little strip when I am free—when my boys have done their schooling. I shall go back.'

He turned towards her and Miriam smiled into the soft brown eyes and tried to think of something to say.

'My grandfather was a gentleman-farmer.'

'Ah—that does not surprise me—but what a very English expression!'

'Is it?'

'Well, it sounds so to us. We Swiss are very democratic.'

'I think I'm a radical.'

Pastor Lahmann lifted his chin and laughed softly.

'You are a vairy ambitious young lady.'

'Yes.'

Pastor Lahmann laughed again.

'I, too, am ambitious. I have a good Swiss ambition.'

Miriam smiled into the mild face.

'You have a beautiful English provairb which expresses my ambition.'

Miriam looked, eagerly listening, into the brown eyes that came round to meet hers, smiling:

> 'A little land, well-tilled,
> A little wife, well-willed,
>   Are great riches.'

Miriam seemed to gaze long at a pallid, rounded man with smiling eyes. She saw a garden and fields, a firelit interior, a little woman smiling and busy and agreeable moving quickly about. . . . and Pastor Lahmann—presiding. It filled her with fury to be regarded as one of a world of little tame things to be summoned by little man to be well-willed wives. She must make him see that she did not even recognize such a thing as 'a well-willed wife.' She felt her gaze growing fixed and moved to withdraw it and herself.

'Why do you wear glasses, mademoiselle?'

The voice was full of sympathetic wistfulness.

'I have a severe myopic astigmatism,' she announced, gathering up her music and feeling the words as little hammers on the newly seen, pallid, rounded face.

'Dear me . . . I wonder whether the glasses are really necessary. . . . May I look at them? . . . I know something of eye-work.'

Miriam detached her tightly fitting pince-nez and, having given them up, stood with her music in hand anxiously watching. Half her vision gone with her glasses, she saw only a dim black-coated knowledge, near at hand, going perhaps to help her.

'You wear them always—for how long?'

'Poor child, poor child, and you must have passed through all your schooling with those lame, lame eyes . . . let me see the eyes . . . turn a little to the light . . . so.'

Standing near and large he scrutinized her vague gaze.

'And sensitive to light, too. You were vairy, vairy blonde, even more blonde than you are now, as a child, mademoiselle?'

'Na guten Tag, Herr Pastor.'

Fräulein Pfaff's smiling voice sounded from the little door.

Pastor Lahmann stepped back.

Miriam was pleased at the thought of being grouped with him in the eyes of Fräulein Pfaff. As she took her glasses from his outstretched hand she felt that Fräulein would recognize that they had established a kind of friendliness. She halted for a moment at the door, adjusting her glasses, amiably uncertain, feeling for something to say.

Pastor Lahmann was standing in the middle of the room examining his nails. Fräulein, at the window, was twitching a curtain into place. She turned and drove Miriam from the room with speechless, waiting eyes.

The sunlight was streaming across the hall. It seemed gay and home-like. Pastor Lahmann had made her forget she was a governess. He had treated her as a girl. Fräulein's eyes had spoiled it. Fräulein was angry about it for some extraordinary reason.

'Don't let her *do* it, Miss Henderson.'

Fräulein Pfaff's words broke the silence accompanying the servant's progress from Gertrude whose soup-plate she had first seized, to Miriam, more than half-way down the table.

Startled into observation, Miriam saw the soup-spoon of her neighbour whisked, dripping, from its plate to the uppermost of Marie's pile, and Emma shrinking back with a horrified face against Jimmie who was leaning forward entranced with watching. . . . The whole table was watching. Marie, having secured Emma's plate to the base of her pile clutched Miriam's spoon. Miriam moved sideways as the spoon swept up, saw the desperate, hard, lean face bend towards her for a moment as her plate was seized, heard an exclamation of annoyance from Fräulein and little sounds from all round the table. Marie had passed on to Clara. Clara received her with plate and spoon held firmly together and motioned her, before she would relinquish them, to place her load upon the shelf of the lift.

Miriam felt she was in disgrace with the whole table. . . . She sat flaring, rapidly framing phrase after phrase for the lips of her judges . . . 'slow and awkward' . . . 'never has her wits about her. . . .'

'Don't let her do it, Miss Henderson. . . .' Why should Fräulein fix upon *her* to teach her common servants? Struggling through her resentment was pride in the fact that she did not know how to handle soup-plates. Presently she sat refusing absolutely to accept the judgment silently assailing her on all hands.

'You are not very domesticated, Miss Henderson.'

'No,' responded Miriam quietly, in joy and fear.

Fräulein gave a short laugh.

Goaded, Miriam plunged forward.

'We were never even allowed in the kitchen at home.'

'I see. You and your sisters were brought up like countesses, wie Gräfinnen,' observed Fräulein Pfaff drily. Miriam's whole body was on fire . . . 'and your sisters and your sisters,' echoed through and through her. Holding back her tears she looked full at Fräulein and met the brown eyes. She met them until they turned away and Fräulein broke into smiling generalities. Conversation was released all round the table. Emphatic undertones reached her from the English side. 'Fool' . . . 'simply idiotic.'

'I 've done it now,' mused Miriam calmly, on the declining tide of her wrath.

Pretending to be occupied with those about her, she sat examining the look Fräulein had given her . . . she hates me. . . . Perhaps she did from the first. . . . She did from the first. . . . I shall have to go . . . and suddenly, lately, she has grown worse. . . .

CHAPTER X

WALKING along a narrow muddy causeway by a little river overhung with willows, girls ahead of her in single file and girls in single file behind, Miriam drearily recognized that it was June. The month of roses, she thought, and looked out across the flat green fields. It was not easy to walk along the slippery pathway. On one side was the little grey river, on the other long wet grass, repellent and depressing. Not far ahead was the roadway which led, she supposed, to the farm where they were to drink new milk. She would have to walk with someone when they came to the road, and talk. She wondered whether this early morning walk would come, now, every day. Her heart sank at the thought. It had been too hot during the last few days for any going out at midday, and she had hoped that the strolling in the garden, sitting about under the chestnut tree and in the little wooden garden room off the *saal* had taken the place of walks for the summer.

She had got up reluctantly, at the surprise of the very early gonging. Mademoiselle had guessed it would be a 'milk-walk.' Pausing in the bright light of the top landing as Mademoiselle ran downstairs, she had seen through the landing window the deep peak of a distant gable casting an unfamiliar shadow—a shadow sloping the wrong way, a morning shadow. She remembered the first time, the only time, she had noticed such a shadow—getting up very early one morning while Harriett and all the household were still asleep—and how she had stopped dressing and gazed at it as it stood there cool and quiet and alone across the mellow face of a neighbouring stone porch—had suddenly been glad that she was alone and had wondered why that shadowed porch-peak was more beautiful than all the summer things she knew, and had felt at that moment that nothing could touch or trouble her again.

She could not find anything of that feeling in the early day

outside Hanover.   She was hemmed in, and the fields were so
sad she could not bear to look at them.   The sun had disappeared since they came out.   The sky was grey and low and
it seemed warmer already than it had been in the midday sun
during the last few days.   One of the girls on ahead hummed
the refrain of a student-song:

> In der Ecke steht er
> Seinen Schnurbart dreht er
> Siehst du wohl, da steht er schon
> Der versoff'ne Schwiegersohn.

Miriam felt very near the end of endurance.

Elsa Speier who was just behind her, became her inevitable
companion when they reached the roadway.   A farm-house
appeared about a quarter of a mile away.

Miriam's sense of her duties closed in on her.   Trying
not to see Elsa's elaborate clothes and the profile in which
she could find no meaning, no hope, no rest, she spoke to
her.

'Do you like milk, Elsa?' she said cheerfully.

Elsa began swinging her lace-covered parasol.

'If I like milk?' she repeated presently, and flashed mocking
eyes in Miriam's direction.

Despair touched Miriam's heart.

'Some people don't,' she said.

Elsa hummed and swung her parasol.

'Why should I like milk?' she stated.

The muddy farmyard, lying back from the roadway and
below it, was steamy and choking with odours.   Miriam who
had imagined a cool dairy and cold milk frothing in pans, felt a
loathing as warmth came to her fingers from the glass she held.
Most of the girls were busily sipping.   She raised her glass
once towards her lips, snuffed a warm reek, and turned away
towards the edge of the group, to pour out the contents of her
glass, unseen, upon the filth-sodden earth.

Passing languidly up through the house after breakfast,

unable to decide to spend her Saturday morning as usual at a
piano in one of the bedrooms, Miriam went, wondering, in
response to a quiet call from Fräulein Pfaff, into the large room
shared by the Bergmanns and Ulrica Hesse. Explaining that
Clara was now to take possession of the half of Elsa Speier's
room that had been left empty by Minna—'poor Minna now
with her good parents seeking health in the Swiss mountains,
schooldays at an end, at an end, at an end,' she repeated mourn-
fully, Fräulein indicated that Clara's third of the large room
would now be Miriam's.

Miriam stood incredulous at her side as she indicated a
large empty chest of drawers, a white covered bed in a deep
corner away from the window, a small drawer in the dressing-
table and five pegs in a large French wardrobe. Emma was
going very gravely about the room collecting her work-basket
and things for *raccommodage*. She flung one ecstatic glance
at Miriam as she went away with these.

'I shall hold you responsible here amongst these dear
children, Miss Henderson,' fluted Fräulein, quietly gathering
up a few last things of Minna's collected on the bed, 'our dear
Ulrica and our little Emma,' she smiled, passing out, leaving
Miriam standing in the wonderful room.

'My goodney,' she breathed, gathering gently clenched fists
close to her person. She stood for a few moments; she felt
like a visitor . . . embroidered toilet covers, polished furniture, gold and cream crockery, lace curtains, white beds, the
large screen cutting off her third of the room . . . then she
rushed headlong upstairs, a member of the downstairs landing,
to collect her belongings.

On the landing just outside the door of the garret bedroom
stood a huge wicker travelling basket; a clumsy umbrella with
a large knobby handle, like a man's umbrella, lay on the top of
it partly covering a large pair of goloshes.

She was tired and very warm by the time everything was
arranged in her new quarters.

Taking a last look round she caught the eye of Eve's
photograph gazing steadily at her from the chest of drawers.
. . . It would be quite easy now that this had happened

to write and tell them that the Pomerania plan had come to nothing.

Evidently Fräulein approved of her, after all.

In the schoolroom she found the *raccommodage* party gathered round the table. At its head sat Mademoiselle, her arms flung out upon the table and her face buried against them.

'Cheer up, Mademoiselle,' said Jimmie as Miriam took an empty chair between Gertrude and the Martins.

Timidly meeting Gertrude's eye Miriam received her half-smile, watched her eyebrows flicker faintly up and the little despairing shrug she gave as she went on with her mending.

'Ah, mamma*zell*chen c'est pas mal, ne soyez triste, mein Gott mammazellchen es ist aber nichts!' chided Emma consolingly from her place near the window.

'Oh! je ne veux pas, je ne veux pas,' sobbed Mademoiselle.

No one spoke; Mademoiselle lay snuffling and shuddering. Solomon's scissors fell on to the floor. 'Mais pour*quoi* pas, Mademoiselle?' she interrogated as she recovered them.

'Pourquoi, pourquoi!' choked Mademoiselle. Her suffused little face came up for a moment towards Solomon. She met Miriam's gaze as if she did not see her. 'Vous me demandez pourquoi je ne veux pas partager ma chambre avec une femme mariée?' Her head sank again and her little grey form jerked sharply as she sobbed.

'Probably a widder, Mademoiselle,' ventured Bertha Martin, 'oon voove.'

'*Verve*, Bertha,' came Millie's correcting voice and Miriam's interest changed to excited thoughts of Fräulein—not hating her, and choosing Mademoiselle rather than herself to sleep with the servant, a new servant—the things on the landing—Mademoiselle refusing to share a room with a married woman . . . she felt about round this idea as Millie's prim, clear voice went on . . . her eyes clutched at Mademoiselle, begging to understand . . . she gazed at the little down-flung head, fine little tendrils frilling along the edge of her hair, her little hard

grey shape, all miserable and ashamed. It was dreadful.
Miriam felt she could not bear it. She turned away. It was
a strange new thought that any one should object to being with
a married woman . . . would she object? or Harriett? Not
unless it were suggested to them. . . . Was there some special
refinement in this French girl that none of them understood?
Why should it be refined to object to share a room with a
married woman? A cold shadow closed in on Miriam's mind.

'I don't care,' said Millie almost quickly, with a crimson face.
'It 's a special occasion. I think Mademoiselle ought to com-
plain. If I were in her place I should write home. It 's not
right. Fräulein has no right to make her sleep with a servant.'

'Why can't the servant sleep in one of the back attics?'
asked Solomon.

'Not furnished, my sweetheart,' said Gertrude, 'and you
know, Kinder, you 're all running on very fast about servants—
the good Frau is our housekeeper.'

'Will she have meals with us?'

'Gewiss, Jimmie, meals.'

'Mon Dieu, vous êtes terribles, toutes!' came Mademoiselle's
voice. It seemed to bite into the table. 'Oh, c'est grossière!'
She gathered herself up and escaped into the little schoolroom.

'Armes, armes Momzell,' wailed Ulrica gently, gazing out
of the window.

'Som one should go, go you, Hendchen,' urged Emma.

'Don't for goodness' sake, Hendy,' begged Jimmie, 'not you,
she 's wild about you going downstairs,' she whispered.

Miriam struggled with her gratification. 'Oh go, som one;
go you, Clara!'

'Better leave her alone,' ruled Gertrude.

'We miss old Minna, don't we?' concluded Bertha.

The heat grew intense.

The air was more and more oppressive as the day went on.

Clara fainted suddenly just after dinner, and Fräulein,
holding a little discourse on clothing and an inquiry into

wardrobes, gave a general permission for the reduction of garments to the minimum and sent everyone to rest uncorseted until tea-time, promising a walk to the woods in the cool of the evening. There was a sense of adventure in the house. It was as if it were being besieged. It gave Miriam confidence to approach Fräulein for permission to rearrange her trunk in the basement. She let Fräulein understand that her removal was not complete, that there were things to do before she could be properly settled in her new room.

'Certainly, Miss Henderson, you are quite free,' said Fräulein instantly, as the girls trooped upstairs.

Miriam knew she wanted to avoid an afternoon shut up with Emma and Ulrica and she did not in the least want to lie down. It seemed to her a very extraordinary thing to do. It surprised and disturbed her. It suggested illness and weakness. She could not remember ever having lain down in the day-time. There had been that fortnight in the old room at home with Harriett . . . chicken-pox and new books coming, and games, and Sarah reading the *Song of Hiawatha* and their being allowed to choose their pudding. She could not remember feeling ill. Had she ever felt ill? . . . Colds and bilious attacks. . . .

She remembered with triumph a group of days of pain two years ago. She had forgotten. . . . Bewilderment and pain . . . her mother's constant presence . . . everything, the light everywhere, the leaves standing out along the tops of hedgerows as she drove with her mother, telling her of pain and she alone in the midst of it . . . for always . . . pride, long moments of deep pride. . . . Eve and Sarah congratulating her, Eve stupid and laughing . . . the new bearing of the servants . . . Lilly Belton's horrible talks fading away to nothing.

Fräulein had left her and gone to her room. Every door and window on the ground floor stood wide, excepting that leading to Fräulein's little double rooms. She wondered what the rooms were like and felt sorry for Fräulein, tall and gaunt, moving about in them alone, alone with her own dark eyes, curtains hanging motionless at the windows . . . was it really bad to tight-lace? The English girls, except Millie and Solomon, all had small waists. She wished she knew. She placed her large hands round her waist. Drawing in her breath she could almost make them meet. It was easier to play tennis with stays . . . how dusty the garden looked, baked. She wanted to go out with two heavy watering-cans, to feel them pulling her arms from their sockets, dragging her shoulders down, throwing out her chest, to spray canful after canful through a great wide rose, sprinkling her ankles sometimes, and to grow so warm that she would not feel the heat. Bella Lyndon had never worn stays; playing rounders so splendidly, lying on the grass between the games with her arms under her head . . . simply disgusting, someone had said . . . who . . . a disgusted face . . . nearly all the girls detested Bella.

Going through the hall on her way down to the basement, she heard the English voices sounding quietly out into the afternoon from the rooms above. Flat and tranquil they sounded, Bertha and Jimmie she heard, Gertrude's undertones, quiet words from Millie. She felt she would like a corner in the English room for the afternoon, a book and an occasional remark—*Mr Barnes of New York*—she would not be able to read her three yellow-backs in the German bedroom. She felt at the moment glad to be robbed of them. It would be much better, of course. There was no sound from the German rooms. She pictured sleeping faces. It was cooler in the basement—but even there the air seemed stiff and dusty with the heat.

Why did the hanging garments remind her of All Saints' Church and Mr Brough? . . . she must tell Harriett that in her letter . . . that day they suddenly decided to help in the church decorations . . . she remembered the smell of the soot on the holly as they had cut and hacked at it in the cold garden, and Harriett overturning the heavy wheelbarrow on the way to church, and how they had not laughed because they both felt solemn, and then there had just been the three Anwyl girls and Mrs Anwyl and Mrs Scarr and Mr Brough in the church-room, all being silly about Birdy Anwyl roasting chestnuts, and how silly and affected they were when a piece of holly stuck in her skirt.

Coming up the basement stairs in response to the tea-gong, Miriam thought there were visitors in the hall and hesitated; then there was Pastor Lahmann's profile disappearing towards the door and Fräulein patting and dismissing two of his boys. His face looked white and clear and firm and undisturbed. Miriam wanted to arrest him and ask him something—what he thought of the weather—he looked so different from her memory of him in the *saal* two Saturdays ago—two weeks— four classes she must have missed. Why? Why was she missing Pastor Lahmann's classes? How had it happened? Perhaps she would see him in class again. Perhaps next week. . . .

The other visitors proved to be the Bergmanns in new dresses. Miriam gazed at Clara as she went down the school-room to her corner of the table. She looked like . . . a hostess. It seemed absurd to see her sit down to tea as a schoolgirl. The dress was a fine black muslin stamped all over with tiny fish-shaped patches of mauve. It was cut to the base of the neck and came to a point in front where the soft white ruching was fastened with a large cameo brooch. Clara's pallid worried face had grown more placid during the hot inactive days, and to-day her hard mouth looked patient and determined and responsible. She seemed quite independent of her surroundings. Miriam found herself again and again consulting her calm face. Her presence haunted Miriam throughout tea-time. Emma was sweet, pink and bright after her rest, in a bright light brown muslin dress dotted with white spots. . . .

Funny German dresses, thought Miriam, funny . . . and old. Her mind hovered and wondered over these German dresses—did she like them or not—something about them— she glanced at Elsa, sitting opposite in the dull faint electric blue with black lace sleeves she had worn since the warm weather set in. Even Ulrica, thin and straight now . . . like a pole . . . in a tight flat dress of saffron muslin sprigged with brown leaves, seemed to be included in something that made all these German dresses utterly different from anything the English girls could have worn. What was it? It was crowned by the Bergmanns' dresses. It had begun in a summer dress of Minna's, black with a tiny sky-blue spot and a heavy ruche round the hem. She thought she liked it. It seemed to set the full tide of summer round the table more than the things of the English girls—and yet the dresses were ugly—and the English girls' dresses were not that . . . they were nothing . . . plain cottons and zephyrs with lace tuckers—no ruches. It was something . . . somehow in the ruches—the ruches and the little peaks of neck.

A faint scent of camphor came from the Martins across the way, sitting in their cool creased black-and-white check cotton dresses. They still kept to their hard white collars and cuffs. As tea went on Miriam found her eyes drawn back and back again to these newly unpacked camphor-scented dresses . . . and when conversation broke after moments of stillness . . . shadowy foliage . . . the still hot garden . . . the sunbaked wooden room beyond the sunny *saal*, the light pouring through three rooms and bright along the table . . . it was to the Martins' check dresses that she glanced.

It was intensely hot, but the strain had gone out of the day; the feeling of just bearing up against the heat and getting through the day had gone; they all sat round . . . which was which? . . . Miriam met eye after eye—how beautiful they all were, looking out from faces and meeting hers—and her eyes came back unembarrassed to her cup, her solid butter-brot and the sunlit angle of the garden-wall and the bit of tree just over Fräulein Pfaff's shoulder. She tried to meet Mademoiselle's eyes, she felt sure their eyes could meet. She wondered intensely what was in Elsa's mind behind her faint hard blue dress. She wanted to hear Mademoiselle's voice; Mademoiselle was almost invisible in her corner near the door, the new housekeeper was sitting at her side very upright and close to the table. Once or twice she felt Fräulein's look; she sustained it, and glowed happily under it without meeting it;

she referred back contentedly to it after hearing herself laugh out once—just as she would do at home; once or twice she forgot for a moment where she was. The way the light shone on the housekeeper's hair, bright brown and plastered flatly down on either side of her bright white-and-crimson face, and the curves of her chocolate and white striped cotton bodice, reminded her sharply of something she had seen once, something that had charmed her . . . it was in the hair against the hard white of the forehead and in the flat broad cheeks with the hard, clear crimson colouring nearly covering them . . . something in the way she sat, standing out against the others. . . . Judy on her left hand, with almost the same colouring, looked small and gentle and refined.

Tea was over. Fräulein decided against a walk and they all trooped into the *saal*. No programme was suggested; they all sat about unoccupied. There was no centre; Fräulein Pfaff was one of them. The little group near her in the shady half of the sunlit summer-house was as quietly easy as those who sat far back in the *saal*. Miriam had got into a low chair near the *saal* doors whence she could see across the room, through the summer-house window, through the gap between the houses across the way, to the far-off afternoon country. Its colours gleamed, a soft confusion of tones, under the heat-haze. For a while she sat with her eyes on Fräulein's thin profile, clean and cool and dry in the intense heat . . . 'she must be looking out towards the lime-trees.' . . . Ulrica sat drooped on a low chair near her knees . . . 'sweet beautiful head' . . . the weight of her soft curved mouth seemed too much for the delicate angles of her face and it drooped faintly, breaking their sharp lines. Miriam wished all the world could see her. . . . Presently Ulrica raised her head, as Elsa and Clara broke into words and laughter near her, and her drooping lips flattened gently back into their place in the curve of her face. She gazed out through the doorway of the summer-house

with her great despairing eyes . . . the housekeeper was
rather like a Dutch doll . . . but that was not it.

The sun had set.   Miriam had found a little thin volume of
German poetry in her pocket. She sat fumbling the leaves.
She felt the touch of her limp straightening hair upon her
forehead. It did not matter. Twilight would soon come, and
bed-time. But it must have been beginning to get like that
at tea-time. Perhaps the weather would get even hotter.
She must do something about her hair . . . if only she could
wear it turned straight back.

There was a stirring in the room; beautiful forms rose and
stood and spoke and moved about. Someone went to the door.
It opened gently with a peaceful sound on to the quiet hall and
footsteps ran upstairs. Two figures going out from the *saal*
passed in front of the two still sitting quietly grouped in the
light of the summer-house. They were challenged as they
passed and turned soft profiles and stood talking. Behind the
voices—flutings, single notes, broken phrases—long undisturbed warblings came from the garden birds.

Clara was at the piano. Tall behind her stood Millie's
gracious shapeless baby-form.

As Millie's voice, climbing carefully up and down the even
stages of Solveig's song, reached the second verse, Miriam tried
to separate the music from the words. The words were
wrong. She half saw a fair woman with a great crown of
plaited hair and very broad shoulders singing the song in the
Hanover concert-room, in Norwegian. She remembered the
moment of taking her eyes away from the singer and the platform, and feeling the crowded room and the airlessness, and
then the song going steadily on from note to note as she
listened . . . no triils and no tune . . . saying something.
It stood in the air. All the audience were saying it. And then
the fair-haired woman had sung the second verse as though it
were something about herself—tragically . . . tragic muse.
. . . It was not *her* song, standing there in the velvet dress.

. . . She stopped it from going on. There was nothing but the movement of the lace round her shoulders and chest, her expanded neck, quivering, and the pressure in her voice. . . . And then there had been Herr Bossenberger, hammering and shouting it out in the *saal* with Millie, and everything in the schoolroom, even the dust on the paper-rack, standing out clearer and clearer as he bellowed slowly along. And then she had got to know that everybody knew about it; it was a famous song. There were people singing it everywhere in German and French and English—a girl singing about her lover. . . . It was not that; even if people sang it like that, if a real girl had ever sung something like that, that was not what she meant . . . 'the winter may pass' . . . yes, that was all right—and mountains with green slopes and narrow torrents —and a voice going strongly out and ceasing, and all the sky filled with the sound—and the song going on, walking along, thinking to itself. . . . She looked about as Millie's voice ceased trembling on the last high note. She hoped no one would hum the refrain. There was no one there who knew anything about it. . . . Judy? Judy knew, perhaps. Judy would never hum or sing anything. If she did, it would be terrible. She knew so much. Perhaps Judy knew every-thing. She was sitting on the low sill of the window behind the piano, sewing steel beads on to a shot silk waistband held very close to her eyes. Minna could. Minna might be sitting in her plaid dress on the window-seat with her embroidery, her smooth hair polished with bay-rum, humming Solveig's song.

The housekeeper brought in the milk and rolls and went away downstairs again. The cold milk was very refreshing, but the room grew stifling as they all sat round near the little centre table with the french window nearly closed, shutting off the summer-house and garden. Everybody in turn seemed to be saying 'Ik kenne meine Tasse sie ist svatz.' Bertha had begun it, holding up her white glass of milk as she took it from the tray and exactly imitating the housekeeper's voice.

'Platt Deutsch spricht-sie, ja?' Clara had said. It seemed

as if there were no more to be said about the housekeeper. At prayers when they were all saying 'Vater unser,' she heard Jimmie murmur, 'Ik kenne meine Tasse.'

Fräulein Pfaff came upstairs behind the girls and ordered silence as they went to their rooms. 'Hear, all, children,' she said in German in the quiet clear even tone with which she had just read prayers, 'no one to speak to her neighbour, no one to whisper or bustle, nor to-night to brush her hair, but each to compose her mind and go quietly to her rest. Thus acting, the so great heat shall injure none of us and peaceful sleep will come. Do you hear, children?'

Answering voices came from the bedrooms. She entered each room, shifting screens, opening each window for a few moments, leaving each door wide.

'Each her little corner,' she said in Miriam's room, 'fresh water set for the morning. The heavens are all round us, my little ones; have no fear.'

Gently sighing and moaning, Ulrica moved about in her corner. Emma dropped a slipper and muttered consolingly. Thankfully Miriam listened to Fräulein's short, deprecating footsteps pacing up and down the landing. She was safe from the dreadful challenge of conversation with her pupils. She felt hemmed in in the stifling room with the landing full of girls all round her. She wanted to push away her screen, push up the hot white ceiling. She wished she could be safely upstairs with Mademoiselle and the height of the candle-lit garret above her head. It could not possibly be hotter up there than in this stifling room with its draperies and furniture and gas.

Fräulein came in very soon and turned out the light with a formal good-night greeting. For a while after all the lights were out, she continued pacing up and down.

Across the landing someone began to sneeze rapidly, sneeze after sneeze. 'Ach, die Millie!' muttered Emma sleepily. For several minutes the sneezing went on. Sighs and impatient

movements sounded here and there. 'Ruhig, Kinder, ruhig.
Millie shall soon sleep peacefully, as all.'

Miriam could not remember hearing Fräulein Pfaff go away
when she woke in the darkness feeling unendurably oppressed.
She flung her sheet aside and turned her pillow over and
pushed her frilled sleeves to her elbows. How energetic I am,
she thought, and lay tranquil. There was not a sound. 'I
shall never be able to sleep down here, it's too awful,' she
murmured, and puffed and shifted her head on the pillow.

The win-ter may—pass. . . . The win-ter . . . may pass.
The winter may . . . pass. The Academy . . . a picture in
very bright colours . . . a woman sitting by the roadside with
a shawl round her shoulders and a red skirt and red cheeks
and bright green country behind her . . . people moving
about on the shiny floor, someone just behind saying, 'that is
plein-air, these are the plein-airistes'—the woman in the
picture was like the housekeeper. . . .

A brilliant light flashed into the room . . . lightning—how
strange the room looked—the screens had been moved—the
walls and corners and little beds had looked like daylight.
Someone was talking across the landing. Emma was awake.
Another flash came and movements and cries. Emma screamed
aloud, sitting up in bed. 'Ach Gott! Clara! *Clara!*' she
screamed. Cries came from the next room. A match was
struck across the landing, and voices sounded. Gertrude was
in the room lighting the gas and Clara tugging down the blind.
Emma was sitting with her hands pressed to her eyes, quickly
gasping, 'Ach Clara! Mein Gott! Ach Gott!' On Ulrica's bed
nothing was visible but a mound of bedclothes. The whole landing was astir. Fräulein's voice called up urgently from below.

Miriam was the last to reach the schoolroom. The girls
were drawn up on either side of the gaslit room—leaving the

shuttered windows clear. She moved to take a chair at the end of the table in front of the *saal* doors. 'Na!' said Fräulein sharply from the sofa-corner. 'Not there! In full current!' Her voice shook. Miriam drew the chair to the end of the row of figures and sat down next to Solomon Martin. The wind rushed through the garden, the thunder rattled across the sky. 'Oh, Clara! Fräulein! Nein!' gasped Emma. She was sitting opposite, between Clara and Jimmie, with flushed face and eyes strained wide, twisting her linked hands against her knees. Jimmie patted her wrist, 'It 's all right, Emmchen,' she muttered cheerfully. 'Nein, Christina!' jerked Fräulein sharply. 'I will not have that! To touch the flesh! You understand, all! That you know. All! Such immodesty!'

Miriam leaned forward and glanced. Fräulein was sitting very upright on the sofa in a shapeless black cloak with her hands clasped on her breast. Near her was Ulrica in her trailing white dressing-gown, her face pressed against the back of the sofa. In the far corner, the other side of Fräulein, sat Gertrude in her grey ulster, her knees comfortably crossed, a quilted scarlet silk bedroom-slipper sticking out under the hem of her ulster.

The thunder crashed and pounded just above them. Everyone started and exclaimed. Emma flung her arms up across her face and sat back in her chair with a hooting cry. From the sofa came a hidden sobbing and gasping. 'Ach Himmel! Ach Herr *Jé*-sus! Ach du *lie*-ber, *lie*-ber Gott!'

Miriam wished they could see the lightning and be prepared for the crashes. If she were alone she would watch for the flashes and put her fingers in her ears after each flash. The shock of the sound was intolerable to her. Once if had broken, she drank in the tumult joyfully. She sat tense and miserable, longing to get to bed. She wondered whether it would be of any use to explain to Fräulein that they would be safer in their iron bedsteads than anywhere in the house. She tried to distract her thoughts. . . . Fancy Jimmie's name being Christina. . . . It suited her exactly, sitting there in her little striped dressing-gown with its 'toby' frill. How Harriett would scream if she could see them all sitting round. But she and

Harriett had once lain very quiet and frightened in a storm by the sea—the thunder and lightning had come together, and someone had looked in and said, 'There won't be another like that, children.' 'My boots, I should hope not,' Harriett had said.

For a while it seemed as though cannon-balls were being thumped down and rumbled about on the floor above; then came another deafening crash. Jimmie laughed and put up her hand to her loosely-pinned top-knot as if to see whether it were still there. Outcries came from all over the room. After the first shock, which had made her sit up sharply and draw herself convulsively together, Miriam found herself turning towards Solomon Martin who had also stirred and sat forward. Their eyes met full, and consulted. Solomon's lips were compressed, her perspiring face was alight and determined. Miriam felt that she looked for long into those steady, oily, half-smiling brown eyes. When they both relaxed she sat back, catching a sympathetic challenging flash from Gertrude. She drew a deep breath and felt proud and easy. Let it bang, she said to herself. I must think of doors suddenly banging—that never makes me jumpy—and she sat easily breathing.

Fräulein had said something in German in a panting voice, and Bertha had stood up and said, '*I'll* get the Bible, Fräulein.'

'Ei! Bewahre! Ber-ta!' shouted Clara. 'Stay only here! Stay only here!'

'Nein, Bertha, nein, mein Kind,' moaned Fräulein sadly.

'It's really perfectly all right, Fräulein,' said Bertha, getting quietly to the door.

As Fräulein opened the great book on her knees, the rain hissed down into the garden.

'Gott sei Dank,' she said, in a clear child-like voice. 'It dot besser wenn da regnet?' inquired the housekeeper, looking round the room. She began vigorously wiping her face and neck with the skirt of the short cotton jacket she wore over her red petticoat.

Ulrica broke into steady weeping.

Fräulein read Psalms, ejaculating the short phrases as if they were petitions, with a pause between each. When the thunder came she raised her voice against it and read more rapidly.

As the storm began to abate, a little party of English went to the kitchen and brought back milk and biscuits and jam.

'You will be asleep, Miss Hendershon?' Miriam started at the sound of Ulrica's wailing whisper. Fräulein had just gone. She had been sitting on the end of Emma's bed talking quietly of self-control and now Emma was asleep. Ulrica's corner had been perfectly quiet. Miriam had been lying listening to the steady swishing of the rain against the chestnut leaves.

'No; what is it?'

'Oh, most wonderful. Ich bin so empfindlich. I am so sensible.'

'Sensitive?'

'Oh, it was most wonderful. Only hear and I shall tell you. This evening when the storm leave himself down it was exactly as my Konfirmation.'

'Yes.'

'It was as my Konfirmation. I think of that wonderful day, my white dress, the flower-bouquet and how I weeped always. Oh, it was all of most beautifullest. I am so sensible.'

'Oh, yes,' whispered Miriam.

'I weeped so! All day I have weeped! The all whole day! And my mozzer she console me I shall not weep. And I weep. Ach! It was of most beautifullest.'

Miriam felt as if she were being robbed. . . . This was Ulrica. . . . 'You remember the Konfirmation, miss?'

'Oh, yes, I remember.'

'Have you weeped?'

'We say *cry*, not weep, except in poetry—weinen, to cry.'

'Have you cry?'

'No, I didn't cry. But we mustn't talk. We must go to sleep. Good night.'

'Gute Nacht. Ach, wie empfindlich bin ich, wie empfindlich. . . .'

Miriam lay thinking of how she and Harriett on their confirmation morning had met the vicar in the Upper Richmond Road, having gone out, contrary to the desire expressed by him at his last preparation class, and how he had stopped and greeted them. She had tried to look vague and sad and to murmur something in spite of the bull's-eye in her cheek, and had suddenly noticed as they stood grouped that Harriett's little sugar-loaf hat was askew and her brown eye underneath it was glaring fixedly at the vicar above the little knob in her cheek—and how they somehow got away and went, gently reeling and colliding, moaning and gasping down the road out of hearing.

Early next morning Judy came in to tell Emma and Ulrica to get up at once and come and help the housekeeper make the rooms tidy and prepare breakfast. Miriam lay motionless while Emma unfolded and arranged the screens. Then she gazed at the ceiling. It was pleasant to lie tranquil, open-eyed and unchallenged, while others moved busily about. Two separate, sudden and resounding garglings almost startled her to thought, but she resisted, and presently she was alone in the strange room. She supposed it must be cooler after the storm. She felt strong and languid. She could feel the shape and weight of each limb; sounds came to her with perfect distinctness; the sounds downstairs and a low-voiced conversation across the landing, little faint marks that human beings were making on the great wide stillness, the stillness that brooded along her white ceiling and all round her and right out through the world; the faint scent of her soap-tablet reached her from the distant washstand. She felt that her short sleep must have been perfect, that it had carried her down and down into the heart of tranquillity where she still lay awake, and drinking as if at a source. Cool streams seemed to be flowing in her brain, through her heart, through every vein, her breath was like a live cool stream flowing through her.

She remembered that she had dreamed her favourite dream

—floating through clouds and above tree-tops and villages. She had almost brushed the tree-tops, that had been the happiest moment, and had caught sight of a circular seat round the trunk of a large old tree, and a group of white cottages.

She stirred; her hands seemed warm on her cool chest and the warmth of her body sent up a faint pleasant sense of personality. 'It 's me,' she said, and smiled.

'Look here, you 'd better get up, my dear,' she murmured.

She wanted to have the whole world in and be reconciled. But she knew that if any one came, she would contract and the expression of her face would change and they would hate her or be indifferent. She knew that if she even moved she would be changed.

'Get up.'

She listened for a while to two voices across the landing. Millie's thick and plaintive with her hay-fever and Bertha's thin and cold and level and reassuring. . . . Bertha's voice was like the morning, clean and cool. . . . Then she got up and shut the door.

The sky was a vivid grey—against its dark background the tops of heavy masses of cloud were standing up just above the roof-line of the houses beyond the neighbouring gardens. The trees and the grey roofs and the faces of the houses were staringly bright. They were absolutely stiff, nothing was moving, there were no shadows.

A soft distant rumble of thunder came as she was dressing. . . . The storm was still going on . . . what an extraordinary time of day for thunder . . . the excitement was not over . . . they were still a besieged party . . . all staying at the Bienenkorb together. . . . How beautiful it sounded rumbling away over the country in the morning. When she had finished struggling with her long thick hair and put the hairpins into the solid coil on the top of her head and tied the stout doubled door-knocker plait at her neck, she put on the rose-madder blouse. The mirror was lower and twice as large as the one in the garret, larger than the one she had shared with Harriett. 'How jolly I look,' she thought, 'jolly and big somehow. Mother would like me this morning. I *am* German-looking to-day, pinky red, and yellow hair. But I haven't got a German expression and I don't smile like a German. . . . She smiled. . . . Silly, baby-face! Doll! Never mind. I look jolly. She looked gravely into her eyes. . . . There's something about my expression.' Her face grew wistful. 'It isn't vain to like it. It's something. It isn't me. It's something I am, somehow. Oh, *do* stay,' she said, 'do be like that always.' She sighed and turned away saying in Harriett's voice, 'Oo—crumbs! This is no place for *me*.'

The sky seen from the summer-house was darker still. There were no massed clouds, nothing but a hard even dark copper-grey, and away through the gap the distant country was bright like a little painted scene. On the horizon, the hard dark sky shut down. At intervals thunder rumbled evenly, far away. Miriam stood still in the middle of the summer-house floor. It was half-dark; the morning *saal* lay in a hot sultry twilight. The air in the summer-house was heavy and damp. She stood with her half-closed hands gathered against her. 'How perfectly magnificent,' she murmured, gazing out through the hard half-darkness to where the brightly coloured world lay in a strip and ended against the hard sky.

'Yes . . . yes,' came a sad low voice at her side.

For a second Miriam did not turn. She drank in the quiet 'yes, yes,' the hard fixed scene seemed to move. Who loved it too, the dark sky and the storm? Then she focused her companion who was standing a little behind her, and gazed at Fräulein; she hardly saw her, she seemed still to see the outdoor picture. Fräulein made a movement towards her; and then she saw for a moment the strange grave young look in her eyes. Fräulein had looked at her in that moment as an equal. It was as if they had embraced each other.

Then Fräulein said sadly, 'You like the storm-weather, Miss Henderson?'

'Yes.'

Fräulein sighed, looking out across the country. 'We are

in the hollow of His hand,' she murmured. 'Come to your breakfast, my child,' she chided, smiling.

There was no church. Late in the afternoon, when the sky lifted, they all went to the woods in their summer dresses and hats. They had permission to carry their gloves, and Elsa Speier's parasol and lace scarf hung from her wrist. The sky was growing higher and lighter, but there was no sun. They entered the dark woods by a little well-swept pathway and for a while there was a strip of sky above their heads; but presently the trees grew tall and dense, the sky was shut out and their footsteps and voices began to echo about them as they straggled along, grouping and regrouping as the pathway widened and narrowed, gathering their skirts clear of the wet undergrowth. They crossed a roadway, and two carriage loads of men and women, talking and laughing and shouting, with shining red faces passed swiftly by, one close behind the other. Beyond the roadway the great trees towered up in a sort of twilight. There were no flowers here, but bright fungi shone here and there about the roots of the trees and they all stood for a moment to listen to the tinkling of a little stream.

Pathways led away in all directions. It was growing lighter. There were faint chequers of light and shade about them as they walked. The forest was growing golden all round them, lifting and opening, old and green, clearer and clearer. There were bright jewelled patches in amongst the trees; the boles of the trees shone out sharp grey and silver and flaked with sharp green leaves away and away until they melted into a mist of leafage. Singing sounded suddenly away in the wood; a sudden strong shouting of men's voices singing together like one voice in four parts, four shouts in one sound.

'O *Sonnenschein*! O *Sonnenschein*!'

Between the two exclamatory shouts, the echo rang through the woods and the listening girls heard the sharp drip, drip and murmur of the little stream near by, then the voices swung on into the song, strongly interwoven, swelling and lifting; dropping to a soft even staccato and swelling strongly out again.

> 'Wie scheinst du mir in's Herz hinein,
> Weck'st drinnen lauter Liebeslust,
> Dass mir so enge wird die Brust
> O *Sonn*enschein!   O *Sonn*—enschein!'

When the voices ceased there was a faint distant sound of crackling twigs and the echo of talking and laughter.

'Ach, Studenten!'

'Irgend ein Männergesangverein.'

'I think we ought to get back, Gertrude.   Fräulein *said* only an hour altogether and it 's church to-night.'

'We 'll get back, Millennium mine—never fear.'

As they began to retrace their steps, Clara softly sang the last line of the song, the highest note ringing, faint and clear, away into the wood.

'Ho-*lah* !'   A mighty answering shout rang through the wood.   It was like a word of command.

'Oh, come along home; Clara, what are you dreaming of?'

'Taisez-vous, taisez-vous, Clarah! C'est honteux, mon Dieu!'

CHAPTER XI

THE next afternoon they all drove in a high, wide brake with an awning, five miles out into the country to have tea at a forest-inn. The inn appeared at last standing back from the wide roadway along which they had come, creamy-white and grey-roofed, long and low and with overhanging eaves, close against the forest. They pulled up and Pastor Lahmann dropped the steps and got out. Miriam, who was sitting next to the door, felt that the long sitting in two rows confronted in the hard afternoon light, bumped and shaken and teased with the crunchings and slitherings of the wheels, the grinding and squeaking of the brake, had made them all enemies. She had sat tense and averted, seeing the general greenery, feeling that the cool flowing air might be great happiness, conscious of each form and each voice, of the insincerity of the exclamations and the babble of conversation that struggled above the noise of their going, half seeing Pastor Lahmann opposite to her, a little insincerely smiling man in an alpaca suit and a soft felt hat. She got down the steps without his assistance. With whom should she take refuge? . . . no Minna. There were long tables and little round tables standing about under the trees in front of the inn. Some students in Polytechnik uniform were leaning out of the upper window.

The landlord came out. Every one was out of the brake and standing about. Tall Fräulein was taking short padding steps towards the inn-door. A strong grip came on Miriam's arm and she was propelled rapidly along towards the farther greenery. Gertrude was talking to her in loud rallying tones, asking questions in German and answering them herself. Miriam glanced round at her face. It was crimson and quivering with laughter. The strong laughter and her strong features seemed to hide the peculiar roughness of her skin and

154

coarseness of her hair. They made the round of one of the long tables. When they were on the far side Gertrude said, 'I think you 'll see a friend of mine to-day, Henderson.'

'D' you mean Erica's brother?'

'There 's his chum anyhow at yondah window.'

'Oh, I say.'

'Hah! Spree, eh? Happy thought of Lily's to bring us here.'

Miriam pondered, distressed. 'You must tell me which it is if we see him.'

Their party was taking possession of a long table near by. Returning to her voluble talk, Gertrude steered Miriam towards them.

As they settled round the table under the quiet trees, the first part of Weber's *Invitation* sounded out through the upper window. The brilliant tuneless passages bounding singly up the piano, flowing down entwined, were shaped by an iron rhythm.

Every one stirred. Smiles broke. Fräulein lifted her head until her chin was high, smiled slowly until the fullest width was reached and made a little chiding sound in her throat.

Pastor Lahmann laughed with raised eyebrows. 'Ah! la valse . . . les étudiants.'

The window was empty. The assault settled into a gently-leaping, heavily-thudding waltz.

As the waiter finished clattering down a circle of cups and saucers in front of Fräulein, the unseen iron hands dropped tenderly into the central melody of the waltz. The notes no longer bounded and leaped but went dreaming along in an even, slow, swinging movement.

It seemed to Miriam that the sound of a far-off sea was in them, and the wind and the movement of distant trees and the shedding and pouring of far-away moonlight. One by one, delicately and quietly the young men's voices dropped in, and the sea and the wind and the trees and the pouring moonlight came near.

When the music ceased Miriam hoped she had not been gazing at the window. It frightened and disgusted her to see

that all the girls seemed to be sitting up and . . . being bright
. . . affected. She could hardly believe it. She flushed with
shame. . . . Fast, horrid . . . perfect strangers . . . it was
terrible . . . it spoilt everything. Sitting up like that and
grimacing. . . . It was different for Gertrude. How happy
Gertrude must be. She was sitting with her elbows on the
table laughing out across the table about something. . . .
Millie was not being horrid. She looked just as usual, pudgy
and babyish and surprised and half resentful . . . it was her
eyebrows. Miriam began looking at eyebrows.

There was a sudden silence all round the table. Standing
at Fräulein's side was a young student, holding his peaked cap
in his hand and bowing with downcast eyes. Above his pallid
scarred face his hair stood upright. He bowed at the end of
each phrase. Miriam's heart bounded in anticipation. Would
Fräulein let them dance after tea, on the grass?

But Fräulein, with many smiles and kind words, denied the
young man's formally repeated pleadings. They finished tea
to the strains of a funeral march.

They were driving swiftly home through the twilight. The
warm scents of the woods stood across the roadway. They
breathed them in. Sitting at the forward end of the brake,
Miriam could turn and see the shining of the road and the
edges of the high woods.

Underneath the awning, faces were growing dim. Warm
at her side was Emma. Emma's hand was on her arm under a
mass of fern and grasses. Voices quivered and laughed.
Miriam looked again and again at Pastor Lahmann sitting
almost opposite to her, next to Fräulein Pfaff. She could look
at him more easily than at either of the girls. She felt that
only he could feel the beauty of the evening exactly as she did.
Several times she met and quietly contemplated his dark eyes.
She felt that there was someone in those eyes who was neither
tiresome nor tame. She was looking at someone to whom
those boys and that dead wife were nothing. At first he had

met her eyes formally, then with obvious embarrassment, and at last simply and gravely. She felt easy and happy in this communion. Dimly she was conscious that it sustained her, it gave her dignity and poise. She thought that its meaning must, if she observed it at all, be quite obvious to Fräulein and must reveal her to her. Presently her eyes were drawn to meet Fräulein's and she read there a disgust and a loathing such as she had never seen. The woods receded, the beauty dropped out of them. The crunching of the wheels sounded out suddenly. What was the good of the brake-load of grimacing people? Miriam wanted to stop it and get out and stroll home along the edge of the wood with the quiet man.

'Haben die Damen vielleicht ein *Rad* verloren?'

A deep voice on the steps of the brake. . . . 'Have the ladies lost a wheel, perhaps?' Miriam translated helplessly to herself during a general outbreak of laughter. . . .

In a moment a brake overtook them and drove alongside in the twilight. The drivers whipped up their horses. The two vehicles raced and rumbled along, keeping close together. Fräulein called to their driver to desist. The students slackened down too and began singing at random, one against the other; those on the near side standing up and bowing and laughing. A bouquet of fern fronds came in over Judy's head, missing the awning and falling against Clara's knees. She rose and flung it back and then every one seemed to be standing up and laughing and throwing.

They drove home, slowly, side by side, shouting and singing and throwing. Warm, blinding masses of fragrant grass came from the students' brake and were thrown to and fro through the darkness lit by the lamps of the two carriages.

CHAPTER XII

TOWARDS the end of June there were frequent excursions.

Into all the gatherings at Waldstrasse the outside world came like a presence. It removed the sense of pressure, of being confronted and challenged. Everything that was said seemed to be incidental to it, like remarks dropped in a low tone between individuals at a great conference.

Miriam wondered again and again whether her companions shared this sense with her. Sometimes when they were all sitting together she longed to ask, to find out, to get some public acknowledgment of the magic that lay over everything. At times it seemed as if could they all be still for a moment— it must take shape. It was everywhere, in the food, in the fragrance rising from the opened lid of the tea-urn, in all the needful unquestioned movements, the requests, the handings and thanks, the going from room to room, the partings and assemblings. It hung about the fabrics and fittings of the house. Overwhelmingly it came in through oblongs of window giving on to stairways. Going upstairs in the light pouring in from some uncurtained window, she would cease for a moment to breathe.

Whenever she found herself alone she began to sing, softly. When she was with others a head drooped or lifted, the movement of a hand, the light falling along the detail of a profile could fill her with happiness.

It made companionship a perpetual question. At rare moments there would come a tingling from head to foot, a faint buzzing at her lips and at the tip of each finger. At these moments she could raise her eyes calmly to those about her and drink in the fact of their presence, see them all with perfect distinctness, but without distinguishing one from the other. She wanted to say, 'Isn't it extraordinary? Do you realize?' She felt that if only she could make her meaning clear all difficulties must vanish. Outside in the open, going forward to some goal through sunny mornings, gathering at inns, wading through the scented undergrowth of the woods, she would dream of the secure return to Waldstrasse, their own beleaguered place. She saw it opening out warm and familiar back and back to the strange beginning in the winter. They would be there again to-night, singing.

One morning she knew that there was going to be a change. The term was coming to an end. There was to be a going away. The girls were talking about 'Norderney.'

'Going to Norderney, Hendy?' Jimmie said suddenly.

'Ah!' she responded mysteriously. For the rest of that day she sat contracted and fearful.

'You shall write and inquire of your good parents what they would have you do. You shall tell them that the German pupils return all to their homes; that the English pupils go for a happy holiday to the sea.'

'Oh yes,' said Miriam conversationally, with trembling breath.

'It is of course evident that since you will have no duties to perform, I cannot support the expense of your travelling and your maintenance.'

'Oh no, of course not,' said Miriam, her hands pressed against her knee.

She sat shivering in the warm dim *saal* shaded by the close sun-blinds. It looked as she had seen it with her father for the first time, and Fräulein sitting near seemed to be once more in the heavy panniered blue velvet dress.

She waited stiff and ugly till Fräulein, secure and summer-clad, spoke softly again.

'You think, my child, you shall like the profession of a teacher?'

'Oh yes,' said Miriam, from the midst of a tingling flush.

'I think you have many qualities that make the teacher. . . .
You are earnest and serious-minded. . . . Grave. . . . Sometimes perhaps overgrave for your years. . . . But you have a
serious fault—which must be corrected if you wish to succeed
in your calling.'

Miriam tried to pull her features into an easy inquiring
seriousness. A darkness was threatening her. 'You have a
most unfortunate manner.'

Without relaxing, Miriam quivered. She felt the blood
mount to her head.

'You must adopt a quite, quite different manner. Your
influence is, I think, good, a good English influence in its most
general effect. But it is too slightly so and of too much in-
direction. You must exert it yourself, in a manner more alive,
you must make it your aim that you shall have a responsible
influence, a direct personal influence. You have too much of
chill and formality. It makes a stiffness that I am willing to
believe you do not intend.'

Miriam felt a faint dizziness.

'If you should fail to become more genial, more simple and
natural as to your bearing, you will neither make yourself
understood nor will you be loved by your pupils.'

'No——' responded Miriam, assuming an air of puzzled
and interested consideration of Fräulein's words. She was
recovering. She must get to the end of the interview and get
away and find the answer. Far away beneath her fear and
indignation, Fräulein was answered. She must get away and
say the answer to herself.

'To truly fulfil the most serious role of the teacher you must
enter into the personality of each pupil and must sympathize
with the struggles of each one upon the path on which our feet
are set. Efforts to good kindliness and thought for others must
be encouraged. The teacher shall be sunshine, human sunshine, encouraging all effort and all lovely things in the personality of the pupil.'

Fräulein rose and stood, tall. Then her half-tottering,
decorous footsteps began. Miriam had hardly listened to her
last words. She felt tears of anger rising and tried to smile.

'I shall say now no more. But when you shall hear from your good parents, we can further discuss our plans.' Fräulein was at the door.

Fräulein left the *saal* by the small door and Miriam felt her way to the schoolroom. The girls were gathering there ready for a walk. Some were in the hall and Fräulein's voice was giving instructions: 'Machen Sie schnell, Miss Henderson,' she called.

Fräulein had never before called to her like that. It had always been as if she did not see her but assumed her ready to fall in with the general movements.

Now it was Fräulein calling to her as she might do to Gertrude or Solomon. There was no hurried whisper from Jimmie telling her to 'fly for her life.'

'Ja, Fräulein,' she cried gaily and blundered towards the basement stairs. Mademoiselle was standing averted at the head of them; Miriam glanced at her. Her face was red and swollen with crying.

The sight amazed Miriam. She considered the swollen suffusion under the large black hat as she ran downstairs. She hoped Mademoiselle did not see her glance. . . . Mademoiselle, standing there all disfigured and blotchy about something . . . it was nothing . . . it couldn't be anything. . . . If any one were dead she would not be standing there . . . it was just some silly prim French quirk . . . her dignity . . . someone had been 'grossière' . . . and there she stood in her black hat and black cotton gloves. . . . Hurriedly putting on her hat and long lace scarf she decided that she would not change her shoes. Somewhere out in the sunshine a hurdy-gurdy piped out the air of *Dass du mich liebst, das wusst ich*. She glanced at the frosted barred window through which the dim light came into the dressing-room. The piping notes, out of tune, wrongly emphasized, slurring one into the other, followed her across the dark basement hall and came faintly to her as she went slowly upstairs. There was no hurry. Every one was talking busily in the hall, drowning the sound of her footsteps. She had forgotten her gloves. She went back into the cool grey musty rooms. A little crack in an upper pane

shone like a gold thread.   The barrel-organ piped.   As she
stooped to gather up her gloves from the floor she felt the cold
stone firm and secure under her hand.   And the house stood
up all round her with its rooms and the light lying along stairways and passages, and outside the bright hot sunshine and the
roadways leading in all directions, out into Germany.

How could Fräulein possibly think she could afford to go to
Norderney?   They would all go.   Things would go on.   She
could not go there—nor back to England.   It was cruel . . .
just torture and worry again . . . with the bright house all
round her—the high rooms, the dark old pianos, strange old
garret, the unopened door beyond it.   No help anywhere.

As they walked, she laughed and talked with the girls,
responding excitedly to all that was said.   They walked along
a broad and almost empty boulevard in two rows of four and
five abreast, with Mademoiselle and Judy bringing up the rear.
The talk was general and there was much laughter.   It was the
kind of interchange that arose when they were all together and
there was anything 'in the air,' the kind that Miriam most
disliked.   She joined in it feverishly.   It's perfectly natural
that they should all be excited about the holidays she told
herself, stifling her thoughts.   But it must not go too far.
They wanted to be jolly. . . . If I could be jolly too they
would like me.   I must not be a wet blanket. . . . Mademoiselle's voice was not heard.   Miriam felt that the steering
of the conversation might fall to any one.   Mademoiselle was
extinguished.   She must exert her influence.   Presently she
forgot Mademoiselle's presence altogether.   They were all
walking along very quickly. . . . If she *were* going to Norderney
with the English girls she must be on easy terms with them.

'Ah, ha!' somebody was saying.

'Oh—ho!' said Miriam in response.

'Ih—hi!' came another voice.

'Tre-la-la,' trilled Bertha Martin gently.

'You mean Turrah-lahee-tee,' said Miriam.

'Good for you, Hendy,' blared Gertrude, in a swinging middle tone.

'Chalk it up. Chalk it up, children,' giggled Jimmie.

Millie looked pensively about her with vague disapproval. Her eyebrows were up. It seemed as if anything might happen; as if at any moment they might all begin running in different directions.

'*Cave*, my dear brats, be artig,' came Bertha's cool even tones.

'Ah! we are observed.'

'No, we are not observed. The observer observeth not.'

Miriam saw her companions looking across the boulevard. Following their eyes, she found the figure of Pastor Lahmann walking swiftly, bag in hand, in the direction of an opening into a side street.

'Ah!' she cried gaily. 'Voilà Monsieur; courrez, Mademoiselle!'

At once she felt that it was cruel to draw attention to Mademoiselle when she was dumpy and upset.

'What a fool I am,' she moaned in her mind. 'Why can't I say the right thing?'

'Ce n'est pas moi,' said Mademoiselle, 'qui fait les avances.'

The group walked on for a moment or two in silence. Bertha Martin was swinging her left foot out across the kerb with each step, giving her right heel a little twirl to keep her balance.

'You are very clever, Bair-ta,' said Mademoiselle, still in French, 'but you will never make a prima ballerina.'

'Hulloh!' breathed Jimmie, 'she's perking up.'

'Isn't she,' said Miriam, feeling that she was throwing away the last shred of her dignity.

'What was the matter?' she continued, trying to escape from her confusion.

Mademoiselle's instant response to her cry at the sight of Pastor Lahmann rang in her ears. She blushed to the soles of her feet. . . . How could Mademoiselle misunderstand her insane remark? What did she mean? What did she really think of her? Just kind old Lahmann—walking along there in the outside world. . . . *She* did not want to stop him. . . .

He was a sort of kinsman for Mademoiselle . . . that was
what she had meant. Oh, why couldn't she get away from all
these girls? . . . indeed—and again she saw the hurrying
figure which had disappeared leaving the boulevard with its
usual effect of a great strange ocean—he could have brought
help and comfort to all of them if he had seen them and stopped.
Pastor Lahmann—Lahmann—perhaps she would not see him
again. Perhaps he could tell her what she ought to do.

'Oh, my dear,' Jimmie was saying, 'didn't you know?—a
fearful row.'

Mademoiselle's laughter tinkled out from the rear.

'A row?'

'Fearful!' Jimmie's face came round, round-eyed under
her white sailor hat that sat slightly tilted on the peak of her
hair.

'What about?'

'Something about a letter or something, or some letters or
something—I don't know. Something she took out of the
letter-box, it was unlocked or something and Ulrica saw her,
and told Lily!'

'Goodness!' breathed Miriam.

'Yes, and Lily had her in her room, and Ulrica, and poor
little Petite couldn't deny it. Ulrica said she did nothing but
cry and cry. She's been crying all the morning, poor little
pig.'

'Why did she want to take anything out of the box?'

'Oh, I don't know. There was a fearful row anyhow.
Ulrica said Lily talked like a clergyman—wie ein Pfarrer. . . .
I don't know. Ulrica said she was *opening* a letter. *I* don't
know.'

'But she can't read German or English. . . .'

'*I* don't know. Ask me another.'

'It is *extraordinary*.'

'What's extraordinary?' asked Bertha from the far side of
Jimmie.

'Petite and that letter.'

'Oh.'

'What did the Kiddy *want*?'

'Oh, my dear, don't ask me to explain the peculiarities of the French temperament.'

'Yes, but all the letters in the letter-box would be English or German, as Hendy says.'

Bertha glanced at Miriam. Miriam flushed. She could not discuss Mademoiselle with two of the girls at once.

'Rum go,' said Bertha.

'You're right, my son. It's rum. It's all over now, anyhow. There's no accounting for tastes. Poor old Petite.'

Miriam woke in the moonlight. She saw Mademoiselle's face as it had looked at tea-time, pale and cruel, silent and very old. Someone had said she had been in Fräulein's room again all the afternoon. . . . Fräulein had spoken to her once or twice during tea. She had answered coolly and eagerly . . . disgusting . . . like a child that had been whipped and forgiven. . . . How could Fräulein dare to forgive anybody?

She lay motionless. The night was cool. The screens had not been moved. She felt that the door was shut. After a while she began in imagination a conversation with Eve.

'You *see* the trouble was,' she said and saw Eve's downcast believing, admiring, sympathetic face, 'Fräulein talked to me about manner, she simply wanted me to grimace, *simply*. *You* know—be like other people.'

Eve laughed. 'Yes, I know.'

'You see? *Simply*.'

'Well, if you wanted to stay, why couldn't you?'

'I simply couldn't; you know how people are.'

'But you can act so splendidly.'

'But you can't keep it up.'

'Why not?'

'*Eve*. There you are, you see, you always go back.'

'I mean I think it would be simply lovely. If I were clever like you I should do it all the time, be simply always gushing and "charming."'

Then she reminded Eve of the day they had walked up the

lane to the Heath talking over all the manners they would like to have—and how Sarah suddenly in the middle of supper had caricatured the one they had chosen. 'Of course you overdid it,' she concluded, and Eve crimsoned and said, 'Oh yes, I know it was my fault. But you could have begun all over again in Germany and been quite different.'

'Yes, I know, I thought about that. . . . But if you knew as much of the world as I do. . . .'

Eve stared, showing a faint resentment.

Miriam thought of Eve's many suitors, of her six months' betrothal, of her lifelong peace-making, her experiment in being governess to the two children of an artist—a little green-robed boy threatening her with a knife.

'Yes, but I mean if you had been about.'

'I know,' smiled Eve confidently. 'You mean if I were you. Go on. I know. Explain, old thing.'

'Well, I mean of course if you are a governess in a school you *can't* be jolly and charming. You can't be idiotic or anything. . . . I did think about it. Don't tell anybody. But I thought for a little while I might go into a family—one of the girls' families—the German girls, and begin having a German manner. Two of the girls asked me. One of them was ill and went away—that Pomeranian one I told you about. Well, then, I didn't tell you about that little one and her sister—they asked me to go to them for the holidays. The youngest said —it was *so* absurd—"you shall marry my bruzzer—he is mairchant—very welty"—absurd.'

'*Not* absurd—you probably *would* have, away from that school.'

'D' you think so?'

'Yes, you would have been a regular German, fat and jolly and laughing.'

'I know. My dear, I thought about it. You may imagine. I wondered if I ought.'

'Why didn't you try?'

Why not? Why was she not going to try? Eve would, she was sure, in her place. . . .

Why not grimace and be very 'bright' and 'animated' until

the end of the term and then go and stay with the Bergmanns for two months and be as charming as she could? . . . Her heart sank. . . . She imagined a house, every one kind and blond and smiling. Emma's big tall brother smiling and joking and liking her. She would laugh and pretend and flirt like the Pooles and make up to him—and it would be lovely for a little while. Then she would offend someone. She would offend every one but Emma—and get tired and cross and lose her temper. Stare at them all as they said the things everybody said, the things she hated; and she would sit glowering, and suddenly refuse to allow the women to be familiar with her. . . . She tried to see the brother more clearly. She looked at the screen. The Bergmanns' house would be full of German furniture. . . . At the end of a week every bit of it would reproach her.

She tried to imagine him without the house and the family, not talking or joking or pretending . . . alone and sad . . . despising his family . . . needing her. He loved forests and music. He had a great, strong, solid voice and was strong and sure about everything and she need never worry any more.

> Seit ich ihn gesehen
> Glaub' ich blind zu sein.

There would be a garden and German springs and summers and sunsets and strong kind arms and a shoulder. She would grow so happy. No one would recognize her as the same person. She would wear a band of turquoise-blue velvet ribbon round her hair and look at the mountains. . . . No good. She could never get out to that. Never. She could not pretend long enough. Everything would be at an end long before there was any chance of her turning into a happy German woman.

Certainly with a German man she would be angry at once. She thought of the men she had seen—in the streets, in cafés and gardens, the masters in the school, photographs in the girls' albums. They had all offended her at once. Something in their bearing and manner. . . . Blind and impudent. . . . She thought of the interview she had witnessed between Ulrica and her cousin—the cousin coming up from the estate in Erfurth, arriving in a carriage, Fräulein's manner, her smiles and hints; Ulrica standing in the *saal* in her sprigged saffron muslin dress curtseying . . . with bent head, the cousin's condescending laughing voice. It would never do for her to go into a German home. She must not say anything about the chance of going to the Bergmanns'—even to Eve.

She imagined Eve sitting listening in the window space in the bow that was carpeted with linoleum to look like parquet flooring. Beyond them lay the length of the Turkey carpet darkening away under the long table. She could see each object on the shining sideboard. The silver biscuit-box and the large epergne made her feel guilty and shifting, guilty from the beginning of things.

'You see, Eve, I thought, counting it all up, that if I came home it would cost less than going to Norderney and that all the expense of my going to Germany and coming back is less than what it would have cost to keep me at home for the five months I've been here—I wish you'd tell everybody that.'

She turned about in bed; her head was growing fevered.

She conjured up a vision of the backs of the books in the bookcase in the dining-room at home. . . . *Iliad* and *Odyssey* . . . people going over the sea in boats and someone doing embroidery . . . that little picture of Hector and Andromache in the corner of a page . . . he in armour . . . she, in a trailing dress, holding up her baby. Both, silly. . . . She wished she had read more carefully. She could not remember anything in Lecky or Darwin that would tell her what to do . . . *Hudibras* . . . *The Atomic Theory* . . . *Ballads and Poems*, D. G. Rossetti . . . Kinglake's *Crimea* . . . Palgrave's *Arabia* . . . *Crimea*. . . . *The Crimea*. . . . Florence Nightingale; a picture somewhere; a refined face, with cap and strings. . . . She must have smiled. . . . Motley's *Rise of* . . . *Rise of* . . . Motley's *Rise of the Dutch Republic*. . . . Motley's *Rise of the Dutch Republic* and the *Chronicles of the Schönberg-Cotta Family*. She held to the memory of these

two books. Something was coming from them to her. She
handled the shiny brown gold-tooled back of Motley's *Rise* and
felt the hard graining of the red-bound *Chronicles*. . . . There
were green trees outside in the moonlight. . . . in Luther's
Germany . . . trees and fields and German towns and then
Holland. She breathed more easily. Her eyes opened
serenely. Tranquil moonlight lay across the room. It surprised her like a sudden hand stroking her brow. It seemed to
feel for her heart. If she gave way to it her thoughts would go.
Perhaps she ought to watch it and let her thoughts go. It
passed over her trouble like her mother did when she said,
'Don't go so deeply into everything, chickie. You must learn
to take life as it comes. Ah-eh, if I were strong I could show
you how to enjoy life. . . .' Delicate little mother, running
quickly downstairs clearing her throat to sing. But mother
did not know. She had no reasoning power. She could not
help because she did not know. The moonlight was sad
and hesitating. Miriam closed her eyes again. Luther . . .
pinning up that notice on a church door. . . . (Why is Luther
like a dyspeptic blackbird? Because the Diet of Worms did
not agree with him.) . . . and then leaving the notice on the
church door and going home to tea . . . coffee . . . some
evening meal . . . Käthe . . . Käthe . . . happy Käthe.
. . . They pinned up that notice on a Roman Catholic church
. . . and all the priests looked at them . . . and behind the
priests were torture and dark places . . . Luther looking up to
God . . . saying you couldn't get away from your sins by
paying money . . . standing out in the world and Käthe
making the meal at home . . . Luther was fat and German.
Perhaps his face perspired . . . *Eine feste Burg* ; a firm for-
tress . . . a round tower made of old brown bricks and no
windows. . . . No need for Käthe to smile. . . . She had
been a nun . . . and then making a lamplit meal for Luther
in a wooden German house . . . and Rome waiting to kill them.

Darwin had come since then. There were people . . .
distinguished minds, who thought Darwin was true.

No God. No Creation. The struggle for existence.
Fighting. . . . Fighting. . . . Fighting. . . . Everybody groping

and fighting. . . . Fräulein. . . . Some said it was true . . . some
not. They could not both be right. It was probably true
. . . only old-fashioned people thought it was not. It was
true. Just that—monkeys fighting. But who began it? Who
made Fräulein? Tough leathery monkey. . . .

Then nothing matters. Just one little short life. . . .

> A few more years shall roll . . .
> A few more seasons pass. . . .

There was a better one than that . . . not so organ-grindery.

> Swift to its close ebbs out· life's little day;
> Earth's joys grow dim, its glories fade away;
> Change and decay in all around I see.

Wow-wow-wow-whiney-caterwauley. . . .

Mr Brough quoted Milton in a sermon and said he was a
materialist. . . . Pater said it was a bold thing to say. . . .
Mr Brough was a clear-headed man. She couldn't imagine
how he stayed in the Church. . . . She hoped he hated that
sickening, sickening, idiot humbug, Eve . . . meek . . . with
silly long hair . . . 'divinely smiling' . . . Adam was like a
German . . . English too. . . . Impudent bombastic creature
. . . a sort of man who would call his wife 'my dear.' There
was a hymn that even pater liked . . . the tune was like a
garden in the autumn. . . .

> O . . . Strength and *Stay*—up— . . . Holding—all
> Cre—ay—ay—tion. . . . Who . . . ever Dost
> Thy . . . self—un . . . Moved—a—Bide. . . .
> Thyself unmoved abide. . . . Thyself unmoved
> abide . . . Unmoved abide. . . .
> Unmoved abide. . . . Unmoved Abide . . .

. . . Flights of shining steps, shallow and very wide—going
up and up and growing fainter and fainter, and far away at the
top a faint old face with great rays shooting out all round it
. . . the picture in the large *Pilgrim's Progress*. . . . God in
heaven. . . . I belong to Apollyon . . . a horror with ex-

pressionless eyes . . . darting out little spiky flames . . . if
only it would come now . . . instead of waiting until the
end. . . .

She clasped her hands closely one in the other. They felt
large and strong. She stopped her thoughts and stared for a
long while at the faint light in the room. . . . 'It's physically
impossible' someone had said . . . the only hell thinkable is
remorse . . . remorse. . . .

Sighing impatiently she turned about . . . and sighed again,
breathing deeply and rattling and feeling very hungry. . . .
There will be breakfast, even for me. . . . If they knew me
they would not give me breakfast. . . . No one would . . . I
should be in a little room and one after another would come
and be reproachful and shocked . . . and then they would go
away and be happy and forget. . . .

Sarah would come. Whatever it was, Sarah would come.
She read the Bible and marked pieces. . . . But she would
rush in without saying anything, with a red face and bang down
a plate of melon. . . . What did God do about people like
Sarah? Perhaps Apollyon could be made to come at once—
sweeping in like a large bat—be torn to bits—those men at
that college said he had come to them. They swore—one
after the other and the devil came in through one of the carved
windows and carried one of them away. . . . I have my
doubts . . . Pater's face laughing—I have my doubts, ooof—
P-ooof. She flung off the outer covering and felt the strong
movements of her limbs. Hang! Hang! *Hang!* DAMN. . . .

If there's no God, there's no Devil . . . and everything
goes on. . . . Fräulein goes on having her school. . . . What
does she really think? . . . Out in the world people don't
think. . . . They grimace. . . . Is there anywhere where
there are no people? . . . be a gipsy. . . . There are always
people. . . .

'What a perfect morning . . . what a perfect morning,'
Miriam kept telling herself, trying to see into the garden.

There was a bowl of irises on the breakfast-table—it made everything seem strange. There had never been flowers on the table before. There was also a great dish of *Pumpernickel* besides the usual food. Fräulein had enjoined silence. The silence made the impression of the irises stay. She hoped it might be a new rule. She glanced at Fräulein two or three times. She was pallid white. Her face looked thinner than usual and her eyes larger and keener. She did not seem to notice any one. Miriam wondered whether she were thinking about cancer. Her face looked as it had done when once or twice she had said, 'Ich bin so bange vor Krebs.' She hoped not. Perhaps it was the problem of evil. Perhaps she had thought of it when she put the irises on the table.

She gazed at them, half-feeling the flummery petals against the palm of her hand. Fräulein seemed cancelled. There was no need to feel self-conscious. She was not thinking of any of them. Miriam found herself looking at high grey stone basins, with stems like wine-glasses and large square fluted pedestals, filled with geraniums and calceolarias. They had stood in the sunshine at the corners of the lawn in her grandmother's garden. She could remember nothing else but the scent of a greenhouse and its steamy panes over her head . . . lemon thyme and scented geranium.

How lovely it would be to-day at the end of the day. Fräulein would feel happy then . . . or did elderly people fear cancer all the time ? . . . It was a great mistake. You should leave things to Nature. . . . You were more likely to have things if you thought about them. But Fräulein would think and worry . . . alone with herself . . . with her great dark eyes and bony forehead and thin pale cheeks . . . always alone, and just cancer coming. . . . I shall be like that one day . . . an old teacher, and cancer coming. It was silly to forget all about it and see Granny's calceolarias in the sun . . . all that had to come to an end. . . . To forget was like putting off repentance. Those who did not put it off saw when the great waters came, a shining figure coming to them through the flood. . . . If they did not they were like the man in a nightcap, his mouth hanging open—no teeth—and skinny hands, playing cards on his death-bed.

After bed-making, Fräulein settled a mending party at the window-end of the schoolroom table. She sent no emissary, but was waiting herself in the schoolroom when they came down. She hovered about putting them into their places and inquiring about the work of each one.

She arranged Miriam and the Germans at the *saal* end of the table for an English lesson. Mademoiselle was not there. Fräulein herself took the head of the table. Once more she enjoined silence—the whole table seemed waiting for Miriam to begin her lesson.

The three or four readings they had done during the term alone in the little room had brought them through about a third of the blue-bound volume. Hoarsely whispering, then violently clearing her throat and speaking suddenly in a very loud tone, Miriam bade them resume the story. They read and she corrected them in hoarse whispers. No one appeared to be noticing. A steady breeze coming through the open door of the summer-house flowed past them and along the table, but Miriam sat stifling, with beating temples. She had no thoughts. Now and again in correcting a simple word she was not sure that she had given the right English rendering. Behind her distress two impressions went to and fro—Fräulein and the *raccommodage* party sitting in judgment and the whole roomful waiting for cancer.

Very gently at the end of half an hour Fräulein dismissed the Germans to practise.

Herr Schraub was coming at eleven. Miriam supposed she was free until then and went upstairs.

On the landing she met Mademoiselle coming downstairs with mending.

'Bossy coming?' she said feverishly in French; 'are you going to the *saal*?'

Mademoiselle stood contemplating her.

'I 've just been giving an English lesson, oh, mon Dieu,' she proceeded.

Mademoiselle still looked, gravely and quietly.

Miriam was passing on. Mademoiselle turned and said hurriedly in a low voice. 'Elsa says you are a fool at lessons.'

'Oh,' smiled Miriam.

'You think they do not speak of you, hein? Well, I tell you they speak of you. Jimmie says you are as fat as any German. She laughed in saying that. Gertrude, too, thinks you are a fool. Oh, they say things. If I should tell you all the things they say you would not believe.'

'I dare say,' said Miriam heavily, moving on.

'Every one, all say things, I tell you,' whispered Mademoiselle turning her head as she went on downstairs.

Miriam ran into the empty summer-house tearing open a well-filled envelope. There was a long letter from Eve, a folded half-sheet from mother. Her heart beat rapidly. Thick, straight rain was seething down into the garden.

'Come and say good-bye to Mademoiselle, Hendy.'

'Is she *going*?'

'Umph.'

'Little Mademoiselle?'

'Poor little beast!'

'Leaving?'

'Seems like it—she 's been packing all the morning.'

'Because of that letter business?'

'Oh, I dunno. Anyhow there 's some story of some friend of Fräulein's travelling through to Besançon to-day and Mademoiselle's going with her and we 're all to take solemn leave and she 's not coming back next term. Come on.'

Mademoiselle, radiantly rosy under her large black French hat, wearing her stockinette jacket and grey dress, was standing at the end of the schoolroom table—the girls were all assembled and the door into the hall was open.

The housekeeper was laughing and shouting and imitating

the puffing of a train. Mademoiselle stood smiling beside her with downcast eyes.

Opposite them was Gertrude with thin white face, blue lips and hotly blazing eyes fixed on Mademoiselle. She stood easily with her hands clasped behind her.

She must have an appalling headache thought Miriam. Mademoiselle began shaking hands.

'I say, Mademoiselle,' began Jimmie quietly and hurriedly in her lame French, as she took her hand, 'have you got another place?'

'A place?'

'I mean what are you going to do next term, petite?'

'Next term?'

'We want to know about your plans.'

'But I remain now with my parents till my marriage!'

'Petite!!! Fancy never telling us.'

Exclamations clustered round from all over the room.

'Why should I tell?'

'We didn't even know you were engaged!'

'But of course. Certainly I marry. I know quite well who is to marry me.'

The room was taking leave of Mademoiselle almost in silence. The English were standing together. Miriam heard their voices. ''Dieu, m'selle, 'dieu, m'selle,' one after the other and saw hands and wrists move vigorously up and down. The Germans were commenting, 'Ah, she is engaged—ah, what— en-gaged. Ah, the rascal! Hör mal——'

Miriam dreaded her turn. Mademoiselle was coming near . . . so cheap and common-looking with her hard grey dress and her cheap jacket with the hat hiding her hair and making her look skinny and old. She was a more dreadful stranger than she had been at first. . . . Miriam wished she could stay. She could not let any one go away like this. They would not meet again and Mademoiselle was going away detesting her and them all, going away in disgrace and not minding and going to be married. All the time there had been that waiting for her. She was smiling now and showing her babyish teeth. How could Jimmie hold her by the shoulders?

'Venez, mon enfant, venez à l'instant,' called Fräulein from the hall.

Mademoiselle made her hard little sound with her throat.

'Why doesn't she go?' thought Miriam as Mademoiselle ran down the room. 'Adieu, adieu evaireeboddie—alla——'

'Are all here?'

Jimmie answered and Fräulein came to the table and stood leaning for a moment upon one hand.

The door opened and the housekeeper shone hard and bright in the doorway.

'Wäsche angekommen!'

'Na, gut,' responded Fräulein quietly.

The housekeeper disappeared.

'Fräulein looks like a dead body,' thought Miriam.

Apprehension overtook her . . . 'there's going to be some silly fuss.'

'I shall speak in English, because the most that I shall say concerns the English members of this household and its heavy seriousness will be, by those who are not English, sufficiently understood.'

Miriam flushed, struggling for self-possession. She determined not to listen. . . . 'Damn . . . Devil . . .' she exhorted herself . . . 'humbugging creature. . . .' She felt the blood throbbing in her face and her eyes and looked at no one. She was conscious that little movements and sounds came from the Germans, but she heard nothing but Fräulein's voice which had ceased. It had been the clear-cut, low-breathing tone she used at prayers. 'Oh, Lord, bother, damnation,' she reiterated in her discomfiture. The words echoing through her mind seemed to cut a way of escape. . . .

'That dear child,' smiled Fräulein's voice, 'who has just left us, came under this roof . . . nearly a year ago.

'She came, a tender girl (Mademoiselle—Mademoiselle, oh, goodness!) from the house of her pious parents, fromme Eltern, fromme Eltern,' Fräulein breathed these words slowly out and a deep sigh came from one of the Germans, 'to reside with us. She came in the most perfect confidence with the aim to complete her own simple education, the pious and simple nurture of a Protestant French girl, and with the aim also to remove for a period something of the burden lying upon the shoulders of those dear parents in the upbringing of herself and her brothers and sisters.' (And then to leave home and be married—how easy, how easy!)

'Honourably—honourably she has fulfilled each and every duty laid upon her as institutrice in this establishment.

'Sufficient to indicate this fulfilment of duty is the fact that she was happy and that she made happy others——'

Fräulein's voice dropped to its lowest note and grew fuller in tone.

'Would that I could here complete what I have to say of the sojourn of little Aline Ducorroy under this roof. . . . But that I cannot do.

'That I cannot do.

'It has been the experience of this pure and gentle soul to come, under this roof, in contact with things not pure.'

Fräulein's voice had become breathless and shaking. Both her hands sought the support of the table.

'This poor child has had unwillingly to suffer the fact of associating with those not pure.'

'Ach, Fräulein! What you say!' ejaculated Clara.

In the silence the leaves of the chestnut tree tapped one against the other. Miriam listened to them . . . there must be a little breeze blowing across the garden. Why had she not noticed it before? Were they all hearing it?

'With—those—not pure.'

'Here, in this my school.'

Miriam's heart began to beat angrily.

'She has been forced, here, in this school, to hear talking'— Fräulein's voice thickened—'of men, . . .'

'*Männer—geschichten . . . hier!*'

'*Männer—geschichten.*' Fräulein's voice rang out down the table. She bent forward so that the light from both the windows behind her fell sharply across her grey-clad shoulders and along the top of her head. There was no condemnation, Miriam felt, in those broad grey shoulders—they were innocent. But the head, shining and flat, the wide parting, the sleekness of the hair falling thinly and flatly away from it—angry, dreadful skull. She writhed away from it. She would not look any more. She felt her neck was swelling inside her collar-band.

Fräulein whispered low.

'Here, in my school, here standing round this table are those who talk of—men.

'Young girls . . . who talk . . . of men.'

While Fräulein waited, trembling, several of the girls began to snuffle and sob.

'Is there, can there be in the world anything that is more base, more vile, more impure? Is there? Is there?'

Miriam wished she knew who was crying. She tried to fix her thoughts on a hole in the table-cover. 'It could be darned. . . . It could be darned.'

'You are brought here together, each and all of you here together in the time of your youth. It is, it should be, for you, the most beautiful occasion. Can you find anything more terrible than that such occasion where all may work and influence each other—for all life—in purity and goodness—that such occasion should be used—impurely? Like a dawn, like a dawn for purity should be the life of a maiden. Calm, and pure and with holy prayer.'

Miriam repeated these words in her mind, trying to dwell on the beauty of Fräulein's middle tones. 'And the day shall come, I shall wish, for all of you, that the sanctity of a home shall be within your hands. What then shall be the shame, what the regret of those who before the coming of that sacred time did think thoughts of men, did speak of them? *Shame, shame,*' whispered Fräulein amidst the sobbing of the girls.

'With the thoughts of those who have this impure nature I can do nothing. For them it is freely to acknowledge this evil in the heart and to pray that the heart may be changed and made clean.

'But a thing I can do and I do. . . . I will have no more of this talking. In my school I will have no more. . . . Do you hear, all? Do you hear?'

She struck the table with both fists and brandished them in mid-air.

'Eh-h,' she sneered. 'I know, *I* know who are the culprits. I have always known.' She gasped. 'It shall cease—these talks—this vile talk of men. Do you understand? It shall cease. I—will—not—have—it. . . . The school shall be clean . . . from pupil to pupil . . . from room to room. . . . Every day . . . every hour. . . . Shameless!' she screamed. 'Shameless. Ah! I know. I know you.' She stood with her arms folded, swaying, and gave a little laugh. 'You think to deceive me. You do not deceive me. I know. I have known and I shall know. This school is mine. Mine! My place! I will have it as I will have it. That is clear and plain, and you all shall help me. I shall say no more. But I shall know what to do.'

Mechanically Miriam went downstairs with the rest of the party. With the full force of her nerves she resisted the echoes of Fräulein's onslaught, refusing to think of anything she had said and blotting out her image every time it rose. The essential was that she would be dismissed, as Mademoiselle had been dismissed. That was the upshot of it all for her. Fräulein was a mad, silly, pious female who would send her away and go on glowering over the Bible. She would have to go, go, *go* in a sort of disgrace.

The girls were talking all round her, excitedly. She despised them for showing that they were disturbed by Fräulein's despotic nonsense. As they reached the basement she remembered the letter crushed in her hand and sat down on the last step to glance through it.

'Dearest Mim. I have a wonderful piece of news for you. I wonder what you will say? It is about Harriett. She has asked me to tell you as she does not like to write about it herself.'

With steady hands Miriam turned the closely-written sheets

reading a phrase here and there . . . 'regularly in the seat behind us at All Saints' for months—saw her with the Pooles at a concert at the Assembly Rooms and made up his mind then—the moment he saw her—joined the tennis-club—they won the doubles handicap—a beautiful Slazenger racquet— only just over sixteen—for years—of course Mother says it 's just a little foolish nonsense—but I am not sure that she really thinks so—Gerald took me into his confidence—made a solemn call—*admirably* suited to each other—rather a long melancholy good-looking face—they look such a contrast—the big Canadian Railway—not exactly a clerk—something rather above that, to do with making drafts of things and so on. Very sweet and charming—my own young days—that I have reached the great age of twenty-three—resident post in the country— two little girls—we think it very good pay—I shall go in September—plenty of time—that you should come home for the long holidays. We are all looking forward to it—the tennis-club—your name as a holiday member—the American tournament in August—Harry was the youngest lady member like you—of course Harry could not let you come without knowing —find somebody travelling through—Fräulein Pfaff—expect to see you looking like a flour-sack with a string tied round its waist—all the dwarf roses in bloom—hardly any strawberries —we shall see you soon—everybody sends.'

Miriam got up and swung the half-read letter above her head like a dumb-bell.

She looked about her like a stranger—everything was as it had been the day she came—the little cramped basement hall —the strange German girls—small and old looking, poking about amongst the baskets. She hardly knew them. She passed half-blindly amongst them with her eyes wide. The little dressing-room seemed full of bright light. She saw every one at once clearly. All the English girls were there. She knew every line of each of them. They were her old friends. They knew her. Looking at none of them, she felt she embraced them all, closely, and that they knew it. They shone. They were beautiful. She wanted to cry aloud. She was English and free. She had nothing to do with this

German school. Baskets at her feet made her pick her way. Solomon was kneeling at one, sorting and handing out. At a little table under the window, Millie stood jotting pencil notes in a pocket-book. Judy was at her side. The others were grouped about the piano. Gertrude sat on the keyboard, her legs dangling.

Miriam plumped down on a full basket.

'Hullo, Hendy, old chap, *you* look all right!'

Miriam looked fearlessly up at the faces that were turned towards her. Again she seemed to see all of them at once. The circle of her vision seemed huge. It was as if the confining rim of her glasses were gone and she saw equally from eyes that seemed to fill her face. She drew all their eyes to her. They were waiting for her to speak. For a moment it seemed as if they stood there lifeless. She had drawn all their meaning and all their happiness into herself. She could do as she wished with them—their poor little lives.

They stood waiting for some word from her. She dropped her eyes and caught the flash of Gertrude's swinging steel buckles.

'Wasn't Fräulein angry?' she said carelessly.

Someone pushed the door to.

'Sly old bird.'

'Fancy imagining we shouldn't see through Mademoiselle leaving.'

'H'm,' said Miriam.

'I knew Mademoiselle *would* sneak if she had half a chance.'

'Yes, ever since she got so thick with Elsa.'

'Oh!—Elsa.'

'You bet Fräulein looks down on the two of them in her heart of hearts.'

'M'm—she's fairly sick, Jemima, with the lot of us this time.'

'Mademoiselle told her some pretty things,' laughed Gertrude. 'Lily thinks we're lost souls—nearly all of us.'

'Onny swaw, my dears, onny swaw.'

'It's all very well. But there's no knowing what Mademoiselle would make her believe. She'd got reams about you, Hendy—nothing bad enough.'

'H'm,' said Miriam, 'I can imagine——'

Her thoughts brought back a day when she had shown Mademoiselle the names in her birthday-book and dwelt on one page and let Mademoiselle understand that it was *the* page —brown eyes—*les yeux bruns foncés*. Why did Mademoiselle and Fräulein think that bad—want to spoil it for her? She had said nothing about the confidences of the German girls to any one. Elsa must have found that out from Clara.

'Oh, well it's all over now. Let's be thankful and think no more about it.'

'All very fine, Jemima. You're going home.'

'Thank goodness.'

'And not coming back. Lucky Pigleinchen.'

'Well, so am I,' said Miriam, 'and I'm not coming back.'

'I say! Aren't you coming to Norderney?' Gertrude flashed dark eyes at her.

'Can't you come to Norderney?' said Judy thickly, at her elbow.

'Well, you see there are all sorts of things happening at home. I *must* go. One of my sisters is engaged and another going away. I must go home for a while. Of course I *might* come back.'

'Think it over, Henderson, and see if you can't decide in our favour.'

'We shall have another Miss Owen.'

Miriam struggled up out of her basket. 'But I thought you all *liked* Miss Owen!'

'Ho! Goodness! Too simple for words.'

'You never told us you had any sisters, Hendy,' said Jimmie, tapping her on the wrist.

'What a pity you're going just as we're getting to know you,' Judy smiled shyly and looked on the floor.

'Well—I'm off with my bundle,' announced Gertrude. 'To be continued in our next. Think it over, Hendy. Don't desert us. Hurry up, my room. It'll be tea-time before we're straight. Come on, Jim.'

Miriam moved, with Judy following at her elbow, across the room to Millie. She looked up with her little plaintive frown.

Miriam could not remember what her plans were. 'Let's
see,' she said, 'you're going to Norderney, aren't you?'
'I'm not going to Norderney,' said Millie almost tearfully.
'I only wish I were. I don't even know I'm coming back
next term.'
'Aren't you looking forward to the holidays?'
'I don't know. I'd rather be staying here if I'm not coming
back after.'
'To stay in Germany? You'd rather do that than anything?'
'*Rather.*'
'Here, with Fräulein Pfaff?'
'Of course, here with Fräulein Pfaff. I'd rather be in
Germany than anything.'
Millie stood staring, with her pout and her slightly raised
eyebrows, at the frosted window.
'Would you stay here in the school for the holidays if
Fräulein were staying?'
'I'd do anything,' said Millie, 'to stay in Germany.'
'You know,' said Miriam gazing at her, 'so would I—any
mortal thing.'
Millie's eyes had filled with tears.
'Then why don't ye stay?' said Judy, with gentle gruffness.

The house was shut up for the night.
Miriam looked up at the clock dizzily as she drank the last
of her coffee. It marked half-past eleven. Fräulein had told
her to be ready at a quarter to twelve. Her hands felt large
and shaky and her feet were cold. The room was stifling—
bare and brown in the gaslight. She left it and crept through
the hall where her trunk stood, and up the creaking stairs.
She turned up the gas. Emma lay asleep with red eyelids and
cheeks. Miriam did not look at Ulrica. Hurriedly and
desolately she packed her bag. She was going home empty-
handed. She had achieved nothing. Fräulein had made not
the slightest effort to keep her. She was just nothing again—
with her Saratoga trunk and her hand-bag. Harriett had

achieved. Harriett. She was just going home with nothing to say for herself.

'The carriage is here, my child. Make haste.'

Miriam pushed things hurriedly into her bag. Fräulein had gone downstairs.

She was ready. She looked numbly round the room. Emma looked very far away. She turned out the gas. The dim light from the landing shone into the room. She stood for a moment in the doorway looking back. The room seemed to be empty. There seemed to be nothing in it but the black screen standing round the bed that was no longer hers.

'Good-bye,' she murmured and hurried downstairs.

In the hall Fräulein began to talk at once, talking until they were seated side by side in the dark cab.

Then Miriam gazed freely at the pale profile shining at her side. Poor Fräulein Pfaff, getting old.

Fräulein began to ask about Miriam's plans for the future. Miriam answered as to an equal, elaborating a little account of circumstances at home, and the doings of her sisters. As she spoke she felt that Fräulein envied her her youth and her family at home in England—and she raised her voice a little and laughed easily and moved, crossing her knees in the cab.

She used sentimental German words about Harriett—a description of her that might have applied to Emma—little emphatic tender epithets came to her from the conversations of the girls. Fräulein praised her German warmly and asked question after question about the house and garden at Barnes and presently of her mother.

'I can't talk about her,' said Miriam shortly.

'That is English,' murmured Fräulein.

'She's such a little thing,' said Miriam, 'smaller than any of us.' Presently Fräulein laid her gloved hand on Miriam's gloved one. 'You and I have, I think, much in common.'

Miriam froze—and looked at the gas-lamps slowly swinging by along the boulevard. 'Much will have happened in England whilst you have been here with us,' said Fräulein eagerly.

They reached a street—shuttered darkness where the shops were, and here and there the yellow flare of a café. She

strained her eyes to see the faces and forms of men and women
—breathing more quickly as she watched the characteristic
German gait.

There was the station.

Her trunk was weighed and registered. There was something to pay. She handed her purse to Fräulein and stood
gazing at the uniformed man—ruddy and clear-eyed—clear
hard blue eyes and hard clean clear yellow moustaches—
decisive untroubled movements. Passengers were walking
briskly about and laughing and shouting remarks to each other.
The train stood waiting for her. The ringing of an enormous
bell brought her hands to her ears. Fräulein gently propelled
her up the three steps into a compartment marked Damen-
Coupé. It smelt of biscuits and wine.

A man with a booming voice came to examine her ticket.
He stood bending under the central light, uttering sturdy
German words. Miriam drank them in without understanding. He left the carriage very empty. The great bell
was ringing again. Fräulein, standing on the top step, pressed
both her hands and murmured words of farewell.

'Leb' wohl, mein Kind, Gott segne dich.'

'Good-bye, Fräulein,' she said stiffly, shaking hands.

The door was shut with a slam—the light seemed to go down.
Miriam glanced at it—half the dull green muslin shade had
slipped over the gas-globe. The carriage seemed dark. The
platform outside was very bright. Fräulein had disappeared.
The train was high above the platform. Politely smiling,
Miriam scrambled to the window. The platform was moving,
the large bright station moving away. Fräulein's wide smile
was creasing and caverning under her hat from which the veil
was thrown back.

Standing at the window Miriam smiled sharply. Fräulein's
form flowed slowly away with the platform.

Groups passed by smiling and waving.

Miriam sat down.

She leaped up, to lean from the window.

The platform had disappeared.

BACKWATER

CHAPTER I

A SWARTHY turbaned face shone at Miriam from a tapestry screen standing between her and the ferns rising from a basket framework in the bow of the window. Consulting it at intervals as the afternoon wore on, she found that it made very light of the quiet propositions that were being elaborated within hearing of her inattentive ears. Looking beyond it she could catch glimpses between the crowded fernery, when a tram was not jingling by, of a close-set palisade just across the roadway and, beyond the palisade, of a green level ending at a row of Spanish poplars. The trams seemed very near and noisy. When they passed by the window, the speakers had to raise their voices. Otherwise the little drawing-room was very quiet, with a strange old-fashioned quietness. It was full of old things, like the Gobelin screen, and old thoughts like the thoughts of the ladies who were sitting and talking there. She and her mother had seemed quite modern, fussy, worldly people when they had first come into the room. From the moment the three ladies had come in and begun talking to her mother, the things in the room, and the view of the distant row of poplars had grown more and more peaceful, and now at the end of an hour she felt that she, and to some extent Mrs Henderson too, belonged to the old-world room with its quiet green outlook shut in by the poplars. Only the trams were disturbing. They came busily by, with their strange jingle-jingle, plock-plock, and made her inattentive. Why were there so many people coming by in trams? Where were they going? Why were all the trams painted that hard, dingy blue?

The sisters talked quietly, outlining their needs in smooth gentle voices, in small broken phrases, frequently interrupting and correcting each other. Miriam heard dreamily that they wanted help with the lower school, the children from six to eight years of age, in the mornings and afternoons, and in the evenings a general superintendence of the four boarders. They kept on saying that the work was very easy and simple; there were no naughty girls—hardly a single naughty girl—in the school; there should be no difficult superintendence, no exercise of authority would be required.

By the time they had reached the statement of these modifications Miriam felt that she knew them quite well. The shortest, who did most of the talking and who had twinkling eyes and crooked pince-nez and soft reddish cheeks and a little red-tipped nose, and whose small coil of sheeny grey hair was pinned askew on the top of her head—stray loops standing out at curious angles—was Miss Jenny, the middle one. The very tall one sitting opposite her, with a delicate wrinkled creamy face and coal-black eyes and a peak of ringletted smooth coal-black hair, was the eldest, Miss Deborah. The other sister, much younger, with neat smooth green-grey hair and a long, sad, greyish face and faded eyes, was Miss Haddie. They were all three dressed in thin fine black material and had tiny hands and little softly-moving feet. What did they think of the trams?

'Do you think you could manage it, chickie?' said Mrs Henderson suddenly.

'I think I could.'

'No doubt, my dear, oh, no doubt,' said Miss Jenny with a little sound of laughter as she tapped her knee with the pince-nez she had plucked from their rakish perch on the reddened bridge of her nose.

'I don't think I could teach Scripture.'

An outbreak of incoherent little sounds and statements from all three taught her that Miss Deborah took the Bible classes of the whole school.

'How old is Miriam?'

'Just eighteen. She has put up her hair to-day.'

'Oh, poor child, she need not have done that.'

'She is a *born* teacher. She used to hold little classes amongst her schoolfellows when she was only eight years old.'

Miriam turned sharply to her mother. She was sitting with her tired look—bright eyes, and moist flushed face. How had she heard about the little classes? Had there been little classes? She could not remember them.

'She speaks French like a Parisienne.'

That was that silly remark made by the woman in the train coming home from Hanover.

'Eh—we thought—it was in Germany she was——'

'Yes, but I learned more French.'

The sisters smiled provisionally.

'She shared a room with the Mademoiselle.'

'Oh—er—hee—hay—perhaps she might speak French with the gels.'

'Oh no, I couldn't *speak*.'

There was a tender little laugh.

'I don't know French conversation.'

'Well, well.'

The sisters brought the discussion to an end by offering twenty pounds a year in return for Miriam's services, and naming the date of the beginning of the autumn term.

On the way to the front door they all looked into the principal schoolroom. Miriam saw a long wide dining-room table covered with brown American cloth. Shelves neatly crowded with books lined one wall from floor to ceiling. Opposite them at the far end of the room was a heavy grey marble mantelpiece, on which stood a heavy green marble clock frame. At its centre a gold-faced clock ticked softly. Opposite the windows were two shallow alcoves. In one stood a shrouded blackboard on an easel. The other held a piano with a high slender back. The prancing outward sweep of its lid gave Miriam the impression of an afternoon dress.

Miss Deborah drew up one of the Venetian blinds. They all crowded to the window and looked out on a small garden backed by trees and lying in deep shadow. Beyond were more gardens and the brownish backs of small old brick houses. Low walls separated the school garden from the gardens on either side.

'On our right we have a school for the deaf and dumb,' said Miss Perne; 'on the other side is a family of Polish Jews.'

'Mother, why *did* you pile it on?'

They would soon be down at the corner of Banbury Park where the tram lines ended and the Favourite omnibuses were standing in the muddy road under the shadow of the railway bridge. Through the jingling of the trams, the dop-dop of the hoofs of the tram-horses and the noise of a screaming train thundering over the bridge, Miriam made her voice heard, gazing through the spotted veil at her mother's quivering features.

'They might have made me do all sorts of things I can't do.'

Mrs Henderson's voice, breathless with walking, made a little sound of protest, a narrowed sound that told Miriam her amusement was half annoyance. The dark, noisy bridge, the clatter and rattle and the mud through which she must plunge to an omnibus exasperated her to the limit of her endurance.

'I'd got the post,' she said angrily; 'you could see it was all settled and then you went saying those things.'

Glancing at the thin shrouded features she saw the faint lift of her mother's eyebrows and the firmly speechless mouth.

'Piccadilly—jump on, chickie.'

'Let's go outside now it's fine,' said Miriam crossly.

Reaching the top of the omnibus she hurried to the front seat on the left-hand side.

'That's a very windy spot.'

'No it isn't, it's quite hot. The sun's come out now. It's rained for weeks. It won't rain any more. It'll be hot. You won't feel the wind. Will you have the corner, mother?'

'No, chick, you sit there.'

Miriam screwed herself into the corner seat, crossing her knees and grazing the tips of her shoes.

'This is the only place on the top of a bus.'

Mrs Henderson sat down at her side.

'I always make Harriett come up here when we go up to the West End.'

'Of course it's the only place,' she insisted in response to her mother's amused laugh. 'No one smoking or talking in front; you can see out in front and you can see the shops if there are any, and you're not falling off all the time. The bus goes on the left side of the road and tilts to the left.'

The seats were filling up and the driver appeared clambering into his place.

'Didn't you ever think of that? Didn't you ever think of the bus tilting that way?' persisted Miriam to her mother's inattentive face. 'Fancy never thinking of it. It's beastly on the other side.'

The omnibus jerked forward.

'You ought to be a man, Mimmy.'

'I liked that little short one,' said Miriam contentedly as they came from under the roar of the bridge. 'They were awfully nice, weren't they? They seemed to have made up their mind to take me before we went. . . . So I think they like us. I wonder why they like us. Didn't you think they liked us? Don't you think they are awfully nice?'

'I do. They are very charming ladies.'

'Yes, but wasn't it awfully rum their liking us in that funny way?'

'I'm sure I don't see why they should 'not.'

'Oh, mother, you know what I mean. I like them. I'm perfectly sure I shall like them. D'you remember the little one saying all girls ought to marry? Why did she say that?'

'They are dear funny little O.M.'s,' said Mrs Henderson merrily. She was sitting with her knees crossed, the stuff of her brown canvas dress was dragged across them into an ugly fold by the weight of the velvet panel at the side of the skirt. She looked very small and resourceless. And there were the Pernes with their house and their school. They were old maids. Of course. What then?

'I never dreamed of getting such a big salary.'

'Oh, my chickie, I'm afraid it isn't much.'

'It is, mother, it's lovely.'

'Oh—eh—well.'

Miriam turned fiercely to the roadway on her left.

She had missed the first swing forward of the vehicle and the first movements of the compact street.

They were going ahead now at a steady even trot. Her face was bathed in the flow of the breeze.

Little rivulets played about her temples, feeling their way through her hair. She drew off her gloves without turning from the flowing roadway. As they went on and on down the long road, Miriam forgot her companion in the tranquil sense of being carried securely forward through the air away from people and problems. Ahead of her, at the end of the long drive, lay three sunlit weeks, bright now in the certainty of the shadow that lay beyond them . . . 'the junior school' . . . 'four boarders.'

They lumbered at last round a corner and out into a wide thoroughfare, drawing up outside a newly-built public-house. Above it rose row upon row of upper windows sunk in masses of ornamental terra-cotta-coloured plaster. Branch roads, laid with tram-lines led off in every direction. Miriam's eyes followed a dull blue tram with a grubby white-painted seatless roof jingling busily off up a roadway where short trees stood all the way along in the small dim gardens of little grey houses. On the near corner of the road stood a wide white building bulging into heavy domes against the sky. Across its side, large gilt letters standing far apart spelled out 'Banbury Empire.'

'It must be a theatre,' she told herself in astonishment. 'That's what they call a suburban theatre. People think it is really a theatre.'

The little shock sent her mind feeling out along the road they had just left. She considered its unbroken length, its shops, its treelessness. The wide thoroughfare, up which they now began to rumble, repeated it on a larger scale. The pavements were wide causeways reached from the roadway by stone steps, three deep. The people passing along them were unlike any she knew. There were no ladies, no gentlemen, no girls or young men such as she knew. They were all alike. They were . . . She could find no word for the strange impression they made. It coloured the whole of the district through which they had come. It was part of the new world to which she was pledged to go on September 18th. It was her world already; and she had no words for it. She would not be able to convey it to others. She felt sure her mother had not noticed it. She must deal with it alone. To try to speak about it, even with Eve, would sap her courage. It was her secret. A strange secret for all her life as Hanover had been. But Hanover was beautiful, with distant country through the *saal* windows, its colours misty in the sunlight; the beautiful, happy town and the woodland villages so near. This new secret was shabby, ugly and shabby. The half-perceived something persisted unchanged when the causeways and shops disappeared and long rows of houses streamed by, their close ranks broken only by an occasional cross-road. They were large, high, flat-fronted houses with flights of grey stone steps leading to their porchless doors. They had tiny railed-in front gardens crowded with shrubs. Here and there long narrow strips of garden pushed a row of houses back from the roadway. In these longer plots stood signboards and show-cases. 'Photographic Studio,' 'Commercial College,' 'Eye Treatment,' 'Academy of Dancing.' . . . She read the announcements with growing disquietude.

Rows of shops reappeared and densely crowded pavements, and then more high straight houses.

She roused herself at last from her puzzled contemplation and turned to glance at her mother. Mrs Henderson was looking out ahead. The exhausted face was ready, Miriam saw, with its faintly questioning eyebrows and tightly-held lips, for emotional response. She turned away uneasily to the spellbound streets.

'Useless to try to talk about anything. . . . Mother would be somehow violent. She would be overpowering. The strange new impressions would be dissolved.'

But she must do something, show some sign of companionship. She began humming softly. The air was so full of
clamour that she could not hear her voice. The houses and
shops had disappeared. Drab brick walls were passing slowly
by on either side. A goods' yard. She deepened her humming, accentuating her phrases so that the sound might reach
her companion through the reverberations of the clangour of
shunting trains.

The high brick walls were drawing away. The end of the
long roadway was in sight. Its widening mouth offered no
sign of escape from the disquieting strangeness. The open
stretch of thoroughfare into which they emerged was fed by
innumerable lanes of traffic. From the islands dotted over its
surface towered huge lamp standards branching out thin arms.
As they rattled noisily over the stone setts they jolted across
several lines of tramway and wove their way through currents
of traffic crossing each other in all directions.

'I wonder where we're going—I wonder if this is a Piccadilly
bus,' Miriam thought of saying. Impossible to shout through
the din.

The driver gathered up his horses and they clattered
deafeningly over the last open stretch and turned into a smooth
wide prospect.

'Oh bliss, wood-paving,' murmured Miriam.

A mass of smoke-greyed, sharply steepled stone building
appeared on the right. Her eyes rested on its soft shadows.

On the left a tall grey church was coming towards them,
spindling up into the sky. It sailed by, showing Miriam a
circle of little stone pillars built into its tower. Plumy trees
streamed by, standing large and separate on moss-green grass
railed from the roadway. Bright white-faced houses with
pillared porches shone through from behind them and blazed
white above them against the blue sky. Wide side-streets
opened showing high balconied houses. The side-streets
were feathered with trees and ended mistily.

Away ahead were edges of clean bright masonry in profile, soft tufted heads of trees, bright green in the clear light. At the end of the vista the air was like pure saffron-tinted mother-of-pearl.

Miriam sat back and drew a deep breath.

'Well, chickie?'

'What's the matter?'

'Why, you've been very funny!'

'How?'

'You've been so dummel.'

'No, I haven't.'

'Oh—eh.'

'How d'you mean I've been funny?'

'Not speaking to poor old mum-jam.'

'Well, you haven't spoken to me.'

'No.'

'I shan't take any of my summer things there,' said Miriam.

Mrs Henderson's face twitched.

'Shall I?'

'I'm afraid you haven't very much in the way of thick clothing.'

'I've only got my plaid dress for every day and my mixy grey for best and my dark blue summer skirt. My velveteen skirt and my nainsook blouse are too old.'

'You can wear the dark blue muslin blouse with the blue skirt for a long time yet with something warm underneath.'

'My grey's very grubby.'

'You look very well in it indeed.'

'I don't mean that. I mean it's all gone sort of dull and grubby over the surface when you look down it.'

'Oh, that's your imagination.'

'It isn't my imagination and I can see how Harriett's looks.'

'You both look very nice.'

'That's not the point.'

'Don't make a mountain out of a molehill, my chick.'

'I'm not making anything. The simple fact is that the grey dresses are piggy.'

Mrs Henderson flushed deeply, twining and untwining her silk-gloved fingers.

'She thinks that's "gross exaggeration." That's what she wants to say,' pondered Miriam wearily.

They turned into Langham Place.

She glanced to see whether her mother realized where they were.

'Look, we're in the West End, mother! Oh, I'm not going to think about Banbury Park till it begins!'

They drew up near the Maison Nouvelle.

'*Stanlake* is,' said a refined emphatic voice from the pavement. Miriam did not look for the speaker. The quality of the voice brought her a moment's realization of the meaning of her afternoon's adventure. She was going to be shut up away from the grown-up things, the sunlit world, and the people who were enjoying it. She would be shut up and surrounded in Wordsworth House, a proper schooly school, amongst all those strange roadways. It would be cold English pianos and dreadful English children—and trams going up and down that grey road outside.

As they went on down Regent Street she fastened, for refuge from her thoughts, upon a window where softly falling dresses of dull olive stood about against a draped background of pale dead yellow. She held it in her mind as shop after shop streamed by.

'These shops are extremely *récherché*.'

'It's old Regent Street, mother,' said Miriam argumentatively. 'Glorious old Regent Street. Ruby wine.'

'Ah, Regent Street.'

'We always walk up one side and down the other. Up the dolls' hospital side and down Liberty's. Glory, glory, ruby wine.'

'You *are* enthusiastiç.'

'But it's so glorious. Don't you think so?'

'Sit back a little, chickie. One can't see the windows. You're such a solid young woman.'

'You 'll see our A B C soon. You know. The one we go
to after the Saturday pops. You 've been to it. You came to
it the day we came to Madame Schumann's farewell. It 's just
round here in Piccadilly. Here it is. Glorious. I must make
the others come up once more before I die. I always have a
scone. I don't like the aryated bread. We go along the
Burlington Arcade too. I don't believe you 've ever been
along there. It 's simply perfect. Glove shops and fans and
a smell of the most exquisite scent everywhere.'

'Dear me. It must be very captivating.'

'Now we shall pass the parks. Oh, isn't the sun A1 copper
bottom!'

Mrs Henderson laughed wistfully.

'What delicious shade under those fine old trees. I almost
wish I had brought my *en-tout-cas*.'

'Oh no, you don't really want it. There will be more breeze
presently. The bus always begins to go quicker along here. It 's
the Green Park, that one. Those are clubs that side, the West
End clubs. It 's fascinating all the way along here to Hyde Park
Corner. You just see Park Lane going up at the side. Park
Lane. It goes wiggling away, straight into heaven. We 've
never been up there. I always read the name at the corner.'

'You ridiculous chick—ah, there is the Royal Academy of
Arts.'

'Oh yes, I wonder if there are any Leightons this year.'

'Or Leader. Charles Leader. I think there is nothing
more charming than those landscape scenes by Leader.'

'I 've got three bally weeks. I can see Hyde Park. We 've
got ages yet. It goes on being fascinating right down through
Kensington and right on up to the other side of Putney Bridge.'

'Dear me. Isn't it fascinating after that?'

'Oh, not all that awful walk along the Upper Richmond
Road—not until our avenue begins——'

Miriam fumbled with the fastening of the low wide gate as
her mother passed on up the drive. She waited until the

footsteps were muffled by the fullness of the may-trees linking their middle branches over the bend in the drive. Then she looked steadily down the sunflecked asphalted avenue along which they had just come. The level sunlight streamed along the empty roadway and the shadows of the lime-trees lay across the path and up the oak palings. Her eyes travelled up and down the boles of the trees, stopping at each little stunted tuft of greenery. She could no longer hear her mother's footsteps. There was a scented coolness in the shady watered garden. Leaning gently with her breast against the upper bars of the gate she broke away from the sense of her newly-made engagement.

She scanned the whole length of the shrouded avenue from end to end and at last looked freely up amongst the interwoven lime-trees. Long she watched, her eyes roaming from the closely-growing leaves where the green was densest to the edges of the trees where the light shone through. 'Gold and green,' she whispered, 'green and gold, held up by firm brown stems bathed in gold.'

When she reached the open garden beyond the bend she ran once round the large centre bed where berberus and laurestinus bushes stood in a clump ringed by violas and blue lobelias and heavily scented masses of cherry-ripe. Taking the shallow steps in two silent strides she reached the shelter of the deep porch. The outer door and the door of the vestibule stood open. Gently closing the vestibule she ran across the paved hall and opened the door on the right.

Harriett, in a long fawn canvas dress with a deep silk sash, was standing in the middle of the drawing-room floor with a large pot of scented geraniums in her arms.

'Hullo!' said Miriam.
Putting down her pot Harriett fixed brown eyes upon her and began jumping lightly up and down where she stood. The small tips of her fawn glacé kid shoes shone together between the hem of her dress and the pale green of the carpet.
'What are you doing?' said Miriam quietly shutting the door behind her and flushing with pleasure.

Harriett hopped more energetically. The blaze from the western window caught the paste stone in the tortoise-shell comb crowning her little high twist of hair and the prisms of the lustres standing behind her on the white marble mantelpiece.

'What you doing, booby?'

'Old conservatory,' panted Harriett.

Miriam looked vaguely down the length of the long room to where the conservatory doors stood wide open. As she gazed at the wet tiling Harriett ceased hopping and kicked her delicately. 'Well, gooby?'

Miriam grinned.

'You 've got it. I knew you would. The Misses Perne have engaged Miss Miriam Henderson as resident teacher for the junior school.'

'Oh yes, I 've got it,' smiled Miriam. 'But don't let 's talk about that. It 's just an old school, a house. I don't know a bit what it 'll be like. I 've got three bally blooming weeks. Don't let 's talk about it.'

'Awri.'

'What about Saturday?'

'It 's all right. Ted was at the club.'

'Was he!'

'Yes, old scarlet face, he were.'

'I 'm *not*.'

'He came in just before closing time and straight up to me and sat where you were. He looked sick when I told him, and so fagged.'

'It was awfully hot in town,' murmured Miriam tenderly.

She went to the piano and struck a note very softly.

'He played a single with the duffer and lost it.'

'Oh, well, of course, he was so tired.'

'Yes, but it wasn't that. It was because you weren't there. He 's simply no good when you 're not there, now. He 's perfectly different.'

Miriam struck her note again.

'Listen, that 's E flat.'

'Go on.'

'That's a chord in E flat. Isn't it lovely? It sounds perfectly different in C. Listen. Isn't it funny?'

'Well, don't you want to know why it's all right about Saturday?'

'Yes, screamingly.'

'Well, that's the perfectly flabbergasting thing. Ted simply came to say they've got a man coming to stay with them and can he bring him.'

'My dear! What a heavenly relief. That makes twelve men and fourteen girls. That'll do.'

'Nan Babington's hurt her ankle, but she swears she's coming.' Harriett sniffed and sank down on the white rug drawing her knees up to her chin.

'You shouldn't say "swears."'

'Well, you bet. She simply loves our dances.'

'Did she say she did?'

'She sat on the pavilion seat with Bevan Seymour all the afternoon and I was with them when Ted was playing with the duffer. She told Bevan that she didn't know anywhere else where the kids arranged the dances, and everything was so jolly. It's *screaming*, my dear, she said.'

'It's horrid the way she calls him "my dear." Your ring is simply dazzling like that, Harry. D' you see? It's the sun.'

'Of course it'll mean she'll sit out in a deck chair in the garden with Bevan all the time.'

'How disgusting.'

'It's her turn for the pavilion tea on Saturday. She's coming in her white muslin and then coming straight on here with two sticks and wants us to keep her some flowers. Let's go and have tea. It'll be nearly dinner-time.'

'Has Mary made a cake?'

'I dunno. Tea was to be in the breakfast-room when you came back.'

'Why not in the conservatory?'

'Because, you silly old crow, I'm beranging it for Saturday.'

'Shall we have the piano in there?'

'Well, don't you think so?'

'Twenty-six of us. Perhaps it'll be more blissful.'

'If we have the breakfast-room piano in the hall it 'll bung up the hall.'

'Yes, but the Erard bass is so perfect for waltzes.'

'And the be-rilliant Collard treble is so all right in the vatoire.'

'I thought it was Eve and I talked about the Collard treble.'

'Well, I was there.'

'Anyhow we 'll have the grand in the conservatory. Oh, Bacchus! Ta-ra-ra-boom-deay.'

'*Tea*,' said a rounded voice near the keyhole.

'Eve!' shouted Miriam.

The door opened slightly. 'I know,' said the voice.

'Come *in*, Eve,' commanded Miriam, trying to swing the door wide.

'I know,' said the voice quivering with the effort of holding the door. 'I know all about the new Misses Perne and the new man—Max Sonnenheim—Max.'

'This way out,' called Harriett from the conservatory.

'Eve,' pleaded Miriam, tugging at the door, 'let me get at you. Don't be an idiot.'

A gurgle of amusement made her loosen her hold.

'I 'm not trying, you beast. Take your iron wrists away.'

A small white hand waggled fingers through the aperture.

Miriam seized and covered it. 'Come in for a minute,' she begged. 'I want to see you. What have you got on?'

'*Tea*.'

The hand twisted itself free and Eve fled through the hall.

Miriam flung after her with a yell and caught at her slender body. 'I 've a great mind to drag down your old hair.'

'Tea,' smiled Eve serenely.

'All *right*, I 'm coming, damn you, aren't I?'

'Oh, Mimmy!'

'Well, damn *me*, then. Somebody in the house must swear. I say, Eve?'

'What?'

'Nothing, only I *say*.'

'Um.'

CHAPTER II

Miriam extended herself on the drawing-room sofa which had been drawn up at the end of the room under the open window.

The quintets of candles on the girandoles hanging on either side of the high overmantel gave out an unflickering radiance, and in the centre of the large room the chandelier, pulled low, held out in all directions bulbs of softly tinted light.

In an intensity of rose-shaded brilliance pouring from a tall standard lamp across the hearthrug stood a guest with a fiddle under her arm fluttering pages on a music stand. The family sat grouped towards her in a circle.

On her low sofa, outside the more brilliant light, Miriam made a retreating loop in the circle of seated forms, all visible as she lay with her eyes on the ceiling. But no eyes could meet and pilfer her own. The darkness brimmed in from the window on her right. She could touch the rose-leaves on the sill and listen to the dewy stillness of the garden.

'What shall I play?' said the guest.

'What have you there?'

'Gluck . . . *Klassische Stücke* . . . *Cavatina.*'

'Ah, Gluck,' said Mr Henderson, smoothing his long knees with outspread fingers.

'Have you got the Beethoven thing?' asked Sarah.

'Not here, Sally.'

'I saw it—on the piano—with chords,' said Sarah excitedly.

'Chords,' encouraged Miriam.

'Yes, I think so,' muttered Sarah taking up her crochet. 'I dare say I'm wrong,' she giggled, throwing out a foot and hastily withdrawing it.

'I can find it, dear,' chanted the guest.

Miriam raised a flourishing hand. The crimsoned oval of

Eve's face appeared inverted above her own. She poked a
finger into one of the dark eyes and, looking at the screwed-up
lid, whispered voicelessly, 'Make her play the *Romance* first
and *then* the *Cavatina* without talking in between. . . .'

Eve's large soft mouth pursed a little, and Miriam watched
steadily until dimples appeared. 'Go on, Eve,' she said, re-
moving her hand.

'Shall I play the Beethoven first?' inquired the guest.

'Mm—and then the *Cavatina*,' murmured Miriam, as if
half asleep, turning wholly towards the garden, as Eve went to
collect the piano scores.

She seemed to grow larger and stronger and easier as the
thoughtful chords came musing out into the night and hovered
amongst the dark trees. She found herself drawing easy
breaths and relaxing completely against the support of the hard
friendly sofa. How quietly every one was listening. . . .

After a while, everything was dissolved, past and future and
present and she was nothing but an ear, intent on the meditative
harmony which stole out into the garden.

When the last gently strung notes had ceased she turned
from her window and found Harriett's near eye fixed upon her,
the eyebrow travelling slowly up the forehead.

'Wow,' mouthed Miriam.

Harriett screwed her mouth to one side and strained her
eyebrow higher.

The piano introduction to the *Cavatina* drowned the comments on the guest's playing and the family relaxed once more
into listening.

'Pink anemones, eh,' suggested Miriam softly.

Harriett drew in her chin and nodded approvingly.

'Pink anemones,' sighed Miriam, and turned to watch
Margaret Wedderburn standing in her full-skirted white dress
on the hearthrug in a radiance of red and golden light. Her

heavily waving fair hair fell back towards its tightly braided basket of plaits from a face as serene as death. From between furry eyelashes her eyes looked steadfastly out, robbed of their everyday sentimental expression.

As she gazed at the broad white forehead, the fine gold down covering the cheeks and upper lip, and traced the outline of the heavy chin and firm, large mouth and the steady arm that swept out in rich 'cello-like notes the devout theme of the lyric, Miriam drifted to an extremity of happiness.

. . . To-morrow the room would be lit and decked and clear. Amongst the crowd of guests, he would come across the room, walking in his way. . . . She smiled to herself. He would come 'sloping in' in his way, like a shadow, not looking at any one. His strange friend would be with him. There would be introductions and greetings. Then he would dance with her silently and not looking at her, as if they were strangers, and then be dancing with someone else . . . with smiling, mocking, tender brown eyes and talking and answering and all the time looking about the room. And then again with her, cool and silent and not looking. And presently she would tell him about going away to Banbury Park.

Perhaps he would look wretched and miserable again, as he had done when they were alone by the piano the Sunday before she went to Germany. . . . 'Play *Abide with me*, Miriam; play *Abide with me*.' . . .

To-morrow there would be another moment like that. He would say her name suddenly, as he had done last week in the Babingtons' dance, very low, half-turning towards her. She would be ready this time and say his name and move instead of being turned to stone. Confidently the music assured her of that moment.

She lay looking quietly into his imagined face till the room had gone. Then the face grew dim and far off and at last receded altogether into darkness. That darkness was dreadful.

It was his own life. She would never know it. However well
they got to know each other they would always be strangers.
Probably he never thought about her when he was alone. Only
of Shakespeare and politics. What would he think if he knew
she thought of him? But he thought of her when he saw her.
That was utterly certain; the one thing certain in the world.
. . . That day, coming along Putney Hill with mother, tired
and dull and trying to keep her temper, passing his house,
seeing him standing at his window, alone and pale and serious.
The sudden lightening of his face surprised her again, violently,
as she recalled it. It had lit up the whole world from end to
end. He did not know that he had looked like that. She had
turned swiftly from the sudden knowledge coming like a blow
on her heart, that one day he would kiss her. Not for years
and years. But one day he would bend his head. She
wrenched herself from the thought, but it was too late. She
thanked heaven she had looked; she wished she had not; the
kiss had come; she would forget it; it had not touched her, it
was like the breath of the summer. Everything had wavered;
her feet had not felt the pavement. She remembered walking
on, exulting with hanging head, cringing close to the ivy
which hung from the top of the garden wall, sorry and pitiful
towards her mother, and every one who would never stand
first with Ted.
. . . There were girls who let themselves be kissed for fun.
. . . Playing 'Kiss in the Ring,' being kissed by someone they
did not mean to always be with, all their life . . . how sad and
dreadful. Why did it not break their hearts?

Meg Wedderburn was smiling on her hearthrug, being
thanked and praised. Her brown violin hung amongst the
folds of her skirt.
'People *do* like us,' mused Miriam, listening to the peculiar
sympathy of the family voice.
Meg was there, away from her own home, happy with them,
the front door shut, their garden and house all round her and

her strange luggage upstairs in one of the spare rooms.   Nice
Meg. . . .

After breakfast the next morning Miriam sat in a low carpet
chair at a window in the long bedroom she shared with Harriett.
It was a morning of blazing sunlight and bright blue.   She
had just come up through the cool house from a rose-gathering
tour of the garden with Harriett.   A little bunch of pink
anemones she had picked for herself were set in a tumbler on
the wash-hand-stand.

She had left the door open to hear coming faintly up from
the far-away drawing-room the tap-tap of hammering that told
her Sarah and Eve were stretching the drugget.

On her knee lay her father's cigarette-making machine and a
parcel of papers and tobacco.   An empty cigarette tin stood
upon the window-sill.

She began packing tobacco into the groove of the machine,
distributing and pressing it lightly with the tips of her fingers,
watching, as she worked, the heavy pink cups of the anemones
and the shining of their green stalks through the water.   They
were, she reflected, a little too much out.   In the sun they
would have come out still more.   They would close up at
night unless the rooms grew very hot.   Slipping the paper
evenly into the slot she shut the machine and turned the
roller.   As the sound of the loosely working cogs came up
to her she revolted from her self-imposed task.   She was
too happy to make cigarettes.   It would use up her happiness
too stupidly.

She was surprised by a sudden suggestion that she should
smoke the single cigarette herself.   Why not?   Why had she
never yet smoked one?   She glanced at the slowly swinging
door.   No one would come.   She was alone on the top floor.
Every one was downstairs and busy.   The finished cigarette
lay on her knee.   Taking it between her fingers, she pressed a
little hanging thread of tobacco into place.   The cigarette felt
pleasantly plump and firm.   It was well made.   As she rose

to get matches, the mowing machine sounded suddenly from the front lawn. She started and looked out of the window, concealing the cigarette in her hand. It was the gardener with bent shoulders pushing with all his might. With some difficulty she unhitched the phosphorescent match-box from its place under the gas-bracket and got back into her low chair, invisible from the lawn.

The cool air flowed in garden-scented. She held the cigarette between two fingers. The match hissed and flared as she held it carefully below the sill, and the flame flowed towards her while she set the paper alight. Raising the cigarette to her lips she blew gently outwards, down through the tobacco. The flame twisted and went out, leaving the paper charred. She struck another match angrily, urging herself to draw, and drew little panting breaths with the cigarette well in the flame. It smoked. Blowing out the match she looked at the end of the cigarette. It was glowing all over and a delicate little spiral of smoke rose into her face. Quickly she applied her lips again and drew little breaths, opening her mouth wide between each breath and holding the cigarette sideways away from her. The end glowed afresh with each breath. The paper charred evenly away and little flecks of ash fell about her.

A third of the whole length was consumed. Her nostrils breathed in smoke and, as she tasted the burnt flavour, the sweetness of the unpolluted air all around her was a new thing. The acrid tang in her nostrils intoxicated her. She drew more boldly. There was smoke in her mouth. She opened it quickly, sharply exhaling a yellow cloud oddly different from the grey spirals wreathing their way from the end of the cigarette. She went on drawing in mouthful after mouthful of smoke, expelling each quickly with widely-opened lips, turning to look at the well-known room through the yellow haze and again at the sky, which drew nearer as she puffed at it. The sight of the tree-tops scrolled with her little clouds brought her a sense of power. She had chosen to smoke and she was smoking, and the morning world gleamed back at her. . . .

The morning gleamed. She would choose her fate. It should be amongst green trees and sunshine. That daunted lump who had accepted the post at Banbury Park had nothing to do with her. Morning gladness flooded her, and her gladness of the thought of the evening to come quickened as it had done last night into certainty.

She burned the last inch of the cigarette in the grate, wrapped with combings from the toilet-tidy in a screw of paper. When all was consumed she carefully replaced the summer bundle of ornamental mohair behind the bars.

Useless to tell any one. No one would believe she had not felt ill. She found it difficult to understand why any one should feel sick from smoking. Dizzy perhaps . . . a little drunk. Pater's tobacco was very strong, some people could not smoke it. . . . She had smoked a whole cigarette of strong tobacco and liked it. Raising her arms above her head she worked them upwards, stretching every muscle of her body. No, she was anything but ill.

Leaving the window wide, she went on to the landing. The smell of tobacco was everywhere. She flung into each room in turn, throwing up windows and leaving doors propped ajar.

Harriett coming up the garden with a basket of cut flowers saw her at the cook's bedroom window.

'What on earth you doing thayer!' she shrieked, putting down her basket.

Hanging from the window Miriam made a trumpet of her hands.

'Something blew in!'

All preparations for the evening were made and the younger members of the household were having a late tea in the break-fast-room. 'We've done the alcoves,' said Sarah explosively, 'in case it rains.'

Nan Babington sat up in her long chair to bring her face round to the deep bay where Sarah stood.

'My *dear*! Seraphina! And she's doing the pink bows! *Will* some saint take my cup? Ta. . . . My dear, how *perfectly* screaming.'

Miriam raised her head from the petal-scattered table, where she lay prone side by side with Harriett, to watch Nan sitting up in her firm white dress beaming at Sarah through her slanting eye.

'What flowers you going to wear, Nan?'

Nan patted her sleek slightly Japanese-looking hair. '*Ah* . . . splashes of scarlet, my dear. Splashes of scarlet. One in my hair and one here.' She patted the broad level of her enviable breast towards the left shoulder.

'Almost *on* the shoulder, you know—arranged flat, *can't* be squashed and showing as you dance.'

'Geraniums! Oom. You've got awfully good taste. What a frightfully good effect. Bright red and bright white. Clean. Go on, Nan.'

'*Killing*,' pursued Nan. 'Tom said at breakfast with his mouth absolutely *full* of sweetbread, "it'll rain"'—growled, you know, with his mouth *crammed* full. "Never mind, Tommy," said Ella with the *utmost* promptitude, "they're sure to have alcoves." "Oomph," growled Tommy, pretending not to care. *Naughty* Tommy, naughty, *naughty* Tommy!'

'Any cake left?' sighed Miriam, sinking back amongst her petals and hoping that Nan's voice would go on.

'You girls are the most adorable individuals I ever met. . . . *Did* anybody see Pearlie going home this afternoon?'

Every one chuckled and waited.

'My *dears*! My *dears*!! Bevan *dragged* me along to the end of the pavilion to see him enter up the handicaps with his new automatic pen—*awfully* smashing—and I was just hobbling the last few yards past the apple-trees when we *saw* Pearlie hand-in-hand with the Botterford boys, prancing along the asphalt court—*prancing*, my dears!'

Miriam and Harriett dragged themselves up to see. Nan

bridled and swayed from listener to listener, her wide throat gleaming as she sang out her words.

'Prancing—with straggles of grey hair sticking out and that *tiny* sailor hat cocked *almost* on to her nose. My dear, you sh'd 've *seen* Bevan! He put up his eyeglass, my dears, for a *fraction* of a second,' Nan's head went up—'Madame Pompadour,' thought Miriam—and her slanting eyes glanced down her nose, 'and dropped it, clickety-click. You sh'd 've *seen* the expression on his angelic countenance.'

'I say, she is an awful little creature, isn't she?' said Miriam, watching Eve bend a crimson face over the tea-tray on the hearthrug. 'She put her boots on the pavilion table this afternoon when all those men were there—about a mile high they are—with tassels. Why *does* she go on like that?'

'Men like that sort of thing,' said Sarah lightly.

'Sally!'

'They do. . . . I believe she drinks.'

'Sally! My *dear*!'

'I believe she *does*. She's always having shandygaff with the men.'

'Oh, well, perhaps she doesn't,' murmured Eve.

'Chuck me a lump of sugar, Eve.'

Miriam subsided once more amongst the rose petals.

'Bevvy thinks I oughtn't to dance.'

'Did he say so?'

'Of course, my dear. But old Wyman said I could, every third, except the Lancers.'

'You sh'd 've seen Bevvy's face. "Brother Tommy doesn't object," I said. "He's going to look after me!" "*Is* he?" said Bevvy in his *most* superior manner.'

'What a fearful scrunching you're making,' said Harriett, pinching Miriam's nose.

'Let's go and dress,' said Miriam, rolling off the table.

'How many times has she met him?' asked Miriam as they went through the hall.

'I dunno. Not many.'

'I think it's simply hateful.'

'Mimmy!' It was Nan's insinuating voice.

'Coming,' called Miriam. 'And, you know, Tommy needn't think he can carry on with *Meg* in an alcove.'

'*What* would she think? Let's go and tell Meg she must dress.'

'Mimmy!'

Miriam went back and put her head round the breakfast-room door.

'Let me see you when you're dressed.'

'Why?'

'I want to kiss the back of your neck, my dear; love kissing people's necks.'

Miriam smiled herself vaguely out of the room, putting away the unpleasant suggestion.

'I wish I'd got a dress like Nan's,' she said, joining Harriett in the dark lobby.

'I say, somebody's been using the *Financial Times* to cut up flowers on. It's all wet.' Harriett lifted the limp newspaper from the marble-topped coil of pipes and shook it.

'Hang it up somewhere.'

'Where? Everything's cleared up.'

'Stick it out of the lavatory window and pull the window down on it.'

'Awri, you hold the door open.'

Miriam laughed as Harriett fell into the room.

'Blooming boot-jack.'

'Is it all right in there? Are all the pegs clear? Is the washing-basin all right?'

A faint light came in as Harriett pushed up the frosted pane.

'Here's a pair of boots all over the floor and your old Zulu hat hanging on a peg. The basin's all right except a perfectly foul smell of nicotine. It's pater's old feather.'

'That doesn't matter. The men won't mind that. My old hat can stay. There are ten pegs out here and all the slab, and there's hardly anything on the hall-stand. That's it. Don't cram the window down so as to cut the paper. That'll do. Come on.'

'I wish I had a really stunning dress,' remarked Miriam, as they tapped across the wide hall.

'You needn't.'

The drawing-room door was open. They surveyed the sea of drugget, dark grey in the fading light. '*Pong*-pong-*pong* de-doodle, *pong*-pong-*pong* de-doodle,' murmured Miriam as they stood swaying on tiptoe in the doorway.

'Let 's have the gas and *two* candlesticks, Harry, on the dressing-table under the gas.'

'All right,' mouthed Harriett in a stage whisper, making for the stairs as the breakfast-room door opened.

It was Eve. 'I say, Eve, I 'm *scared*,' said Miriam, meeting her.

Eve giggled triumphantly.

'Look here. I shan't come down at first. I 'll play the first dance. I 'll get them all started with "Bitter-Sweet."'

'Don't worry, Mim.'

'My *dear*, I simply don't know how to face the evening.'

'You do,' murmured Eve. 'You are proud.'

'What of ?'

'You know quite well.'

'What ?'

'He 's the nicest boy we know.'

'But he 's not my boy. Of course not. You 're insane. Besides, I don't know who you 're talking about.

'Oh, well, we won't talk. We 'll go and arrange your chignon.'

'I 'm going to have simply twists and perhaps a hair ornament.'

Miriam reached the conservatory from the garden door and set about opening the lid of the grand piano. She could see at the far end of the almost empty drawing-room a little ruddy, thick-set, bearded man with a roll of music under his arm talking to her mother. He was standing very near to her, surrounding her with his eager presence. 'Mother 's wonderful,' thought Miriam, with a moment's adoration for Mrs Henderson's softly-smiling girlish tremulousness. Listening to the man's hilarious expostulating narrative voice she fumbled hastily for her waltz amongst the scattered piles of music.

As she struck her opening chords she watched her mother gently quell the narrative and steer the sturdy form towards a group of people hesitating in the doorway. 'Have they had coffee?' she wondered anxiously. 'Is Mary driving them into the dining-room properly?' Before she had reached the end of her second page every one had disappeared. She paused a moment and looked down the brightly lit empty room —the sight of the cold sheeny drugget filled her with despair. The hilarious voice resounded in the hall. There couldn't be many there yet. Where they all looking after them properly? For a moment she was tempted to leave her piano and go and make some desperate attempt at geniality. Then the sound of the pervading voice back· again in the room and brisk footsteps coming towards the conservatory drove her back to her music. The little man stepped quickly over the low moulding into the conservatory.

'Ah, Mariamne,' he blared gently.

'Oh, ßennett, you angel, how *did* you get here so early?' responded Miriam, playing with zealous emphasis.

'Got old Barrowgate to finish off the out-patients,' he said with a choke of amusement.

'I say, Mirry, don't you play. Let me take it on. You go and ply the light fantastic.' He laid his hands upon her shoulders and burred the tune she was playing like a muted euphonium over the top of her head. 'No. It's all right. Go and get them dancing. Get over the awfulness—*you* know.'

'Get over the awfulness, eh? Oh, I'll get over the awfulness.'

'Ssh—are there many there?'

They both looked round into the drawing-room.

Nan Babington was backing slowly up and down the room supported by the outstretched arms of Bevan Seymour, her black head thrown back level with his, the little scarlet knot in

her hair hardly registering the smooth movements of her
invisible feet.

'They seem to have begun,' shouted Bennett in a whisper
as Harriett and her fiancé swung easily circling into the room
and were followed by two more couples.

'Go and dance with Meg. She only knows Tommy
Babington.'

'Like the lid up?'

Miriam's rhythmic clangour doubled its resonance in the
tiled conservatory as the great lid of the piano went up.

'Magnifique, Mirry, parfaitement magnifique,' intoned
Tommy Babington, appearing in the doorway with Meg on
his arm.

'Bonsoir, Tomasso.'

'You are like an expressive metronome.'

'Oh—nom d'un pipe.'

'You would make a rhinoceros dance.'

Adjusting his pince-nez he dexterously seized tall Meg and
swung her rapidly in amongst the dancers.

'Sarah 'll say he 's had a Turkish bath,' thought Miriam,
recalling the unusual clear pallor of his rather overfed face.
'Pleated shirt. That 's to impress Meg.'

She felt all at once that the air seemed cold. It was not like
a summer night. How badly the ferns were arranged. Nearly
all of them together on the staging behind the end of the piano;
not enough visible from the drawing-room. Her muscles were
somehow stiffening into the wrong mood. Presently she would
be playing badly. She watched the forms circling past the gap
in the curtains and slowed a little. The room seemed fairly full.

'That 's it—perfect, Mim,' signalled Harriett's partner,
swinging her by. She held to the fresh rhythm and passing
into a tender old waltz tune that she knew by heart gave herself
to her playing. She need not watch the feet any longer. She
could go on for ever. She knew she was not playing altogether
for the dancers. She was playing to two hearers. But she
could not play that tune if they came. They would be late.

But they must be here now. Where were they? Were they
having coffee? Dancing? She flung a glance at the room
and met the cold eye of Bevan Seymour. She would not look
again. The right feeling for the dreamy old tune came and
went uncontrollably. Why did they not come? Presently
she would be cold and sick and done for, for the evening. She
played on, harking back to the memory of the kindly challenge
in the eyes of her brother-in-law to be, dancing gravely with a
grave Harriett—fearing her . . . writing in her album:

> She was his life,
> The ocean to the river of his thoughts—
> Which terminated all.

. . . cold, calm little Harriett. Her waltz had swung soft and
low and the dancers were hushed. Only Tommy Babington's
voice still threaded the little throng.

Someone held back the near curtain. A voice said quietly,
'Here she is.'

Ted's low, faintly-mocking voice filled the conservatory.

He was standing very near her, looking down at her with his
back to the gay room. Yesterday's dream had come more
than true, at once, at the beginning of the evening. He had
come straight to her with his friend, not dancing, not looking
for a partner. They were in the little green enclosure with her.
The separating curtains had fallen back into place.

Behind the friend who stood leaning against the far end of
the piano, the massed fernery gleamed now with the glow of
concealed fairy lamps. She had not noticed it before. The
fragrance of fronds and moist warm clumps of maidenhair and
scented geraniums inundated her as she glanced across at the
light falling on hard sculptured waves of hair above a white
handsome face.

Her music held them all, protecting the wordless meeting.
Her last night's extremity of content was reality, being lived
by all three of them. It centred in herself. Ted stood within
it, happy in it. The friend watched, witnessing Ted's confession. Ted had said nothing to him about her, about any of
them, in his usual way. But he was disguising nothing now
that he had come.

At the end of her playing she stood up faintly dizzy, and held out towards Max Sonnenheim's familiar strangeness hands heavy with happiness and quickened with the sense of Ted's touch upon her arm. The swift crushing of the strange hands upon her own, steadied her as the curtains swung wide and a group of dancers crowded in.

'Don't tell N. B. we 've scrubbed the coffin, Miriorama— she 'll sit there all the evening.'

'That was my sister and my future brother-in-law,' said Miriam to Max Sonnenheim as Harriett and Gerald ran down the steps and out into the dark garden.

'Your sister and brother-in-law,' he responded thoughtfully.

He was standing at her side at the top of the garden steps staring out into the garden and apparently not noticing the noisy passers-by. If they stood there much longer, Ted, who had not been dancing, would join them. She did not want that. She would put off her dance with Ted until later. The next dance she would play herself and then perhaps dance again with Max. Once more from the strange security of his strongly swinging arms she would meet Ted's eyes, watching and waiting. She must dance once more with Max. She had never really danced before. She would go to Ted at last and pass on the spirit of her dancing to him. But not yet.

'I will show you the front garden,' she said, running down the steps.

He joined her and they walked silently round the side of the house, through the kitchen yard and out into the deserted carriage drive. She thought she saw people on the front lawn and walked quickly, humming a little tune, on down the drive.

Max crunched silently along a little apart from her, singing to himself.

Both sides of the front gate were bolted back and their footsteps carried them straight out on to the asphalted avenue extending right and left, a dim tunnel of greenery, scarcely lit by the lamps out in the roadway. With a sudden sense of daring, Miriam determined to assume the deserted avenue as part of the garden.

The gate left behind, they made their way slowly along the high leafy tunnel.

They would walk to the end of the long avenue and back again. In a moment she would cease humming and make a remark. She tasted a new sense of ease, walking slowly along with this strange man without 'making conversation.' He was taking her silence for granted. All her experience so far had been of companions whose uneasiness pressed unendurably for speech, and her talking had been done with an irritated sense of the injustice of aspersions on 'women's tongues,' while no man could endure a woman's silence . . . even Ted, except when dancing; no woman could, except Minna, in Germany. Max must be foreign, of course, German—of *course*. She could, if she liked, talk of the stars to him. He would neither make jokes nor talk science and want her to admire him, until all the magic was gone. Her mood expanded. He had come just at the right moment. She would keep him with her until she had to face Ted. He was like a big ship towing the little barque of her life to its harbour.

His vague humming rose to a little song. It was German. It was the *Lorelei*. For a moment she forgot everything but pride in her ability to take her share in both music and words.

'You understand German!' he cried.

They had reached the end of the avenue and the starlit roadway opened ahead, lined with meadows.

'Ach, wie schön,' breathed Max.

'Wie schön.' Miriam was startled by the gay sound of her own voice. It sounded as if she were alone, speaking to herself. She looked up at the spangled sky. The freshening air streamed towards them from the meadows.

'We *must* go back,' she said easily, turning in again under the trees.

The limes seemed heavily scented after their breath of the open. They strolled dreamily along keeping step with each other. They would make it a long quiet way to the gate. Miriam felt strangely invisible. It was as if in a moment a voice would come from the clustering lime-trees or from the cluster of stars in the imagined sky.

'Wie süss,' murmured Max, 'ist treue Liebe.'

'How dear,' she translated mentally, 'is true love.' Yes, that was it, that was true, the German phrase. Ted was dear, dear. But so far away. Coming and going, far away.

'Is it?' she said with a vague, sweet intonation, to hear more.

'Wie süss, wie süss,' he repeated firmly, flinging his arm across her shoulders.

The wildly shimmering leafage rustled and seemed to sing. She walked on horrified, cradled, her elbow resting in her companion's hand as in a cup. She laughed, and her laughter mingled with the subdued lilting of the voice close at her side. Ted was waiting somewhere in the night for her. Ted. Ted. Not this stranger. But why was Ted not bold like this? Primly and gently she disengaged herself.

She and Ted would walk along through the darkness and it would shout to them. Day-time colours seemed to be shining through the night. . . . She turned abruptly to her companion.

'Aren't the lime-trees jolly?' she said conversationally.

'You will dance again with me?'

'Yes, if you like.'

'I must go so early.'

'Must you?'

'To-morrow morning early I go abroad.'

'Hullo!'

'Where were *you* all that last dance?'

Nan Babington's voice startled her as they came into the bright hall through the open front door.

She smiled towards Nan, sitting drearily with a brilliant smile on her face watching the dancers from a long chair drawn up near the drawing-room door, and passed on into the room with her hand on her partner's arm. They had missed a dance and an interval. It must have been a Lancers and now there was another waltz.

Several couples were whirling gravely about. Amongst them she noted Bevan Seymour, upright and slender, dancing

with Harriett with an air of condescending vivacity, his bright
teeth showing all the time.   Her eyes were ready for Ted.   She
was going to meet his for the first time—just one look, and then
she would fly for her life anywhere, to anybody.   And he
would find her and make her look at him again.   Ted.   He
was not there.   People were glancing at her, curiously.   She
veiled her waiting eyes and felt their radiance stream through
her, flooding her with strength from head to foot.   How
battered and ordinary every one had looked, frail and sick,
stamped with a pallor of sickness.   How she pitied them all.

'Let us take a short turn,' said Max, and his arms came
around her.   As they circled slowly down the length of the
room she stared at his black shoulder a few inches from her
eyes.   His stranger's face was just above her in the bright
light; his strange black-stitched glove holding her mittened
hand.   His arms steadied her as they neared the conservatory.

'Let us go out,' she heard him say, and her footsteps were
guided across the moulding, her arm retained in his.   Meg
Wedderburn was playing and met her with her sentimental
smile.   In the gloom at her side, just beyond the shaded candle
stood Ted, ready to turn the music, his disengaged hand holding
the bole of the tall palm.   He dropped his hands and turned as
they passed him, almost colliding with Miriam.   'Next dance
with me,' he whispered neatly.   'Will you show me your
coffin?' asked Max as they reached the garden steps.

'It's quite down at the end beyond the kitchen garden.'

'There are raspberry canes all along here, on both sides—
trailing all over the place; the gardener puts up stakes and
things but they manage to trail all over the place.'

'Ah, yes.'

'Some of them are that pale yellow kind, the colour of
champagne.   You can just see how they trail.   Isn't it funny
how dark they are, and yet the colour's there all the time, isn't
it?   They are lovely in the day, lovely leaves and great big
fruit, and in between are little squatty gooseberry bushes, all
kinds, yellow and egg-shaped like plums, and little bright green

round ones and every kind of the ordinary red kind. Do you know the little bright green ones, quite bright green when they 're ripe, like bright green chartreuse?'

'No. The green chartreuse of course I know. But green ripe gooseberries I have not seen.'

'I expect you only know the unripe green ones they make April fool of.'

'April fool?'

'I mean *gooseberry* fool. Do you know why men are like green gooseberries?'

'No. Why are they? Tell me.'

'Perhaps you would not like it. We are passing the apple trees now; quarendens and stibbards.'

'Tell me. I shall like what you say.'

'Well, it 's because women can make fools of them whenever they like.'

Max laughed; a deep gurgling laugh that echoed back from the wall in front of them.

'We are nearly at the end of the garden.'

'I think you would not make a man a fool. No?'

'I don't know. I 've never thought about it.'

'You have not thought much about men.'

'I don't know.'

'But they, they have thought about you.'

'Oh, I 'm sure I don't know.'

'You do not care, perhaps?'

'I don't know, I don't know, I don't know. Here 's the coffin. I 'm afraid it 's not very comfortable. It 's so low.'

'What is it?'

'It 's an overturned seedling box. There 's grass all round. I wonder whether·it 's damp,' said Miriam suddenly invaded by a general uncertainty.

'Oh, we will sit down, it will not be damp. Your future brother-in-law has not scrubbed also the ivy on the wall,' he pursued as they sat down on the broad low seat, 'it will spoil your blouse.'

Miriam leaned uncomfortably against the intervening arm.

'Isn't is a perfectly lovely night?' she said.

'I feel that you would not make of a man a fool. . . .'

'Why not?'

'I feel that there is no poison in you.'

'What *do* you mean?' People . . . poisonous . . . What a horrible idea.

'Just what I say.'

'I know in a way. I think I know what you mean.'

'I feel that there is no poison in you. I have not felt that before with a woman.'

'Aren't women awful?' Miriam made a little movement of sympathy towards the strange definiteness at her side.

'I have thought so. But you are not as the women one meets. You have a soul serene and innocent. With you it should be well with a man.'

'I don't know,' responded Miriam. 'Is he telling me I am a fool?' she thought. 'It's true, but no one has the courage to tell me.'

'It is most strange. I talk to you here as I will. It is simple and fatal'; the supporting arm became a gentle encirclement and Miriam's heart beat softly in her ears. 'I go to-morrow to Paris to the branch of my father's business that is managed there by my brother. And I go then to New York to establish a branch there. I shall be away then, perhaps a year. Shall I find you here?'

A quick crunching on the gravel pathway just in front of them made them both hold their breath to listen. Someone was standing on the grass near Max's side of the coffin. A match spat and flared and Miriam's heart was shaken by Ted's new, eager, frightened voice. 'Aren't you *ever* going to dance with me again?'

She had seen the whiteness of his face and his cold, delicate, upright figure. In spirit she had leapt to her feet and faltered his name. All the world she knew had fallen into newness. This was certainty. Ted would never leave her. But it was Max who was standing up and saying richly in the blackness left by the burnt-out match, 'All in good time, Burton. Miss Miriam is engaged to me for this dance.' Her faint 'of course, Ted,' was drowned in the words which her partner sang after the footsteps retreating rapidly along the gravel path: 'We 're just coming!'

'I suppose they 've begun the next dance,' she said, rising decisively and brushing at her velvet skirt with trembling hands.

'Our dance. Let us go and dance our dance.'

They walked a little apart steadily along up through the kitchen garden, their unmatched footsteps sounding loudly upon the gravel between remarks made by Max. Miriam heard them and heard the voice of Max. But she neither listened nor responded.

She began to talk and laugh at random as they neared the lawn lit by the glaring uncurtained windows.

Consulting his scrutinizing face as they danced easily in the as yet half-empty room, he humming the waltz which swung with their movement, she found narrow, glinting eyes looking into her own; strange eyes that knew all about a big business and were going to Paris and New York. His stranger's face was going away, to be washed and shaved innumerable times, keeping its assurance in strange places she knew nothing about.

Here, just for these few hours, laughing at Ted. A phrase flashed through her brain, 'He 's brought Ted to his senses.' She flushed and laughed vaguely and danced with a feeling of tireless strength and gaiety. She knew the phrase was not her own. It was one Nan Babington could have used. It excited her. It meant that real things were going to happen, she could bear herself proudly in the room. She rippled complacently at Max. The room was full of whirling forms, swelling and shrinking as they crossed and recrossed the line between the clear vision rimmed by her glasses and the surrounding bright confusion. Swift, rhythmic movement, unbroken and unjostled, told her how well they were dancing. She was secure, landed in life, dancing carelessly out and out to a life of her own.

'I go; I see you again in a year,' said Max suddenly, drawing up near the door where Mrs Henderson stood sipping coffee with Sarah and Bennett.

'Where is Burton?' he asked in the midst of his thanks and leave-taking.

They all hesitated. Miriam suddenly found herself in the presence of a tribunal.

Bennett's careless 'Oh, he 's gone; couldn't stay,' followed her as she flung upstairs to Meg Wedderburn's empty room. Why had her mother looked so self-conscious and Sarah avoided her eye . . . standing there like a little group of conspirators.

People were always inventing things. 'Bother—damnational silliness,' she muttered, and began rapidly calculating. Ted gone away. Little Ted hurt and angry. To-morrow. Perhaps he wouldn't come. If he didn't she wouldn't see him before she went. The quiet little bead of ruby-shaded gas reproached her. Meg's eyes would be sad and reproachful in this quiet neatness. Terror seized her. She wouldn't see him. He had finished his work at the Institution. It was the big Norwich job next week.

CHAPTER III

Miriam propped *The Story of Adèle* open against the three Bibles on the dressing-table. It would be wasteful to read it upstairs. It was the only story-book amongst the rows of volumes which filled the shelves in the big schoolroom and would have to last her for tea-time reading the whole term. The *Fleurs de l'Eloquence*? Shiny brown leather covered with little gold buds and tendrils, fresh and new although the parchment pages were yellow with age. The Fleurs were so short . . . that curious page signed 'Froissart' with long s's, coming to an end just as the picture of the French court was getting clear and interesting. That other thing, *The Anatomy of Melancholy*. Fascinating. But it would take so much reading, on and on forgetting everything; all the ordinary things, seeing things in some new way, some way that fascinated people for a moment if you tried to talk about it and then made them very angry, made them hate and suspect you. Impossible to take it out and have it on the schoolroom table for tea-time reading. What had made the Pernes begin allowing tea-time reading? Being shy and finding it difficult to keep conversation going with the girls for so long? They never did talk to the girls. Perhaps because they did not see through them and understand them. North London girls. So different from the Fairchild family and the sort of girls they had been accustomed to when they were young. Anyhow, they hardly ever had to talk to them. Not at breakfast or dinner-time when they were all three there; and at tea-time when there was only one of them, there were always the books. How sensible. On Sunday afternoons, coming smiling into the schoolroom, one of them each Sunday—perhaps the others were asleep— reading aloud; the Fairchild family, smooth and good and happy, every one in the book surrounded with a sort of light, going on and on towards heaven, tea-time seeming so nice and mean and ordinary afterwards—or a book about a place in the

226

north of England called Saltcoats, brine, and a vicarage and
miners; the people in the book horrible, not lit up, talking about
things and being gloomy and not always knowing what to do,
never really sure about Heaven like the Fairchild family,
black brackish book. *The Fairchild Family* was golden and
gleaming.

The Anatomy of Melancholy would not be golden like *The
Fairchild Family* . . . 'the cart was now come alongside a
wood which was exceedingly shady and beautiful'; 'good
manners and civility make everybody lovely'; but it would be
round and real, not just chilly and moaning like *Saltcoats*. The
title would be enough to keep one going at tea-time. An*at*—
omy of *Mel*—ancholy, and the look of the close-printed pages
and a sentence here and there. The Pernes would not believe
she really wanted it there on the table. The girls would stare.
When *The Story of Adèle* was finished she would have to find
some other book; or borrow one. Nancie Wilkie, sitting at
tea with her back to the closed piano facing the great bay of
dark green-blinded window, reading *Nicholas Nickleby*. Just
the very one of all the Dickens volumes that would be likely to
come into her hands. Impossible to borrow it when Nancie
had finished with it. Impossible to read a book with such a
title. *David Copperfield* was all right; and *The Pickwick Papers*.
Little Dorritt—A Tale of Two Cities—The Old Curiosity Shop.
There was something suspicious about these, too.

Adèle—The Story of Adèle. The book had hard, unpleasant
covers with some thin cottony material—bright lobelia blue—
—strained over them and fraying out at the corners. Over
the front of the cover were little garlands and festoons of
faded gold, and in the centre framed by an oval band of
brighter gold was the word Adèle, with little strong tendrils
on the lettering. There was some secret charm about the book.
The strong sunlight striking the window just above the coarse
lace curtains that obscured its lower half, made the gilding
shine and seem to move a whole wild woodland. The coarse
white toilet cover on the chest of drawers, the three Bibles,

the little cheap mahogany - framed looking - glass, Nancie
Wilkie's folding hand-glass, the ugly gas bracket sticking out
above the mirror, her own bed in the corner with its coarse
fringed coverlet, the two alien beds behind her in the room, and
the repellent washstand in the far corner became friendly as the
sun shone on the decorated cover of the blue and gold book.

She propped it open again and began tidying her hair. It
must be nearly tea-time. A phrase caught her eye. 'The old
château where the first years of Adèle's life were spent was
situated in the midst of a high-walled garden. Along one side
of the château ran a terrace looking out over a lovely expanse of
flower-beds. Beyond was a little pleasaunce surrounded by a
miniature wall and threaded by little pathways lined with rose
trees. Almost hidden in the high wall was a little doorway.
When the doorway was open you could see through into a
deep orchard.' The first tea-bell rang. The figure of Adèle
flitting about in an endless summer became again lines of black
print. In a moment the girls would come rushing up. Miriam
closed the book and turned to the dazzling window. The sun
blazed just above the gap in the avenue of poplars. A bright
yellow pathway led up through the green of the public cricket
ground, pierced the avenue of poplars and disappeared through
the further greenery in a curve that was the beginning of its
encirclement of the park lake. Coming slowly along the
pathway was a little figure dressed bunchily in black. It
looked pathetically small and dingy in the bright scene. The
afternoon blazed round it. It was something left over. What
was the explanation of it? As it came near it seemed to change.
It grew real. It was hurrying eagerly along, quite indifferent
to the afternoon glory, with little rolling steps that were like the
uneven toddling of a child, and carrying a large newspaper
whose great sheets, although there was no wind, balled out
scarcely controlled by the small hands. Its feathered hat had
a wind-blown rakish air. On such a still afternoon. It was
thinking and coming along, thinking and thinking and a little
angry. What a rum little party, murmured Miriam, despising
her words and admiring the wild thought-filled little bundle of
dingy clothes. Beastly, to be picking up that low kind of

slang—not real slang. Just North London sneering. Goo—
what a *rum* little party, she declared aloud, flattening herself
against the window. Hotly flushing, she recognized that she had
been staring at Miss Jenny Perne hurrying in to preside at tea.

'We 've been to Jones's this afternoon, Miss Jenny.'
Each plate held a slice of bread and butter cut thickly all the
way across a household loaf, and the three-pound jar of home-
made plum jam belonging to Nancie Wilkie was going the
round of the table. It had begun with Miriam, who sat on
Miss Jenny's right hand, and had Nancie for neighbour. She
had helped herself sparingly, unable quite to resist the en-
hancement of the solid fare, but fearing that there would be no
possibility of getting anything from home to make a return in
kind. Things were so bad, the dance had cost so much. One
of Mary's cakes, big enough for five people, would cost so much.
And there would be the postage.

Piling a generous spoonful on to her own thick slice, Nancie
coughed facetiously and repeated her remark which had produced no result but a giggle from Charlotte Stubbs who sat
opposite to her.

'Eh? Eh? What?'

Miss Jenny looked down the table over the top of her newspaper without raising her head. Her pince-nez were perched
so that one eye appeared looking through its proper circle, the
other glared unprotected just above a rim of glass.

'Miss Haddie took us to Jones's this afternoon,' said Nancie
almost voicelessly. Miriam glanced at the too familiar sight of
Nancie's small eyes vanishing to malicious points. She was
sitting as usual very solid and upright in her chair, with her
long cheeks pink flushed and her fine nose white and cool and
twitching, her yellow hair standing strongly back from her
large white brow. She stabbed keenly in her direction as
Miriam glanced, and Miriam turned and applied herself
to her bread and jam. If she did not eat she would not
get more than two slices from the piled dishes before the

others had consumed four and five apiece and brought tea to an end.

'Eh? What for? Why are ye laughing, Nancie?'

'I 'm not laughing, Miss Jenny.' Nancie's firm lips curved away from her large faultless teeth. 'I 'm only smiling and telling you about our visit to Jones's.'

Miss Jenny's newspaper was lowered and her pince-nez removed.

'Eh? What d' ye say? Nonsense, Nancie, you know you were laughing. Why do you say you weren't? What do you mean? Eh?'

'I 'm sorry, Miss Jennie. Something tickled me.'

'Yes. Don't be nonsensical. D' ye see? It 's nonsensical to say no when you mean yes. D' ye understand what I mean, Nancie? It 's bad manners.' Hitching on her pince-nez, Miss Jenny returned to her paper.

Miriam gave herself up to the luxury of reading *Adèle* to the accompaniment of bread and jam. She would not hurry over her bread and jam. As well not have it. She would sacrifice her chance of a third slice. She reflected that it would be a good thing if she could decide never to have more than two slices, and have them in peace. Then she could thoroughly enjoy her reading. But she was always so hungry. At home she could not have eaten thick bread and butter. But here every slice seemed better than the last. When she began at the hard thick edge there always seemed to be tender places on her gums, her three hollow teeth were uneasy and she had to get through worrying thoughts about them—they would get worse as the years went by, and the little places in the front would grow big and painful and disfiguring. After the first few mouthfuls of solid bread a sort of padding seemed to take place and she could go on forgetful.

'They 'd got,' said Trixie Sanderson in a velvety tone, 'they 'd got some of their Christmas things out, Miss Jenny.' She cleared her throat shrilly on the last word and toned off the sound with a sigh. Inaudible laughter went round the table, stopping at Miriam, who glanced fascinated across at Trixie. Trixie sat in her best dress, a loosely made brown velveteen

with a deep lace collar round her soft brown neck. Her neck
and her delicate pale face were shaded by lively silky brown
curls. She held her small head sideways from her book with
a questioning air. One of her wicked swift brown eyes was
covered serenely with its thin lid.

She uttered a second gentle sigh and once more cleared her
throat, accompanying the sound with a rapid fluttering of the
lowered lid.

Miriam condemned her, flouting the single eye which tried
to search her, hating the sudden, sharp dimpling which came
high up almost under Trixie's cheek bones in answer to her
own expression.

'Miss Jenny,' breathed Trixie in a high tone, twirling one
end of the bow of black ribbon crowning her head.

Beadie Fetherwell, at the far end of the table opposite the
tea-tray, giggled aloud.

'Eh? What? Did somebody speak?' said Miss Jenny,
looking up with a smile. 'Are ye getting on with yer teas?
Are ye ready for second cups?'

'Beadie spoke,' murmured Trixie, glancing at Beadie whose
neat china doll's face was half hidden between her cup and the
protruding edge of her thatch of light gold curls.

Miriam disgustedly watched Beadie prolong the irritating
comedy by choking over her tea.

It was some minutes before the whole incident was made
clear to Miss Jenny. Reading was suspended. Every one
watched while Charlotte Stubbs, going carefully backwards,
came to the end at last of Miss Jenny's questions, and when
Miss Jenny rapidly adjudicating—*well!* you're all very naughty
children. I can't think what's the matter with you? Eh?
Ye shouldn't do it. I can't think what possesses you. What
is it, eh? Ye shouldn't do it. D'you see?—and having
dispensed the second allowance of tea with small hesitating
preoccupied hands, returned finally to her newspaper, it was
Charlotte who sat looking guilty. Miriam stole a glance at the
breadth of her broad flushed face, at its broadest as she hung
over her book. Her broad flat nose shone with her tea-
drinking, and her shock of coarse brown-gold hair, flatly

brushed on the top, stuck out bushily on either side, its edges lit by the afternoon glow from the garden behind her. The others were unmoved. Trixie sat reading, the muscles controlling her high dimples still faintly active. She and Nancie and Beadie, whose opaque blue eyes fixed the table just ahead of her book with their usual half-squinting stare, had entered on their final competition for the last few slices.

Miriam returned to her book. The story of Adèle had moved on through several unassimilated pages. 'My child,' she read, 'it is important to remember'—she glanced on, gathering a picture of a woman walking with Adèle along the magic terrace, talking—words and phrases that fretted dismally at the beauty of the scene. Examining later chapters she found conversations, discussions, situations, arguments, 'fusses' —all about nothing. She turned back to the early passage of description and caught the glow once more. But this time it was overshadowed by the promise of those talking women. That was all there was. She had finished the story of Adèle.

A resounding slam came up from the kitchen.

'Poor cook—another tooth,' sighed Trixie.

Smothering a convulsion, Miriam sat dumb. Her thwarted expectations ranged forth beyond control, feeling swiftly and cruelly about for succour where she had learned there was none. . . . Nancie, her parents abroad, her aunt's house at Cromer, with a shrubbery, the cousin from South Africa coming home to Cromer, taking her out in a dog-cart, telling her she was his guiding star, going back to South Africa; everything Nancie said and did, even her careful hair-brushing and her energetic upright walk, her positive brave way of entering a room, coming out through those malicious pin-points—things she said about the Misses Perne and the girls, things she whispered and laughed, little rhymes she sang with her unbearable laugh.

. . . Beadie, still shaking at intervals in silent servile glancing laughter, her stepmother, her little half-brother who had fits, her holidays at Margate, 'you'd look neat, on the seat, of a bicyka made for two'—Beadie brought Miriam the utmost sense of imprisonment within the strange influence that had

threatened her when she first came to Banbury Park.   Beadie
was in it, was an unquestioning part of it.   She felt that she
could in some way, in some one tint or tone, realize the whole
fabric of Beadie's life on and on to the end, no matter what
should happen to her.   But she turned from the attempt—any
effort at full realization threatened complete despair.   Trixie
too, with a home just opposite the Banbury Empire. . . .
Miriam slid over this link in her rapid reflections—a brother
named Julian who took instantaneous photographs of girls,
numbers and numbers of girls, and was sometimes 'tight.' . . .
    Charlotte.   Charlotte carried about a faint suggestion of
relief.   Miriam fled to her as she sat with the garden light on
her hair, her lingering flush of distress rekindled by her amusement, her protective responsible smile beaming out through
the endless blue of her eyes.   Behind her painstaking life at
the school was a country home, a farm somewhere far away.
Of course it was dreadful for her to be a farmer's daughter.
She evidently knew it herself and said very little about it   But
her large red hands, so strange handling school-books, were
comforting; and her holland apron with its bib under the fresh
colouring of her face—do you like butter?   A buttercup under
your chin—brought to Miriam a picture of the farm, white
amidst bright greenery, with a dairy and morning cock-crow
and creamy white sheep on a hillside.   It was all there with her
as she sat at table reading *The Lamplighter*.   The sound of her
broad husky voice explaining to Miss Jenny had been full of it.
But it was all past.   She too had come to Banbury Park.   She
did not seem to mind Banbury Park.   She was to study hard
and be a governess.   She evidently thought she was having a
great chance—she was fifteen and quite 'uncultured '   How
could she be turned into a governess?   A sort of nursery
governess, for farms, perhaps.   But farms did not want books
and worry.   Miriam wanted to put her back into her farm,
and sometimes her thoughts wearily brushed the idea of going
with her.   Perhaps, though, she had come away because her
father could not keep her?   The little problem hung about her
as she sat sweetly there, common and good and strong.   The
golden light that seemed to belong specially to her came from

a London garden, an unreal North London garden. Resounding in its little spaces were the blatterings and shouts of the deaf and dumb next door.

Miss Jenny left the *Standard* with Miriam after tea, stopping suddenly as she made her uncertain way from the tea-table to the door and saying absently, 'Eh, you 'd better read this, my dear. There 's a leader on the Education Commission. Would ye like to ? Yes, I think you 'd better.' Miriam accepted the large sheets with hesitating expressions of thanks, wondering rather fearfully what a leader might be and where she should find it. She knew the word. Her mother read 'the leaders' in the evening—'excellent leader' she sometimes said, and her father would put down his volume of *Proceedings of the British Association*, or Herbert Spencer's *First Principles*, and condescendingly agree. But any discussion generally ended in his warning her not to believe a thing because she saw it in print, and a reminder that before she married she had thought that everything she saw in print was true, and quite often he would go on to general remarks about the gullibility of women, bringing in the story of the two large long-necked pearly transparent drawing-room vases with stems and soft masses of roses and leaves painted on their sides that she had given too much for at the door to a man who said they were Italian. Brummagem, Brummagem, he would end, mouthing the word and turning back to his book with the neighing laugh that made Miriam turn to the imagined picture of her mother in the first year of her married life, standing in the sunlight at the back door of the Babington house, with the varnished coach-house door on her right and the cucumber frames in front of her sloping up towards the bean-rows that began the kitchen garden; with her little scalloped bodice, her hooped skirt, her hair bunched in curls up on her high pad and falling round her neck, looking at the jugs with grave dark eyes. And that neighing laugh had come again and again all through the years until she sat meekly, flushed and suffering under the fierce

gaslight, feeling every night of her life winter and summer as
if the ceiling were coming down on her head, and read 'leaders'
cautiously, and knew when they were written in 'a fine, chaste,
dignified style.' But that was *The Times*. The *Standard* was
a penny rag, and probably not worth considering at all. In any
case she would not read it at evening study. She had never had
a newspaper in her hand before as far as she could remember.
The girls would see that she did not know how to read it, and it
would be snubby towards them to sit there as if she were a Miss
Perne, scrumpling a great paper while they sat with their books.
So she read her text-books, a page of Saxon Kings with a ten-
line summary of each reign, a list of six English counties with
their capitals and the rivers the capitals stood on and the
principal industries of each town, devising ways of remembering
the lists and went on to Bell's *Standard Elocutionist*. She had
found the book amongst the school books on the school-room
shelves. It was a 'standard' book and must therefore be about
something she ought to know something about if she were to
hold her own in this North London world. There had been
no 'standard' books at school and the word offended her. It
suggested fixed agreement about the things people ought to
know and that she felt sure must be wrong, and not only wrong
but 'common' . . . standard readers . . . standard pianoforte
tutors. She had learned to read in *Reading Without Tears*, and
gone on to *Classical Poems and Prose for the Young*, her arithmetic book instead of being a thin cold paper-covered thing
called Standard I, had been a pleasant green volume called
'Barnard Smith,' that began at the beginning and went on to
compound fractions and stocks. There was no Morris's
Grammar at Banbury Park, no Wetherell or English Accidence,
no bits from *Piers Plowman* and pages of scraps of words with
the way they changed in different languages, and quotations,
just sentences that had made her long for more . . . 'up-clomb'
. . . 'the mist up-clomb.' She opened Bell's *Standard
Elocutionist* apprehensively, her mind working on possible
meanings for elocutionist. She thought of ventriloquist and
wondered dismally whether it was a book of conjuring tricks.
It was poems, poems and prose, all mixed up together anyhow.

The room was very still, the girls all sitting reading with their
backs to the table so that nobody 'poked.' She could not go on
vaguely fluttering pages, so she read a solid-looking poem that
was not divided up into verses.

'Robert of Sicily, brother of Pope Urbane And Valmond
Emperor of Allemaine, Apparelled in magnificent attire, With
retinue of many a knight and squire, On St John's eve, at
vespers, proudly sat And heard the priests chant the *Mag-
nificat*.' Should she go on? It was like the pieces in Scott's
novels, the best bits, before the characters began to talk.

'. . . and bay the moon than such a Roman and bay the
moon than such a Roman,' muttered Nancie rapidly, swinging
her feet. It would not be fair to read a thing that would take
her right away and not teach her anything, whilst the girls were
learning their things for Monday. She hesitated and turned
a page. The poem, she saw, soon began to break up into
sentences with quotation signs; somebody making a to-do.
Turning several pages at once, she caught sight of the word
Hanover. 'Hamelin Town's in Brunswick, by famous Hanover city.' That was irresistible. But she must read it one
day away from the gassy room and the pressure of the girls.
The lines were magic; but the rush that took her to the German
town, the sight and smell and sound of it, the pointed houses,
wood fires, the Bürghers, had made her cheeks flare and
thrown her out of the proper teacher's frame of mind. She
wanted to stand up and pull up the blinds hiding the garden
and shout the poem aloud to the girls. They would stare and
giggle and think she had gone mad. 'The mountain has gone
mad,' Nancie would mutter. 'There is a mountain in Banbury
Park, covered over with yellow bark,' Nancie's description of
herself. That was how the girls saw her stiff hair—and they
thought she was 'about forty.' Well, it was true. She was,
practically. She went on holding Bell up before her face, open
at a page of prose, and stared at the keyboard of the piano just
beyond her crossed knees. It aroused the sight and sense of
the strangely moving hands of the various girls whose afternoon
practice it was her business to superintend, their intent faces,
the pages of bad unclassical music, things with horrible names,

by English composers, the uselessness of the hours and terms
and years of practice.

Presently the bread and butter and milk came up for the
girls, and then there was prayers—the three servants lined up
in front of the bookshelves; cook wheezing heavily, tall and
thin and bent, with a sloping mob cap and a thin old brown
face with a forehead that was like a buttress of shiny bone, and
startling dark eyes that protruded so that they could be seen
even when she sat looking down into her lap; and Flora the
parlourmaid, short and plump and brown with the expression
of perfectly serene despair that was part of Miriam's daily
bread; and Annie the housemaid, raw pink and gold and grinning slyly at the girls—Miss Perne, sitting at the head of the
table with the shabby family Bible and the book of family
prayers, Miss Jenny and Miss Haddie one on each side of the
fireplace, Miss Jenny's feet hardly reaching the floor as she sat
bunched on a high schoolroom chair, Miss Haddie in her cold
slate-grey dress sitting back with her thin hands clasped in her
lap, her grey face bent devotionally so that her chin rested on
her thin chest, her eyes darting from the servants to the girls
who sat in their places round the table during the time it took
Miss Perne to read a short psalm.   Miriam tried to cast down
her eyes and close her ears. All that went on during that
short interval left her equally excluded from either party. She
could not sit gazing at Flora, and Miss Perne's polite unvarying
tone brought her no comfort. She sometimes thought long-
ingly of prayers in Germany, the big quiet *saal* with its high
windows, its great dark doors, its annexe of wooden summer-
room, Fräulein's clear, brooding undertone, the pensive calm
of the German girls; the strange mass of fresh melodious
sound as they all sang together. Here there seemed to be
everything to encourage and nothing whatever to check the
sudden murmur, the lightning swift gesture of Nancie or
Trixie.
  The moment Miss Perne had finished her psalm, they all
swung round on to their knees. Miriam pressed her elbows

against the cane seat of her chair and wondered what she should
say to Miss Jenny at supper about the newspaper, while Miss
Perne decorously prayed that they might all be fed with the
sincere milk of the Word and grow thereby.

After the Lord's Prayer, a unison of breathy mutterings
against closed fingers, they all rose. Then the servants filed
out of the room followed by the Misses Perne. Miss Perne
stopped in the doorway to shake hands with the girls on their
way to bed before joining her sisters in the little sitting-room
across the hall. One of the servants reappeared almost at
once with a tray, distributed its contents at the fireplace end
of the long table and rang the little bell in the hall on her way
back to the kitchen. The Misses Perne filed back across the
hall.

'Eh, Deborah, are ye sure?' said Miss Jenny, getting into
her chair at Miss Perne's right hand.

Perhaps the newspaper would not be mentioned after all.
If it were she would simply say she had been preparing for
Monday and was going to read it after supper. Anyhow
there was never any threat with the Pernes of anything she
would not be able to deal with. She glanced to see what there
was to eat, and then, feeling Miss Haddie's eye from across the
table, assumed an air of interested abstraction to cover her
disappointment. Cold white blancmange in a round dish
garnished with prunes, bread and butter, a square of cream
cheese on a green-edged dessert plate, a box of plain biscuits,
the tall bottle of lime juice and the red glass jug of water.
Nothing really sweet and nice—the blancmange would be
flavoured with laurel—prussic acid—and the prunes would be
sweet in the wrong sort of way—wholesome, just sweet fruit.
Cheese—how could people eat cheese?

'Well, my dear, I tell you only what I saw with my own eyes
—Polly Allen and Eunice Dupont running about in the park
without their hats.'

'Ech,' syphoned Miss Haddie, drawing her delicate green-

grey eyebrows sharply towards the deep line in the middle of
her forehead. She did not look up but sat frowning sourly
into her bowl of bread and milk, ladling and pouring the milk
from the spoon.

Miriam kept a nervous eye on her acid preoccupation. No
one had seen the behaviour of her own face, how one corner of
her mouth had shot up so sharply as to bring the feeling of a
deeply denting dimple in her cheek. She sat regulating her
breathing and carefully extracting the stone from a prune.

'Did ye speak to them?' asked Miss Jenny, fixing her tall
sister over her pince-nez.

Miss Perne sat smilingly upright, her black eyes blinking
rapidly at the far-off bookshelves.

'I did *not* speak to them——'

'Eh, Deborah, why not?' scolded Miss Jenny as Miss Perne
drew breath.

'I did *not* speak to them,' went on Miss Deborah, beaming
delightedly at the bookcase, 'for the very good reason that I
was not sufficiently near to them. I was walking upon the
asphalt pathway surrounding the lake and had just become
engaged in conversation with Mrs Brinkwell, who had stopped
me for the purpose of giving me further details with regard to
Constance's prolonged absence from school, when I saw Polly
and Eunice apparently chasing one another across the recreation ground, in the condition I have described to you.'

Miriam, who had felt Miss Haddie's scorn-filled eyes playing
watchfully over her, sat pressing the sharp edge of her high
heel into her ankle.

'Eh, my dear, what a pity you couldn't speak to them.
They 've no business at all in the recreation ground where the
rough boys go.'

'Well, I have described to you the circumstances, my dear,
and the impossibility of my undertaking any kind of inter-
vention.'

'Eh, well, Deborah my dear, I think I should have done
something. Don't you think you ought? Eh? Called someone perhaps—eh?—or managed to get at the gels in some way
—dear, dear, what is to be done? You see it is hardly of any

use to speak to them afterwards. You want to catch them
red-handed and make them feel ashamed of themselves.'

'I am fully prepared to admit, my dear Jenny, the justice of
all that you say. But I can only repeat that in the circumstances in which I found myself I was entirely unable to
exercise any control whatever upon the doings of the gels.
They were running; and long before I was free from Mrs
Brinkwell they were out of sight.'

Miss Perne spoke in a clear, high, narrative tone that seemed
each moment on the point of delighted laughter, her delicate
head held high, her finely wrinkled face puckering with re-
strained pleasure. Miriam saw vividly the picture in the park,
the dreadful, mean, grubby lake, the sad asphalt pathway all
round it, the shabby London greenery, the October wind
rushing through it, Miss Perne's high, stylish arrowy figure
fluttered by the wind, swaying in her response to Mrs Brinkwell's story, the dreadful asphalt playground away to the left,
its gaunt swings and bars—gallows. . . . Ingoldsby—the girls
rushing across it, and held herself sternly back from a vision of
Miss Perne chasing the delinquents down the wind. Why did
Miss Perne speak so triumphantly? As much as to say There,
my dear Jenny, there's a problem you can't answer. She
enjoyed telling the tale and was not really upset about the girls.
She spoke exactly as if she were reading aloud from *Robinson
Crusoe*. Miss Haddie was watching again, flashing her ·eyes
about as she gently spooned up her bread and milk. Miriam
wished she knew whether Miss Haddie knew how difficult it
was to listen gravely. She was evidently angry and disgusted.
But still she could watch.

'Did you go that way at all afterwards—the way the girls
went?'

'I did not,' beamed Miss Perne, turning to Miss Jenny as if
waiting for a judgment.

'Well, eh, I'm sure, really, it's most diffikilt. What is one
to do with these gels? Now, Miriam, here's something for
you to exercise your wits upon. What would ye do, eh?'

Miriam hesitated. Memories kept her dumb. Of course
she had never rushed about in a common park where rough

boys came. At the same time—if the girls wanted to rush about and scream and wear no hats, nobody had any right to interfere with them . . . they ought to be suppressed though, North London girls, capable of anything in the way of horridness . . . the Pernes did not seem to see how horrid the girls were in themselves, common and knowing and horrid. 'Dear, funny little O.M.'s' . . . they were something much more than that. They were wrong about the hats, but it was good, heavenly to be here like this with them. She turned to Miss Jenny, her mind in a warm confusion, and smiled into the little red face peering delicately from out its disorderly Gorgon loops.

'Well?'

'My dear Jenny,' said Miss Haddie's soft hollow voice, 'how should the child judge?'

Miriam's heart leapt. She smiled inanely and eagerly accepted a second helping of blancmange suddenly proffered by Miss Perne, who was drawing little panting breaths and blinking sharply at her.

'Nonsense, Haddie. Come along, my dear, it's a chance for you. Come along.'

'Tomboys,' said Miss Haddie indignantly.

Miriam drew a breath. It was wrong, they were not tomboys—she knew they had not run like tomboys—they had scuttled, she was sure—horrid girls, that was what they were, nothing the Pernes could understand. The Pernes ought not to be bothered with them.

'Well,' she said, feeling a sudden security, 'are we responsible for them out of school hours?'

Miss Haddie's eyebrows moved nervously, and Miss Perne's smile turned to a dubious mouthing.

'Eh, there you are. D'ye see, Deborah? That's it. That's the crucial point. Are we responsible? I'm sure I can't say. That places the whole difficulty in a nutshell. Here are these gels, not even day-boarders. How far can we control their general behaviour? Eh? I'm sure I don't know.'

'My dear Jenny,' said Miss Haddie quickly, her hollow voice reverberating as if she were using a gargle, 'it's quite obvious that we can't have gels known to belong to the school running about in the park with nothing on.'

'I agree, my dear Haddie. But, as Jenny says, how are we to prevent such conduct?'

'Don't let us lose sight of Miriam's point. *Are* we responsible for their play-times? I suppose we're *not*, you know, Deborah, really after all. Not directly, perhaps. But surely we are *indirectly* responsible. *Surely*. We ought to be able to make it impossible for them to carry on in this unseemly fashion.'

'Yes, yes,' said Miss Deborah eagerly, 'surely.'

'Is it education?' suggested Miriam.

'That's it, my dear. It is education. That's what's wanted. That's what these gels want. I don't know, though. All this talk of education. It ought to be the thing. And yet look at these two gels. Both of them from Miss Cass's. There's her school now. Famous all over London. Three hundred gels. We've had several here. And they've all had that objectionable noisy tone. Eh, Deborah? I don't know. How is it to be accounted for? Eh?'

'I've never heard of Miss Cass's,' said Miriam.

'My *dear* child! It's not possible! D'ye mean to say ye don't know Miss Cass's high school?'

'Oh, if it's a high school, of *course*.'

All three ladies waited, with their eyes on her, making a chorus of inarticulate sounds.

'Oh well, high schools are simply fearful.'

Miriam glowed in a tide of gentle cackling laughter.

'Well, you know, I think there's something in it,' giggled Miss Jenny softly. 'It's the number perhaps. That's what I always say, Deborah. Treating the gels like soldiers. Like a regiment. D'ye see? No individual study of the gels' characters——'

'Well. However that may be, I am sure of one thing. I am sure that on Monday Polly and Eunice must be reprimanded. Severely reprimanded.'

'Yes. I suppose they must. They're nice gels at heart, you know. Both of them. That's the worst of it. Well, I hardly mean that. Only so often the naughty gels are so thoroughly—well—nice, likeable at bottom, ye know, eh? I'm sure. I don't know.'

Miriam sat on in the schoolroom after supper with the newspaper spread out on the brown American cloth table cover under the gas. She found a long column headed 'The Royal Commission on Education.' The Queen, then, was interesting herself in education. But in England the sovereign had no power, was only a figure-head. Perhaps the Queen had been advised to interest herself in education by the Privy Council and the Conservatives, people of leisure and cultivation. A commission was a sort of command—it must be important, something the Privy Council had decided and sent out in the Queen's name.

She read her column, sitting comfortlessly between the window and the open door. As she read the room grew still. The memory of the talking and clinking supper-table faded, and presently even the ticking of the clock was no longer there. She raised her head at last. No wonder people read newspapers. You could read about what was going on in the country, actually what the Government was doing at that very moment. Of course; men seemed to know such a lot because they read the newspapers and talked about what was in them. But anybody could know as much as the men sitting in the arm-chairs if they chose; read all about everything, written down for everybody to see. That was the freedom of the press —*Areopagitica*, that the history books said so much about, and was one of those new important things, more important than facts and dates. Like the Independence of Ireland. Yet very few people really talked like newspapers. Only angry men with loud voices. Here was the free press that Milton had gone to prison for. Certainly it made a great difference. The room was quite changed. There was hardly any pain in the silent cane-seated chairs. There were really people making the world better. Now. At last. Perhaps it was rather a happy fate to be a teacher in the Banbury Park school and read newspapers. There were plenty of people who could neither read nor write. Someone had a servant like that who did all the marketing and never forgot anything or made any mistake over the change—none the worse for it, pater said, people who wanted book-learning could get it, there must always be hewers of wood, drawers of water; *laissez-faire*. But Gladstone did not believe that. At this moment Gladstone was saying that because the people of England as a whole were uneducated their 'condition of ignorance' affected the whole of the 'body politic.' That was Gladstone. He had found that out . . . with large moist silky eyes like a dog, and pointed collars, seeing things as they were and going to change them. . . . Miriam stirred uneasily as she felt the beating of her heart. . . . If only she were at home how she could rush up and down the house and shout about it and shake Mary by the shoulders. She shrank into herself and sat stiffly up, suddenly discovering she was lounging over the table. As she moved she reflected that probably Gladstone's being so very dark made him determined that things should not go on as they were. In that case Gladstonians would be dark—perhaps not musical. Someone had said musical people were a queer soft lot. *Laissez-faire*. Lazy fair. But perhaps it was possible to be fair and musical and to be a Gladstonian too. You can't have your cake and eat it. No. It was a good thing, one's best self knew it was a good thing that someone had found out why people were so awful; like a dentist finding out a bad tooth however much it hurt. Only if education was going to be the principal thing and all teachers were to be 'qualified' it was no use going on. Miss Jenny had said private schools were doomed.

For a long time she sat blankly contemplating the new world that was coming. Every one would be trained and efficient but herself. She was not strong enough to earn a living and qualify as a teacher at the same time. The day's work tired her to death. She must hide somewhere. . . . She would not be wanted. . . . If you were not wanted. . . . If you knew you were not wanted—you ought to get out of the way.

Chloroform. Someone had drunk a bottle of carbolic acid.
The clock struck ten. Gathering up the newspaper she
folded it neatly, put it on the hall-table and went slowly upstairs, watching the faint reflection of the half-lowered hall gas
upon the polished balustrade. The staircase was cold and airy.
Cold rooms and landings stretched up away above her into the
darkness. She became aware of a curious buoyancy rising
within her. It was so strange that she stood still for a moment
on the stair. For a second, life seemed to cease in her and the
staircase to be swept from under her feet. . . . 'I 'm alive.'
. . . It was as if something had struck her, struck right through
her impalpable body, sweeping it away, leaving her there
shouting silently without it. I 'm alive. . . . I 'm alive. Then
with a thump her heart went on again and her feet carried her
body, warm and happy and elastic, easily on up the solid stairs.
She tried once or twice deliberately to bring back the breathless
moment standing still on a stair. Each time something of it
returned. 'It 's me, *me*; this is *me* being alive,' she murmured
with a feeling under her like the sudden drop of a lift. But
her thoughts distracted her. They were eagerly talking to her,
declaring that she had had this feeling before. She opened her
bedroom door very quietly. The air of the room told her that
Nancie and Beadie were asleep. Going lightly across to the
chest of drawers dressing-table by the window as if she were
treading on air, she stood holding its edge in the darkness.
Two forgotten incidents flowed past her in quick succession;
one of waking up on her seventh birthday in the seaside villa
alone in a small dark room and suddenly saying to herself that
one day her father and mother would die and she would still
be there and, after a curious moment when the darkness seemed
to move against her, feeling very old and crying bitterly; and
another of standing in the bow of the dining-room window at
Barnes looking at the raindrops falling from the leaves through
the sunshine and saying to Eve, who came into the room as she
watched, 'D' you know, Eve, I feel as if I 'd suddenly wakened
up out of a dream.' The bedroom was no longer dark. She
could see the outlines of everything in the light coming from
the street lamps through the half-closed Venetian blinds.

Beadie sighed and stirred. Miriam began impatiently preparing for bed without lighting the gas. 'What 's the use of feeling like that if it doesn't stay? It doesn't change anything. Next time I 'll make it stay. It might whisk me right away. There 's something in me that can't be touched or altered. Me. If it comes again. If it 's stronger every time. . . . Perhaps it goes on getting stronger till you die.'

CHAPTER IV

WHEEZING, cook had spread a plaster of dampened ashy cinders upon the basement schoolroom fire and gone bonily away across the oilcloth in her heelless boots. As the door closed, Miriam's eye went up from her book to the little slope of grass showing above the concrete wall of the area. The grass gleamed along the edge of a bank of mist. In the mist the area railings stood hard and solid against the edge of empty space. Several times she glanced at the rich green, feeling that neither 'emerald,' 'emerald velvet,' nor 'velvety enamel' quite expressed it. She had not noticed that there was a mist shutting in and making brilliant the half-darkness of the room at breakfast-time, only feeling that for some reason it was a good day. 'It's fog—there's a sort of fog,' she said, glowing. The fog made the room with the strange brilliant brown light on the table, on the horsehair chairs, on the shabby length of brown and yellow oilcloth running out to the bay of the low window, seem to be rushing through space, alone. It was quite safe, going on its journey—towards some great good.

The back door, just across the little basement hall, scrooped inwards across the oilcloth, jingling its little bell, and was banged to. The flounter-*crack* of a raincloak smartly shaken out was followed by a gentle scrabbling in a shoe-box,—the earliest girl, peaceful and calm, a wonderful sort of girl, coming into the empty basement quietly getting off her things, with all the rabble of the school coming along the roads, behind. The jingling door was pushed open again just as her slippered feet ran upstairs. 'Khoo—what a filthy day!' said a vibrating hard mature voice. Miriam glanced at her time-table, history—dictation—geography—sums—writing—and shrank to her utmost air of preoccupation lest either of the elder girls should look in.

Sounds increased in the little hall, loud abrupt voices, short rallying laughs, the stubbing and stamping of feet on the oil-cloth. At the expected rattling of the handle of her own door she crouched over her book. The door opened and was quietly closed again. A small figure flung itself forward. Miriam was clutched by harsh serge-clad arms. As she moved, startled, firm cracked lips were pressed against her cheek-bone. 'Good morning, Burra,' she said, turning to put an arm round the child. She caught a glimpse of broad cheeks bulging firmly against a dark bush of short hair. Large, fierce, blood-shot eyes glared close to her own. 'Hoo—*angel*.' The little gasping body stiffened against her shoulder, pinning down her arm. The crimson face tried to reach her breast. 'Have you changed your boots,' said Miriam coldly. 'Hoo—*hoo*.' The short hard fingers hurt her. 'Go and get them off at once.' Head down Burra rushed at the door, colliding with the in-coming figure of a neat little girl dressed in velvet-trimmed red merino, with a rose and white face and short gentle gold hair. She put a little pile of books on the table and stood still near to Miriam, with her hands behind her. They both looked down the room out of the window, with quiet unsmiling faces. 'What have you been doing since Friday, Gertie?' Miriam said presently. 'We went for a walk,' said Gertie in a neat liquid little voice, dimpling and faintly raising her eyebrows.

The eight little girls who made up the upper class of the junior school stood in a close row as near as possible to Miriam's chair at the head of the table. They were silent and fresh and eagerly crowded, waiting for her to begin. She kept them silent for a few moments for the pleasure of having them there with her. She knew that Miss Perne, sitting in the window space with the youngest class drawn up in a half-circle for their Scripture lesson, was an approving presence, keeping her own little class at a level of quiet question and answer that made a background rather than a disturbance for the adventure of the elder girls. 'Not too close together,' said Miriam at last, gathering herself with a deep breath; 'throw back your shoulders and stand straight. Don't lump down on your heels. Let your weight come on the ball of your feet. Are you all all right? Don't poke your heads forward.' As the girls eagerly manœuvred themselves, willingly carrying out her instructions even to turning their heads to face the opposite wall, she caught most of the eyes in turn smiling their eager affectionate conspiracy and, restraining her desire to get up then and there and clasp the little figures one by one, began the lesson. Four of the girls, two square-built Quakeresses with straight brown frocks, deep slow voices and dreamy eyes, a white-faced, tawny-haired, thin child with an eager stammer, and a brilliant little Jewess knew the 'principal facts and dates' of the reign of Edward I by rote backwards and forwards in response to any form of question. Burra hung her head and knew nothing. Beadie Featherwell, dreadfully tall, a head taller, with her twelve years, than the tallest child in the lower school, knew no more than Burra, and stood staring at the wall and biting her lips. A stout child with open mouth and snoring breath answered with perfect exactitude from the book, but her answers bore no relationship to the questions, and Gertie could only pipe replies if the questions were so put as to contain part of the answer. The white-faced girl was beginning to gnaw her fingers by the time the questioning was at an end.

'Well now, what is the difficulty,' said Miriam, 'of getting hold of the events of this queer little reign?' Everybody laughed and was silent again at once because Miriam's voice went on, trying to interest both herself and the successful girls in inventing ways of remembering all the things that had to be 'hooked on to the word Edward.' In less than ten minutes even the stout snoring girl could repeat the reign successfully, and for the remainder of their time they talked aimlessly.

The children stood at ease, saying whatever occurred to them, even the snoring girl secured from ridicule by Miriam's consideration of whatever was offered. Their adventure took them away from their subject into what Miriam knew 'clever' people would call 'side issues.' 'Nothing is a side issue,' she told herself passionately with her eyes on the green glare beyond the window. The breaking up of Miss Perne's class left the whole of the lower school on her hands for the rest of the morning.

By half-past twelve she was sitting alone and exhausted with aching throat at her place at the head of the table.

'Koo, *isn't* it a filthy day!' Polly Allen, a short heavy girl with a sallow pitted face, thin ill-nourished hair and kind swiftly moving grey eyes, marched in out of the dark hall with flapping bootlaces. In the bay she sat down and began to lace up her boots. The laces flicked carelessly upon the linoleum as she threaded, profaning the little sanctuary of the window space. 'Oh me bones, me poor old bones,' she muttered. 'Eunice!' her hard mature voice vibrated through the room. 'Eunice Dupont!'

'What's the jolly row?' said a slow voice at the door. 'Wot's the bally shindy, beloved?'

'Like a really beautiful Cheshire cat,' Miriam repeated to herself, propped studiously on her elbows, shrinking, and hoping that if she did not look round, Eunice's carved brown curls, her gleaming, slithering opaque oval eyes and her short upper lip, the strange evil carriage of her head, the wicked lines of her figure, would be withdrawn. 'Cheshire, Cheshire,' she scolded inwardly, feeling the pain in her throat increase.

'Nothing. Wait for me. That's all. Oh, my lungs, bones *and* et ceteras. It's old age, I suppose, Uncle William.'

'Well, hurry your old age up, that's all. I'm ready.'

'Well, don't go away, you funny cuckoo, you can wait, can't you?'

A party of girls straggled in one by one and drifted towards Polly in the window space.

'It's the parties I look forward to.'

'Oh, look at her tie!'

'My tie? Six-three at Crisp's.'

The sounds of Polly's bootlacing came to an end. She sat holding a court. 'Doesn't look forward to parties? She must be a funny cuckoo!'

'Dancing's divine,' said a smooth deep smiling voice. 'Reversing. Khoo! with a fella. Khooo!'

'You surprise me, Edie. You do indeed. Hoh. Shocking.'

'Shocking? Why? What do you mean, Poll?'

'Nothing. Nothing. Riang doo too.'

'*I* don't think dancing's shocking. How can it be? You're barmy, my son.'

'Ever heard of Lottie Collins?'

'Ssh. Don't be silly.'

'I don't see what Lottie Collins has got to do with it. My mother thinks dancing's all right. That's good enough for me.'

'Well—I'm not your mother.'

'Nor any one else's.'

'Khoo, *Mabel*.'

'Who wants to be any one's mother?'

'Not me. Ug. Beastly little brats.'

'Oh shut *up*. Oh you *do* make me tired.'

'Kids are jolly. A1. I hope I have lots.'

Surprised into amazement, Miriam looked up to consult the face of Jessie Wheeler, the last speaker—a tall flat-figured girl with a strong squarish pale face, hollow cheeks, and firm colourless lips. Was it being a Baptist that made her have such an extraordinary idea? Miriam's eyes sought refuge from the defiant beam of her sea-blue eyes in the shimmering cloud of her hair. The strangest hair in the school; negroid in its intensity of fuzziness, but saved by its fine mesh.

'Don't you adore kiddies, Miss Henderson?'

'I think they're rather nice,' said Miriam quickly, and returned to her book.

'I should jolly well think they were,' said Jessie fervently.

'Hope your husband'll think so too, my dear,' said Polly, getting up.

'Oh, of course, I should only have them if the fellow wanted me to.'

'You haven't got a fella yet, madam.'

'Of course not, cuckoo. But I shall.'

'Plenty of time to think about that.'

'Hoo. Fancy never having a fellow. I should go off my nut.'

When they had all disappeared, Miriam opened the windows. There was still someone moving about in the hall and, as she stood in the instreaming current of damp air looking wearily at the concrete, a girl came into the room. 'Can I come in a minute?' she said, advancing to the window. 'I want to speak to you,' she pursued when she reached the bay. She stood at Miriam's side and looked out of the window. Half-turning, Miriam had recognized Grace Broom, one of the elder first-class girls who attended only for a few subjects. She was a dark short-necked girl with thick shoulders; a receding mouth and boldly drawn nose and chin gave her a look of shrewd elderliness. The heavy mass of hair above the broad sweep of her forehead, her heavy frame and leisurely walk added to this appearance. She wore a high-waisted black serge pinafore dress with black crape vest and sleeves.

'Do you mind me speaking to you?' she said in a hot voice. Her black-fringed brown eyes were fixed on the garden railings where people passed by and Miriam never looked.

'No,' said Miriam shyly.

'You know why we're in mourning?'

Miriam stood silent with beating heart, trying to cope with the increasing invasion.

'Our father's dead.'

Hurriedly Miriam noted the superstitious tone in the voice. . . . This is a family that revels in plumes and hearses. She glanced at the stiff rather full crape sleeve nearest to her and sought about in her mind for help as she said with a blush, 'Oh, I see.'

'We've just moved.'

'Oh yes, I see,' said Miriam, glancing fearfully at the heavy scroll of profile and finding it expressive and confused.

'We've got a house about a quarter as big as where we used to live.'

Miriam found it impossible to respond to this confession and still tried desperately to sweep away the sense of the figure so solidly planted at her side.

'I 've asked our aunt it we can ask you to come to tea with us.'

'Thank you very much,' said Miriam in one word.

'When could you come?'

'Oh, I 'm afraid I couldn't come. It would be impossible.

'Oh no. You must come. I shall ask Aunt Lucy to write to Miss Perne.'

'I really couldn't come. I shouldn't be able to ask you back.'

'That doesn't matter,' panted the relentless voice. 'I 've wanted to speak to you ever since you came.'

When next Miriam saw the black-robed Brooms and their aunt file past the transept where were the Wordsworth House sittings, she felt that to visit them might perhaps not be the ordeal she had not dared to picture. It would be strange. Those three heavy black-dressed women. Their small new house. She imagined them sitting at tea in a little room. Why was Grace so determined that she should sit there too? Grace had a life and a home and was real. She did not know that things were awful. Nor did Florrie Broom, nor the aunt. But yet they did not look like 'social' people. They were a little different. Not worldly. Not pious either. Nor intellectual. What could they want with her? She had soon forgotten them and the congregation assumed its normal look. As the service went on the thoughts came that came every Sunday. An old woman with a girl at her side were the only people whose faces were within Miriam's line of vision from her place at the wall end of the Wordsworth House pew. The people in front of them were not even in profile, and those behind were hidden from her by the angle of the transept wall. To her right she could just see, rising above the heads in the rows of pews in front of her, the far end of the chancel screen. The faces grouped in the transept on the opposite side of the church were a blur. The two figures sat or knelt or stood in a heavy silence. They neither sang nor prayed. Their faces remained unaltered during the whole service. To Miriam they were its most intimate part. During the sermon she rarely raised her eyes from the space they filled for her as they sat thrown into relief by the great white pillar. Their faces were turned towards the chancel. They could see its high dim roof and distant altar, the light on the altar, flowers, shining metal, embroideries, the maze of the east window, the white choir. They showed no sign of seeing these things. The old woman's heavy face with its heavy jaw-bone seemed to have been dead for years under its coffin-shaped black bonnet. Her large body was covered by a mantle of thickly-ribbed black material trimmed with braid and bugles. That bright yellow colour meant liver. Whatever she had she was dying of it. People were always dying when they looked like that. But it was a bad way to die. The real way was the way of that lady trailing about over the Heath near Roehampton, dying by inches of an internal complaint, with her face looking fragile—like the little alabaster chapel in the nursery with a candle alight inside. She was going to die, walking about alone on the Heath in the afternoons. Her family going on as usual at home; the greengrocer calling. She knew that everybody was alone and that all the fuss and noise people made all day was a pretence. . . . What to do? To be walking about with a quiet face meeting death. Nothing could be so alone as that. The pain, and struggle, and darkness. . . . That was what the old woman feared. She did not think about death. She was afraid and sullen all the time. Stunned, sitting there with her cold, common daughter. She had been common herself as a girl, but more noisy, and she had married and never thought about dying, and now she was dying and hating her cold daughter. The daughter, sitting there with her stiff slatey-blue coat and skirt, her indistinct hat tied with a thin harsh veil to her small flat head—what a home with her in it all the time! She would never laugh. Her poor-looking cheeks were yellowish, her fringe dry, without gloss. She would move her mouth, when she spoke, sideways, with a snarling curl of one-half of the upper lip, and have that resentful way of speaking that all North Londoners have, and the maddening North London accent. The old woman's voice would be deep and hollow. . . . The girl moving heavily about the house wearing boots and stiff dresses and stiff stays showing their outline through her clothes. They would be bitter to their servant and would not trust her. What was the good of their being alive . . . a house and a water-system and drains and cooking, and they would take all these things for granted and grumble and snarl . . . the gas-meter man would call there. Did men like that resent calling at houses like that? No. They'd just say, 'The ole party she sez to me.' How good they were, these men. Good and kind and cheerful. Someone ought to prevent the extravagance of keeping whole houses and fires going for women like that. They ought to be in an institution. But they never thought about that. They were satisfied with themselves. They were self-satisfied because they did not know what they were like. . . . *Why* should you have a house, and tradesmen calling?

'*Jehoiakin!*' The rush of indistinct expostulating sound coming from the pulpit was accompanied for a moment by reverberations of the one clearly bawled word. The sense of the large cold church, the great stone pillars, the long narrow windows faintly stained with yellowish green, the harsh North London congregation, stirred and seemed to settle down more securely. She saw the form of the vicar in the light grey stone pulpit standing up short and neat against the cold grey stone wall, enveloped in fine soft folds, his small puckered hands beautifully cuffed, his plump crumpled little face, his small bald head fringed with little saffron-white curls, his pink pouched busy mouth. What was it all about? Pompous, pottering, going on and on and on—in the Old Testament. The whole church was in the Old Testament. . . . *Honour* thy father and thy mother. How horribly the words would echo through the great cold church. *Why* honour thy father and thy mother? What had they done that was so honourable? Everybody was dying in cold secret fear. Christ, the son of God, was part of it all, the same family . . . vindictive. Christmas and Easter, hard white cold flowers, no real explanation. 'I came not to destroy but to fulfil.' The stagnant blood flushed in her face and tingled in her ears as the words occurred to her. Why didn't everybody die at once and stop it all?

Miss Haddie paused at the door of her room and wheeled suddenly round to face Miriam who had just reached the landing.

'You 've not seen my little corner,' she tweedled breathlessly, throwing open her door.

Miriam went in. 'Oh how nice,' she said fearfully, breathing in the freshness of a little square sun-filled muslin-draped, blue-papered room. Taking refuge at the white-skirted window, she found a narrow view of the park, greener than the one she knew. The wide yellow pathway going up through the cricket ground had shifted away to the right.

'It 's really a—a—a dressing-room from your room.'

'Oh,' said Miriam vivaciously.

'There 's a door, a—a—a door. I dare say you 've noticed.'

'Oh! *That 's* the door in our cupboard!' The dim door behind the hanging garments led to nothing but to Miss Haddie's room. She began unbuttoning her gloves.

Miss Haddie was hesitating near a cupboard, making little sounds.

'I suppose we must all make ourselves tidy now,' said Miriam.

'I thought you didn't look very happy in church this morning,' cluttered Miss Haddie rapidly.

Miriam felt heavy with anger. 'Oh,' she said clumsily, 'I had the most frightful headache.'

'Poor child. I thought ye didn't look yerself.'

The window was shut. But the room was mysteriously fresh, far away from the school. A fly was hovering about the muslin window blind with little reedy loops of song. The oboe . . . in the quintet, thought Miriam suddenly. 'I don't know,' she said, listening. The flies sang like that at home. She had heard them without knowing it. She moved in her place by the window. The fly swept up to the ceiling, wavering on a deep note like a tiny gong. . . . Hot sunny refined lawns, roses in bowls on summer-house tea-tables, refined voices far away from the Caledonian Road.

'Flies don't *buzz*,' she said passionately. 'They don't *buzz*. Why do people say they buzz?' The pain pressing behind her temples slackened. In a moment it would be only a glow.

Miss Haddie stood with bent head, her face turning from side to side, with its sour hesitating smile, her large eyes darting their strange glances about the room.

'Won't you sit down a minute? They haven't sounded the first bell yet.' Miriam sat down on the one little white-painted, cane-seated chair near the dressing-table. 'Eh—eh,' said Miss Haddie, beginning to unfasten her veil. 'She doesn't approve of general conversation,' thought Miriam. 'She's a female. Oh well, she'll have to see I'm not.'

'What gave you yer headache?'

'Oh well, I don't know. I suppose I was wondering what it was all about.'

'I don't think I quite understand ye.'

'Well, I mean—what that old gentleman was in such a state of mind about.'

'D'ye mean Mr La Trobe!'

'Yes. Why do you laugh?'

'I don't understand what ye mean.'

Miriam watched Miss Haddie's thin fingers feeling for the pins in her black toque. 'Of course not,' she thought, looking at the unveiled shrivelled cheek. . . . 'thirty-five years of being a lady.'

'Oh well,' she sighed fiercely.

'What is it ye mean, my dear?'

—'couldn't make head or tail of a thing the old dodderer said'—no 'old boy,' no—these phrases would not do for Miss Haddie.

'I couldn't agree with *anything* he said.'

Miss Haddie sat down on the edge of the little white bed burying her face in her hands and smoothing them up and down with a wiping movement.

'One can always criticize a sermon,' she said reproachfully.

'Well, why not?'

'I mean to say ye *can*,' said Miss Haddie from behind her fingers, 'but, but ye shouldn't.'

'You can't help it.'

'Oh yes, ye can. If ye listen in the right spirit,' gargled Miss Haddie hurriedly.

'Oh, it isn't only the sermon, it's the whole thing,' said Miriam crimsoning.

'Ye mustn't think about the speaker,' went on Miss Haddie in faint hurried rebuke. 'That's wrong. That sets people running from church to church. You must attend your own parish church in the right spirit, let the preacher be who—who —what he may.'

'Oh, but I think that's positively *dangerous*,' said Miriam gravely. 'It simply means leaving your mind open for whatever they choose to say. Like Rome.'

'Eh, no—o—o,' flared Miss Haddie dropping her hands, 'nonsense. Not like Rome at all.'

'But it *is*. It's giving up your conscience.'

'You're very determined,' laughed Miss Haddie bitterly.

'I'm certainly not going to give my mind up to a parson for him to do what he likes with. That's what it is. That's what they do. I've seen it again and again. I've heard people talking about sermons,' finished Miriam with vivacious intentness.

Miss Haddie sat very still with her hands once more pressed tightly against her face.

'Oh, my dear. This is a dreadful state of affairs. I'm afraid you're all wrong. That's not it at all. If you listen only for the good, the good will come to you.'

'But these men don't know. How should they? They don't agree amongst themselves.'

'Oh, my dear, that is a very wrong attitude. How long have ye felt like this?'

'Oh, all my life,' responded Miriam proudly.

'I'm very sorry, my dear.'

'Ever since I can remember. Always.'

There were ivory-backed brushes on the dressing-table.

Miriam stared at them and let her eyes wander on to a framed picture of an agonized thorn-crowned head.

'Were you—have ye—eh—have ye been confirmed?'

'Oh yes.'

'Did ye discuss any of your difficulties with yer vicar?'

'Not I. I knew his mind too well. Had heard him preach for years. He would have run round my questions. He wasn't capable of answering them. For instance, supposing I had asked him what I 've *always* wanted to know. How can people, ordinary people, be expected to be like Christ, as they say, when they think Christ was supernatural? Of course, if He was supernatural, it was easy enough for Him to be as He was; if He was not supernatural, then there 's nothing in the whole thing.'

'My *dear* child! I 'm dreadfully sorry ye feel like that. I 'd no idea ye felt like that, poor child. I knew ye weren't quite happy always; I mean I 've thought ye weren't quite happy in yer mind sometimes, but I 'd no idea—eh, eh, have ye ever consulted anybody—anybody able to give ye advice?'

'There you are. That 's exactly the whole thing! *Who* can one consult? There isn't anybody. The people who are qualified are the people who have the thing called faith, which means that they beg the whole question from the beginning.'

'Eh—dear—me—Miriam—child!'

'Well, I 'm made that way. How can I help it if faith seems to me just an abnormal condition of the mind with fanaticism at one end and agnosticism at the other?'

'My dear, ye believe in God?'

'Well, you see, I see things like this. On one side a prime cause with a certain object unknown to me, bringing humanity into being; on the other side humanity, all more or less miserable, never having been consulted as to whether they wanted to come to life. If that is belief, a South Sea Islander could have it. But good people, people with faith, want me to believe that one day God sent a saviour to rescue the world from sin and that the world can never be grateful enough and must become as Christ. Well. If God made people he is responsible and ought to save them.'

'What do yer parents think about yer ideas?'

'They don't know.'

'Ye 've never mentioned yer trouble to them?'

'I did ask pater once when we were coming home from the *Stabat Mater* that question I 've told you about.'

'What did he say?'

'He couldn't answer. We were just by the gate. He said he thought it was a remarkably reasonable dilemma. He laughed.'

'And ye 've never had any discussion of these things with him?'

'No.'

'Ye 're an independent young woman,' said Miss Haddie.

Miriam looked up. Miss Haddie was sitting on the edge of her bed. A faint pink flush on her cheeks made her eyes look almost blue. She was no longer frowning. 'I 'm something new—a kind of different world. She is wondering. I must stick to my guns,' mused Miriam.

'I 'll not ask ye,' said Miss Haddie quietly and cheerfully, 'to expect any help from yer fellow creatures since ye 've such a poor opinion of them. But ye 're not happy. Why not go straight to the source?'

Miriam waited. For a moment the sheen on Miss Haddie's silk sleeves had distracted her by becoming as gentle and un-challenging as the light on her mother's dresses when there were other people in the room. She had feared the leaping out of some emotional appeal. But Miss Haddie had a plan. Strange secret knowledge.

'I should like to ask ye a question.'

'Yes?'

'Well, I 'll put it in this way. While ye 've watched the doings of yer fellow creatures ye 've forgotten that the truth ye 're seeking is a—a Person.'

Miriam pondered.

'That 's where ye ought to begin. And how about—what—what about—I fancy ye 've been neglecting the—the means of grace. . . . I think ye have.' Miss Haddie rose and crossed the room to a little bookshelf at the head of her bed, talking happily on. 'Upright as a dart,' commented Miriam mentally, waiting for the fulfilment of the promise of Miss Haddie's cheerfulness. Against the straight lines of the wall-paper Miss Haddie showed as swaying slightly backwards from the waist as she moved.

The first bell rang and Miriam got up to go. Miss Haddie came forward with a small volume in her hands and held it out, standing close by her and keeping her own hold on the volume. 'Ye 'll find no argument in it. Not but I think a few sound arguments would do ye good. Give it a try. Don't be stiff-necked. Just read it and see.' The smooth soft leather slipped altogether into Miriam's hands and she felt the passing contact of a cool small hand and noted a faint fine scent coming to her from Miss Haddie's person.

In her own room she found that the soft binding of the book had rounded corners and nothing on the cover but a small plain gold cross in the right-hand corner. She feasted her eyes on it as she took off her things. When the second bell rang she glanced inside the cover. 'Preparation for Holy Communion.' Hurriedly hiding it in her long drawer under a pile of linen, she ran to the door. Running back again she took it out and put it, together with her prayer-book and hymn-book, in the small top drawer.

The opportunity to use Miss Haddie's book came with Nancie's departure for a week-end visit. Beadie was in the deeps of her first sleep and the room seemed empty. The book lay open on her bed. She noted as she placed it there when she began preparing for bed that it was written by a bishop, a man she knew by name as being still alive. It struck her as extraordinary that a book should be printed and read while the author was alive, and she turned away with a feeling of shame from the idea of the bishop, still going about in his lawn sleeves and talking, while people read a book that he had written in his study. But it was very interesting to have the book to look at, because he probably knew about modern people with doubts and would not think about them as 'infidels'—'an honest agnostic has my sympathy,' he might say, and it was possible he did not believe in eternal punishment. If he did he would not have had his book printed with rounded edges and that beautiful little cross . . . *Line upon Line* and the *Pilgrim's Progress* were not meant for modern minds. Archbishop Whateley had a 'chaste and eloquent wit' and was a 'great gardener.' A witty archbishop fond of gardening was simply aggravating and silly.

Restraining her desire to hurry, Miriam completed her toilet and at last knelt down in her dressing-gown. Its pinked neck-fiill fell heavily against her face as she leant over the bed. Tucking it into her neck she clasped her outstretched hands, leaving the book within the circle of her arms. The attitude seemed a little lacking in respect for the beautifully printed gilt-edged pages. Flattening her entwined hands between herself and the edge of the bed, she read very slowly that just as for worldly communion men cleanse and deck their bodies so for attendance at the Holy Feast must there be a cleansing and decking of the spirit. She knelt upright, feeling herself very grave. The cold air of the bedroom flowed round her, carrying conviction. Then that dreadful feeling at early service, kneeling like a lump in the pew, too late to begin to be good, the exhausted moments by the altar rail—the challenging light on the shining brass rod, on the priest's ring and the golden lining of the cup, the curious bite of the wine in the throat—the sullen disappointed home-coming; all the strange failure was due to lack of preparation. She knelt for some moments, without thoughts, breathing in the cleansing air, sighing heavily at intervals. What she ought to do was clear. A certain time for preparation could be taken every night, kneeling up in bed with the gas out if Nancie were awake, and a specially long time on Saturday night. The decision took her back to her book. She read that no man can cleanse himself, but it is his part to examine his conscience and confess his sins with a prayer for cleansing grace.

The list of questions for self-examination as to sins past and present in thought, word, and deed brought back the sense of her body with its load of well-known memories. Could they be got rid of? She could cast them off, feel them sliding away like Christian's Burden. But was that all? Was it being reconciled with your brother to throw off ill-feeling without letting him know and telling him you were sorry for unkind deeds and words? Those you met would find out the change; but all the others—those you had offended from your youth up —all your family? Write to them. A sense of a checking of the tide that had seemed to flow through her finger-tips came with this suggestion, and Miriam knelt heavily on the hard floor, feeling the weight of her well-known body. The wall-paper attracted her attention and the honeycomb pattern of the thick fringed white counterpane. She shut the little book and rose from her knees. Moving quickly about the room, she turned at random to her washhand basin and vigorously re-washed her hands in its soapy water. The Englishman, she reflected as she wasted the soap, puts a dirty shirt on a clean body, and the Frenchman a clean shirt on a dirty body.

CHAPTER V

MIRIAM felt very proud of tall Miss Perne when she met her in the hall at the beginning of her second term. Miss Perne had kissed her and held one of her hands in two small welcoming ones, talking in a gleeful voice. 'Well, my dear,' she said at the end of a little pause, 'you 'll have a clear evening. The gels do not return until to-morrow, so you 'll be able to unpack and settle yerself in comfortably. Come and sit with us when ye 've done. We 'll have supper in the sitting-room. M' yes.' Smiling and laughing she turned eagerly away. 'Of course, Miss Perne,' said Miriam in a loud wavering voice, arresting her, 'I enjoyed my holidays; but I want to tell you how glad I am to be back here.'

'Yes, yes,' said Miss Perne hilariously, 'we 're all glad.'

There was a little break in her voice, and Miriam saw that she would have once more taken her in her arms.

'I like being here,' she said hoarsely, looking down, and supported herself by putting two trembling fingers on the hall table. She was holding back from the gnawing of the despair that had made her sick with pain when she heard once more the jingle-jingle, plock-plock of the North London trams. This strong feeling of pride in Miss Perne was beating it down. 'I 'm very glad, my dear,' responded Miss Perne in a quivering, gleeful falsetto. 'If you can't have what you like you must like what you have,' said Miriam over and over to herself as she went with heavy feet up the four flights of stairs.

A candle was already burning in the empty bedroom. 'I 'm back. I 'm back. It 's all over,' she gasped as she shut the door. 'And a jolly good thing too. This is my place. I can keep myself here and cost nothing and not interfere with anybody. It 's just as if I 'd never been away. It 'll always be like that now. Short holidays, gone in a minute, and then the long term. Getting out of touch with everything, things happening, knowing nothing about them, going home like a visitor, and people talking to you about things that are only theirs now, and not wanting to hear about yours . . . not about the little real everyday things that give you an idea of anything, but only the startling things that are not important. You have to think of them, though, to make people interested—awful, awful, awful; really only putting people further away afterwards, when you 've told the thing and their interest dies down and you can't think of anything else to say. "Miss Perne's hair is *perfectly* black—as black as coal, and she 's the eldest, just *fancy*." Then everybody looks up. "My room 's downstairs, the room where I teach, is in the basement. Directly breakfast is over——"

'"Basement? What a pity! Basement rooms are awfully bad," and by the time you have stopped them exclaiming and are just going to begin, you see that they are fidgeting and thinking about something else. . . . Eve had listened a little; because she wanted to tell everything about her own place and had agreed that nobody really wanted to hear the details. . . . The landscapes from the windows of the big country house, all like pictures by Leader, the stables and laundry, a "laundry-maid" who was sixty-five, the eldest pupil with seven muslin dresses in the summer, and being scolded because she swelled out after two helpings of meat and two of pie and cream, and the youngest almost square in her little covert coat, and with a square face and large blue eyes, and the puppies who went out in a boat at Weston-super-Mare and were sea-sick. . . . Eve did not seem to mind the family being common. Eve was changing. "They are so jolly and strong. They enjoy life. They 're like other people." . . . "D' you think that 's jolly? Would you like to be like that—like other people?" "Rather. I mean to be." "Do you?" "Of course it can't be done all at once. But it 's good for me to be there. It 's awfully jolly to be in a house with no worry about money and plenty of jolly food. Mrs Green is so strong and clever. She can do anything. She 's good for me, she keeps me going." "Would you like to be like her?" "Of course. They 're all so jolly—even when they 're old. Her sister 's forty and she 's still pretty; not given up hope a bit." "*Eve!*"'

Eve had listened; but not agreed about the teaching, about making the girls see how easy it was to get hold of the things and then letting them talk about other things. 'I see how you do it, and I see why the girls obey you, of course.' Funny. Eve thought it was hard and inhuman. That's what she really thought.

Two newly-purchased lengths of spotted net veiling were lying at the top of her lightly packed trunk partly folded in uncrumpled tissue paper. She took the crisp dye-scented net very gently into her hands, getting, sitting alone on the floor by her trunk, the full satisfaction that had failed her in the shop with Harriett's surprise at her sudden desire flowing over the counter and infecting the charm of baskets full of cheap stockings and common bright-bordered handkerchiefs, some of which had borders so narrow and faint as really hardly to show when they were scrumpled up. 'Veiling, moddom? Yes, moddom,' the assistant had retorted when she had asked for a veil. 'Wot on *earth* fower?' . . . Without answering Harriett she had bought two. There was no need to have bought two. One could go back in the trunk as a store. They would be the beginning of gradually getting a 'suitable outfit,' 'things convenient for you.' She got up to put a veil in the little top drawer very carefully; trying it across her face first. It almost obliterated her features in the dim candle-light. It would be the greatest comfort on winter walks, warm and like a rampart. 'You've no idea how warm it keeps you,' she could say if anybody said anything. She arranged her clothes very slowly and exactly in her half of the chest of drawers. 'My appointments ought to be an influence in the room— until all my things are perfectly refined I shan't be able to influence the girls as I ought. I must begin it from now. At the end of the term I shall be stronger. From strength to strength.' She wished she could go to bed at once and prepare for to-morrow lying alone in the dark with the trams going up and down outside as they would do night by night for the rest of her life.

The nine o'clock post brought a letter from Harriett. Miriam carried it upstairs after supper. Placing it unopened on a chair by the head of her bed under the gas-bracket she tried to put away the warm dizzy feeling it brought her in an elaborate toilet that included the placing in readiness of every-thing she would need for the morning. When all was complete she was filled with a peace that promised to remain indefinitely as long as everything she had to do should be carried out with unhurried exactitude. It could be made to become the atmosphere of her life. It would come nearer and nearer and she would live more and more richly into it until she had grown like those women who were called blessed. . . . She looked about her. The plain room gave her encouragement. It became the scene of adventure. She tip-toed about it in her night-gown. All the world would come to her there. Flora knew. Flora was the same, sweeping the floors and going to bed in an ugly room with two other servants; but she was in it alone sometimes and knew. . . .

'One verse to-night will be enough.' Opening her Bible at random she read, 'And not only so, but we glory in tribulations also: knowing that tribulation worketh patience.' Eagerly closing the volume she knelt down smiling. 'Oh do let tribu-lation work patience in me,' she murmured, blushing, and got up staring gladly at the wall behind her bed. Shaking her pillow lengthwise against the ironwork head of the bed, she established herself with the bed-clothes neatly arranged, sitting up to read Harriett's letter before turning out the gas:

'Toosday morning—You 've not gone yet, old tooral-ooral, but I 'm writing this because I know you 'll feel blue this evening, to tell you not to. Becos, it 's *no* time to Easter and becos here 's a great piece of news. The last of the Neville Subscription Dances comes in the Easter holidays and *you 're to come*. D' ye *'ear*, Liza? Gerald says if you can't stump up he 's going to get you a ticket, and anyhow you 've got to come. You 'll enjoy it just as much as you did the first and probably more, because most of the same people will be there. So Goodni'. Mind the lamp-post, Harry. P.S.—Heaps of love, old silly. You 're just the same. It 's no bally good pre-tending you 're not.'

Miriam felt her heart writhe in her breast. 'Get thee

behind me, Harry,' she said, pushing the letter under the pillow and kneeling up to turn out the gas. When she lay down again her mind was rushing on by itself. . . .

Harry doesn't realize a bit how short holidays are. Easter—nothing. Just one dance and never seeing the people again. I was right just now. I was on the right track then. I must get back to that. It's no good giving way right or left; I must make a beginning of my own life. . . . I wish I had been called 'Patience' and had thin features. . . . Adam Street, Adelphi. . . . 'Now do you want to be dancing out there with one of those young fellows, my dear girl—No? That's a very good thing for me. I'm an old buffer who can't manage more than every other dance or so. But if you do me the honour of sitting here while those young barbarians romp their Lancers? . . . Ah, this is excellent—I want you to talk to me. You needn't mind me. Hey? What? I've known that young would-be brother-in-law of yours for many years and this evening I've been watching your face. Do you mind that, dear girl, that I've watched your face? In all homage. I'm a staunch worshipper of womanhood. I've seen rough life as well as suave. I'm an old gold-digger—Ustralia took many years of my life; but it never robbed me of my homage for women. . . .

'That's a mystery to me. How you've allowed your young sister to overhaul you. Perhaps you have a Corydon hidden away somewhere—or don't think favourably of the bonds of matrimony? Is that it?

'You are not one to be easily happy. But that is no reason why you should say you pity any one undertaking to pass through life at your side. Don't let your thoughts and ideas allow you to miss happiness. Women are made to find and dispense happiness. Even intense women like yourself. But you won't find it an easy matter to discover your mate.

'Have you ever thought of committing your ideas to paper? There's a book called *The Confessions of a Woman*. It had a great sale and its composition occupied the authoress for only six weeks. You could write in your holidays.

'Think over what I 've told you, my dear, dear girl. And don't forget old Bob Greville's address. You 're eighteen. He 's only eight; eight Adam Street. The old Adam. Waiting to hear from the new Eve—whenever she 's unhappy.'

He would be there again, old flatterer, with his steely blue eyes and that strong little Dr Conelly—Conelly who held you like a vice and swung you round and kept putting you back from him to say things. 'If only you knew the refreshment it is to dance with a girl who can talk sense and doesn't *giggle*. . . . Yes yes yes, women are *physically* incapable of keeping a secret. . . . Meredith, he 's the man. He understands woman as no other writer——' And the little dark man—De Vigne— who danced like a snake. . . . Tired? Divinely drowsy? That 's what I like. Don't talk. Let yourself go. Little snail, Harriett called him. And that giant, Conelly's friend, whirling you round the room like a gust, with his eyes fixed far away in the distance and dropping you with the chaperones at the end of the dance. If *he* had suddenly said 'Let yourself go' . . . He too would have become a snail. God has made life ugly.

Dear Mr Greville, dear *Bob*. Do you know anything about a writer called Meredith? If you have one of his books I should like to read it. No. Dear Bob, I 'm simply wretched. I want to talk to you.

Footsteps sounded on the stairs—the servants, coming up-stairs to bed. No dancing for them. Work, caps, and aprons. And those *strange* remote rooms upstairs to sleep in that nobody ever saw. Probably Miss Perne went up occasionally to look at them and see that they were all right; clean and tidy. . . . They had to go up every night, carrying little jugs of water and making no noise on the stairs, and come down every morning. They were the servants—and there would never be any dancing. Nobody thought about them. . . . They could not get away from each other, and cook. . . .

To be a general servant would be very hard work. Perhaps impossible. But there would be two rooms, the kitchen at the bottom of the house, and a bedroom at the top, your own. It would not matter what the family was like. You would look after them, like children, and be alone to read and sleep. . . . Toothache. Cheap dentists; a red lamp; 'painless extractions' . . . having to go there before nine in the morning, and be alone in a cold room, the dentist doing what he thought best and coming back to your work crying with pain, your head wrapped up in a black shawl. Hospitals; being quite helpless and grateful for wrong treatment; coming back to work, ill. Sinks and slops . . . quinsey, all alone . . . growths . . . consumption.

Go to sleep. It would be better to think in the morning. But then this clear first impression would be gone and school would begin and go on from hour to hour through the term, mornings and afternoons and evenings, dragging you along further and further and changing you, months and months and years until it was too late to get back and there was nothing ahead.

The thing to remember, to keep in mind all the time, was to save money—not to spend a single penny that could be saved, to be determined about that so that when the temptation came you could just hang on until it was past.

No fun in the holidays, no money spent on flowers and gloves and blouses. Keeping stiff and sensible all the time. The family of the two little Quaker girls had a home library, with lists, an inventory, lending each other their books and talking about them, and albums of pressed leaves and flowers with the Latin names, and went on wearing the same plain clothes. . . . You had to be a certain sort of person to do that.

It would spoil the holidays to be like that at home. Every penny must be spent, if only on things for other people. Not spending would bring a nice strong secret feeling, and a horrid expression into one's eyes.

The only way was to give up your family and stay at your work, like Flora, and have a box of half-crowns in your drawer. . . . Spend and always be afraid of 'rainy days'—or save and never enjoy life at all.

But going out now and again in the holidays, feeling stiff and governessy and just beginning to learn to be oneself again when it was time to go back and not enjoying life . . . your money was spent and people forgot you, and you forgot them and went back to your convent to begin again.

Save, save. Sooner or later saving must begin. Why not at once. Harry, it's no good. I'm old already. I've got to be one of those who have to give everything up.

I wonder if Flora is asleep?

That's settled. Go to sleep. Get thee behind me. Sleep . . . the dark cool room. Air; we breathe it in and it keeps us alive. Everybody has air. Manna. As much as you want, full measure, pressed down and running over. . . . Wonderful. There is somebody giving things, whatever goes . . . something left. . . . Somebody seeing that things are not quite unbearable, . . . but the pain, the pain all the time, mysterious black pain. . . .

Into thy hands I commit my spirit. *In manus* something. . . . You understand if nobody else does. But *why* must I be one of the ones to give everything up? *Why* do you make me suffer so?

CHAPTER VI

PIECEMEAL statements in her letter home brought Miriam now and again a momentary sense of developing activities, but she did not recognize the completeness of the change in her position at the school until half-way through her second term she found herself talking to the new pupil teacher. She had heard apathetically of her existence during supper-table conversations with the Misses Perne at the beginning of the term. She was an Irish girl of sixteen, one of a large family living on the outskirts of Dublin, and would be a boarder, attending the first class for English and earning pocket money by helping with the lower school. As the weeks went on and Miriam grew accustomed to hearing her name—Julia Doyle—she began to associate it with an idea of charm that brought her a sinking of heart. She knew her position in the esteem of the Pernes was secure. But this new young teacher would work strange miracles with the girls. She would do it quite easily and unconsciously. The girls would be easy with her and would laugh and one would have to hear them.

However, when at last her arrival was near and the three ladies discussed the difficulty of having her met, Miriam plied them until they reluctantly gave her permission to go, taking a workman's train that would bring her to Euston station at seven o'clock in the morning.

At the end of an hour spent pacing the half-dark platform exhausted with cold and excitement and the monotonously reiterated effort to imagine the arrival of one of Mrs Hungerford's heroines from a train journey, Miriam, whose costume had been described in a letter to the girl's mother, was startled, wandering amidst the vociferous passengers at the luggage end of the newly arrived train, by a liquid colourless intimate voice at her elbow. 'I think I'll be right to say how d' you do.'

She turned and saw a slender girl in a middle-aged toque and

an ill-cut old-fashioned coat and skirt. What were they to say
to each other, two dowdy struggling women both in the same
box? She must get her to Banbury Park as quickly as possible.
It was dreadful that they should be seen together there on the
platform in their rag-bag clothes. At any rate they must not
talk. 'Oh, I'm very pleased to see you. I'm glad you've
come. I suppose the train must have been late,' she said
eagerly.

'Ah, we'll be late I dare venture. Haven't an idea of the
hour.'

'Oh, yes,' said Miriam emphatically, 'I'm sure the train's
late.'

'Where'll we find a core?'

'What?'

'We'll need a core for the luggage.'

'Oh yes, a cab. We must get a cab. We'd better find a
porter.'

'Ah, I've a man here seeking out my things.'

Inside the cab Julia's face shone chalky white, and Miriam
found that her eyes looked like Weymouth Bay—the sea in
general, on days when clouds keep sweeping across the sun.
When she laughed she had dimples and the thick white rims
of her eyelids looked like piping cord round her eyes. But she
was not pretty. There were lines in her cheeks as well as
dimples, and there was something apologetic in her little gusty
laugh. She laughed a good deal as they started off, saying
things, little quiet remarks that Miriam could not understand
and did not seem to be answers to her efforts to make conversation. Perhaps she was not going the right way to make
her talk. Perhaps she had not said any of the things she
thought she had said.

She cleared her throat and looked out of the window thinking
over a possible opening.

'I've never been so glad over anything in my life as hearing
you're one of the teachers,' said Julia presently.

'The Pernes call me by my name, so I suppose you will, too,
as you're a teacher,' said Miriam headlong.

'That's awfully sweet of you,' replied Julia laughing and

blushing a clear deep rose. 'It makes any one feel at home. I'll be looking out till I hear it.'

'It's——' Miriam laughed. 'Isn't it funny that people don't like saying their own names.'

'I wish you'd tell me about your teaching. I'm sure you're awf'ly clever.'

Miriam gave her a list of the subjects she taught in the lower school.

'You know all there is to know.'

'Oh well, and then I take top girls now for German and the second class for French reading, and two arithmetic classes in the upper school, and a "shell" of two very stupid girls to help with their College of Preceptors.'

'You're frightening me.'

Miriam looked out of the cab window, hardly hearing Julia's next remark. The drab brick walls of King's Cross station were coming towards them. When they had got themselves and Julia's luggage out of the cab and into the train for Banbury Park, she was still pondering uneasily over her own dislike of appearing as a successful teacher. This stranger saw her only as a teacher. That was what she had become. If she was really a teacher now, just that in life, it meant that she must decide at once whether she really meant to teach always. Every one now would think of her as a teacher; as someone who was never going to do anything else, when really she had not even begun to think about doing any of the things that professional teachers had to do. She was not qualifying herself for examinations in her spare time, as her predecessor had done. Supposing she did. This girl Julia would certainly expect her to be doing so. What then? If she were to work very hard and also develop her character, when she was fifty she would be like Miss Cramp; good enough to be a special visiting teacher, giving just a few lectures a week at several schools, talking in a sad voice, feeling ill and sad, having a yellow face and faded hair and not enough saved to live on when she was too old to work. Prospect, said the noisy train. That was it, there was no prospect in it. There was no prospect in teaching. What was there a prospect in, going along in this North London train with this girl who took her at her word?

She turned eagerly to Julia who was saying something and laughing unconcernedly as she said it. 'If you'd like to know what it is I've come over for, I'll tell you at once. I've come over to learn Chopang's Funeral March. It's all I think about. When I can play Chopang's Funeral March, I'll not call the Queen me aunt.'

'Well, my dear child, I'm sure I wish I could arrange your life for ye,' said Miss Haddie that evening. She was sitting on the edge of the schoolroom table, having come in at ten o'clock to turn out the gas and found Miriam sitting unoccupied. The room was cold and close with the long-burning gas, and Miriam had turned upon her with a scornful half laugh when she had playfully exclaimed at finding her there so late. Miss Haddie was obviously still a little excited. She had presided at schoolroom tea and Julia had filled the room with Dublin— the bay, the streets, the jarveys and their outside cars, her journey, the channel boat, her surprise at England.

'Eh, what's the matter, Miriam, my dear?' For some time Miriam had parried her questions, fiercely demanding that her mood should be understood without a clue. Presently they had slid into an irritated discussion of the respective values of sleep before and sleep after midnight, in the midst of which Miriam had said savagely, 'I wish to goodness I knew what to do about things.'

Miss Haddie's kindly desire gave her no relief. What did she mean but the hopelessness of imagining that anybody could do anything about anything. Nobody could ever understand what any one else really wanted. Only some people were fortunate. Miss Haddie was one of the fortunate ones. She had her share in the school and many wealthy relatives and the very best kind of good clothes and a good deal of strange old-fashioned jewellery. And whatever happened there was money and her sisters and relatives to look after her without feeling it a burden because of the expense. And there she sat at the table looking at what she thought she could see in another person's life.

'If only one knew in the least what one *ought* to do,' said Miriam crossly.

Miss Haddie began speaking in a halting murmur, and Miriam rushed on with flaming face. 'I suppose I shall have to go on teaching all my life, and I can't think how on earth I 'm going to do it. I don't see how I can work in the evenings, my eyes get so tired. If you don't get certificates there 's no prospect. And even if I did my throat is simply agonies at the end of each morning.'

'Eh! my dear child! I 'm sorry to hear that. Why have ye taken to that? Is it something fresh?'

'Oh no, my throat always used to get tired. Mother's is the same. We can't either of us talk for ten minutes without feeling it. It 's perfectly awful.'

'But, my dear, oughtn't ye to see someone—have some advice? I mean ye ought to see a doctor.'

Miriam glanced at Miss Haddie's concerned face and glanced away with a flash of hatred. 'Oh no. I s'pose I shall manage.'

'D' ye think yer wise—letting it go on?'

Miriam made no reply.

'Well now, my dear,' said Miss Haddie, getting down off the table, 'I think it 's time ye went to bed.'

'Phm,' said Mirriam impatiently, 'I suppose it is.'

Miss Haddie sat down again. 'I wish I could help ye, my dear,' she said gently.

'Oh, no one can do that,' said Miriam in a hard voice.

'Oh yes,' murmured Miss Haddie cheerfully, 'there 's One who can.'

'Oh yes,' said Miriam, tugging a thread out of the fraying edge of the table cover. 'But it 's practically impossible to discover what on earth they mean you to do.'

'N—aiche, my dear,' she said in an angry guttural, 'ye 're always led.'

Miriam tugged at the thread and bit her lips.

'Why do ye suppose ye 'll go on teaching all yer life? Perhaps ye 'll marry.'

'Oh no.'

'Ye can't tell.'

'Oh, I never shall—in any case now.'

'Have ye quarrelled with him?'

'Oh, well, *him*,' said Miriam roundly, digging a pencil point between the grainings of the table-cover. 'It 's *they*, I think, goodness knows, I don't know; it 's so perfectly extraordinary.'

'You 're a very funny young lady.'

'Well, I shan't marry *now* anyhow.'

'Have ye refused somebody?'

'Oh well—there was someone—who went away—went to America—who was coming back to see me when he came back——'

'Yes, my dear?'

'Well, you see, he 's handed in his checks.'

'Eh, my dear—I don't understand,' said Miss Haddie thwarted and frowning.

'Aw,' said Miriam, jabbing the table, 'kicked the bucket.'

'My dear child, you use such strange language—I can't follow ye.'

'Oh well, you see, he went to America. It was in New York. I heard about it in January. He caught that funny illness. You know. Influenza—and died.'

'Eh, my poor dear child, I 'm very sorry for ye. Ye *do* seem to have troubles.'

'Ah well, yes, and then the queer thing is that he was really only the friend of my real friend. And it was my real friend who told me about it and gave me a message he sent me and didn't like it, of course. Naturally.'

'Well *really*, Miriam,' said Miss Haddie, blushing, with a little laugh half choked by a cough.

'Oh yes, then of course one meets people—at dances. It 's appalling.'

'I wish I understood ye, my dear.'

'Oh well, it doesn't make any difference now. I shall hardly ever meet anybody now.'

Miss Haddie pondered over the table with features that worked slightly as she made little murmuring sounds. 'Eh no. Ye needn't think that. Ye shouldn't think like that. . . . Things happen sometimes . . . just when ye least expect it.'

'Not to me.'

'Oh, things will happen to ye—never fear. . . . Now, my dear child, trot along with ye off to bed.'

Miriam braced herself against Miss Haddie's gentle shaking of her shoulders and the quiet kiss on her forehead that followed it.

The strengthening of her intimacy with Miss Haddie was the first of the many changes brought to Miriam by Julia Doyle. At the beginning of the spring term her two room mates were transferred to Julia's care. The two back rooms became a little hive of girls over which Julia seemed to preside. She handled them all easily. There was rollicking and laughter in the back bedrooms, but never any sign that the girls were 'going too far,' and their escapades were not allowed to reach across the landing. Her large front room was, Miriam realized as the term went on, being secretly and fiercely guarded by Julia.

The fabric of the days, too, had changed. All day—during the midday constitutional when she often found Julia at her side walking in her curious springy lounging way and took the walk in a comforting silence resting her weary throat, during the evenings of study and the unemployed intervals of the long Sundays—Julia seemed to come between her and the girls. She mastered them all with her speech and laughter. Miriam felt that when they were all together Julia was always in some hidden way on the alert. She never jested with Miriam but when they were alone, and rarely then. Usually she addressed her in a low tone and as if half beside herself with some over-powering emotion. It was owing, too, to Julia's presence in the school that an unexpected freedom came to Miriam every day during the hour between afternoon school and tea-time.

Persuaded by the rapid increase towards the end of the winter term of the half-feverish exhaustion visiting her at the end of each day, she had confided in her mother, who had wept at this suggestion of an attack on her health and called in the family doctor. 'More air,' he said testily, 'air and move-ment.' Miriam repeated this to Miss Perne, who at once arranged that she should be free, if she chose, to go out every afternoon between school and tea-time.

At first she went into the park every day. It was almost empty during the week at that hour. The cricket green was sparsely decked with children and their maids. A few strollers were left along the poplar avenue and round the asphalt-circled lake; but away on the further slopes usually avoided in the midday walks because the girls found them oppressive, Miriam discovered the solitary spring air. Day by day she went as if by appointment to meet it. It was the same wander-ing eloquent air she had known from the beginning of things. Whilst she walked along the little gravel pathways winding about over the clear green slopes in the flood of afternoon light, it stayed with her. The day she had just passed through was touched by it; it added a warm promise to the hours that lay ahead—tea-time, the evening's reading, the possible visit of Miss Haddie, the quiet of her solitary room, the coming of sleep.

One day she left the pathways and strayed amongst pools of shadow lying under the great trees. As she approached the giant trunks and the detail of their shape and colour grew clearer her breathing quickened. She felt her prim bearing about her like a cloak. The reality she had found was leaving her again. Looking up uneasily into the forest of leaves above her head she found them strange. She walked quickly back into the sunlight, gazing reproachfully at the trees. There they were as she had always known them; but between them and herself was her governess's veil, close drawn, holding them sternly away from her. The warm comforting communicative air was round her, but she could not recover its secret. She looked fearfully about her. To get away somewhere by her-self every day would not be enough. If that was all she could have, there would come a time when there would be nothing anywhere. For a day or two she came out and walked feverishly about in other parts of the park, resentfully questioning the empty vistas. One afternoon, far away, but coming towards her as if in answer to her question, was the figure of a man walking quickly. For a moment her heart cried out to him. If he would come straight on and, understanding, would walk into her life and she could face things knowing that he was there, the light would come back and would stay until the end— and there would be other lives, on and on. She stood transfixed, trembling. He grew more and more distinct and she saw a handbag and the outline of a bowler hat; a North London clerk hurrying home to tea. With bent head she turned away and dragged her shamed heavy limbs rapidly towards home.

Early in May came a day of steady rain. Enveloped in a rain-cloak and sheltered under her lowered umbrella she ventured down the hill towards the shops. Near the railway arch the overshadowed street began to be crowded with jostling figures. People were pouring from the city trams at the terminus and coming out of the station entrance in a steady stream. Hard intent faces, clashing umbrellas, the harsh snarling monotone of the North London voice, gave her the feeling of being an intruder. Everything seemed to wonder what she was doing down there instead of being at home in the schoolroom. A sudden angry eye above a coarse loudly talking mouth all but made her turn and go with instead of against the tide; but she pushed blindly on and through and presently found herself in a quiet street just off the station road looking into a shop window. . . . '1 lb. super cream-laid boudoir note —with envelopes—1s.' Her eyes moved about the window from packet to packet, set askew and shining with freshness. If she had not brought so much note-paper from home she could have bought some. Perhaps she could buy a packet as a Christmas present for Eve and have it in her top drawer all the time. But there was plenty of note-paper at home. She

half turned to go, and turning back fastened herself more closely
against the window, meaninglessly reading the inscription on
each packet. Standing back at last, she still lingered. A
little blue-painted tin plate sticking out from the side of the
window announced in white letters 'Carter Paterson.' Miriam
dimly wondered at the connection. Underneath it hung a
cardboard printed in ink, 'Circulating Library, 2d. weekly.'
This was still more mysterious. She timidly approached the
door and met the large pleasant eye of a man standing back in
the doorway.

'Is there a library here?' she said with beating heart.

She stood so long reading and re-reading half-familiar titles,
Cometh up as a Flower, *Not like other Girls*, *The Heir of Redcliffe*,
books that she and Harriett had read and books that she felt
were of a similar type, that tea was already on the schoolroom
table when she reached Wordsworth House with an unknown
volume by Mrs Hungerford under her arm. Hiding it upstairs, she came down to tea and sat recovering her composure
over her paper-covered *Cinq Mars*, a relic of the senior Oxford
examination now grown suddenly rich and amazing. To-day
it could not hold her. *The Madcap* was upstairs, and beyond
it an unlimited supply of twopenny volumes, and Ouida.
Red-bound volumes of Ouida on the bottom shelf had sent her
eyes quickly back to the safety of the upper rows. Through
the whole of tea-time she was quietly aware of a discussion
going on at the back of her mind as to who it was who had
told her that Ouida's books were bad; evil books. She remembered her father's voice saying that Ouida was an extremely
able woman, quite a politician. Then of course her books
were all right, for grown-up people. It must have been someone at a dance who had made her curious about them, someone
she had forgotten. In any case, whatever they were, there was
no one now to prevent her reading them if she chose. She
would read them if she chose. Write to Eve about it first.
No. Certainly not. Eve might say 'Better not, my dear.
You will regret it if you do. You won't be the same.' Eve
was different. She must not be led by Eve in any case. She
must leave off being led by Eve—or anybody. The figures

sitting round the table, bent over their books, quietly disinclined for conversation or mischief under the shrewd eye of Miss Haddie, suddenly looked exciting and mysterious. But perhaps the man in the shop would be shocked. It would be impossible to ask for them; unless she could pretend she did not know anything about them.

For the last six weeks of the summer term she sat up night after night propped against her upright pillow and bolster under the gas-jet reading her twopenny books in her silent room. Almost every night she read until two o'clock. She felt at once that she was doing wrong; that the secret novel-reading was a thing she could not confess, even to Miss Haddie. She was spending hours of the time that was meant for sleep, for restful preparation for the next day's work, in a 'vicious circle' of self-indulgence. It was sin. She had read somewhere that sin promises a satisfaction that it is unable to fulfil. But she found when the house was still and the trams had ceased jingling up and down outside that she grew steady and cool and that she rediscovered the self she had known at home, where the refuge of silence and books was always open. Perhaps that self, leaving others to do the practical things, erecting a little wall of unapproachability between herself and her family that she might be free to dream alone in corners, had always been wrong. But it was herself, the nearest most intimate self she had known. And the discovery that it was not dead, that her six months in the German school and the nine long months during which Banbury Park life had drawn a veil even over the little slices of holiday freedom, had not even touched it, brought her warm moments of reassurance. It was not perhaps a 'good' self, but it was herself, her own familiar secretly happy and rejoicing self—not dead. Her hands lying on the coverlet knew it. They were again at these moments her own old hands, holding very firmly to things that no one might touch or even approach too nearly, things, everything, the great thing that would some day communicate itself to someone through these secret hands with the strangely thrilling finger-tips. Holding them up in the gas-light she dreamed over their wisdom. They knew everything and held their secret, even from her. She eyed them, com-muned with them, passionately trusted them. They were not 'artistic' or 'clever' hands. The fingers did not 'taper' nor did the outstretched thumb curl back on itself like a frond —like Nan Babington's. They were long, the tips squarish and firmly padded, the palm square and bony and supple, and the large thumb-joint stood away from the rest of the hand like the thumb-joint of a man. The right hand was larger than the left, kindlier, friendlier, wiser. The expression of the left hand was less reassuring. It was a narrower, lighter hand, more flexible, less sensitive and more even in its touch—more smooth and manageable in playing scales. It seemed to belong to her much less than the right; but when the two were firmly interlocked they made a pleasant curious whole, the right clasping more firmly, its thumb always uppermost, its fingers separated firmly over the back of the left palm, the left hand clinging, its fingers close together against the hard knuckles of the right.

It was only when she was alone and in the intervals of quiet reading that she came into possession of her hands. With others they oppressed her by their size and their lack of feminine expressiveness. No one could fall in love with such hands. Loving her, someone might come to tolerate them. They were utterly unlike Eve's plump, white, inflexible little palms. But they were her strength. They came between her and the world of women. They would be her companions until the end. They would wither. But the bones would not change. The bones would be laid, unchanged and wise, in her grave.

She began her readings with Rosa Nouchette Carey. Read-ing her at home, after tea by the breakfast-room fireside with red curtains drawn and the wind busy outside amongst the ever-green shrubs under the window, it had seemed quite possible that life might suddenly develop into the thing the writer described. From somewhere would come an adoring man who believed in heaven and eternal life. One would grow very good; and after the excitement and interest had worn off one would go on, with firm happy lips being good and going to church and making happy matches for other girls or quietly disapproving of everybody who did not believe just in the same way and think about good girls and happy marriages and heaven; keeping such people outside. Smiling, wise and happy inside in the warm; growing older, but that did not matter because the adored man was growing older too.

Now it had all changed. The quiet house and fireside, gravity, responsibility, a greying husband, his reading profile always dear, both of them going on towards heaven, 'all tears wiped away,' tears and laughter of relief after death, still seemed desirable. But 'women.' . . . Those awful, awful women, she murmured to herself stirring in bed. I never thought of all the *awful* women there would be in such a life. I only thought of myself and the house and the garden and the man. What an escape! Good God in heaven, what an escape! Far better to be alone and suffering and miserable here in the school, alive. . . .

Then there 'll be whole heaps of books, millions of books I can't read—perhaps nearly all the books. She took one more volume of Rosa, in hope, and haunted its deeps of domesticity. 'I 've gone too far.' . . . If Rosa Nouchette Carey knew me, she 'd make me one of the bad characters who are turned out of the happy homes. I 'm some sort of bad unsimple woman. Oh, damn, damn, she sighed. I don't know. Her hands seemed to mock her, barring her way.

Then came a series of Mrs Hungerford—all the volumes she had not already read. She read them eagerly, inspirited. The gabled country houses, the sunlit twilit endless gardens, the deep orchards, the falling of dew, the mists of the summer mornings, masses of flowers in large rooms with carved oaken furniture, wide staircases with huge stained windows throwing down strange patches of light on shallow thickly carpeted stairs. These were the things she wanted; gay house-parties, people with beautiful wavering complexions and masses of shimmering hair catching the light, fragrant filmy diaphanous dresses; these were the people to whom she belonged—a year or two of life like that, dancing and singing in and out the houses and gardens; and then marriage. Living alone, sadly estranged, in the house of a husband who loved her and with whom she was in love, both of them thinking that the other had married because they had lost their way in a thunderstorm or spent the night sitting up on a mountain-top or because of a clause in a will, and then one day both finding out the truth. . . . That is what is meant by happiness . . . happiness. But these things could only happen to people with money. She would never have even the smallest share of that sort of life. She might get into it as a governess—some of Mrs Hungerford's heroines were governesses—but they had clouds of hair and were pathetically slender and appealing in their deep mourning. She read volume after volume, forgetting the titles—the single word 'Hungerford' on a cover inflamed her. Her days became an irrelevance and her evenings a dreamy sunlit indulgence. Now and again she wondered what Julia Doyle would think if she knew what she was reading and how it affected her—whether she would still watch her in the way she did as she went about her work pale and tired, whether she would go on guarding her so fiercely?

At last exasperated, tired of the mocking park, the mocking happy books, she went one day to the lower shelf, and saying very calmly, 'I think I'll take a Ouida,' drew out *Under Two Flags* with a trembling hand. The brown-eyed man seemed to take an interminable time noting the number of the book, and when at last she got into the air her limbs were heavy with sadness. That night she read until three o'clock and finished the volume the next night at the same hour, sitting upright when the last word was read, refreshed.   From that moment the red-bound volumes became the centre of her life.   She read *Moths* and *In Maremma* slowly word by word, with an increasing steadiness and certainty.   The mere sitting with the text held before her eyes gave her the feeling of being strongly confronted.   The strange currents which came whenever she was alone and at ease flowing to the tips of her fingers, seemed to flow into the book as she held it and to be met and satisfied. As soon as the door was shut and the gas alight, she would take the precious, solid trusty volume from her drawer and fling it on her bed, to have it under her eyes while she undressed.   She ceased to read her Bible and to pray.   Ouida, Ouida, she would muse with the book at last in her hands.   I want bad things—strong bad things. . . . It doesn't matter, Italy, the sky, bright hot landscapes, things happening.   I don't care what people think or say.   I am older than any one here in this house.   I am myself.

. . . If you had loved, if you loved, you could die, laughing, gasping out your life on a battlefield, fading by inches in a fever-swamp, or living on, going about seamed and old and ill.   Whatever happened to you, if you had cared, fearing nothing, neither death nor hell. God came. He would welcome and forgive you. Life, struggle, pain. Happy laughter with twisted lips—all waiting somewhere outside, beyond.   It would come.   It must be made to come.

Who was there in the world?   Ted had failed.   Ted belonged to the Rosa Nouchette Carey world.   He would marry one of those women.   Bob knew.   Bob Greville's profile was real.   Sitting on the wide stairs at the Easter Subscription Dance, his soft fine white hair standing up, the straight line of polished forehead, and fine nose and compressed lips, the sharp round chin with the three firm folds underneath it, the point of his collar cutting across them, the keen blue eyes looking straight out ahead, across Australia. The whole face listening. He had been listening to her nearly all the evening. Now and again quiet questions. She could go on talking to him whenever she liked. Go to him and go on talking, and talking, safely, being understood. Talking on and on. But he was old. Living old and alone in chambers in Adam Street—Adelphi.

One day just before the end of the summer term, Miss Perne asked Miriam to preside over the large schoolroom for the morning. The first- and second-class girls were settled there at their written examination in English history. Rounding the schoolroom door, she stood for a moment in the doorway. The sunlight poured in through the wide bay window and the roomful of quiet girls seemed like a field. Jessie Wheeler's voice broke the silence. 'It 's the Hen,' she shouted gently. 'It 's the blessed Hen! Oh, *come* on. You going to sit with us ?'

'Yes. Be quiet,' said Miriam.

'Oh, thank goodness,' groaned Jessie, supported by groans and murmurs from all over the room.

'Be quiet, girls, and get on with your papers,' said Miriam in a tone of acid detachment from the top of her tide. She sat feeling that her arms were round the entire roomful, that each girl struggling alone with the list of questions was resting against her breast. 'I 'm going away from them. I must be going away from them,' ran her thoughts regretfully. 'They can't keep me. This is the utmost. I 've won. There 'll never be anything more than this, here. It would always be the same—with different girls. Certainty. Even the sunlight paid a sort of homage to the fathomless certainty she felt. The sunlight in this little schoolroom was telling her of other sunlights, vast and unbroken, somewhere—coming, her own sunlights, when she should have wrenched herself away. It was there; she glanced up again and again to watch it breaking and splashing all over the room. It would come again, but how differently. Quite soon. She might have spared herself all her agonizing. The girls did not know where she belonged. They were holding her. But she would go away, to some huge open space. Leave them—ah, it was unkind. But she had left them already in spirit.

If they could all get up together now and sing, let their voices peal together up and up, throw all the books out of the window, they might go on together, forward into the sunshine, but they would not want to do that. Hardly any of them would want to do that. They would look at her with knowing eyes, and look at the door, and stay where they were.

The room was very close. Polly Allen and Eunice Dupont, sitting together at a little card-table in the darkest corner of the room, were whispering. With beating heart Miriam got up and went and stood before them. 'You two are talking,' she said with her eyes on the thickness of Polly's shoulders as she sat in profile to the room. Eunice, opposite her, against the wall, flashed up at her her beautiful fugitive grin as from the darkness of a wood. History, thought Miriam. What has Eunice to do with history, laws, Henry II, the English Constitution? 'You don't talk,' she said coldly, feeling as she watched her that Eunice's pretty clothes were stripped away and she were stabbing at her soft rounded body, 'at examinations. Can't you see that?' Eunice's pale face grew livid. 'First because it isn't fair and also because it disturbs other people.' You can tell all the people who cheat by their smile, she reflected on her way back. Eunice chuckled serenely two or three times. 'What have these North London girls to do with studies?' . . . There was not a single girl like Eunice at Barnes. Even the very pretty girls were . . . refined.

That afternoon Miriam spent her hour of leisure in calling on the Brooms to inquire for Grace, who had been ill the whole of the term. She found the house after some difficulty in one of the maze of little rows and crescents just off the tram-filled main road. 'She's almost perfect—almost perfection,' said Mrs Philps, the Aunt Lucy Miriam had heard of and seen in church.

They had been together in the little drawing-room talking about Grace from the moment when Miriam was shown in to Mrs Philps sitting darning a duster in a low chair by the closed conservatory door. The glazed closed door, with the little strips of window on either side giving on to a crowded conservatory, made the little room seem dark. To Miriam it seemed horribly remote. Her journey to it had been through immense distances. Threading the little sapling - planted asphalt - pavemented roadways between houses whose unbroken frontage was so near and so bare as to forbid scrutiny, she felt she had reached the centre, the home and secret of North London life. Off every tram-haunted main road, there must be a neighbourhood like this where lived the common-mouthed, harsh-speaking people who filled the pavements and shops and walked in the parks. To enter one of the little houses and speak there to its inmates would be to be finally claimed and infected by the life these people lived, the thing that made them what they were. At Wordsworth House she was held up by the presence of the Pernes and Julia Doyle. Here she was helpless and alone. When she had discovered the number she sought and, crossing the little tiled pathway separated from the pathway next door by a single iron rail, had knocked with the lacquered knocker against the glazed and leaded door, her dreams for the future faded. They would never be realized. They were just a part of the radiance that shone now from the spacious houses she had lived in in the past. The things she had felt this morning in the examination room were that, too. They had nothing to do with the future. All the space was behind. Things would grow less and less.

Admitted to the dark, narrowly-echoing tiled passage, she stated her errand and was conducted past a closed door and the opening of a narrow staircase which shot steeply, carpeted with a narrow strip of surprisingly green velvet carpeting, up towards an unlit landing, and admitted to Mrs Philps.

'Wait a minute, Vashti,' said Mrs Philps, holding Miriam's

hand as she murmured her errand. 'You'll stay tea? Well, if you're sure you can't I'll not press you. Bring the biscuits and the sherry and two white wine-glasses, Vashti. Get them now and bring them in at once. Sit down, Miss Henderson. She's little better than a step-girl. They're all the same.' Whilst she described her niece's illness, Miriam wondered over the immense bundle of little even black sausage-shaped rolls of hair which stuck out, larger than her head and smoothed to a sphere by a tightly drawn net, at the back of her skull. She was short and stout and had bright red cheeks that shone in the gloom and rather prominent large blue eyes that roamed as she talked, allowing Miriam to snatch occasional glimpses of china-filled whatnots and beaded ottomans. Presently Vashti returned clumsily with the wine, making a great bumping and rattling round about the door. 'You stupid thing, you've brought claret. Don't you know sherry when you see it? It's at the back—behind the Harvest Burgundy.' 'I shall have to go soon,' said Miriam, relieved at the sight of the red wine and longing to escape the sherry. Vashti put down the tray and stood with open mouth. Even with her very high heels she looked almost a dwarf. The room seemed less oppressive with the strange long-necked decanter and the silver biscuit box standing on a table in the curious greenish light. Mrs Philps accepted the claret and returned busily to her story, whilst Miriam sipped and glanced at a large print in a heavy black frame leaning forward low over the small white marble mantelpiece. It represented a young knight in armour kneeling at an altar with joined and pointed hands held to his lips. An angel standing in mid-air was touching his shoulder with a sword. 'Why doesn't she kiss the top of his head,' thought Miriam as she sipped her wine. The distant aisles and pillars of the church made the room seem larger than it was. 'I suppose they all look into that church when they want to get away from each other,' she mused as Mrs Philps went on with her long sentences beginning 'And Dr Newman said—' And there was a little mirror above a bulging chiffonier which was also an escape from the confined space. Looking into it, she met Mrs Philps's glowing face with the blue eyes widely staring and fixed upon her own, and heard her declare, with her bunched cherry-coloured lips, that Grace was 'almost perfection.' 'Is she?' she responded eagerly, and Mrs Philps elaborated her theme. Grace, then, with her heavy body and strange hot voice, lying somewhere upstairs in a white bed, was the most important thing in this dark little house. 'She was very near to death then,' Mrs Philps was saying tearfully, 'very near, and when she came round from her delirium, one of the first things she said to me as soon as she was strong enough to whisper, was that she was perfectly certain about there being another life.' Mrs Philps's voice faded and she sat with trembling lips and eyes downcast. '*Did* she!' Miriam almost shouted, half-rising from her seat and turning from contemplating Mrs Philps in the mirror to look her full in the face. The dim green light streaming in from the conservatory seemed like a tide that made everything in the room rock slightly. A touch would sweep it all away and heaven would be there all round them. 'Did she,' whispered Miriam in a faint voice that shook her chest. '"Aunt," she said,' went on Mrs Philps steadily, as the room grew firm round Miriam and the breath she drew seemed like an early morning breath, '"I want to say something quickly," she said, "in case I die. It's that I know—for a positive fact, there is another life."'

'What a perfectly stupendous thing,' said Miriam. 'It's so important.'

'I was much impressed. Of course, I knew she was nearly perfect. But we've not been in the habit of talking about religion. I asked her if she would like to see the vicar. "Oh no," she said, "there's no need. He knows." I doubt if he knows as much as she does. But I didn't make a point of it.'

'Oh, but it's simply wonderful. It's much more important than anything a vicar could say. It's their business to say those things.'

'I don't know about that. But she was so weak that I didn't press it.'

'But it's so important. What a wonderful thing to have in your family. Did she say anything more?'

'She hasn't returned to the subject again. She 's very weak.'

Wild clutching thoughts shook at Miriam. If only Grace could suddenly appear in her nightgown, to be questioned. Or if she herself could stay on there creeping humbly about in this little house, watering the conservatory and darning dusters, being a relative of the Brooms, devoting herself to Grace, waiting on her, hearing all she had to say. What did it matter that the Brooms wore heavy mourning and gloated over funerals, if Grace upstairs in her room had really seen the white light away in the distance far away beyond the noise of the world?

CHAPTER VII

HARRIETT'S ringed fingers had finished dipping and drying the blue and white tea-service. She sat for a moment staring ahead downstream. Sitting opposite her, Gerald watched her face with a half smile. Miriam waited, sitting at her side. It was the first moment of silence since she had come home at midday. From the willow-curtained island against which they were moored came little crepitations and flittings. Ahead of them the river blazed gold and blue, hedged by high spacious trees. '*Come*-to-tea, *come*-to-tea, hurryup-dear,' said a bird suddenly from the island thicket.

'D' you know what bird that is, Gerald?' asked Miriam.

'Not from Adam,' breathed Gerald, swaying on his seat with a little laugh. 'It's a bird. That's all I know.'

'We'd better unmoor, silly,' muttered Harriett briskly, gathering up the tiller ropes.

'Right, *la reine*.'

'Look here, let me do something this time, pull or something.'

'You sit still, my dear.'

'But I should simply love to.'

'You shall pull downstream if you like later on when the bally sun's down. My advice to you now is to go and lounge in the bow.'

'Oh yes, Mim, you try it. Lie right down. It's simply heavenly.'

The boat glided deliciously away upstream as Miriam, relinquishing her vision of Harriett sitting very upright in the stern in her white drill dress, and Gerald's lawn-shirted back and long lean arms grasping the sculls, lay back on the bow cushions with her feet comfortably outstretched under the

293

unoccupied seat in front of her.　Six hours ago, shaking hands
with a roomful of noisy home-going girls—and now nothing
to do but float dreamily in through the gateway of her six
weeks' holiday.　The dust of the school was still upon her; the
skin of her face felt strained and tired, her hands were tired and
hot, her blouse dim with a week of school wear, and her black
skirt oppressed her with its invisible burden of grime.　But
she was staring up at a clean blue sky fringed with tree-tops.
She stretched herself out more luxuriously upon her cushions.
The river smoothly moving and lapping underneath the
boat was like a cradle.　The soft fingers of the air caressed
her temples and moved along the outlines of her face and
neck.　Forty-two days . . . like this.　To-morrow she
would wake up a new person . . . sing, and shout with
Harriett.　She closed her eyes.　The gently lifting water
seemed to come nearer; the invading air closed in on her.
She gave herself ecstatically to its touch; the muscles of her
tired face relaxed and she believed that she could sleep; cry
or sleep.

It was Gerald who had worked this miraculous first day for
her.　'Boating' hitherto had meant large made-up parties of
tennis-club people, a fixed day, uneasy anticipations as to the
weather, the carrying of hampers of provisions and crockery,
spirit lamps and kettles, clumsy hired randans, or little fleets
of stupidly competing canoes, lack of space, heavy loads to pull,
the need for ceaseless chaff, the irritating triumphs of clever
'knowing' girls in smart clothes, the Pooles, or really beautiful
people, like Nan Babington and her cousin.　Everything they
said sounding wonderful and seeming to improve the scenery;
the jokes of the men, even Ted always joked all the time, the
misery of large picnic teas on the grass, and in the end
great weariness and disappointment, the beauty of the river
and the trees only appearing the next day or perhaps long
afterwards.

This boat was Gerald's own private boat, a double-sculling
skiff, slender and gold-brown, beautifully fitted and with a
locker containing everything that was wanted for picnicking.
They had arranged their expedition at lunch-time, trained to

Richmond, bought fruit and cakes and got the boat's water-keg filled by one of Redknap's men. Gerald knew how to do things properly. He had always been accustomed to things like this boat. He would not care to have anything just anyhow. 'Let's do the thing decently, *la reine*.' He would keep on saying that at intervals until Harriett had learned too. How he had changed her since Easter when their engagement had been openly allowed. The clothes he had bought for her, especially this plain drill dress with its neat little coat. The long black tie fastened with the plain heavy cable broach pinned in lengthwise half-way down the ends of the tie, which reached almost to her black belt. That was Gerald. Her shoes, the number of pairs of light, expensive, beautifully made shoes. Her bearing, the change in her voice, a sort of roundness about her old Harryish hardness. But she was the same Harry, the Harry she had seen for the first time snorting with anger over Mr Marth's sentimental singing at the Assembly Rooms concert. 'My hat, wasn't *la reine* fuming!' He would forgive her all her ignorance. It was her triumph. What an extraordinary time Harry would have. Gerald was well-off. He had a private income behind his Canadian Pacific salary. His grandfather had been a diplomatist, living abroad nearly all the time, and his wealthy father and wealthy mother with a large fortune of her own had lived in a large house in Chelsea, giving dinner parties and going to the opera until nearly all the capital had gone, both dying just in time to leave enough to bring Gerald in a small income when he left Haileybury. And the wonderful thing was that Gerald liked mouching about and giggling. He liked looking for hours in shop windows and strolling on the Heath. Liked bulls-eyes.

Everything had disappeared into a soft blackness; only on the water a faint light was left. It came and went; sometimes there was nothing but darkness and the soft air. The small paper lantern swinging at the bow made a little blot of light that was invisible from the stroke seat. The boat went swiftly and easily. Miriam felt she could go on pulling for hours at the top of her strength through the night. Leaning forward, breasting the featureless darkness, sweeping the sculls back at the full reach of her arms, leaning back and pressing her whole weight upwards from the foot-board against the pull of the water, her body became an outstretched elastic system of muscles, rhythmically working against the smooth dragging resistance of the dark water. Her sleeves were rolled up, her collar-stud unfastened, her cool drowsy lids drooped over her cool eyes. Each time she leaned backwards against her stroke, pressing the foot-board, the weight of her body dragged at a line of soreness where the sculls pressed her hands, and with the final fling of the water from the sculls a little stinging pain ran along the pads of her palms. To-morrow there would be a row of happy blisters.

'You needn't put more beef into it than you like, Mirry.' Gerald's voice came so quietly out of the darkness that it scarcely disturbed Miriam's ecstasy. She relaxed her swing and, letting the sculls skim and dip in short easy strokes, sat glowing.

'I 've never pulled a boat alone before.'

'It shows you can't be a blue-stocking, thank the Lord,' laughed Gerald.

'Who said I was?'

'I 've always understood you were a very wise lady, my dear.'

'Nobody told you she was a blue-stocking, silly. You invented the word yourself.'

'I ? I invented blue-stocking?'

'Yes, you, silly. It 's like your saying women never date their letters just because your cousins don't.'

'*Vive la reine*. The Lord deliver me from blue-stockings, anyhow.'

'All *right*, what *about* it? There aren't any here!'

'You 're not one, anyhow.'

The next day, after tea, Eve arrived home from Gloucestershire.

Miriam had spent the day with Harriett. After breakfast, bounding silently up and downstairs, they visited each room in turn, chased each other about the echoing rooms and passages of the basement and all over the garden. Miriam listened speechlessly to the sound of Harriett's heels soft on the stair carpet, ringing on the stone floors of the basement, and the swish of her skirts as she flew over the lawn, following, surrounding, responding to Miriam's wild tour of the garden. Miriam listened and watched, her eyes and ears eagerly gathering and hoarding visions. It could not go on. Presently some claim would be made on Harriett and she would be alone. But when they had had their fill of silently rushing about, Harriett piloted her into the drawing-room and hastily began opening the piano. A pile of duets lay on the lid. She had evidently gathered them there in readiness. Wandering about the room, shifting the familiar ornaments, flinging herself into chair after chair, Miriam watched her and saw that her strange quiet little snub face was lit and shapely. Harriett, grown-up, serene and well-dressed and going to be married in the spring, was transported by this new coming together. When they had played the last of the duets that they knew well, Harriett fumbled at the pages of a bound volume of operas in obvious uncertainty. At any moment Miriam might get up and go off and bring their sitting together on the long cretonne-covered duet stool to an end. 'Come on,' roared Miriam gently, 'let's try this'; and they attacked the difficult pages. Miriam counted the metre, whispered it, intoned and sang it, carrying Harriett along with shouts 'go *on*, go *on*' when they had lost each other. They smashed their way along, by turns playing only a single note here and there into the framework of Miriam's desperate counting, or banging out cheerful masses of discordant tones, anything, to go on driving their way together through the pages while the sunlight streamed half seen into the conservatory and the flower-filled garden crowded up against the windows, anything to come out triumphantly together at the end and to stop satisfied, the sounds of the house, so long secretly known to them both, low now around them, heard by them together, punctuating their joy. The gong sounded for lunch. 'Eve,'

Miriam remembered suddenly, 'Eve 's coming this afternoon.' The thought set gladness thundering through her as she rose from the piano. 'Let 's go for a walk after lunch,' she muttered. Harriett blushed.

'Awri,' she responded tenderly.

The mile of gently rising roadway leading to the Heath was overarched by huge trees. Shadowy orchards, and the silent sunlit outlying meadows and park land of a large estate, streamed gently by them beyond the trees as they strode along through the cool leaf-scented air. They strode speechlessly ahead as if on a pilgrimage, keeping step. Harriett's stylish costume had a strange unreal look in the great lane, under the towering trees. Miriam wondered if she found the lane dull and was taking it so boldly because they were walking along it together. Obviously she did not want to talk. She walked along swiftly and erect, looking eagerly ahead as if, when they reached the top and the Heath and the windmill, they would find something they were both looking for. Miriam felt she could glance about unnoticed and looked freely, as she had done so many hundreds of times before, at the light on the distant meadows and lying along the patches of undergrowth between the trunks of the trees. They challenged and questioned her silently as they had always done, and she them, in a sort of passionate sulkiness. They gave no answer, but the scents in the cool tree-filled air went on all the time offering steady assurance, and presently as walking became an un-conscious rhythm and the question of talk or no talk had definitely decided itself, the challenge of the light was silenced and the shaded roadway led on to paradise. Was there any one anywhere who saw it as she did? Any one who, looking along the alley of white road, would want to sit down in the roadway or kneel amongst the undergrowth and shout and shout? In the north of London there were all those harsh street voices infesting the trees and the parks. No! they did not exist. There was no North London. Let them die. They did not know the meaning of far-reaching meadows, park - land, deer, the great silent Heath, the silent shoulders of the windmill against the far-off softness of the sky. Harsh streetiness . . . cunning, knowing . . . do you *blame* me? . . . or charwomanishness, smarmy; churchy or chapelish sentimentality. Sentimentality. No need to think about them.

'Never the time and the place and the loved one all together.' Who said that? Was it true? Dreadful. It couldn't be. So many people had seen moonlit gardens, together. All the happy people who were sure of each other. 'I say, Harriett,' she said at the top of her voice, bringing Harriett curvetting in the road just in front of her. 'I say, listen.' Harriett ran up the remaining strips of road and out on to the Heath. It was ablaze with sunlight—as the river and the trees had been yesterday—a whole day of light and Eve on her way home, almost home. Harriett must not know how she was rushing to meet Eve; with what tingling fingers. 'Oh, what I was going to ask you was whether you can see the moonlight like it is when you are alone, when Gerald is there.'

'. . . It isn't the same as when you are alone,' said Harriett quietly, arranging the cuff of her glove.

'Do explain what you mean.'

'Well, it's different.'

'I see. You don't know how.'

'It's quite different.'

'Does Gerald like the moonlight?'

'*I* dunno. I never asked him.'

'Fancy the Roehampton people living up here all the time.'

'There's their old washing going flip-flap over there.'

Harriett was finding out that she was back in the house with Eve.

'Let's rush to the windmill. Let's sing.'

'Come on; only we can't rush and sing too.'

'Yes we can, come on.' Running up over hillocks and stumbling through sandy gorse-grown hollows they sang a hunting song, Miriam leading with the short galloping phrases, Harriett's thinner voice dropping in, broken and uncertain, with a strange brave sadness in it that went to Miriam's heart.

'Eve, you look exactly like Dudley's gracious lady in these things. Don't you feel like it?' Eve stopped near the landing window and stood in her light green canvas dress with its pale green silk sleeves shedding herself over Miriam from under her rose-trimmed white chip hat. Miriam was carrying her light coat and all the small litter of her journey. 'Go on up,' she said, 'I want to talk,' and Eve hurried on, Miriam stumblingly following her, holding herself in, eyes and ears wide for the sight and sound of the slender figure flitting upstairs through the twilight. The twilight wavered and seemed to ebb and flow, suggesting silent dawn and full midday, and the house rang with a soundless music.

'It was Mrs Wallace who suggested my *wearing* all my best things for the journey,' panted Eve; 'they don't get crushed with packing and they needn't get dirty if you 're careful.'

'You look exactly like Dudley's gracious lady. You know you do. You know it perfectly well.'

'They do seem jolly, now I 'm back. They don't seem anything down there. Just ordinary, with everybody in much grander things.'

'How do you mean, grander? What sort of things?'

'Oh, all sorts of lovely white dresses.'

'It is extraordinary about all those white dresses,' said Miriam emphatically, pushing her way after Eve into Sarah's bedroom. 'Can I come in? I 'm coming in. Sarah says it 's because men like them, and she gets simply sick of girls in white and cream dresses all over the place in the summer, and it 's a perfect relief to see any one in a colour in the sun. They have red sunshades sometimes, but Sarah says that 's not enough; you want people in colours. I wonder if there 's anything in it?'

'Of course there is,' said Sarah, releasing the last strap of Eve's trunk.

'They 'd *all* put on coloured things if it weren't for that.'

'Men tell them.'

'Do they?'

'The engaged men tell them—or brothers.'

'I can't think how you get to know these things, sober Sally.'

'Oh, you can tell.'

'Well, then, *why* do men like silly white and cream dresses, pasty, whitewashy clothes altogether?'

'It 's something they want; it looks different to them.'

'Sarah knows all sorts of things,'· said Miriam excitedly, watching the confusion of the room from the windows. 'She says she knows why the Pooles look down and smirk; their dimples and the line of their chins; that men admire them looking down like that. *Isn't* it frightful. Disgusting. And men don't seem to see through them.'

'It 's those kind of girls get on best.'

Miriam sighed.

'Oh well, don't let 's think about them. Not to-night, anyhow,' cooed Eve.

'Sarah says there are much more awful reasons. I can't think how she finds them all out. Sober Sally. I know she 's right. It 's too utterly sickening somehow, for words,'

'Mim.'

'*Pooh*—barooo, *baroooo*.'

'Mim——'

'Damnation.'

'Mimmy-*Jim*.'

'I said DAMNATION.'

'Oh, it 's all right. What have we got to do with horrid, knowing people.'

'Well, they 're there, all the time. You can't get away from them. They 're all over the place. Either the knowing ones or the simpering ones. It 's all the same in the end'

Eve quietly began to unpack. 'Oh well,' she smiled, 'we 're

all different when there are men about to when we 're by ourselves. We all make eyes, in a way.'

'Eve! What a perfectly beastly thing to say.'

'It isn't, my dear,' said Eve pensively. 'You should see yourself; *you* do.'

'Sally, *do* I ?'

'Of course you do,' giggled Eve quietly, 'as much as anybody.'

'Then I 'm the most crawling thing on the face of the earth,' thought Miriam, turning silently to the tree-tops looming softly just outside the window; 'and the worst of it is I only know it at moments now and again.' The tree-tops, serene with some happy secret, cast her off, and left her standing with groping crisping fingers unable to lift the misery that pressed upon her heart. 'God, what a filthy world! God what a filthy world!' she muttered. 'Every one hemmed and hemmed and hemmed into it.' Harriett came in and stepped up on to the high canopied bed. ''Ullo,' she said in general, setting herself tailor-fashion in the middle of the bed so that the bright twilight fell full upon her head and the breast and shoulders of her light silk-sleeved dress. Humming shreds of a violin obbligato, Eve rustled out layer after layer of paper-swathed garments, to be gathered up by Sarah moving solidly about between the wardrobe and the chest of drawers in her rather heavy boots. There would not be any talk. But silently the room filled and overflowed. Turning at last from her window, Miriam glanced at her sisters and let her thoughts drop into the flowing tide. Harry, sitting there sharp and upright in the fading light, coming in to them with her future life streaming out behind her, spreading and shining and rippling, herself the radiant point of that wonderful life, actually there, neatly enthroned amongst them, one of them, drawing them all with her out towards its easy security; Eve, happy with her wardrobe of dainty things, going fearlessly forward to some unseen fate, not troubling about it. Sarah's strange clean clear channel of wisdom. Where would it lead ? It would always drive straight through everything.

All these things meant that the mere simple awfulness of

things at home had changed. These three girls she had known so long as fellow-prisoners, and who still bore at moments in their eyes, their movements, the marks of the terrors and uncertainties amongst which they had all grown up, were going on, out into life, scored and scarred, but alive and changeable, able to become quite new. Memories of strange crises and the ageing, deadening shifts they had invented to tide them over humiliating situations were here crowded in the room together with them all. But these memories were no longer, as they had so often been, the principal thing in the room whenever they were all gathered silently together. If Eve and Harriett had got away from the past and now had happy eyes and mouths. . . . Sarah's solid quiet cheerfulness, now grown so large and free that it seemed even when she was stillest to knock your mind about like something in a harlequinade. . . . Why had they not all known in the past that they would change? Why had they been so oppressed whenever they stopped to think?

Those American girls in *Little Women* and *Good Wives* made fun out of everything. But they had never had to face real horrors and hide them from everybody; mewed up.

When it was nearly dark Sarah lit the gas. Harriett had gone downstairs. Miriam lowered the Venetian blinds, shutting out the summer. To-morrow it would be there again, waiting for them when they woke in the morning. In her own and Harriett's room the daylight would be streaming in through the Madras muslin curtains, everything in the room very silent and distinct; nothing to be heard but the little flutterings of birds under the eaves. You could listen to it for ever if you kept perfectly still. When you drew back the curtains the huge day would be standing outside clear with gold and blue and dense with trees and flowers.

Sarah's face was uneasy. She seemed to avoid meeting any one's eyes. Presently she faced them, sitting on a low rocking chair with her tightly clasped hands stretched out beyond her knees. She glanced fearfully from one to the other and bit her lips. 'What now,' thought Miriam. The anticipated holidays disappeared. Of course. She might have known they would. For a moment she felt sick, naked, and weak. Then she braced herself to meet the shock. I must sit tight, I must sit tight and not show anything. Eve's probably praying. Oh, make haste, Sally, and get it over.

'What's the matter, Sally?' said Eve in a low voice.

'Oh, Eve and Mim, I'm awfully sorry.'

'You'd better tell us at once,' said Eve, crimsoning.

'Haven't you noticed anything?'

Miriam looked at Sarah's homely prosperous face. It couldn't be anything. It was a nightmare. She waited, pinching her wrist.

'What is it, Sally?' breathed Eve, tapping her green-clad knee. Clothes and furniture and pictures . . . houses full of things and people talking in the houses and having meals and pretending, talking, and smiling and pretending.

'It's mother.'

'What on earth do you mean, Sarah?' said Miriam angrily.

'She's ill. Bennett took her to a specialist. There's got to be—she's got to have an operation.'

Miriam drew up the blind with a noisy rattle, smiling as Eve frowned impatiently at the noise. Driving the heavy sash up as far as it would go, she leaned her head against the open frame. The garden did not seem to be there. The tepid night air was like a wall, a black wall. For a moment a splintered red light, like the light that comes from a violent blow on the forehead, flashed along it. Sarah and Eve were talking in strange voices, interrupting each other. It would be a relief to do something, faint or something selfish. But she must hear what they were saying; listen to both the voices cutting through the air of the hot room. Propped weak-limbed against the window, open-mouthed for air she forced herself to hear, pressing her cold hands closely together. The gaslight that had seemed so bright, hardly seemed to light the room at all.

Everything looked small, even Grannie's old Chippendale bed-
stead and the double-fronted wardrobe. The girls were little
monkey ghosts babbling together beside Eve's open trunk.
Did they see that it was exactly like a grave?

The sun shone through the apple-trees, making the small
half-ripe apples look as though they were coated with enamel.

It was quite clear that if they did go away together, the four
of them, she, Eve, Gerald, and Harriett to Brighton or somewhere, they would be able to forget. You could tell that from
the strange quiet easy tone of Harriett's and Gerald's voices.
There would be the Aquarium. She supposed they would go
to the Aquarium, with its strange underground smell of stagnant sea air, and stare into the depths of those strange green
tanks and watch the fish flashing about like shadows or skimming by near the front of the tank with the light full on their
softly tinted scales. Harriett sat steadily at her side on the
overturned seed-box, middle-aged and responsible, quietly
discussing the details of the plan with Gerald, cross-legged at
their feet on the grass plot. They had not said anything about
the reasons for going; but of course Gerald must know all that.
He knew everything now, all about the money troubles, all the
awful things, and it seemed to make no difference to him.
He made light of it. It was humiliating to think that he had
come just as things had reached their worst, the house going
to be sold, pater and mother and Sarah going into lodgings in
September, and the maddening helpless worry about mother
and all the money for that. And yet it was a good thing
he had known them all in the old house and seen them there,
even pretending to be prosperous. But the house and garden
was nothing to him. Just a house and garden. Harriett's
house and garden, and he was going to take Harriett away.
The house and garden did not matter.

She glanced at the sunlit fruit trees, the thickets of the
familiar kitchen garden, the rising grass bank at the near end
of the distant lawn, the eloquent back of the large red house.

He could not see all the things there were there, all the long years, or know what it was to have that cut away and nothing ahead but Brighton Aquarium with Harriett and Eve, and then the school again, and disgraceful lodgings in some strange place; no friends and every one looking down on them. She met his eyes and they both smiled.

'Keep her perfectly quiet for the next few weeks, that's the idea, and when it's all over she'll be better than she's ever been in her life.'

'D' you think so?'

'I don't think, I know she will; people always are. I've known scores of people have operations. It's nothing nowadays. Ask Bennett.'

'Does he think she'll be better?'

'Of course.'

'Did he say so?'

'Of *course* he did.'

'Well, I s'pose we'd really better go.'

'Of course, we're going.'

'I'm going to look for a place in a family, after next term. I shall give notice when I get back. You get more money in a family, Eve says, and home life, and if you haven't a home they're only too glad to have you there in the holidays too.'

'You take my advice, my dear girl. Don't go into a family. Eve'll find it out before she's much older.'

'I must have more money.'

'Mirry's so silly. She insists on paying her share of Brighton. Isn't she an owl?'

'Oh well, of course, if she's going to make a point of spending her cash when she needn't, she'd better find a more paying job. That's certain sure.'

CHAPTER VIII

'You know I'm funny. I never talk to young ladies.'

Miriam looked leisurely at the man walking at her side along the grass-covered cliff; his well-knit frame, his well-cut blue serge, the trimness of collar and tie, his faintly blunted regular features, clean ruddy skin and clear expressionless German blue eyes. Altogether he was rather like a German, with his red and white and gold and blue colouring and his small military moustache. She could imagine him snapping abruptly in a booming chest voice: 'Mit Frauen spreche ich über*haupt* nicht.' But he spoke slowly and languidly, he was an Englishman and somehow looked like a man who was accustomed to refined society. It was true he never spoke at the boarding-house meals, excepting an occasional word with his friend, and he had been obliged to join their Sunday walk because his friend was so determined to come. Still he was not awkward or clumsy, either at table or now. Only absolutely quiet, and then saying such a startling rather rude thing quite suddenly. One could stare at him to discover the reason of his funny speech, because evidently he was quite common, not a bounder but quite a common young man, speaking of women as 'young ladies.' Then how on earth did he manage to look distinguished? Oppressed and ill at ease, she turned away to the far-reaching green levels and listened to the sea tumbling heavily far below against the cliffs. Away ahead, Eve and her little companion walking jauntily along, his tight dust-coloured curls exposed to the full sunlight, his cane swinging round as he talked and laughed, seemed to be turning inland towards the downs. They had seen Ovingdean in the distance, stupid Ovingdean that everybody had talked about at breakfast, and were finding the way. How utterly silly. They did not see how utterly silly it was to make up your mind to 'go to Ovingdean' and then go to Ovingdean. How utterly silly everybody and everything was.

Eve looked very straight and slim and was walking happily, bending her head a little as she always did when she was listening. Their backs looked happy. And here she was, forced to walk with this nice-looking, strange solid heavyish man and his cold insulting remark; almost the only thing he had said since they had been alone together. It had been rather nice walking along the top of the cliff side by side saying nothing. They walked exactly in step and his blunted features looked quite at ease; and she had gone easily along disposing of him with a gentle feeling of proprietorship, and had watched the gentle swing and movement of the landscape as they swung along. It seemed secure and painless and was gradually growing beautiful, and then suddenly she felt that he must have his thoughts, men were always thinking, and would be expecting her to be animated and entertaining. Lumpishly she had begun about the dullness of the beach and promenade on Sundays and the need to find something to do between dinner and tea—lies. All conversation was a lie. And somehow she had led him to his funny German remark.

'How do you mean?' she said at last, anxiously. It was very rude intruding upon him like that. He had spoken quite simply. She ought to have laughed and changed the conversation. But it was no laughing matter. He did not know what he was saying or how horribly it hurt. A worldly girl would chaff and make fun of him. It was detestable to make fun of men; just a way of flirting. But Sarah said that being rude to men or talking seriously to them was flirting just as much. Not true. Not true. And yet it was true, she did want to feel happy walking along with this man, have some sort of good understanding with him, him as a man with her as a woman. Was that flirting? If so she was just a more solemn underhand flirt than the others, that was all. She felt very sad. Anyhow she had asked her question now. She looked at his profile. Perhaps he would put her off in some way. Then she would walk slower and slower, until Harriett and Gerald caught them up, and come home walking four in a row, taking Harriett's arm. His face had remained quite expressionless.

'Well,' he said at length in his slow well-modulated tone,

'I always take care to get out of the way when there are any young ladies about.'

'When do you mean?' *I* didn't ask you to come, *I* don't want to talk to you, you food-loving, pipe-loving, comfort-loving beast, she thought. But it would be impossible to finish the holiday and go back to the school with this strange statement uninvestigated.

'Well, when my sisters have young ladies in in the evening I always get out of the way.'

Ah, thought Miriam, you are one of those men who flirt with servants and shop-girls . . . perhaps those awful women. . . . Either she must catch Eve up or wait for Harriett . . . not be alone any longer with this man.

'I see. You simply run away from them,' she said scornfully; 'go out for a walk or something.' A small Brixton sitting-room full of Brixton girls—Gerald said that Brixton was something too chronic for words, just like Clapham, and there was that joke about the man who said he would not go to heaven even if he had the chance, because of the strong Clapham contingent that would be there—after all . . .

'I go and sit in my room.'

'Oh,' said Miriam brokenly, 'in the winter? Without a fire?'

Mr Parrow laughed. 'I don't mind about that. I wrap myself up and get a book.'

'What sort of book?'

'I've got a few books of my own; and there's generally something worth reading in *Tit-Bits*.'

How did he manage to look so refined and cultured? Those girls were quite good enough for him, probably too good. But he would go on despising them and one of them would marry him and give him beef-steak puddings. And here he was walking by the sea in the sunlight, confessing his suspicions and fears and going back to Brixton.

'You'll have to marry one of those young ladies one day,' she said abruptly.

'That's out of the question, even if I was a marrying man.'

'Nonsense,' said Miriam, as they turned down the little

pathway leading towards the village. Poor man, how cruel to encourage him to take up with one of those giggling, dressy girls.

'D' you mean to say you 've been never specially interested in anybody?'

'Yes. I never have.'

Ovingdean had to be faced. They were going to look at Ovingdean and then walk back to the boarding-house to tea. Now that she knew all about his home-life, she would not be able to meet his eyes across the table. Two tired elm-trees stood one on either side of the road at the entrance to the village. Here they all gathered and then went forward in a strolling party.

When they turned at last to walk home and fell again into couples as before, Miriam searched her empty mind for something to say about the dim cool musty church, the strange silent deeps of it there amongst the great green downs, the waiting chairs, the cold empty pulpit and the little cold font, and the sunlit front of the old Grange where King Charles had taken refuge. Mr Parrow would know she was speaking insincerely if she said anything about these things. There was a long, long walk ahead. For some time they walked in silence. 'D' you know anything about architecture?' she said at last angrily . . . cruel, silly question. Of course he didn't. But men she walked with ought to know about architecture and be able to tell her things.

'No. That 's a subject I don't know anything about.'

'D' you like churches?'

'I don't know that I 've ever thought about it.'

'Then you probably don't.'

'Oh, well, I don't know about that. I don't see any objection to them.'

'Then you 're probably an atheist.'

'I don't know, I 'm sure.'

'Do you go to church?'

'I can't say I do in the usual way, unless I 'm on a holiday.'

'Perhaps you go for walks instead?'

'Well, I generally stay in bed and have a rest.'

That dreadful room with the dreadful man hiding in it and staying in bed and reading *Tit-Bits* on bright Sunday mornings.

How heavily they were treading on the orange and yellow faces of the Tom Thumbs scattered over the short green grass.

'How much do you think people could marry on?' said Mr Parrow suddenly in a thin voice.

'Oh well, that depends on who they are.'

'I suppose it does do that.'

'And where they are going to live.'

'D'you think any one could marry on a hundred and fifty?'

'Of course,' said Miriam emphatically, mentally shivering over the vision of a tiresome determined cheerful woman with a thin pinched reddish nose, an everlasting grey hat and a faded ulster going on year after year; two or three common children she would never be able to educate, with horribly over-developed characters. It was rather less than the rent of their house. 'Of course, everything would depend on the woman,' she said wisely. After all a hundred and fifty, with no doubt and anxiety about it was a very wonderful thing to have. Probably everybody was wasteful, buying the wrong things and silly things, ornaments and brooches and serviette rings; . . . and not thinking things out and not putting things down in books and not really enjoying managing the hundred and fifty, and always wanting more. It ought to be quite jolly being thoroughly common and living in a small way and having common neighbours doing the same.

'But you think if a man could find a young lady who could agree about prices it would be possible.'

'Of course it would.'

The houses on the eastern ridges of Brighton came into sight in the distance and stood blazing in the sunlight. There was a high half brokendown piece of fencing at the edge of the cliff to their left a little ahead of them, splintered and sunlit.

'How much a week is a hundred and fifty a year?'

'Three pound.'

They gravitated towards the fence and stood vaguely near it looking out across the unruffled glare of the open sea. Why had she always thought that the bright blue and gold ripples seen from the beach and the promenade on jolly weekdays was the best of the sea? It was much more lovely up there, the great expanse in its quiet Sunday loneliness. You could see and think about far-off things instead of just dreaming on the drowsy hot sands, seeing nothing but the rippling stripes of bright blue and bright gold. She put her elbows on the upper bar. Mr Parrow did the same and they stood gazing out across the open sea—Mr Parrow was probably wondering how long they were going to stand silently there and thinking about his tea . . . of course; let him stand—until Eve's voice sounded near them in a dimpling laugh. They walked home in a row, Eve and Mr Green in the centre, asking riddles one against the other. Every time Miriam spoke Mr Parrow laughed or made some little responsive sound.

When Mr Green and Mr Parrow went back to London at the end of the week, Eve and Miriam saw them off at the station. The four went off boldly together down the flight of white stone steps and made their way up into the town.

'Good-bye,' called Miss Meldrum affectionately from the doorway. 'I shall send both of you a copy of the photograph.'

'It's most generous of Miss Meldrum to go to all that expense to give us a pleasant memento,' said Mr Green in his small ringing voice as they all swung out into the clean bare roadway. Miriam felt as if they were a bit of the photograph walking up the hill, and went freely and confidently along with a sense of being steered and guided by Miss Meldrum. Why had she had the group taken—so odd and bold of her, having the photographer waiting in the garden for them before they had finished breakfast, and then laughing and talking and pushing them all about as if they were her dearest friends. It was whilst they were all out in the garden together, hanging about and being arranged, with the photographer's voice like

the voice of a ventriloquist, knocking them coldly about, that
Gerald and Mr Green had arranged about the evening at the
Crystal Palace on the last day of Miriam's holiday. Miriam
had held back from the group, feeling nervous about her hair,
there had been no time to go to their rooms, and had forced
Eve to do the same. Harriett, with a cheerful shiny face, was
sitting on the grass with Gerald in a line with the traveller
from Robinson and Cleaver's, and his thin-voiced sheeny-
haired mocking fiancée. They all looked very small and bald.
The fiancée kept clearing her throat and rearranging her smart
feet and rattling her bangles. The traveller's heavy waxed
moustache was crooked, and his slippery blue eyes looked like
the eyes of an old man. Next to him were two newly arrived
restively sneering young men, one on either side of the saintly-
faced florist's assistant from Wigmore Street, who sat in an
easy pose with her skirt draping gracefully over her feet and her
long white chin propped on her hands. She looked reproachfully about amongst the laughing and talking and seemed to
feel that they were all in church.

Miss Meldrum and Miss Stringer, the two bald Scotch
chemists who went out every evening to look for a comet, the
pale frowning girl from Plaistow with her mad-eyed cousin
whose grey curls bunched in a cherry-coloured velvet band
seemed to say 'death—death' to Miriam more dreadfully out
here amongst the greenery than when she suddenly caught sight
of them at table, sat disconnectedly in chairs behind the squat-
ters on the grass. At the last moment she and Eve were obliged
to fall in at the back of the group with Mr Green and Mr
Parrow, and now the four of them were walking in a row up
the staring white hill, with the evening at the Crystal Palace
ahead of them in far-away London. It was quite right. They
were being like 'other people.' People met and made friends
and arranged to meet again. And then things happened. It
was quite right and ordinary and safe and warm. Of course
Eve and Mr Green must meet again. He was evidently quite
determined that they should. That was what was carrying
them all so confidently up the hill. Perhaps he would in the
end turn into another Gerald. When they turned off into the

unfamiliar Brighton streets, Eve and Mr Green went on ahead. Walking quickly in step along the narrow pavement amongst the unconcerned Brighton townspeople, they looked so small and pitiful.

The brilliant sunlight showed up all the shabbiness of Mr Green's London suit. He looked even smaller than he did in his holiday tweed. Miriam wanted to call to them and stop them, stop Eve's bright figure and her mop of thickly-twisted brown hair and ask her what she was dreaming of, leave the two men there and go back, go out away alone with Eve down to the edge of the sea. She hesitated in her walking, not daring even to glance at her companion who was trudging along with bent head, carrying his large brown leather bag. The street was crowded and she manœuvred so that every one they met should pass between them. Perhaps they would be able to reach the station without being obliged to speak to each other. Parrow. It was either quite a nice name or pitiful; like a child trying to say sparrow. Did he know that to other people it was a strange, important sort of name, rounded like the padding in the shoulders of his coat and his blunted features?

Nobody knew him at all well. Not a single person in the world. If he were run over and killed on the way to the station, nobody would ever have known anything about him. . . . People did die like that . . . probably most people; in a minute, alone and unknown; too late to speak.

Something was coming slowly down the middle of the road-way from amongst the confusion of the distant traffic; an ele-phant—a large grey elephant. Firmly, delicately, undisturbed by the noise of the street, the huge crimson gold-braided howdah it carried on its back, and the strange, coloured things coming along behind it, the thickening of people on the pave-ment and the suddenly increased noise of the town, it came stepping. It was wonderful. 'Wise and beautiful! Wise and beautiful!' cried a voice far away in Miriam's brain. It's a circus said another voice within her. . . . He doesn't know he's in a circus. . . . She hurried forward to reach Eve. Eve turned a flushed face. 'I *say*, it's a circus,' said Miriam bitingly. The blare of a band broke out farther up the street.

People were jostled against them by a clown who came bounding and leaping his way along the crowded pavement, crying incoherent words with a thrilling blatter of laughter. The elephant was close upon them, alone in the road space cleared by its swinging walk. . . . If only every one would be quiet they could hear the soft padding of its feet. Slowly, gently, modestly it went by, followed by a crowd of smaller things; sad-eyed monkeys on horseback in gold coatlets, sullen caged beasts on trolleys drawn by beribboned unblinkered human-looking horses, tall white horses pacing singly by, bearing bobbing princesses and men in masks and cloaks.

Here and there in the long sunlit hours of the holiday by the Brighton sea, Miriam found the far-away seaside holidays of her childhood. Going out one afternoon with Eve and Miss Stringer, walking at Eve's side, listening to the conversation of the two girls, she had felt when they reached the deserted end of the esplanade and proposed turning round and walking home, an uncontrollable desire to be alone, and had left them, impatiently, without a word of excuse and gone on down the grey stone steps and out among the deserted weed-grown sapphire-pooled chalk hummocks at the foot of the cliffs. For a while she was chased by little phrases from Miss Stringer's quiet talking—'if you want people to be interested in you, you must be interested in them'; 'you can get on with everybody if you make up your mind to'—and by the memory of her well-hung clothes and her quiet regular features spoilt by the nose that Gerald said was old-maidish, and her portmanteau full of finery, unpacked on the first-floor landing outside the tiny room she occupied—piles of underlinen startlingly threaded with ribbons.

At the end of half an hour's thoughtless wandering over the weed-grown rocks, she found herself sitting on a little patch of dry silt at the end of a promontory of sea-smoothed hummocks with the pools of bright blue-green fringed water all about her, watching the gentle rippling of the retreating waves over the weedy lower levels. She seemed long to have been listening and watching, her mind was full of things she felt she would never forget, the green-capped white faces of the cliffs, a patch of wet sand dotted with stiffly waiting seagulls, the more distant wavelets ink black and golden pouring in over the distant hummocks, the curious whispering ripples near her feet. She must go back. Her mind slid out making a strange half-familiar compact with all these things. She was theirs, she would remember them all, always. They were not alone, because she was with them and knew them. She had always known them, she reflected, remembering with a quick pang a long, unpermitted wandering out over the cliff edge beyond Dawlish, the sun shining on pinkish sandy scrub, the expression of the bushes; hurrying home with the big rough spaniel that belonged to the house they had hired. She must have been about six years old. She had gone back with a secret, telling them nothing of the sunlight or the bushes, only of a strange lady, sitting on the jetty as she came down over the sands, who had caught her in her arms and horribly kissed her. She had forgotten the lady and been so happy when she reached home that no one had scolded her. And when they questioned her, it seemed that there was only the lady to tell them about. Her mother had looked at her and kissed her. And now she must go back again, and say nothing. The strange promise, the certainty she felt out here on the rocks must be taken back to the Brighton front and the boarding-house. It would disappear as soon as she got back. Here on the Brighton rocks it was not so strong as it had been in Dawlish. And it would disappear more completely. There had been, during the intervening years, holidays with Sarah and Eve and Harriett in seaside lodgings, over which the curious conviction that possessed her now had spread like a filmy veil. But now it would hardly ever come; there were always people talking, the strangers one worked for, or the hard new people like Miss Stringer, people who had a number of things they were always saying.

She tried to remember when the strange independent joy had begun, and thought she could trace it back to a morning in the garden at Babington, the first thing she could remember,

when she had found herself toddling alone along the garden
path between beds of flowers almost on a level with her head
and blazing in the sunlight. Bees with large bodies were sailing
heavily across the path from bed to bed, passing close by her
head and making a loud humming in the air. She could see the
flowers distinctly as she walked quickly back through the afternoon throng on the esplanade; they were sweet williams and
'everlasting' flowers, the sweet williams smelling very strongly
sweet in her nostrils, and one sheeny brown everlasting flower
that she had touched with her nose, smelling like hot paper.

She wanted to speak to someone of these things. Until she
could speak to someone about them she must always be alone.
Always quite alone, she thought, looking out, as she walked,
across the busy stretch of sea between the two piers, dotted
with pleasure boats. It would be impossible to speak to any
one about them unless one felt perfectly sure that the other
person felt about them in the same way and knew that they
were more real than anything else in the world, knew that
everything else was a fuss about nothing. But everybody else
seemed to be really interested in the fuss. That was the
extraordinary thing. Miss Meldrum presiding at the boarding-
house table with her white padded hair and her white face and
bright steady brown eyes, listening to everybody and making
jokes with everybody and keeping things going, sometimes
looked as if she knew it was all a pretence. But if you spoke
to her, she would think you were talking about religion and
would kiss you. She had already kissed Miriam once—for
playing accompaniments to the hymns on a Sunday evening,
and made her feel as if there were some sly secret between them.
If she played the hymns again she would play them stonily . . .
mother would look as she always did if you suddenly began to
talk anything about things in general, as if you were going to
make some concession she had been waiting for all her life.
Now, with the operation and all the uncertainty ahead she
would probably cry. She would want to explain in some way,
as she had done one day long ago; how dreadful it had been . . .
mother, I never feel tired, not really tired, and however I
behave I always feel frightfully happy inside . . . my blessed

chick, it's your splendid health—and the influence of the Holy Spirit. . . . But I hate everybody. . . . What foolish nonsense. You mustn't think such things. You will make yourself unpopular. . . .

She must keep her secret to herself. This Brighton life crushed it back more than anything there had been in Germany or at Banbury Park. In Germany she had found it again and again, and at Banbury Park, though it could never come out and surround her, it was never far off. It lurked just beyond the poplars in the park, at the end of the little empty garden at twilight, amongst the books in the tightly packed bookcase. It was here, too, in and out the sunlit days. As one opened the door of the large, sparely furnished breakfast-room it shone for a moment in the light pouring over the table full of seated forms; it haunted the glittering scattered sand round about the little blank platform where the black and white minstrels stood singing in front of their harmonium, and poured out across the blaze of blue and gold sea ripples, when the town band played Anitra's Dance or the moon-song from the *Mikado*; it lay all along the deserted promenade and roadway as you went home to lunch, and at night it spoke in the flump flump of the invisible sea against the lower woodwork of the pier pavilion.

But every day at breakfast over the eggs, bacon, and tomatoes —knowing voices began their day's talking, the weary round of words and ugly laughter went steadily on, narrow horrible sounds that made you feel conscious of the insides of people's throats and the backs of their noses—as if they were not properly formed. The talk was like a silly sort of battle. . . . Innuendo, Miriam would say to herself, feeling that the word was too beautiful for what she wanted to express; *double entente* was also unsatisfactory. These people were all enemies pretending to be friends. Why did they pretend? Why not keep quiet? Or all sing between their eating, different songs, it would not matter. She and Eve and Harriett and Gerald did sometimes hum the refrains of the nigger minstrels' songs, or one of them would hum a scrap of a solo and all three sing the chorus. Then people were quiet, listening and smiling their evil smiles and Miss Meldrum was delighted. It seemed improper and half-hearted as no one else joined in; but after the first few days the four of them always sang between the courses at dinner. Gerald did not seem to mind the chaffy talk and the vulgar jokes, and would generally join in; and he said strange disturbing things about the boarders, as if he knew all about them. And he and Harriett talked to the niggers too and found out about them. It spoilt them when one knew that they belonged to small London music-halls, and had wives and families and illnesses and trouble. Gerald and Harriett did not seem to mind this. They did not seem to mind anything out of doors. They were free and hard and contemptuous of every one except the niggers and a few very stylish-looking people who sailed along and took no notice of anybody. Gerald said extraordinary, disturbing things about the girls on the esplanade. Miriam and Eve were interested in some of the young men they saw. They talked about them and looked out for them. Sometimes they exchanged glances with them. Were she and Eve also 'on show'; waiting to be given 'half an inch'; would she or Eve be 'perfectly awful in the dark'? Did the young men they specially favoured with their notice say things about them? When these thoughts buzzed about in Miriam's brain she wanted to take a broom and sweep everybody into the sea. . . . She discovered that a single steady unexpected glance, meeting her own, from a man who had the right kind of bearing—something right about the set of the shoulders—could disperse all the vague trouble she felt at the perpetual spectacle of the strolling crowds, the stiffly waiting many-eyed houses, the strange stupid bathing-machines, and send her gaily forward in a glad world where there was no need to be alone in order to be happy. A second encounter was sad, shameful, ridiculous; the man became absurd and lost his dignity; the joyous sense of looking through him right out and away to an endless perspective, of being told that the endlessness was there and telling that the endlessness was there, had gone; the eyes were eyes, solid and mocking and helpless—to be avoided in future; and when they had gone, the sunset or the curious quivering line along the horizon were no longer gateways, but hard barriers, until by some chance one was tranquilly alone again—when the horizon would beckon and lift and the pathway of gold across the sea at sunset call to your feet until they tingled and ached.

Life was ugly and cruel. The secret of the sea and of the evenings and mornings must be given up. It would fade more and more. What was life? Either playing a part all the time in order to be amongst people in the warm, or standing alone with the strange true real feeling—alone with a sort of edge of reality on everything; even on quite ugly common things—cheap boarding-houses, face-towels and blistered window frames.

Since Mr Green and Mr Parrow had left, they had given up going to pier entertainments and had spent most of their time sitting in a close row and talking together, in the intervals of the black and white minstrel concerts and the performances of the town band. They had drifted into this way of spending their time; there was never any discussion or alteration of the day's programme. It worked like a charm and there was no sign of the breaking of the charm. Miriam was sometimes half afraid just as they settled themselves down that someone, probably Gerald or Eve, might say 'Funny, isn't it, how well we four get on,' and that strange power that held them together and kept everything away would be broken before the holiday came to an end. But no one did and they went on sitting together in the morning on the hot sand—the moving living glinting sand that took the sting, as soon as you touched it with your hand, out of everything there might be in the latest letter from home—hearing the niggers from ten to eleven, bathing from eleven to twelve, sitting afterwards fresh and tingling and drowsy in canopied chairs near the band until dinner-time, prowling and paddling in the afternoon and ranging themselves again in chairs for the evening.

They said nothing until almost the end of their time about the passage of the days; but they looked at each other, each time they settled down, with conspiring smiles and then sat, side by side, less visible to each other than the great sunlit sea or the great clean salt darkness, stranded in a row with four easy idle laughing commenting voices, away alone and safe in the gaiety of the strong forgetful air—talking things over. The far-away troublesome crooked things, all cramped and painful and puzzling, came out one by one and were shaken and tossed away along the clean wind. And there was so much for Gerald to hear. He wanted to hear everything—any little thing—'Just like a girl; it's awfully jolly for Harry he's like that. She'll never be lonely,' agreed Miriam and Eve privately. . . . 'He's a perfect dear.' One night, towards the end of their time, they talked of the future. It had begun to press on them. There seemed no more time for brooding even over Eve's fascinating little pictures of life in the big country house, or Miriam's stories and legends of Germany—she said very little about Banbury Park fearing the amazement and disgust of the trio if anything of the reality of North London should reach them through her talk, and guessing the impossibility of their realizing the Pernes—or Gerald's rich memories of the opulence of his early home life, an atmosphere of spending and operas and dinner-parties and receptions and distinguished people. During the evening, in a silent interval, just as the band was tuning up to begin its last tune, Gerald had said with quiet emphasis: 'Well, anyhow, girls, you mark my words, the old man won't make any more money. Not another penny. You may as well make up your minds to that.' Then the band had broken into their favourite Hungarian dance. Three of them sat blissfully back in their deck-chairs, but Miriam remained uncomfortably propped forward, eagerly thinking. The music rushed on, she saw dancers shining before her in wild groups, in the darkness, leaping and shouting, their feet scarcely touching the earth and a wild light darted about them as they shouted and leapt. 'Set Mirry up in some sort of business,' quoted her mind from one of Gerald's recent soliloquies. She knew that she did not want that. But

the dancing forms told her of the absurdity of going back
without protest to the long aching days of teaching in the
little school amongst those dreadful voices which were going,
whatever she did for them, to be dreadful all their lives. Nothing she could do would make any difference to them. They
did not want her. They were quite happy. Her feelings and
thoughts, her way of looking at things, her desire for space and
beautiful things and music and quietude would never be their
desire. Reverence for things—had she reverence? She felt
she must have because she knew they had not; even the old
people; only superstition . . . North London would always
be North London, hard, strong, sneering, money-making,
noisy and trammy. Perhaps the difference between the north
and the south and her own south-west of London was like the
difference between the north and the south of England. . . .
Green's *History of the English People* . . . spinning-jennys
began in the Danish north, hard and cold, with later sunsets.
In the south was Somersetshire lace. North London meant
twenty pounds a year and the need for resignation and determination every day. Eve had thirty-five pounds and a huge
garden and new books and music . . . a book called *Music
and Morals* and interesting people staying in the house. And
Eve had not been to Germany and could not talk French. 'You
are an idiot to go on doing it. It 's wrong. Lazy,' laughed the
dancers crowding and flinging all round her. 'I ought,' she
responded defiantly, 'to stay on and make myself into a certificated teacher.' 'Certificated?' they screamed, wildly sweeping before her in strange lines of light. 'If you do you will be
like Miss Cramp. Certificates—little conceited papers, and
you dead. Certificates would finish you off—Kill—Kill—
Kill—*Kill—Kill!!*' Bang. The band stopped and Miriam
felt the bar of her chair wounding her flesh. The trail of the
dancers flickered away across the sea and her brain was busily
dictating her letter to Miss Perne: 'and therefore I am obliged,
however reluctantly, to take this step, as it is absolutely necessary for me to earn a larger salary at once.'

CHAPTER IX

THE Henderson party found Mr Green and Mr Parrow waiting in the dim plank-floored corridor leading from the station to the main building of the Crystal Palace. When the quiet greetings were over and they had arranged a meeting-place at the end of the evening in case any of the party should be lost, they all tramped on up the resounding corridor. Miriam found herself bringing up the rear with Mr Parrow. They were going on up the corridor, through the Palace and out into the summer evening. They had all come to go out into the summer evening and see the fireworks. All but she had come meaning to get quite near to the 'set pieces' and to look at them. She had not said anything about meaning to get as far away from the fireworks as possible. She had been trusting to Mr Parrow for that. Now that she was with him she felt that perhaps it was not quite fair. He had come meaning to see the fireworks. He would be disappointed. She would be obliged to tell him presently, when they got out into the night. They were all tramping quickly up along the echoing corridor. No one seemed to be talking, just feet, tramp, tramp on the planking, rather quickly. It was like the sound of workmen's feet on the inside scaffolding of a half-built house. The corridor was like something in the Hospital for Incurables . . . that strange old woman sitting in the hall with bent head laughing over her crochet, and Miss Garrett whom they had come to see sitting up in bed, a curtained bed in a ward, with a pleated mob cap all over the top of her head and half-way down her forehead, sitting back against large square pillows with her hands clasped on the neat bed-clothes and a 'sweet, patient' look on her face, coughing gently and spitting, spitting herself to death . . . rushing away out of the ward to wait for mother downstairs in the hall with the curious smells and the dreadful old woman. . . . What was it, chick? . . . Sick, mother, I felt sick, I couldn't stay. It was rage; rage with that dreadful old woman. People probably told her she was patient and sweet, and she had got that trick of putting her head on one side. She was not sweet. She was one of the worst of those dreadful people who would always make people believe in a particular way, all the time. She had a great big frame. If she had done anything but sit as she sat, in that particular way, one could have stayed.

They were all standing looking at some wonderful sort of clock, a calendar-clock—'a triumph of ingenuity,' said Mr Green's bright reedy voice. The building had opened out and rushed up, people were passing to and fro. 'We don't want to stay inside; let's go out,' said Gerald. The group broke into couples again and passed on. Miriam found herself with Mr Parrow once more. Of course she would be with him all the evening. She must tell him at once about the fireworks. She ought not to have come, if she did not mean to see the fireworks. It was mean and feeble to cheat him out of his evening. Why had she come; to wander about with him, not seeing the fireworks? What an idiotic and abominable thing. Now that she was here at his side it was quite clear that she must endure the fireworks. Anything else would be like asking him to wander about with her alone. She did not want to wander about with him alone. She took an opportunity of joining Eve for a moment. They had just walked through a winter garden and were standing at the door of a concert room, all quite silent and looking very shy. 'Eve,' she said hurriedly in a low tone, 'd'you want to see the beastly fireworks?'

'Beastly? Oh, of course, I do,' said Eve in a rather loud embarrassed tone. How dreadfully self-conscious they all were. Somebody seemed to be speaking. 'What *sticks* my family are—I had no idea,' muttered Miriam furiously into Eve's face. Eve's eyes filled with tears, but she stood perfectly still, saying nothing. Miriam wheeled round and stared into the empty concert room. It was filled with a faint bluish light and, beyond the rows of waiting chairs and the empty platform, a huge organ stood piled up towards the roof. The party were moving on. What a queer place the Crystal Palace is . . . what a perfectly horrible place for a concert . . .

pianissimo passages and those feet on those boards tramping
about outside. . . . What a silly muddle. Mr Parrow was
waiting for her to join the others. They straggled along past
booths and stalls, meeting groups of people, silent and lost like
themselves. Now they were passing some kind of stonework
things, reliefs, antique, roped off like the seats in a church.
Just in front of them a short man holding the red cord in his
hands was looking at a group with some ladies. '*Why*,' he
said suddenly in a loud cheerful voice, stretching an arm out
across the rope and pointing to one of the reliefs, 'it 's Auntie
and Grandma!' Miriam stared at him·as they passed, he was
so short, shorter than any of the ladies he was with. 'It 's the
only way to see these things,' he said in the same loud harsh
cheerful voice. Miriam laughed aloud. What a clever man.

'Do you like statues?' said Mr Parrow in a low gentle tone.

'I don't know anything about them,' said Miriam.

'I can't bear fireworks,' she said hurriedly.

They were in the open at last. In the deepening twilight
many people were going to and fro. In the distance soft dark
masses of trees stood out against the sky in every direction.
Not far away the ghostly frames of the set pieces reared against
the sky made the open evening seem as prison-like as the enclosure they had just left. Round about the scaffolding of
these pieces dense little crowds were collecting.

'Don't you want to see the fireworks?'

'I want to get away from them.'

'All right, we 'll get lost at once.'

'It isn't,' she explained a little breathlessly, in relief, suddenly
respecting him, allowing him to thread a way for her through
the increasing crowd towards the open evening, 'that I don't
want to see the fireworks, but I simply can't stand the noise.'

'I see,' laughed Mr Parrow gently. They were making
towards the open evening along a narrow gravel pathway, like
a garden pathway. Miriam hurried a little, fearing that the
fireworks might begin before they got to a safe distance.

'I never have been able to stand a sudden noise. It 's
torture to me to walk along a platform where a train may
suddenly shriek.'

'I see. You 're afraid of the noise.'

'It isn't fear—I can't describe it. It 's agony. It 's like pain. But much much worse than pain. It 's—it 's—annihilating.'

'I see; that 's very peculiar.'

Their long pathway was leading them towards a sweet-scented density, dim bowers and leafy arches appeared just ahead.

'It was much worse even than it is now when I was a little thing. When we went to the seaside I used to sit in the train nearly dead until it had screamed and started. And there was a teacher who sneezed—a noise like a hard scream—at school. She used to go on sneezing—twenty times or so. I was only six and I dreaded going to school, just for that. Once I cried and they took me out of the room. I 've never told any one. Nobody knows.'

'You 've told me.'

'Yes.'

'It 's very interesting. You shan't go anywhere near the fireworks.'

A large rosy flare, wavering steadily against the distant trees, showed up for a moment the shapes and traceries of climbing plants surrounding their retreat. A moment afterwards with a dull boom a group of white stars shot up into the air and hovered, melting one by one as the crowd below moaned and crackled its applause.

Miriam laughed abruptly. 'That 's jolly. How clever people are. But it 's much better up here. It 's like not being too near at the theatre.'

'I think we 've got the best view certainly.'

'But we shall miss the set pieces.'

'The people down there won't see the rosary.'

'What 's that black thing on our left down there?'

'That 's the toboggan run. We ought to go on that.'

'What is it like?'

'It's fine; you just rush down. We must try it.'

'Not for worlds.'

Mr Parrow laughed. 'Oh you must try the toboggan; there's no noise about that.'

'I really couldn't.'

'Really?'

'Absolutely. I mean it. Nothing under the sun would induce me to go on a toboggan.'

They sat watching the fireworks until they were tired of the whistling rockets, showers of stars and golden rain, the flaming bolts that shot up from the Battle of the Nile, the fizzlings and fire spurtings of the set pieces and the recurrent moanings and faint patterings of applause from the crowd.

'I wish they'd do some more coloured flares of light up the trees like they did at first. It was beautiful—more real than these things. "Feu d'artifice" artificial fire—all these noisy things. Why do people always like a noise? Men. All the things men have invented, trains and cannons and things make a frightful noise.'

'The toboggan's not noisy. Come and try the toboggan.'

'Oh no.'

'Well—there's the lake down there. We might have a boat.'

'Do you know how to manage a boat?'

'I've been on once or twice; if you like to try I'll manage.'

'No; it's too dark.' What a plucky man. But the water looked cold. And perhaps he would be really stupid.

A solitary uniformed man was yawning and whistling at the top of the deserted toboggan run. The faint light of a lamp fell upon the square platform and the little sled standing in place at the top of a shiny slope which shot steeply down into blackness.

'We'd better get on,' said Miriam trembling.

'Well, you're very graceful at giving in,' remarked Mr Parrow, handing her into the sled and settling with the man.

He got that sentence out of a book, thought Miriam wildly as she heard the man behind them say 'Ready? Off you go!' . . . Out of a book a book a book—*Oh—ooooh*—how ab*solute*ly

glorious, she yelled as they shot down through the darkness.
Oh, she squealed into the face laughing and talking beside her.
She turned away, shouting, for the final rush, they were flying
—involuntarily her hand flung out, they were tearing headlong
into absolute darkness, and was met and firmly clasped. They
shot slackening up a short incline and stood up still hand in
hand, laughing incoherently.

'Let's walk back and try again,' said Mr Parrow.

'Oh no; I enjoyed it most frightfully; but we mustn't go
again. Besides, it must be fearfully late.'

She pulled at her hand. The man was too near and too big.
His hand was not a bit uncertain like his speech, and for a
moment she was glad that she pulled in vain. 'Very well,'
said Mr Parrow, 'but we must find our way off the grass and
strike the pathway.' Drawing her gently along, he peered
about for the track. 'Let me go,' said her hand dragging gently
at his. 'No,' said the firm enclosure, tightening, 'not yet.'
What does it matter? flashed her mind. Why should I be
such a prude? The hand gave her confidence. It was firm
and strong and perfectly serious. It was a hand like her own
hand and comfortingly strange and different. Gently and
slowly he guided her over the dewy grass. The air that had
rushed so wildly by them a few minutes ago was still and calm
and friendly; the distant crowd harmless and insignificant.
The fireworks were over. The pathway they had missed
appeared under their feet and down it they walked soberly,
well apart, but still hand in hand until they reached the borders
of the dispersing crowd.

CHAPTER X

WHEN Miriam sat talking everything over with the Pernes at supper, on the first night of the term, detached for ever from the things that engrossed them, the school-work, Julia Doyle's future, the peculiarities of the visiting teachers, the problem of the 'unnatural infatuation' of two of the boarders with each other, the pros and cons of a revolutionary plan for taking the girls in parties to the principal London museums, she made the most of her triumphant assertion that she had absolutely nothing in view. She found herself decorously waiting, armed at all points, through the silent interval while the Pernes took in the facts of her adventurous renunciation. She knew at once that she would have to be desperately determined. . . . But after all they could not do anything about it.

Sitting there, in the Perne boat, still taking an oar and determined to fling herself into the sea . . . she ought not to have told them she was leaving them just desperately, without anything else in prospect; because they were so good, not like employers. They would all feel for her. It was just like speaking roughly at home. Well, it was done. She glanced about. Miss Haddie, across the table behind her habitual bowl of bread and milk had a face——the face of a child surprised by injustice. 'I was right——I was right,' Miriam gasped to herself as the light flowed in. 'I 'm escaping——just in time. . . . Emotional tyranny. . . . What a good expression. . . . That 's the secret of Miss Haddie. It was awful. She 's lost me. I 'm free. Emotional tyranny.' . . . 'My hat, Mirry, you 're beyond me. How much do you charge for that one ? Say it again,' she seemed to hear Gerald's friendly voice. Go away Gerald. True. True. All the truth and meaning of her friendship with Miss Haddie in one single flash. How *fearfully* interesting life was. Miss Haddie wrestling with her, fighting for her soul; praying for her, almost driving her to the early service and always ready to quiver over her afterwards and to ask her if she had been happy. . . . And now angry because she was escaping.

She appealed to Miss Deborah and met a flash of her beautiful soft piercing eyes. Her delicate features quivered and wrinkled almost to a smile. But Miss Deborah was afraid of Miss Jenny who was already thinking and embarking on little sounds. Miriam got away for a moment in a tumult, with Miss Deborah. 'Oh,' she shouted to her in the depths of her heart, 'you are heavenly young. You *know*. Life's like Robinson Crusoe. Your god's a great big Robinson Crusoe. You know that anything may happen any minute. And it's all right.' She laughed and shook, staring at the salt-cellar and then across at Miss Haddie whose eyes were full of dark fear. Miss Haddie was alone and outraged. 'She thinks I'm a fraud besides being vulgar . . . life goes on and she'll wonder and wonder about me, puzzled and alone.' . . . She smiled at her her broadest, happiest, home smile, one she had never yet reached at Banbury Park. Flushing scarlet Miss Haddie smiled in return.

'Eh—my dear girl,' Miss Jenny was saying diffidently at her side, 'isn't it a little unwise—very unwise—under the circumstances—with the difficulties—well, in fact with all ye've just told us—have ye thought?' When Miriam reached her broad smile Miss Jenny stopped and suddenly chuckled. 'My *dear* Miriam! I don't know. I suppose we don't know ye. I suppose we haven't really known ye as ye are. But come, have ye thought it out? No, ye haven't,' she ended gravely, looking along the table and flicking with her forefinger the end of her little red nose.

Miriam glanced at her profile and her insecure disorderly bunch of hair. Miss Jenny was formidable. She would recommend certificates. Her eye wavered towards Miss Deborah.

'My dear Jenny,' said Miss Deborah promptly, 'Miriam is not a child. She must do as she thinks best.'

'But don't ye see my point, my dear Deborah? I don't say she's a child. She's a madcap. That's it.' She paused. 'Of course I dare say she'll fall on her feet. Ye're a most extraordinary gel. I don't know. Of course ye can come *back*—or stay here in yer holidays. Ye know *that*, my dear,' she concluded, suddenly softening her sharp little voice.

'I don't *want* to go,' cried Miriam with tear-filled eyes. They were one person in the grip of a decision. Miss Haddie sat up and moved her elbows about. All four pairs of eyes held tears.

'My dear—I wish we could give ye more, Miriam,' murmured Miss Jenny; 'we don't want to lose ye, ye've pulled the lower school together in a remarkable way'; Miss Deborah was drawing little breaths of protest at this descent into gross detail; 'the children are interested. We hear that from the parents. We shall be able to give ye excellent testimonials.'

'Oh, I don't care about that,' responded Miriam desperately. 'Fancy—Great Scott—parents—behind all my sore throats—I've never heard about that. It's all coming out now,' she thought.

'Well—my dear—now——' began Miss Jenny hesitatingly. Feeling herself slipping, Miriam clung harshly to her determination and drew herself up to offer the set of the pretty blouse Gerald and Harriett had bought her in Brighton as a seal on her irrevocable decision to break with Banbury Park. It was a delicate sheeny green silk, with soft tuckers.

'What steps have ye taken?' asked Miss Jenny in a quizzical business-like tone.

'It's very kind of you,' said Miriam formally, and went on to hint vaguely and convincingly at the existence of some place in a family in the country that would be sure to fall to her lot through the many friends to whom Eve had written on her behalf, turning away from the feast towards the freedom of the untenanted part of the room. The sitting had to be brought to an end. . . . In a moment she would be utterly routed. . . . Her lame statements were the end of the struggle. She knew she was demonstrating in her feeble broken tones a sort of blind strength they knew nothing of and that they would leave it at that, whatever they thought; if only there were no more talk.

When they had left the room and Flora came in for the supper things, instead of sitting as usual at the far end of the table pretending to read, she stood planted on the hearthrug watching her. Flora's hands were small and pale and serenely despairing like her face. She cleared the table quietly. She had nothing to hope for. She did not know she had nothing to hope for. Whatever happened she would go quietly on doing things . . . in the twilight . . . on a sort of edge. People would die. Perhaps people had already died in her family. But she would always be the same. One day she would die, perhaps of something hard and slow and painful, with that small yellowish constitution.

She would not be able to go on looking serene and despairing with people round her bed helping her. When she died she would wait quietly with nothing to do, blind and wondering. Death would take her into a great festival—things for her, for herself. She would not believe it and would put up her hands to keep it off. But it would be all round her in great laughter, like the deep roaring and crying of a flood. Then she would cry like a child.

Why was it that for some people, for herself, life could be happy now? It was possible now to hear things laugh just by setting your teeth and doing things; breaking into things, chucking things about, refusing to be held. It made even the dreadful past seem wonderful. All the days here, the awful days, each one awful and hateful and painful.

Flora had gathered up her tray and disappeared, quietly closing the door. But Flora had known and somehow shared her triumph, felt her position in the school as she stood planted and happy in the middle of the Pernes's hearthrug.

'An island is a piece of land entirely surrounded by water.'

Miriam kept automatically repeating these words to herself as the newly returned children clung about her the next morning in the schoolroom. It was a morning of heavy wind and rain and the schoolroom was dark, and chilly with its summer-screened fireplace. The children seemed to her for the first time small and pathetic. She was deserting them. After fifteen months of strange intimacy, she was going away for ever.

During the usual routine days the little girls always seemed large and formidable. She was quite sure they were not so to the other teachers, and she hesitated when she thought over this difference, between the explanation which accounted for their size and redoubtableness by her own feebleness, and the one to which she inclined when she felt her success as a teacher.

She had discovered that the best plan was to stand side by side with the children in face of the things they had to learn, treating them as equals and fellow-adventurers, giving explanations when these were necessary, as if they were obvious and might have been discovered by the children themselves, never as if they were possessions of her own, to be imparted, never claiming a knowledge superior to their own. 'The business of the teacher is to make the children independent, to get them to think for themselves, and that's much more important than whether they get to know facts,' she would say irrelevantly to the Pernes whenever the question of teaching came up. She bitterly resented their vision of children as malleable subordinates. And there were many moments when she seemed to be silently exchanging this determination of hers with her pupils. Good or bad, she knew it was the secret of her influence with them, and so long as she was faithful to it both she and they enjoyed their hours together. Very often she was tired, feeble with fatigue and scamping all opportunities; this too they understood, and never took advantage of her. One or two of them would even, when she failed, try to keep things going on her own method. All this was sheer happiness to her, the bread and wine of her days.

But now and again, perhaps during the mid-morning recess, this impersonal relationship gave way and the children clung fawning all round her, passionately competing for nearness, touching and clinging and snatching for kisses. There was no thought or uprightness or laughter then, their hands were quick and eloquent and their eyes wide and deeply smiling with those strange women's smiles. Sometimes she could respond in kind, answering to their smiles and caresses, making gentle foolish sounds and feeling their passion rise to a frenzy of adoration. The little deprecating consoling sounds that they made as they clung, told her that if she chose steadily to remain always gentle and deprecating and consoling and reproachful she could dominate them as persons and extort in the long run a complete personal obedience to herself, so that they would do their work for her sake and live by and through her, adoring her—as a goddess—and hating her. Even as they fawned, she knew they were torn between their aching desire for a per- fection of tenderness in her and their fear lest she should fulfil the desire. She was always tempted for an instant to yield and fling herself irrevocably into the abyss, letting the children go on one by one into the upper school, carrying as her gift only a passionate memory such as she herself had for one of her nursemaids; leaving her downstairs with an endless suc- cession of new loves, different, but always the same. She would become like a kind of nun, making a bare subsistence, but so beloved always, so quivering and tender and responsive that human love would never fail her and, when strength failed, there would be hands held out to shelter her decline. But the vision never held her for more than a moment. There was something in the thought of such pure personal sentiment that gave her a feeling of treachery towards the children. Mentally she flung them out and off, made them stand upright and estranged. She could not give them personal love. She did not want to; nor to be entangled with them. They were going to grow up into North London women, most of them loudly scorning everything that was not materially profitable; these would remember her with pity—amusement. A few would escape. These would remember her at strange moments that were coming for them, moments when they would recog- nize the beauty of things like the *Psalm of Life* that she had induced them to memorize without understanding it.

This morning a sense of their softness and helplessness went
to her heart. She had taught them so little. But she had
forced them to be impersonal. Almost savagely she had done
that. She had never taken them by a trick. . . .

And now they were going to be Julia's children.

Julia would teach them—alone there in the room with them,
filling the room for them—in her own way. . . .

There would be no more talk about general ideas. . . .

She would have to keep on the 'object' lessons, because the
Pernes had been so pleased with the idea and the children had
liked them. There would still be those moments, with balls
for the solar system and a candle for the sun, and the blinds
down. But there would not be anything like that instant when
all the eyes round the table did nothing but watch the movement of a shadow on a ball . . . the relief afterwards, the
happiness and the moment of intense love in the room—never
to be forgotten, all of them knowing each other, all their
differences gone away, even the clever watchful eyes of the
cheating little Jewess, real and unconscious for a moment.
Julia would be watching the children as much as the shadow,
and the children would never quite forget Julia. She would
get to know a great deal about the children, but there would
be no reverence for big cold outside things. She would teach
them to be kind. 'Little dorlings.' She thought all children
were darlings and talked to them all in her wheedling, coaxing,
adoring way. If one or two were not, it was the fault of the
way they were treated, something in the 'English' way of
dealing with them. Nearly all the elder girls she disapproved
of, they were no longer children—they were English. She
was full of contempt and indignant laughter for them, and of
pity for the 'wee things' who were growing up. Yet she got
on with them all and had the secret of managing them without
letting them see her feelings.

There *was* something specially bad in the English way
of bringing up children. Not the 'education' exactly, but

something else, something in the way they were treated. Something in the way they were brought up made English women so awful—with their smiles. Julia did not smile or smirk. She laughed a great deal, often to tears. And she would often suddenly beam. It was like a light coming from under her thick white skin. Was Julia the answer to the awfulness of Englishwomen? If, as Julia said, the children were all right and only the girls and grown-ups awful, it must be something in the way the children were treated.

Yet Julia was not impersonal.

Miss Deborah, . . . teaching the whole school to be 'good' in the Fairchild way; with her beautiful quivering nodding black head held high—blinking, and not looking at the girls separately—in a grave voice, full of Scripture history, but broken all the time, quivering with laughter and shoutings which she never uttered . . . hilarious, . . . she taught a system of things she had been brought up in. But all the same, she rushed along sweeping the girls with her . . . and the girls believed her. If I taught her system I should have false lips and the girls would not believe me. If ever any one had the courage to tell her of any dreadful thing, she would weep it all away; and the person would begin all over again certainly, as much as possible in the Fairchild way . . . again and again until they died. Supposing a murderer came and sat down in the hall? Supposing Miss Deborah had been brought up as a Thug—killing people from behind? . . .

Miss Jenny, exasperatedly trying to wake all the girls up to the importance of public life, sitting round in their blouses and skirts, half-amused and sometimes trying to argue, because the tone of Miss Jenny's voice made them sorry for the other side. Politics, politics, reading history and the newspapers, the importance of history if you wanted to have any understanding of your own times. To come into the room to take the class after Miss Jenny, always meant finding her stating and protesting and tapping the end of her nose, and the air hot and excited, and the girls in some sort of state of excitement which could only be got over by being very quiet and pretending not to notice them except to be very surprised if there were any disturbance.

Miss Haddie, in horror of their badness, teaching them to master little set tasks because it was shocking to be an idler; loving the sinner but hating the sin much more, with a sort of horror like a girl, a horror in her eyes that was the same as the horror of insects, fearing God who was so close in the room, gloomily, all the time—wanting to teach them all to fawn on Christ. Christ would make everything all right if you made up to him. 'Faint not nor fear, his arms are near. He faileth not and thou art dear.' Awful . . .

And then Julia, making the children love her, herself, as a person. They would all love her in time. Even Burra, after her first grief, would fling herself upon Julia . . . Gertie would not though, ever. Cold, quiet little Gertie, the doctor's daughter. She would make no response however much she were kissed and called a little darling. Gertie even as a child was the English thing that Julia disliked. Julia, with all her success, was not the answer to the problem of why Englishwomen were abominable. She left out so much. 'Julia, you know, I think things are more important than people. Much more. People, if you let them for one single instant, grin and pounce upon you and try to make you forget things. But they're there all the time and you have to go back to them,' and Julia laughing suddenly aloud, 'Ah—you're a duck—a tonic.' And every one was a little afraid of Julia, the children, the boarders whom she managed so high-handedly with her laughter, even the Pernes.

Perhaps Julia's 'personal' way and the English 'personal' way were somehow both wrong and horrid . . . girls' schools were horrid, bound to be horrid, sly, mean, somehow tricky and poisonous. It was a hopeless problem. The English sentimental way was wrong, the way of Englishwomen with children—it made them grow up with those treacherous smiles.

The scientific and 'aesthetic' way, the way of the Putney school—ah, blessed escape! . . . But it left nearly all the girls untouched.

Julia's sentimental way was better than the English sentimental way; its smiles had tears and laughter too, they were not so hypocritical. But it was wrong. It was the strongest thing, though, in the Wordsworth House school.

Julia was not happy. She dreamed fearful dreams. . . . Why did she speak of them as if they were something that no one in this English world into which she had come would understand? She had her strange nights all to herself there across the landing; either lying awake or sleeping and moaning all the time. The girls in her room slept like rocks and did not know that she moaned. They knew she had nightmares and sometimes cried out and woke them. But passing the open door late at night one could hear her moaning softly on every breath with closed lips. That was Julia, her life, all laid bare, moaning. . . . She knows she is alive and that there is no escape from being alive. But it has never made her feel breathless with joy. She laughs all day, at everybody and everything, and at night when she is naked and alone she moans; moan, moan, moan, heart-broken; wind and rain alone in the dark in a great open space.

She sometimes hinted at things, those real unknown things that were her own life unshared by anybody; in a low soft terrible broken voice, with eyes dilated and quivering lips; quite suddenly, with hardly any words. And she would speak passionately about the sea, how she hated it and could not look at it or listen to it; and of woods, the horror of woods, the trees and the shadowiness, making her crisp her hands—ah yes, *les mains crispées*, that was the word; and she had laughed when it was explained to her.

It was not that she had troubles at home. Those things she

seemed to find odd and amusing, like a story of the life of some other person—poverty and one of her sisters 'very peculiar,' another engaged to a scamp and another going to be a shop-assistant, and two more, 'doties' very young, being brought up in the country with an aunt. Everything that happened to people and all the things people did seemed to her funny and amusing, 'tickled her to death.' Harriett's engagement amused her really, though she pretended to be immensely interested and asked numbers of questions in a rich deep awestruck voice . . . blarney. . . . But she wanted to hear everything, and she never forgot anything she was told. And she had been splendid about the operation—really anxious, quite conscious and awake across the landing that awful night and really making you feel she was glad afterwards. 'Poor Mrs Henderson—I was never so glad in my life'—and always seeming to know her without having her explained. She was real there, and so strange in telling the Pernes about it and making it all easy.

Miriam leaned upon Julia more and more as the term went on, hating and fearing her for her secret sorrow and wondering and wondering why she appeared to have such a curious admiration and respect for herself. She could understand her adoration for the Pernes; she saw them as they were and had a phrase which partly explained them, 'no more knowledge of the world than babes'—but what was it in herself that Julia seemed so fiercely and shyly to admire?

She knew she could not let Julia know how she enjoyed washing her hands, in several soapings, in the cold water, before dinner. They would go their favourite midday walk, down the long avenue in the park through the little windings of the shrubbery and into the chrysanthemum show, strolling about in the large greenhouse, all the girls glad of the escape from a set walk, reading over every day the strange names on the little wooden stakes, jokes and gigglings and tiresomenesses all kept within bounds by the happiness that there was, inside the great quiet steamy glass-house, in the strange raw bitter scent of the great flowers, in the strange huge way they stood, with all their differences of shape and colour staring quietly at you, all in the same way with one expression. They were startling, amongst their grey leaves; and they looked startled and held their heads as if they knew they were beautiful. The girls always hurried to get to the chrysanthemums and came away all of them walking in twos, relieved and happy back through the cold park to dinner. But Julia, who loved the flowers, though she made fun of their names in certain moods and dropped them *sotto voce* into the general conversation at the dinner-table would have, Miriam felt sure, scorned her own feeling of satisfaction in the great hand-washing and the good dinner. And she detested pease pudding with the meat, and boiled suet pudding with treacle.

She ate scarcely anything herself, keeping her attention free and always seeming to be waiting for someone to say something that was never said. Her broad-shouldered, curiously buoyant, heavy, lounging, ill-clad form, her thick white skin, her eyes like a grey-blue sea, her dark masses of fine hair had long been for Miriam the deepest nook in the meal-time gatherings—she rested there unafraid of anything the boarders might say or do. She would never be implicated. Julia would take care of that, heading everything off and melting up the difficulties into some absurdity that would set all the Pernes talking. Julia lounged easily there, controlling the atmosphere of the table. And the Pernes knew it unconsciously, they must know it; any English person would know it . . . though they talked about her untidiness and lack of purpose and application. Julia was a deep, deep nook, full of thorns.

Julia had spoiled the news of Sarah's engagement to Bennett Brodie. It had been such a wonderful moment. The thick envelope coming at midday in Bennett's hand-writing—such a surprise—asking Miss Perne's permission to read it at the dinner-table—reading the startling sentences in the firm curved hand—'assert my privilege as your prospective brother-in-law by announcing that I'm on the track of a job that I think will suit you down to the ground,' the curious splash, gravy on the cloth as somebody put the great dish on the table, far-away vexation and funny familiar far-away discomfort all round the table, 'no more of this until I've got full particulars on the tapis; but it may, O Grecian Mariamne, not be without interest to you to hear that that sister of yours does not appear to be altogether averse to taking over the management of the new house and the new practice and the new practitioner, and that the new practitioner is hereby made anew in a sense that is more of an amazement to him than it doubtless will be to your intuitive personality. That life had such happiness in store for him is not the least of the many surprises that have come his way. He can only hope to prove not unworthy; and so a hearty *au revoir* from yours affectionately.' . . . Then Bennett would always be there amongst the home things . . . with his strange way of putting things; he would give advice and make suggestions . . . and Sarah's letter . . . a glance at it showing short sentences, things spoken in a low awe-struck voice. . . . 'We had been to an entertainment together. . . . Coming home along the avenue. I was so surprised. He was so quiet and serious and humble.' . . . All the practical things gone away in a moment, leaving only a sound of deep music, . . . mornings and evenings. Sarah alone now, at last, a person, with mornings and evenings and her own reality in everything. No one could touch her or interfere any more. She was standing aside, herself. She would always be Sarah, someone called Sarah. She need never worry any more, but go on doing things. . . . And then looking up and finding all the table eagerly watching and saying suddenly to Miss Perne 'another of my sisters is engaged' and everybody, even Trixie and Beadie, excited and interested.

The news, the great great news, wonderful Sarah away

somewhere in the background with her miracle—telling it out to
the table of women was a sort of public announcement that life
was moving out on to wider levels.   They all knew it, pinned
there; and how dear and glad they were, for a moment, making it
real, acknowledging by their looks how wonderful it was. Sarah,
floating above them all, caught up out of the darkness of everyday life. . . . And then Julia's eyes—veiled for a moment while
she politely stirred and curved her lips to a smile—cutting
through it all, seeming to say that nothing was really touched
or changed.   But when the table had turned to jealousy and
resentment, and it was time to pretend to hide the shaft of light
and cease to listen to the music, Julia, cool and steady, covered
everything up and made conversation.

And the thought of Julia was always a disturbance in going
to tea with the Brooms.   Grace Broom was the only girl in
the school for whom she had an active aversion.   She put one
or two questions about them: 'You really like going there?'
'You 'll go on seeing them after you leave?' and concluded
carelessly 'that 's a mystery to me——'
Sitting at tea shut in in the Brooms's little dining-room with
the blinds down and the dark red rep curtains drawn and the
gas-light and brilliant fire-light shining on the brilliantly
polished davenport in the window-space and the thick bevelled
glass of the Satsuma-laden mahogany sideboard, the dim
cracked oil-painting of Shakespeare above the mantelshelf, the
dark old landscapes round the little walls, the new picture of
Queen Victoria leaning on a stick and supported by Hindu
servants, receiving a minister, the solid silver tea-service, the
fine heavily-edged linen table-cover, the gleaming, various,
delicately filled dishes, the great bowl of flowers, the heavy,
carven, unmoved, age-long dreaming faces of the three women
with their living interested eyes, she would suddenly, in the
midst of a deep, calm undisturbing silence become aware of
Julia.   Julia would not be impressed by the surroundings, the
strange silent deeps of the room.   She would discover only

that she was with people who revered 'our Queen' and despised 'the working classes.' It would be no satisfaction to her to sit drinking from very exquisite old china, cup after cup of delicious very hot tea, laughing to tears over the story of the curate who knelt insecurely on a high kneeling stool at evening service in a country church and, crashing suddenly down in the middle of a long prayer, went on quietly intoning from the floor, or the madeira cake that leapt from the cake-dish on an at-home day and rolled under the sofa. She would laugh, but she would look from face to face, privately, and wonder. She would not really like the three rather dignified seated forms with the brilliant, tear-filled eyes, sitting on over tea, telling anecdotes, and tales of long strange illnesses suffered by strange hidden people in quiet houses, weddings, deaths, the stories of families separated for life by quarrels over money, stories of far-off holidays in the country; strange sloping rooms and farmhouse adventures; the cow that walked into the bank in a little country town. . . . Mrs Philps's first vision, as a bride, of the English Lakes, the tone of her voice as she talked about all these things.

The getting together and sitting about and laughing in the little room would never be to her like being in a world that was independent of all the other worlds. She would not want to go again and again and sit, just the four women, at tea, talking. The silent, beautifully kept, experienced old furniture all over the house would not fill her with fear and delight and strength. It would be no satisfaction to her to put on her things in front of the huge plate glass of the enormous double-fronted wardrobe in the spare-room, with its old Limoges ware and its faded photographs of the interiors of unknown churches, rows and rows of seats and a faded blur where the altar was, thorn-crowned heads and bold scrolly texts embroidered in crimson and gold silken mounted and oak-framed. And when she went home alone along the quiet, dark, narrow, tree-filled little roadways she would not feel gay and strong and full of personality.

On prize-giving day, Miriam's last day, Julia seemed to

disappear.   For the first time since she had come to the school
it was as if she were not there.   She was neither talking nor
watching nor steering anything at all.   Again and again during
the ceremonies, Miriam looked at her sitting or moving about,
pale and plain and shabby, one of the crowd of girls.

The curious power of the collected girls, their steady profiles,
their movements, their unconcerned security rose and flooded
round Miriam as it had done when she first came to the school.
But she no longer feared it.   It was going on, harsh and unconscious and determined, next term.   She was glad of it; the
certainty thrilled her; she wanted to convey some of her gladness to Julia, but could not catch her eye.

Her gladness carried her through the most tedious part of
the day's performances, the sitting in a listening concourse,
doors open, in the schoolroom, while some ten of the girls
went one by one with stricken faces into the little drawing-
room and played the piece they had learned during the term.
Their shame and confusion, the anger and desperation of their
efforts, the comments of the listeners and their violent ironic
applause, roused her to an intensity of sympathy.   How they
despised the shame-faced tinkling; how they admired the
martyrs.

Their strong indifference seemed to centre in the cold pale
scornful face of Jessie Wheeler, sitting squarely there with
defiant eyes, waiting for the future; the little troop of children
she dreamed of.

These North London girls would be scornful mocking
fiancées.   They would be adored by their husbands.   Secretly
they would forget their husbands in their houses and children
and friends.

Julia was the last player.   She sidled swiftly out of the room;
even her habitual easy halting lounge seemed to have deserted
her; and almost at once, slow and tragic and resignedly weeping,
came the opening notes of Chopin's Funeral March.   Sitting
in the front row of the little batch of children from the lower

school who faced the room from the window bay, Miriam saw, in fancy, Julia's face as she sat at the drawing-room piano— the face she had when she talked of the woods and the sea. The whole of the long march, including the major passage, was the voice of Julia's strange desolation. She played painfully, very slowly and carefully, with tender respectful attention, almost without emphasis. She was not in the least panic-stricken; any one could feel that; but she had none of the musical assurance that would have filled the girls with uneasy admiration and disgust. They were pleased and amused. And far away, Julia was alone with life and death. She made two worlds plain, the scornful world of the girls and her own shadow-filled life.

Miriam longed for the performance to be at an end so that the girls might reassert themselves.

An important stirring was going on at the little table where Miss Cramp sat with the Pernes; only their heads and shoulders showing above the piles of prize-books. Miss Perne stood up and faced the room smiling and gently muttering. Presently her voice grew clear and she was making little statements and pronouncing names, clearly and with gay tender emphasis, the names of tall bold girls in the first class. One by one they struggled to the table and stood gentle and disturbed, with flushed enlightened faces. Not a single girl could stand unconcerned before Miss Perne. Even Polly Allen's brow was shorn of its boldness.

The girls knew. They would remember something of what the Pernes had tried to give them.

The room was unbearably stuffy. The prize-giving was at an end. Miriam's own children had struggled to the table and come back to her for the last time.

Miss Perne was making a little speech . . . about Miss Henderson's forthcoming departure. Why did people do these formal things? She would be expected to make some response. For a moment she had the impulse to get up and rush away through the hall, get upstairs and pack and send for a four-wheeler. But from behind came hands dragging at a fold of her dress and the sound of Burra's hard sobbing. She felt the child's head bowed against her hip. A child at her side twisted its hands together and sat with its head held high, drawing sharp breaths. Miss Perne's voice went on. She was holding up an umbrella, a terrible, expensive, silver-mounted one. The girls had subscribed.

Miriam sat with beating heart waiting for Miss Perne's voice to cease, pressing back towards the support of Burra and other little outstretched clutchings and the general snuffling of her class, grappling with the amazement of hearing from various quarters of the room violent and repeated nose-blowings, and away near the door, in the voice of a girl she had hardly spoken to, a deep heavy contralto sobbing.

Presently she was on her feet with the tightly-rolled silken twist of the umbrella heavy in her hands. Her stiff lips murmured incoherent thanks in a strange thin voice—Harriett's voice with the life gone from it.

HONEYCOMB

CHAPTER I

WHEN Miriam got out of the train into the darkness she knew that there were woods all about her. The moist air was rich with the smell of trees—wet bark and branches—moss and lichen, damp dead leaves. She stood on the dark platform snuffing the rich air. It was the end of her journey. Anything that might follow would be unreal compared to this moment. Little bulbs of yellow light further up the platform told her where she must turn to find the things she must go to meet. 'How lovely the air is here.' . . . The phrase repeated itself again and again, going with her up the platform towards the group of lights. It was all she could summon to meet the new situation. It satisfied her; it made her happy. It was enough; but no one would think it was enough.

But the house was two miles off. She was safe for the present. Throughout the journey from London, the two-mile drive from the station had stood between her and the house. The journey was a long solitary adventure; endless; shielded from thoughts of the new life ahead, and leaving the past winter in the Gunnersbury villa far away; vanquished, almost forgotten. She could recall only the hours she had spent shivering apathetically over small fires; a moment when she had brought a flush of tears to her mother's eyes by suddenly telling her she was maddeningly unreasonable; and another moment, alone with her father, when she had stood in the middle of the hearth-rug, with her hands behind her, and ordered him to abstain from argument with her in the presence of her mother—'because it gives her pain when I have to show you that I am at least as right as you are'—and he had stood cowed and silent. . . . Then the moment of accepting the new post, the last days of fear and isolation and helplessness in hard winter weather, and the setting off in the main line train that had carried her away from everything—into the spring. Sitting in the shabbily upholstered, unexpectedly warm and comfortable main line train, she had seen through the mild muggy air bare woods on the horizon, warm and tawny, and on the near copses a ruddy purpling bloom. Surprise had kept her thoughtless and rapt. Spring—a sudden pang of tender green seen in suburban roadways in April, one day in the Easter holidays, bringing back the forgotten summer and showing you the whole picture of summer and autumn in one moment. But evidently there was another spring, much more real and wonderful, that she had not known—not a clear green thing, surprising and somehow disappointing you, giving you one moment and then rushing your thoughts on through vistas of leafage, but tawny and purple gleamings through soft mist, promising. A vision of spring in dim rich faint colours, with the noisy real rushing spring still to come. A thing you could look at and forget, go back into winter, and see again and again; something to remember when the green spring came, and to think of in the autumn. Perhaps spring was coming all the year round. She looked back, wondering. This was not the first time that she had been in the country in March. Two years ago, when she had first gone out into the world, it had been March . . . the night journey from Barnes to London, and on down to Harwich, the crossing in a snowstorm, the afternoon journey across Holland—grey sky, flat bright green fields, long rows of skeleton poplars. But it was dark before they reached the wooded German country—the spring must have been there, in the darkness. And now, coming to Newlands, she had seen it. The awful blind cold effort of coming to Newlands had brought a new month of spring; there for always. . . . And this was the actual breath of it; here, going through her in the darkness. . . . Someone was at her side, murmuring her name, a footman. She moved with him towards a near patch of light which they reached without going through the station building, and in a moment the door of a little brougham closed upon her with a soft thud. She sat in the softly lit interior, holding her umbrella and her undelivered railway ticket in careful fingers. The footman and a porter were hoisting her Saratoga trunk. Their movements sounded muffled and far-off. The brougham bowled away through the darkness, softly. The lights of the station flickered by and disappeared. The brougham windows were black. No sound but the faint rumble of the wheels along the smooth road. Miriam relaxed and sat back, smiling. For a moment she was conscious of nothing but the soft-toned, softly-lit interior, the softness at her back, the warmth under her feet and her happy smile; then she felt a sudden strength; the smile coming straight up so unexpectedly from some deep where it had been waiting, was new and strong and exhilarating. It would not allow itself to dimple; it carried her forward, tiding her over the passage into new experience and held her back, at the same time; it lifted her and held her suspended over the new circumstances in rapid contemplation. She pressed back more steadily into the elastic softness and sat with bent head, eagerly watching her thoughts . . . this is me; this is right; I 'm *used* to dainty broughams; I can take everything for granted. . . . I must take everything absolutely for granted. . . . The moments passed, carrying her rapidly on. There was a life ahead that was going to enrich and change her as she had been enriched and changed by Hanover, but much more swiftly and intimately. She was changed already. Poverty and discomfort had been shut out of her life when the brougham door closed upon her. For as long as she could endure, and achieve any sort of dealing with the new situation, they had gone, the worry and pain of them could not touch her. Things that rose warm and laughing and expanding within her now, that had risen to the beauty and music and happiness of Germany, that had dried up and seemed to die in the English boarding-school, were going to be met and satisfied . . . she looked down at the hands clasped on her knees, the same hands and knees that had ached with cold through long winter days in the basement schoolroom . . . chilblains . . . the everlasting unforgettable aching of her sore throat . . . things that had made her face yellow and stiff or flushed with fever . . . gone away for ever. Her old self had gone, her governess self. It had really gone weeks ago, got up and left her in that moment when she had read Mrs Corrie's letter in Bennett's villa in the middle of a bleak February afternoon. A voice had seemed to come from the large handwriting scrawling across the faint blue page under the thick neat small address in raised gilt. The same voice, begging her to come for a few weeks and try, seemed to resound gently in the brougham. She had not accepted the situation; she had accepted something in Mrs Corrie's imagined voice, coming to her confidently from the big wealthy house.

The brougham passed a lamp and swerved in through a gate, bowling along over softly crunching gravel. She pressed reluctantly against the cushioned back. The drive had been too short. . . . Bennett's friends had given the Corries wrong ideas about her. They wanted a governess. She was not a governess. There were governesses . . . the kind of person they wanted. It was a mistake; another mistake . . . the brougham made a beautiful dull humming, going along a tree-lined tunnel. . . . What did the Corries want of her, arriving in their brougham? What did they expect her to do? . . .

As the footman opened the door of the brougham, a door far back in the dim porch was flung back, letting out a flood of light and the swift figure of a parlourmaid, who seized Miriam's Gladstone bag and the silver-mounted Banbury Park umbrella and led the way across the porch into the soft golden blaze. The Saratoga trunk had gone away with the brougham, and in a moment the door was closed and Miriam was standing, frightened and alone, in a fire-lit, lamp-lit, thickly carpeted enclosure within sound of a thin chalky voice saying: 'Ello, ello.' It seemed to come from above her. 'Ello—ello—ello —ello,' it said busily, hurrying about somewhere above, as she gazed about the terrifying hall. It was somehow like the box-office of a large theatre, only much better; the lamplight, there seemed to be several lamps, shaded with low-hanging old gold silk, and the rosy light from the huge clear fire in a deep grate, fell upon a thick pale greeny yellow carpet, the little settees with their huge cushions, and the strange-looking pictures set low on dull gold walls. In two directions the hall went dimly away towards low archways screened by silently hanging bead curtains. 'Ello—ello—ello—ello,' said the voice, coming quickly downstairs. Raising her eyes, Miriam saw a pale turquoise-blue silk dress, long and slender with deep frills of black chiffon round the short sleeves and a large frill draping the low-cut bodice, a head and face, sheeny bronze and dead white, coming across the hall.

'Ow-de-do; so glad you 've come,' said the voice, and two thin fingers and a small thin crushed handkerchief were pressed against her half-raised hand.

'Are you famished? Deadly awful journey! I 'm glad you 're tall. Wiggerson 'll take up your things. You must be starvin'. Don't change. There 's only me. Don't be long. I shall tell them to put on the soup.'

Gently propelled towards the staircase, Miriam went mechanically up the wide shallow stairs towards the parlourmaid waiting at the top. Behind her she heard the swift fuffle of Mrs Corrie's dress, the swish of a bead curtain and the thin tuneless voice inaccurately humming in some large near room, 'Jack 's the boy for work; Jack 's the boy for play.' She followed the maid across the landing, walking swiftly, as Mrs Corrie had done—the same greeny carpet, but white walls up here and again strange pictures hung low, on a level with your eyes, strange soft tones . . . crayons? . . . pastels?—what was the word—she was going to live with them, she would be able to look at them—and everything up here, in the soft pink light. There were large lamps with rose-pink shades. The maid held back a pink silk curtain hanging across an alcove, and Miriam went through to the open door of her room. 'Harris will bring up your trunk later, miss—if you like to leave your keys with me,' said the maid behind her. 'Oh yes,' said Miriam carelessly, going on into the room. 'Oh, I don't know where they are. Oh, it doesn't matter, I 'll manage.'

'Very good, miss,' said Wiggerson politely, and came forward to close the bedroom door.

Miriam flung off her outer things and faced herself in the mirror in her plain black hopsack dress with the apple green

velveteen pipings about the tight bodice and the square box
sleeves which filled the square mirror from side to side as she
stood. 'This dress is a nightmare in this room,' she thought,
puffing up her hair under her fringe-net with a hat-pin. 'Never
mind, I mustn't think about it,' she added hurriedly, discon-
certed for a moment by the frightened look in her eyes. The
distant soft flat silvery swell of a little gong sent her hurrying
to the mound of soft bath towel in the wide pale blue washhand basin. She found a bulging copper hot-water jug, brilliantly polished, with a wicker-covered handle. The water
hissed gently into the wide shallow basin, sending up a great
cloud of comforting steam. Dare's soap . . . extraordinary.
People like these being taken in by advertisements . . . awful
stuff, full of free soda, *any* transparent soap is bad for the skin,
must be, in the nature of things . . . makes your skin feel
tight. Perhaps they only use it for their hands. . . . Advertisement will do anything, pater said. . . . Perhaps in houses like
this—plonk, it certainly made a lovely hard ring falling into
the basin—where everything was warm and clean and fragrant,
even Dare's soap could not hurt you. The room behind her
seemed to encourage the idea. But surely it couldn't be her
room. It was a spare room. They had put her into it for her
month on trial. Could it possibly be hers, just her room, if
she stayed . . . the strange, beautiful, beautiful long wide
hang of the faintly pattery faintly blue curtains covering the
whole of the window space; the firelight on them as she came
into the room with Wiggerson, the table with a blotter, there
had been a table by the door with a blotter, as Wiggerson spoke.
She looked round, there it was . . . the blue-covered bed, the
frilled pillows, high silky-looking bed curtains with some sort
of little pattern on them, the huge clear fire, the big wicker chair.

Miriam laughed over her strange hot wine-clear, wine-
flavoured soup . . . *two* things about soup besides taking it
from the side of your spoon, which everybody knows—you *eat*
soup, and you tilt your plate *away*, not towards you (chum

along, chum along and eat your nice hot soup). . . . Her
secure, shy, contented laugh was all right as a response to Mrs
Corrie, sitting at the head of the long table, a tall graceful bird,
thin broad shoulders, with the broad black frill slipping from
them, rather broad thin oval white face, wiry auburn Princess
of Wales fringe coming down into a peak with hollow beaten-
in temples each side of it, auburn coils shining as she moved
her head, and the chalky lisping voice that said little things and
laughed at them and went on without waiting for answers.
But to herself the laugh meant much more than liking Mrs
Corrie and holding her up and begging her to go on. It meant
the large dark room, the dark invisible pictures, the big pieces
of strange dark furniture in gloomy corners, the huge screen
near the door where the parlourmaid came in and out; the
table like an island under the dome of the low-hanging rose-
shaded lamp, the table-centre thickly embroidered with
beetles' wings, the little dishes stuck about, sweets, curiously
crusted brown almonds, sheeny grey-green olives; the misty
beaded glass of the finger bowls—Venetian glass from that
shop in Regent Street—the four various wine glasses at each
right hand, one on a high thin stem, curved and fluted like a
shallow tulip, filled with hock; and, floating in the warmth
amongst all these things the strange, exciting, dry sweet
fragrance coming from the mass of mimosa, a forest of little
powdery blossoms, little stiff grey—the arms of railway signals
at junctions—Japanese looking leaves—standing as if it were
growing, in a shallow bowl under the rose-shaded lamp.

'Mélie 's coming on Friday.'

The parlourmaid set before Miriam a small shapely fish, with
scales like mother-of-pearl and pink fins, lying in a curl of
paper. 'Red mullet,' she exclaimed to herself; 'how on earth
do I know that it 's red mullet ? And those *are* olives, of
course.' Mrs Corrie was humming to herself about Mélie,
as the fork in her thin little fingers plucked fitfully at the
papered fish. 'Do you know planchette ?' she asked, in a faint
sing-song, turning with a little bold pounce to the salt-cellar
close at Miriam's left hand. 'Oh-h-h,' said Miriam intelli-
gently. . . . 'Planchette . . . Planchette . . . *Cloches de Corneville*.

Planquette. Is planchette a part of all this? . . . Planchette, a French dressmaker, perhaps.' She turned fully round to Mrs Corrie and waited, smiling sympathetically. 'It's deadly uncanny,' Mrs Corrie went on, 'I can tell you. *Deadly*.' Her delicate voice stopped, fearfully, and she glanced at Miriam with a laugh. 'I don't believe I know what it is,' said Miriam, sniffing in the scent of the mimosa and savouring the delicate flavour of the fish. These things would go on after planchette was disposed of, she thought, and took a sip of hock.

'It's deadly. I hope Mélie'll bring one. She's a fairy; real Devonshire fairy. She'll make it work. We'll have *such* fun.'

'What is it?' said Miriam a little uneasily. . . . A fairy and a planchette and fun—silly laughter, some tiresome sort of game; a hoax.

'I tell you *all* about it, all, all . . .' intoned Mrs Corrie provisionally, whilst the maid handed the tiny ready-cut saddle of lamb. 'Spinnick? Ah, nicey spinnick; you can leave us that, Stokes. . . . Oh, you *must* have Burgundy—spin-spin and Burgundy; awful good; a thimble-full, half a glass; that's right.'

The clear dry hock had leapt to Miriam's brain and opened her eyes, the Burgundy spread through her limbs, a warm silky tide. The green flavour of the spinach, tasting of earth, and yet as smooth as cream, intoxicated her. Surely nothing could so delicately build up your strength as these small stubby slices of meat so tender that it seemed to crumble under your teeth. . . . 'It's an awful thing. It whirls about and writes with a pencil. Writes. All sorts of things,' said Mrs Corrie, with a little frightened laugh. 'Really. No nonsense. Names. Anythin'. Whatever you're thinkin' about. It's uncanny, I can tell you.'

'It sounds most extraordinary,' said Miriam, with a firm touch of scepticism.

'You wait. Oh—you wait,' sang Mrs Corrie in a whisper. 'I shall find out, I shall find out, if you're not careful, I shall find out his name.'

Miriam blushed violently. 'Ah-ha,' beamed Mrs Corrie

in a soft high monotone. '*I* shall find out. We'll have *such* fun.'

'Do you *believe* in it?' said Miriam, half irritably.

'You wait—you wait—you wait, young lady. Mélie'll be here on Friday day.'

The rich caramel, the nuts and dessert, Mrs Corrie's approval of her refusal of port wine with her nuts, the curious, half-drowsy chill which fell upon the table, darkening and sharpening everything in the room as the broken brown nut-shells increased upon their trellis-edged plates, were under the spell of the strange woman. Mrs Corrie kept on talking about her; Mélie—born in Devonshire, seeing fairies, having second sight, being seen one day staring into space by a sportsman, a fisherman, a sort of poet, who married her and brought her to London. Did Mrs Corrie really believe that she knew everything? 'I believe she's a changeling,' laughed Mrs Corrie at last—'oh, it's cold. Chum-long, let's go.'

'We can't go into my little room,' said Mrs Corrie, turning to Miriam with a little excited catch in her voice, as the bead curtain rattled gently into place behind them. 'It's bein' re-done.' Just ahead of them, beyond a mystery of palms to right and left, a door opened upon warm brilliance. Miriam heard the busy tranquil flickering of a fire. 'I see,' she said eagerly. 'Why does she explain?' she wondered, as they passed into the large clear room. How light it was, fairyland, light and fragrant and very warm. The light was high; creamy bulbs, high up, and creamy colour everywhere, cream and gold stripes, stripy chairs of every shape, some of them with twisted gilt legs, curious oval pictures in soft half-tones, women in hats, strange groups, all tilted forward like mirrors.

'Ooogh—barracky, ain't it? I hate empty droin'-rooms,' said Mrs Corrie, sweeping swiftly about, pushing up great striped easy chairs towards the fire. Miriam stood in a dream, watching the little pale hands in the clear light, dead white fingers, rings, twinkling green and sea blue, and the thin cruel flash of tiny diamonds . . . harpy hands . . . dreadful and clever . . . one of the hands came upon her own and compelled her to drop into a large cushioned chair.

'Like him black?' came the gay voice. Coffee cups tinkled on a little low table near Mrs Corrie's chair. 'I'm glad you're tall. Kummel?'

'She doesn't know German pronunciation,' thought Miriam complacently.

'I suppose I am,' she said, accepting a transparent little cup and refusing the liqueur. Those strange eyes were blue, with dark rings round the iris and there were fine deep wrinkles about the mouth and chin. She looked so picturesque sitting there, like something by an 'old master,' but worn and tired. Why was she so happy—if she thought so many things were deadly awful. . . .

'How's Gabbie Anstruther?'

'Oh—you see—I don't know Mrs Anstruther. They are patients of my future brother-in-law. It was all arranged by letter.'

'About your comin' here, you mean. I say—you'll never get engaged, will you? Promise?'

Miriam got up out of her deep chair and stood, with her elbow on the low mantel, staring into the fire. She heard phrases, from Mrs Anstruther's letter to Bennett, as if they were being spoken by a tiresome grave voice. 'She dotes upon her children. What she really wants is someone to control her; read Shakespeare to her and get her into the air.' Mrs Corrie did not want Shakespeare. That was quite clear. And it was quite clear that she wanted a plain dull woman she could count on; always there, in a black dress. She doted. Someone else, working for her, in her pay, would look after the children and do the hard work.

'The kiddies were 'riffickly 'cited. Wanted to stay up. I hope you're strict, very strict, eh?'

'I believe I'm supposed to understand discipline,' said Miriam stiffly, gazing with weary eyes at the bars of the grate.

'We were in an awful fix before we heard about you. Poor old Bunnikin breakin' down. She adored them—they're

angels. But she hadn't the tiniest bit of a hold over them.
Used to cry when they were naughty. *You* know. Poor
old kiddies. Want them to be awfully clever. Work like a
house afire. I know you're clever. P'raps you won't stay
with my little heathens. Do try and stay. I can see you've
got just what they want. Strong-minded, eh? I'm an
imbecile. So was poor old Bunnikin. D'you like kiddies?'
'Oh, I'm very fond of children,' said Miriam despairingly.
She stared at the familiar bars. They were the bars of the old
breakfast-room grate at home, and the schoolroom bars at
Banbury Park. There they were again, hard and black in the
hard black grate, in the midst of all this light and warmth and
fragrance. Nothing had really changed. Black and hard.
Someone's grate. She was alone again. Mrs Corrie would
soon find out. 'I think children are so *interesting*,' she said
conversationally, struck by a feeling of originality in the remark.
Perhaps children were interesting. Perhaps she would manage
to find the children interesting. She glanced round at Mrs
Corrie. Her squarish white face was worn. Her eyes and
neck looked as though all the life and youth had been washed
away from them by some long sorrow. Her smile was startling
. . . absolute confidence and admiration . . . like mother.
But she would find out if one were not really interested.

That night Miriam roamed about her room from one to
another of the faintly patterned blue hangings. Again and
again she faced each one of them. For long she contemplated
the drapery of the window space, the strange forest-like confusion made, in the faint pattern of tiny leaves and flowers, by
the many soft folds, and turned from it for a distant view of the
draperies of the bed and the French wardrobe. Sitting down
by the fire at last she had them all in her mind's eye. She was
going to be with them all night. If she stayed with them long
enough she would wake one day with red bronze hair and a
pale face and thin white hands. And by that time life would
be all strange draperies and strange inspiring food and mocking

laughing people who floated about hiding a great secret, and servants who were in the plot, admiring and serving it, and despising as much as anybody the vulgar things outside.

Her black dress mocked at these thoughts and she looked about for her luggage. Finding the Saratoga trunk behind the draperies of the French wardrobe, she extracted her striped flannelette dressing-gown and presently sat down again with loosened hair. Entrenched in her familiar old dressing-gown, she felt more completely the power of her surroundings. Whatever should happen in this strange house, she had sat for one evening in possession of this room. It was added for ever to the other things. And this one evening was more real than all the fifteen months at Banbury Park. It was so far away from everything, trams and people and noise—it was in the centre of beautiful exciting life; perfectly still and secure. Creeping to the window she held back the silk-corded rim of a curtain—a deep window-seat, a row of oblong lattices with leaded diamond panes. One of the windows was hasped a few inches open. No sound came in . . . soft moist air and the smell of trees. Nothing but woods all round, everywhere.

The next morning a housemaid tapped at Miriam's door, half an hour after she had called her, to say that her breakfast was laid in the schoolroom. Going out on to the landing she discovered the room by a curious rank odour coming towards her through a half-opened door. Pushing open the door she found a large clear room, barely furnished, carpeted with linoleum and cold in the morning light pouring through an un-draped window. In the grate smoked a half-ignited fire, and one corner of the hearth-rug, caught by a foot, lay turned back. Across one end of the baize-covered table a cloth was laid, and on it stood a small crowded tray: a little teapot, no cosy, some rather thick slices of bread and butter, a small dish of marmalade, a small plate and cup and saucer piled together, and a larger plate on which lay an unfamiliar fish, dark brown, curiously dried and twisted, and giving out a strong salt smoky odour. Miriam sat uncomfortably on the edge of a cane chair getting through her bread and butter and tea and one mouthful of the strong dry fish, feeling, with the door still standing wide, like a traveller snatching a hasty meal at a buffet. She tried to collect her thoughts on education. Little querulous excited sounds came to her from across the wide landing. Presently there came the swift flountering of a print dress across the landing and Wiggerson, long and willowy and capless, with a cold red nose and large red hands, her thin small head looking very young with its revealed bunch of untidy hair, appeared in the schoolroom doorway with an unconscious smile hesitating on her pale lips and in her pale blue eyes. 'It isn't very comfortable for you,' she said in a hurried voice. 'I say, my *word*'; she went to the chilly grate and bent down for the poker. Miriam glanced at the solicitous droop of her long figure. 'Stokes hasn't half laid it,' went on Wiggerson; 'if I were you I should have breakfast in my room. They all do except Mr Corrie when he's at home. The other young lady was daily; she didn't stop. I should, if I were you,' she finished, getting lightly to her feet. She stood between the door and the fireplace, half turned away, and gazing into space with her pale strong eyes, every line in her long pure unconscious figure waiting for Miriam's response.

'Do you *like* me, Wiggerson?' said Miriam within, 'you'll have toothache and neuralgia with that thin head. You're devoted to your relations. You've got a tiresome sickly old mother. You'll never know you're a servant. . . . I think perhaps I will,' she drawled, clearing her throat.

'All right,' said Wiggerson, with a lit face. 'I'll tell them.'

CHAPTER II

As Miriam sat having tea with the children in the dining-room, the brougham drove up to the door. 'There's someone arriving,' she said, hoping to distract the attention of the children from her fumblings with the teapot and the hot water jug. They had certainly never met any one who did not know how to pour out tea. But they were taken in by her bored tone.

'It's only Joey,' said Sybil, frowning tranquilly, her lively penetrating brown eyes fixed on the table just ahead of the small plate nearly covered by a mass of raspberry jam from which she ate with a teaspoon in the intervals of taking small bites from a thin piece of bread and butter held conveniently near her mouth as she sat with one elbow on the table. 'She's always here.' She looked across the table and met the soft brown eyes of the boy. They had been wandering absently about Sybil's square pale face and short straggling red hair as she answered Miriam. 'Jenooshalet,' he said, lisping over the 's' and smiling meditatively.

'Jenoosh,' responded Sybil, and they both laughed drunkenly.

'What I'm finking,' said the boy, putting a teaspoonful of jam into his teacup and speaking with a stammering difficulty that drew deep lines in his thin face; 'what's worrying me is she'll have Rollo after tea instead of us. . . . Vat's what I'm finking.'

'D'you like bays?' said Sybil, throwing a fleeting glance in the direction of Miriam.

'Yes, I do, I think,' said Miriam at random, patting her hair and wondering if the children had been to Weymouth.

'Oh, *Boy*.' Sybil flung her arms tightly round her thin body and sat grinning at her brother. Her old blue and white striped overall, her sparse hair and the ugly large gap between her two large front teeth seemed to set her apart from her surroundings. For a moment it seemed to Miriam that the large quiet room looking through two high windows on to a stretch of tree-shaded lawn, the cheerful little spread of delicate white china at one end of the long table, the preserves and cakes, the cress sandwiches and thin bread and butter were all there for her appreciation alone, the children somehow profane and accidental, having no right to be there. But they had been in these surroundings, the girl for twelve, the boy for eight years. They had never known anything else. For years life had been for them just what it was to-day—breakfast in bed, chirping at their mother from the dressing-rooms where they slept, and scolding at Stokes as she waited on their toilet; jocularly and impatiently learning lessons from little text-books for an hour or so in the morning, spending their afternoons cantering about the commons and along the sandy roadways with the groom; driving with their mother or walking with the governess, and every day coming in at the end of the afternoon to this cosy, dainty grown-up tea, with their strange untroubled brooding faces. They would grow up and be exactly like their parents. They did not know anything about their fate. It was a kind of prison. Perhaps they knew. Perhaps that was what they were always brooding over. No, they did not mind. Their musings were tranquil. They were waiting. They had silent conversations all the time. To be with them after being so long with the straining, determined, openly ambitious children at Banbury Park, was a great relief . . . the way they moved their heads and used their hands . . . the boy's hands were wonderful, the palest fine brown silk, quick eloquent little claws, promising understanding and support. Fine little hands and steady gentle brown eyes.

'Bays.'

'*Bright* bays.'

'Roans.'

'*Strawberry* roans.'

'*Chestnuts.*'

'*Chestnut* bays.'

The children sat facing each other, each with clasped hands, and eyes lit with dreams. Miriam listened. Bay, then, must be that curious liver colour that was neither brown nor chestnut.

'Our ponies are bay,' said Sybil quickly, with flushed face. 'Boy's and mine, the brougham and victoria horses are chestnut bays and we've got two dogs, a whippet bitch, she's in the stables now, and a Great Dane; I'm going to have a Willoughby pug pup on my birthday.'

Mrs Corrie was standing in the hall when the little tea-party came out of the dining-room. She raised her head and stood shaped in the well-cut lines of her long brown and fawn check coat and skirt against the bead curtain that led to the drawing-room, looking across at them. The boy tottered blindly across the hall with arms out-stretched. 'Oh, Rollo, Rollo,' he said brokenly, as he reached her, pressing his hands up against her grey suède waistcoat and his face into her skirt, 'are we going to h—*ave* you?'

Mrs Corrie began singing in a thin laughing voice, taking the boy by the wrists.

'No, no,' he said sharply, 'let me hold you a minute.' But Mrs Corrie danced, forcing his steps as he pressed against her. Up and down the hall they capered while Sybil pranced round them whirling her skirts and clapping her hands. Miriam sank into a settee. The cold March sunlight streaming in through the thinly curtained windows painted the sharply bobbing figures in faint shadows on the opposite wall.

When the dancers were breathless, the little party strayed into the drawing-room. Presently they were gathered at the piano. Mrs Corrie sat on a striped ottoman and, peering closely, picked out the airs of songs that made Miriam stare in amazement. They all sang. Slowly and stumblingly, with many gasps of annoyance from Mrs Corrie, and the children violently assaulting each other whenever either of them got ahead of the halting accompaniment, they sang through all the songs in an album with a brightly decorated paper cover.

But in their performance there was no tune, no rhythm, and the words, spoken out slowly and separately, were intolerable. One song they sang three times. Its chorus,

> Stiboo—stib*ee*,
> Sti-ibbety-*oo*
> Sti-ibbety-b*oo*,
> Stib*ee*,

which Sybil could sing without the piano with an extraordinary flourishing rapidity, pirouetting as she sang, they attacked again and again, slowly and waveringly, fitting the syllables note by note into the printed line of jerkily tailed quavers. . . . They thought this was music. Encouraged at last by the fervour of the halting performance, Miriam found herself seated at the piano attacking the score. They went through the songs from the beginning, three thin blissful wavering tremulous voices, with a careful perfect monotony of emphasis, uninfluenced by any variation of accent or inflection introduced by Miriam into the accompaniment. Looking round as they reached the end she saw flushed rapt faces with happy eyes gleaming through the gathering twilight. They smiled at her as they sang. When they had finished they lit the piano candles, and sang *Stiboo* once more.

'Sti-boo, stibee, sti-ibbety-oo, sti-ibbety boo, stibee,' sang Miriam, getting into the large square bodice of her silkette evening-dress. Its great oblong box-like elbow sleeves more than filled the mirror as she stood. They were stiffened with stout muslin, and stood squarely out from shoulder to elbow, so that the little band of silk, edged with a piping of salmon pink velveteen, which held them round the arm just above the elbow, could only be seen when she raised her arms. The piping was repeated round the square neck of her bodice, cutting in front across the bust just below the collar bone, and at the back just above her shoulder blades. She sang the little refrain at intervals until her toilet was completed by the pinning of a small salmon pink velvet bow against the left side of the hard mass of her coiled hair, and went humming downstairs into the hall. The soles of her new patent leather shoes felt pleasantly smooth against the thick carpet. She went across the hall to prop a foot against the fender and take one more reassuring look at the little disc of steel beads adorning her toe. 'Stiboo——'

'Won't you come in heah?' said a soft staccato bass voice, a woman's voice, but deep and rounded like the voice of a deep-chested watch-dog, barking single soft notes after a furious outbreak.

Miriam looked round. Wiggerson was lighting the big lamp in the dining-room, peering up under the rose-coloured shade. 'In heah,' repeated the deep voice, smiling, and Miriam's eyes discovered that the small door, set back between the dining-room and the window on the left side of the hall door, was open, showing part of a curious soft brown room; a solid brown leather-covered secretaire, with a revolving chair between its pillars of drawers, set back in the bow of a small window, a little bronze lamp with a plain buff-coloured shade standing near a pile of large volumes on the secretaire, a piece of wall covered with a dark silky-looking brown paper shining in the glow of an invisible fire. She went forward across the hall into the room with a polite, pleased, hesitating smile. There was a faint rich exciting odour in the warm little room . . . cigars . . . leather . . . a sort of deep freedom. The rest of the house seemed suddenly far away. Coloured drawings of horses on the little brown walls, two enormous deep low leather arm-chairs drawn up on either side of an enormous fire, a littered mantelshelf. 'I saw you froo the crack,' said a lady, fitted deeply into one of the large chairs. She held out a small hand when Miriam was near enough to take it and said softly and lazily, 'You're the new guvnis, aren't you? I'm Joey Banks.'

'Yes, I came yesterday,' said Miriam serenely.

Sinking into the second arm-chair she crossed her knees and beamed into the fire. What perfect security. . . . She turned to Mr Corrie, unknown and mysteriously away somewhere in London, to thank him for setting her here, protected from the whole world in the deeps of his study chair—all the worry and the noise and the fussing people shut away. If suddenly he came in she would not thank him, but he would know. He would be sitting in the other arm-chair, and she would say, 'What do you think about everything?' Not so much to hear what he thought, but because some of his thoughts would be her thoughts. Thought was the same in everybody who thought at all. She would sit back and rest and hear an understanding voice. He might be heavy and fat. But a leading Q.C. must have thoughts . . . and he had been thin once . . . and there were those books . . . and he would read newspapers; perhaps too many newspapers. He would know almost at once that she thought he read too many newspapers. She would have to conceal that, to hear the voice going on and leaving her undisturbed.

Of course people like this wore evening-dress every day. You could only rest and think and talk and be happy without collars and sleeves—with the cool beaded leather against one's neck and arms in the firelight. . . .

She gazed familiarly into her companion's eyes, taking in her soft crimson silk evening-dress with its wide folded belt of black velvet and the little knots of black about the square sleeves, as the eyes smiled long and easily into hers . . . the smile of one of the girls at the Putney school, the same dark-fringed, caressing, smiling eyes set in delicately bulging pale brown cheeks, the same little frizz of dark hair. She felt for the name, but could only recall the sense of the girl as she had sat, glints of fear and hard watchfulness in the beautiful eyes, trying to copy her neighbour's exercise. This girl's dull hair was fluffed cloudily, and there was no uneasiness in the eyes. Probably she too had been a duffer at school and had had to crib things. But she had left all that behind and her smile was—perfect.

'You look like an Oriental princess,' said Miriam, gazing.

Joey flushed and smiled more deeply, but without making the smallest movement.

'Do I, weally?'

'Exactly,' said Miriam, keeping her own pose with difficulty.

She knew she had flung up her head and spoken emphatically.
But the girl was such a wonderful effect—she wanted her to be
able to see herself . . . she was not quite of the same class as the
Corries, or different, somehow. Miriam gazed on. Raising
the large black cushion a little, turning her head and pressing
her cheek into it, her eyes still on Miriam's, Joey laughed a
short contralto gurgle, bringing sharp dimples and making her
cheeks bulge slightly on either side of the chin.

'I brought it in from Rollo's room,' she said. 'I like bein' in
here. Rollo never comes in; but she always has a fire in here
when she's got people stoppin'. You can pop in here whenever
you like, when Felix isn't at home. It's jolly. I like it.'

Miriam looked into the fire and thought. Joey, too, liked
talking to Mr Corrie in his room when he was not there. He
must be one of those charming sort of men, rather weak, who
went on liking people. Joey was evidently an old friend of
the family and still liked him. She evidently liked even to
mention his name. He couldn't be really anything much . . .
or perhaps Joey didn't really know him at all. Joey did not
live there. She came and went.

'Of course you haven't seen Felix yet, have you?'

'No.'

Joey straightened her head on her pillow.

'It's not the least use me tryin' to describe him to you,' she
breathed in broken tones.

Miriam struggled uneasily with her thoughts . . . a leading
Q.C.—about forty. . . . 'Oh, do try,' she said, a little fearfully
. . . how vulgar . . . just like a housemaid . . . no; Wiggerson would never have said such a thing, nor asked at all.
It was treachery to Mr Corrie. If Joey said anything more
about him, she would never be able to speak to him freely.

'He's divine,' said Joey, smiling into the fire.

How nice of Joey to be so free with her, and want her to like
him too . . . the gong. They both rose and peered into the
little strip of mirror in the small overmantel . . . divine might
mean anything . . . divine . . . oh, quite too utterly too-too
. . . greenery-yellery—Grosvenor-gallery—foot-in-the-grave
young man.

CHAPTER III

THE next day the ground was powdered with snow. Large snowflakes were hurrying through the air, driving to and fro on a harsh wind. The wind snored round the house like a flame and bellowed in the chimneys. An opened window let in the cold air and the smell of the snow. No sound came from the woods. The singing of the birds and the faint sound of the woods had gone.

But when Miriam left her room to go across to the schoolroom and wait for the children, she found spring in the house. The landing was bright with the light streaming through many open doors. Rooms were being prepared. On a large tray on the landing table lay a mass of spring flowers and little flowered bowls of many shapes and sizes filled with fresh water. Stokes and Wiggerson were fluttering in and out of the rooms carrying frilled bed-linen, lace-edged towels and flowered bed-spreads.

People with money could make the spring come as soon as the days lengthened. Clear bright rooms, bright clean paint, soft coloured hangings, spring flowers in the bright light on landings. The warmth from stoves and fires seemed as if it came from the sun. Its glow changed suddenly to the glow of sunlight. It drew the scent of the flowers into the air. And with the new scent of the new flowers something was moving and leaping and dancing in the air. Outside, the wintry weather might go on and on as though the spring would never come.

In a dull cheap villa, there might be a bunch of violets in a bowl on a whatnot. Snuffing very close you could feel the tide of spring wash through your brain. But only in the corner where the violets were. In cold rooms upstairs you could remember the violets and the spring; but the spring did not get into the house.

There was an extraordinary noise going on downstairs.

369

Standing inside the schoolroom door, Miriam listened.   Joey's
contralto laugh coming up in gusts, the sound of dancing feet,
the children shouting names, Mrs Corrie repeating them in her
laughing wavering chalky voice.   Joey; certainly Joey was not
dancing about.   She was probably sitting on the sofa watching
them, and thinking.   Fancy their being so excited about people
coming.   Just like any ordinary people.   She went into the
schoolroom saying over the names to herself.   'Mélie to-day
. . . Dad and Mr Staple-Craven to-morrow . . . the Bean-
pole for Sunday . . . someone they knew very well.   It might
be either a tall man or a tall woman. . . . They made the
house spring-like because people were coming.   Would the
people notice that the house was spring-like?   Would they
realize?   People did not seem to realize anything.   They
would patronize the flowers . . . they ought to feel wild with
joy; join hands and dance round the flowers.

At lunch time the door at the far end of the dining-room
stood open, showing the shrouded length of a billiard-table
and, beyond it, at the far end in the gloom, a squat oak chimney-
piece littered with pipes and other small objects.   The light,
even from the overcast sky, came in so brilliantly that the
holland cover looked almost white.   There must be several
windows; perhaps three.   What a room to have, just for a
billiard-room.   A quiet, mannish room, waiting until it was
wanted, the pockets of the table bulging excitingly under the
cover, the green glass supports under the squat round stoutly
spindling legs, a bit of a huge arm-chair showing near the
fireplace, the end of a sofa, the green shaded lamps low over
the table, the dark untidy mantelpiece, tobacco, books, talks,
billiards.   In there, too, spring flowers stood ready on the
table.   They would be put somewhere on the wide dark
mantel, probably on a corner out of the way.   'We used to
play table-billiards at home,' said Miriam at random, longing to
know what part the billiard-room played in the week-end.

'Billy-billy,' said Mrs Corrie, 'oh, we'll have some fun.
We'll *all* play.'

'It was *such* a bore stretching the webbing,' said Miriam
critically, avoiding Sybil's eager eyes.

'It *must* have been—but how awfully jolly to have billiards. I simply adaw billiards,' said Joey fervently.

'Such a fearful business getting them absolutely taut,' pursued Miriam, feeling how much the cream caramel was enhanced by the sight of the length, beyond the length of the dining-room, of that bright long heavy room. She imagined it lit, and people walking about amongst the curious lights and shadows with cues—and cigarettes; quiet intent faces. English-men. Did the English invent billiards?

'Poor old Joey. Wish you weren't going to the dentist. You won't be here when Mélie comes.'

'Don't mind the dentist a scrap. I 'm looking forward to it. I shall see Mélie to-night.'

She doesn't like her, thought Miriam; people being together is awful; like the creaking of furniture.

Mélie arrived an hour before dinner-time. Miriam heard Mrs Corrie taking her into the room next to her own, with laughter and many phrases. A panting, determined voice, like a voice out of a play, the thick, smooth, rather common voice of a fair-haired, middle-aged lady in a play kept saying, 'The pores, my dear. I must open my pores after the journey. I 'm *choked* with it.'

Presently Mélie's door closed and Mrs Corrie tapped and put her head inside Miriam's door. 'She 's goin' to have a steam bath on her floor, got an injarubber tent on the floor and a spirit lamp. She 's gettin' inside it. Isn't she an old *cure*!'

'She 's thinking more about her food than anything they 're saying; she doesn't really care about them a bit,' thought Miriam at dinner, gazing again and again across at Mrs Staple-Craven's fat little shape, seated opposite herself in a tightly fitting pale blue silk dress whose sleeves had tiny puffs instead of the fashionable large square sleeves. Watching her cross unconscious face, round and blue-eyed and all pure 'milk and roses,' her large yellow head with a tiny twist of hair standing up like the handle of a jug, exactly on the top of the crown, her

fat white hands with thick soft curly fingers and bright pink
nails, the strange blue stare that went from thing to thing on
the table, hearing her thick smooth heedless voice, with its
irrelevant assertions and statements, Miriam wondered . how
she had come to be Mrs Staple-Craven. She was no more
Mrs Staple-Craven than she was sitting at Mrs Corrie's table.
She was not really there. She was just getting through, and
neither Mrs Corrie nor Joey really knew this. At the same
time she was too stout and gluttonous to be still really a fairy in
Devonshire. Where was she? What did she think? She went
on and on because she was afraid someone might ask her that.

Although Joey had been to have her hair dyed, and had not
been to the dentist at all, she was not pretending nearly so
much. She was a little ashamed. Why had she said she was
going to the dentist and come back with sheeny bronzy hair,
ashamed? She had been worrying about her looks. Perhaps
she was more than twenty-one. Nan Babington said no one
need mind being twenty-one if they were engaged, but if not
it was a frantic age to be. Joey was a poor worried thing, just
like any other girl.

When they were safely ensconced round the drawing-room
fire, Mrs Staple-Craven sat very upright in her chair with her
plump little hands on either arm and her eyes fixed on the
blaze. Joey, pleading toothache, had said good night and
gone away with her coffee. There was a moment's silence.

'You 'd never think I 'd been fairly banged to death by the
spirits last night,' said Mrs Staple-Craven in a thick flat reproachful narrative tone. It sounds like a housekeeper giving
an order to a servant she knows won't obey her, thought
Miriam, swishing more comfortably into her chair. If Mrs
Craven would talk there would be no need to do anything.

'Ah-ha,' said Mrs Craven, still looking at the fire, 'something 's pleasing Miss Henderson.'

'Is she rejoicin'? Tell us about the spirits, Mélie. I 'm
deadly keen. Deadly. She mustn't be too delighted. I 've
told her she 's not to get engaged.'

'Engaged?' inquired Mrs Craven, of the fire.

'She 's promised,' said Mrs Corrie, turning off the lights

until only one heavily shaded lamp was left, throwing a rosy glow over Mélie's compact form.

'She won't if she's not under the star, to be sure.'

'Oh, she mustn't think about stars. Why should she marry?'

Miriam looked a little anxiously from one to the other.

'You've shocked her, Julia,' said Mrs Staple-Craven. 'Never mind at all, my dear. You'll marry if you're under the star.'

'Star, star, beautiful star, a handsome one with twenty thousand a year,' sang Mrs Corrie.

'I don't think a man has any right to be handsome,' said Miriam desperately—she must manage to keep the topic going. These women were so terrible—they filled her with fear. She must make them take back what they had said.

'A handsome man's much handsomer than a pretty woman,' said Mrs Craven.

'It's cash, cash, cash—that's what it is,' chanted Mrs Corrie softly.

'Oh, do you?' said Miriam. 'I think a handsome man's generally so weak.'

Mrs Craven stared into the fire.

'You take the one who's got the ooftish, my friend,' said Mrs Corrie.

'But you say I'm not to marry.'

'You shall marry when my poor little old kiddies are grown up. We'll find you a very nice one, with plenty of money.'

'Then you *don't* think marriage is a failure,' said Miriam, with immense relief.

Mrs Corrie leaned towards her with laughter in her clear light eyes. It seemed to fill the room. 'Have some more coffy-drink?'

'No, thanks,' said Miriam, shivering.

'Sing us something—she sings, Mélie—German songs. Isn't she no end clever?'

'Does she?' said Mrs Craven. 'Yes. She's got a singing chin, Sing us a pretty song, my dear.'

As she fluttered the leaves of her Schumann album she saw

Mrs Craven sit back with closed eyes, and Mrs Corrie still sitting forward in her chair with her hands clasped on her knees gazing with a sad white face into the flames.

'Ich grolle nicht, und wenn das Herz auch bricht,' sang Miriam, and thought of Germany. Her listeners did not trouble her. They would not understand. No English person would quite understand—the need, that the Germans understood so well—the need to admit the beauty of things . . . the need of the strange expression of music, making the beautiful things more beautiful, and of words when they were together in the beauty of the poems. Music and poetry told everything—whether you understood the music or the words— they put you in the mood that made things shine—then heart-break or darkness did not matter. Things go on shining until the end; German landscapes and German sunshine and German towns were full of this knowledge. In England there was something besides—something hard.

''Menjous, ain't it?' said Mrs Corrie, as she rose from the piano.

'If we lived aright we should all be singing,' said Mrs Craven, 'it 's natural.'

'You look a duck.'

Miriam stood still at the top of the stairs and looked down into the hall. Mrs Staple-Craven was standing under the largest lamp near the fireplace, looking up at a tall man in a long ulster. Grizzled hair and a long face with a long pointed grizzled beard—she was staring up at him with her eyes 'like saucers' and her face pink, white, gold, 'like a full moon'— how awful for him . . . he 's come down from town probably in a smoking carriage, talking, and there she was, and he had to say something.

'I 've just had my bath,' said Mrs Craven, without altering the angle of her gaze.

'You look a duck,' said the tall man fussily, half turning away.

Standing with his back to the couple, opening letters at the hall table, was a little man in a neat little overcoat with a silk hat tilted back on his head. His figure had a curious crooked jaunty appearance, the shoulders a little crooked and the little legs slightly bent. 'It's Mr Corrie,' mused Miriam, moving backwards as he turned and went swiftly out banging the front door behind him. 'He looks like a jockey'; she got herself back into her room until the hall should be clear. 'He's gone down to the stables.' She listened to the quick jerky little footsteps crunching along the gravel outside her window.

Soon after, the quick little steps sounded on the stairs and the children shouted from their rooms. A door was opened and shut and for five minutes there was a babel of voices. Then the steps came out again and went away down the passage leading off the landing to the bathroom and a little spare room at the further end. They passed the bathroom, and the door of the little room was opened and shut and locked. Everything was silent in the house, but from the room next to hers came the sounds of Mr Craven plunging quickly about and blowing and clearing his throat. She had not heard him come up.

When at last she came downstairs, she found the whole party standing talking in the hall. The second gong was drowning the terrible voices, leaving nothing but gesticulating figures. Presently Mr Staple-Craven was standing before her with Mrs Corrie, and her hand was powerfully wrung and released with a fussy emphatic handshake cancelling the first impression. Mr Craven made some remark in a high voice, lost by Miriam as Mr Corrie came across to her from talking to Joey under a lamp, and took her hand. 'Let me introduce your host,' he said, keeping her hand and placing it on his arm as he turned towards the dining-room, 'and take you into dinner.'

Miriam went across the hall, past the servants waiting on either side of the dining-room door, and down the long room with her hand on the soft sleeve of a neat little dinner jacket, and her footsteps led by the firm, disconnected, jumpy footsteps of the little figure at her side. There was a vague crowd of people coming along behind. 'Come on, everybody,' Mrs Corrie had pealed delicately, and Mrs Craven had said in a thick smooth explanatory voice, 'Of course she's the greatest stranger.'

The table was set with replicas of the little groups of Venetian wine and finger glasses and fine silver and cutlery that had accompanied Miriam's first sense of dining, and when she found herself seated at Mr Corrie's left hand opposite Mrs Craven, with Joey away on her left, facing Mr Craven and Mrs Corrie now far away from her at the door end of the table, it seemed as if these things had been got together only for the use of the men. Why were women there? Why did men and women dine together? She would have liked to sit there and watch and listen, but not to dine—not to be seen dining by Mr Corrie. It was extraordinary, this muddle of men and women with nothing in common. The men must hate it. She knew he did not have such thoughts. All the decanters stood in a little group between him and the great bowl of flaring purple and crimson anemones that stood in the centre of the table, and the way in which he said when her soup came, 'Have some Moselle,' and filled her glass, compelled her to feel welcome to share the ritual of the feast. She sat with bent head wrapped and protected, hearing nothing, as the voices sounded about the table, but the clear sweet narrow rather drawling tones of Mr Corrie's voice. She could hear it talking to men, on racecourses, talking in clubs, laughing richly, rather drunkenly, at improper stories in club smoking-rooms; dining, talking and lunching, dining, talking, talking every day; and sitting there now, wonderfully, giving her security. She knew with perfect certainty that nothing painful or disagreeable or embarrassing could come near her in his presence. But he knew nothing about her; much less than Wiggerson knew.

Joey felt the same, of course. But Joey was laughing and talking in her deep voice and making eyes. No, it was not the same. Joey was not happy.

These people sitting at his table were supposed to be friends. But they knew nothing about him. He made little quiet mocking jokes, and laughed and kept things going. The Staple-Cravens knew nothing at all about him. Mrs Staple-Craven did not care for anybody. She looked about and always spoke as if she were answering an accusation that nobody

had made—a dressmaker persuading you to have something
and talking on and on in fat tones to prevent your asking the
price. . . . Mr Craven only cared for himself. He was weak
and pompous and fussy, with a silly elaborately chivalrous
manner. There was a stillness round the table. Miriam felt
that it centred in her and was somehow her fault. Never
mind. She had successfully got through whitebait and a quail.
She would write home about the quails and whitebait and the
guests and say nothing about her own silence—'Mr Staple-
Craven is a poet . . .'

'Give Mélie some more drink, Percy,' said Mrs Corrie.
'It 's all wrong you two sittin' together.'

'She likes to sit near me, don't you, my duck?' said Mr
Craven, looking about for the wine and bowing to and fro from
his hips.

'You 've been away so long,' murmured Mr Corrie. 'What
sort of a place is Balone to stay in?'

'Oh, nothing of a place in itself, nothing of a place. Why
do you call it Balone?'

'Isn't that right? That 's right enough. Come.'

Miriam waited eagerly, her eyes on Mr Craven's pink face
with the grizzled hair above and below it. How perfectly
awful he must look in his nightshirt, she thought, and flushed
violently. 'Balloyne,' he was saying carefully, showing his
red lips and two rows of unnaturally even teeth. . . . 'Oh,
Lord, they mean Bologne.' Both men were talking together.
'Balloyne is perfectly correct; the correct pronunciation,' said
Mr Craven in a loud testy voice, with loose lips. Mrs Craven
gazed up . . . like a distressed fish . . . into his flushed face.
Mrs Corrie was throwing out her little wavering broken laughs.
Keeping his angry voice, Mr Craven went on. Miriam sat
eagerly up and glanced at Mr Corrie. He was sitting with his
lips drawn down and his eyebrows raised . . . his law-court
face. . . . Suddenly his face relaxed and the dark boyish brown
head with the clear thoughtful brow and the gentle kind eyes
turned towards her. 'Let 's ask Miss Henderson. She shall
be umpire.'

Miriam carefully enunciated the word. The blood sang in

her ears as everyone looked her way. The furniture and all
the room mimicked her. What did it matter, after all, the
right pronunciation? It did matter; not that Balone was
wrong, but the awfulness of being able to miss the right sound
if you had once heard it spoken. There was some awful
meaning in the way English people missed the right sound;
all the names in India, all the Eastern words. How *could* an
English traveller hear hahreem, and speak it hairum, Aswan
and say Ass-ou-ann? It made them miss other things and
think wrongly about them. 'That's more like it,' she heard
Mr Corrie say. There was sheeny braiding round the edges
of his curious little coat. 'Got you there, Craven, got you
there,' he was saying somewhere in his mind . . . his mind went
on by itself repeating things wearily. His small austere face
shone a little with dining; the corners of his thin lips slackened.
'I can read all your thoughts. None of you can disturb my
enjoyment of this excellent dinner; none of you can enhance
it' . . . but he was not quite conscious of his thoughts. Why
did not the others read them? Perhaps they did. Perhaps
they were too much occupied to notice what people were
thinking. Perhaps in society people always were. The
Staple-Cravens did not notice. But they were neither of them
quite sure of themselves. Mrs Corrie was busy all the time
dancing and singing somewhere alone, wistfully. Joey kept
throwing her smile at Mr Corrie—lounging a little, easily,
over the table and saying in her mind, 'I understand you, the
others don't, I do,' and he smiled at her, broadened the smile
that had settled faintly all over his face, now and again in her
direction. But she did not understand him. 'Divine,' perhaps he was, or could be. But Joey did not know him. She
only knew that he had a life of his own and no one else at the
table had quite completely. She did not know that with all his
worldly happiness and success and self-control he was miserable
and lost and needing consolation . . . but neither did he.
Perhaps he never would; would not find it out because he had
so many thoughts and was always talking. So he thought
he liked Joey. Because she smiled and responded. 'Jabez
Balfour,' he was saying slowly, savouring the words and smiling

through his raised wineglass with half closed eyes. That was for Mr Staple-Craven; there was some exciting secret in it. Presently they would be two men over their wine and nuts. Mr Staple-Craven took this remark for himseelf at once, scorning the women with a thick polite insolence. His lips shot out. 'Ah,' he said busily, 'Jabez Balfour, Jabez Balfour; ah,' he swung from side to side from his waist. 'Let me see, Jabez . . .'

'The Liberator scheme,' said Mr Corrie interestedly with a bright young eye. 'They 've got 'im this time; fairly got 'im on the hop.'

Jabez Balfour; what a beautiful name. He could not have done anything wrong. There was a soft glare of anger in Mr Corrie's eyes; as if he were accusing Mr Staple-Craven of some crime, or everybody. Perhaps one would hear something about crime; crime. That 's crime—somebody taking down a book and saying triumphantly, 'that 's crime,' and people talking excitedly about it, in the warm, at dinners . . . like that moment at Richmond Park, the ragged man with panting mouth, running . . . the quiet grass, the scattered deer, the kindly trees, the gentlemen with triumphant faces, running after him; enough, enough, he had suffered enough . . . his poor face, their dreadful faces. He knew more than they did. Crime could not be allowed. People murdering you in your sleep. But criminals knew that—the running man knew. He was running away from himself. He knew he had spoiled the grass and the trees and the deer. To have stopped him and hidden him and let him get over it. His poor face. . . . The awful moment of standing up trying to say or do something, feeling so weak, trembling at the knees, the man's figure pelting along in the distance, the two gentlemen passing, their white waistcoats, homes, wives, bathrooms, stuffiness, indigestion. . . .

'It comes perfectly into line with Biblical records, my dear Corrie: a single couple, two cells originating the whole creation.'

'I 'm maintaining that 's not the Darwinian idea at all. It was not a single couple, but several different ones.'

'We 're not descended from monkeys at all. It 's not natural,' said Mrs Craven loudly, across the irritated voices of the men. Their faces were red. They filled the room with inaccurate phrases, pausing politely between each and keeping up a show of being guest and host. How nice of them. But this was how cultured people with incomes talked about Darwin.

'The great thing Darwin did,' said Miriam abruptly, 'was to point out the power of environment in evolving the different species—selecting.'

'That 's it, that 's it!' sang Mrs Corrie. 'Let 's all select ourselves into the droin'-room.' 'Now I 've offended the men and the women too,' thought Miriam.

Mr Staple-Craven joined the ladies almost at once. He came in, leaving the door open behind him and took a chair in the centre of the fireside circle and sat giving little gasps and sighs of satisfaction, spreading his hands and making little remarks about the colours of the fire, and the shape of the coffee cups. There he was and he would have to be entertained, although he had nothing at all to say and was puzzling about himself and life all the time, behind his involuntary movements and polite smiles and gestures. Perhaps he was uneasy because he knew there was someone saying all the time, 'You 're a silly pompous old man and you think yourself much cleverer than you are.' But it was not altogether that; he was always uneasy, even when he was alone, unless he was rapidly preparing to go and be with people who did not know what he was. If he had been alone with the other three women he would have forgotten for a while and half-liked, half-despised them for their affability.

'The great man 's always at work, always at work,' he said suddenly, in a desperate sort of way. They were like some sort of needlework guild sitting round, just people, in the end; it made the surroundings seem quite ordinary. The room fell to pieces; one could imagine it being turned out, or all the things being sold up and dispersed.

'All work and no play,' scolded Mrs Craven, 'makes Jack . . .'

Miriam heard the swish of the bead curtain at the end of the short passage.

'Heah he *is*,' smiled Joey.

'A miracle,' breathed Mrs Craven, glancing round the circle. Evidently he did not usually come in.

Mr Corrie came quietly into the room with empty hands; in the clear light he looked older than he had done in the dining-room, fuller in the face; grey threads showed in his hair. Every one turned towards him. He looked at no one. His loose little smile had gone. The straight chair into which he dropped with a dreamy careless preoccupied air was set a little back from the fireside circle. No one moved.

'Absorbed the evidence, m'lud?' squeaked Mr Craven.

'Ah-m,' growled his host, clearing his throat.

Why can't they let him alone, Miriam asked herself, and leave him to me, added her mind swiftly. She sat glaring into the fire; the room had resumed it strange magic.

'Do you think it is wrong to teach children things you don't believe yourself? . . .' said Miriam, and her thoughts rushed on. 'You 're an unbeliever and I 'm an unbeliever and both of us despise the thoughts and opinions of "people"; you 're a successful wealthy man and can amuse yourself and forget; I must teach and presently die, teach till I die. It doesn't matter. I can be happy for a while teaching your children, but you know, knowing me a little, what a task that must be; you know I know nothing and that I know that nobody knows anything; comfort me. . . .'

She seemed to traverse a great loop of time, waiting for the answer to her hurried question. Mr Corrie had come into the drawing-room dressed for dinner and sat down near her with a half-smile as she closed the book she was reading and laid it on her knee and looked up, with sentences from *A Human*

Document ringing through her, and by the time her question was out she knew it was unnecessary. But she had flung it out and it had reached him and he had read the rush of thoughts that followed it. She might as well have been silent; better. She had missed some sort of opportunity. What would have happened if she had been quite silent? His answer was swift, but in the interval they had said all they would ever have to say to each other. 'Not in the least,' he said, with a gentle decisiveness.

She flashed thanks at him and sighed her relief. He did not mind about religion. But how far did he understand? She had made him think she was earnest about the teaching children something. He would be very serious about their being 'decently turned out.' She was utterly incapable of turning them out for the lives they would have to lead. She envied and pitied and despised those lives. Envied the ease and despised the ignorance, the awful cruel struggle of society that they were growing up for—no joy, a career and sport for the boy, clubs, the weary dyspeptic life of the blasé man, and for the girl lonely cold hard bitter everlasting 'social' life. She envied the ease. Mr Corrie must know she envied the ease. Did he know that she tried to hide her incapacity in order to go on sharing the beauty and ease?

'It is so difficult,' she pursued helplessly, and saw him wonder why she went on with the subject, and try to read the title of her book. She did not mean to tell him that. That would lead them away; just nowhere. If only she could tell him everything and get him to understand. But that would mean admitting that she was letting the children's education slide; and he was sitting there, confidently, so beautifully dressed for dinner, paying her forty pounds a year not to let the children's education slide. . . . 'It's an opportunity; he's come in here, and sat down to talk to me. I ought to tell him; I'm cheating.' But he had looked for the title of her book, and would have talked, about anything, if she could have talked. He had a little air of deference, quiet kind indulgent deference. His neat little shoulders, bent as he sat turned towards her, were kind. 'I'm too young,' she cried in her mind. If only she could say aloud, 'I 'm too young—I can't do it,' and leave everything to him.

Or leave the children out altogether and talk to him, man to man, about the book. She could not do that. Everything she said would hurt her, poisoned by the hidden sore of her incapability to do anything for his children. He ought to send them to school. But they would not go to a school where anything real was taught. Science, strange things about India and Ireland, the aesthetic movement, Ruskin; making things beautiful. How far away all that seemed, that sacred life of her old school—forgotten. The thought of it was like a breath in the room. Did he know of these things? That sort of school would take the children away, out of this kind of society life. Make them think—for themselves. He did not think or approve of thought. Even the hard Banbury Park people would be nearer to him than any of those things. . . . That was the world. Nearly every one seemed to be in it. He was whimsically trying to read the title of her book with the little half-smile he shared with the boy.

People came in and they both rose. It was over. She sank back miserably into the offering of the moment, retiring into a lamp-lit corner with her book, enclosing herself in its promise.

She sat long that night over her fire, dipping into the strange book, reading passages here and there; feeling them come nearer to her than anything she had read before. She knew at once that she did not want to read the book through; that it was what people called a tragedy, that the author had deliberately made it a tragedy; something black and twisted and painful, came to her out of every page; but seriously to read it right through and be excited about the tragic story seemed silly and pitiful. The thought of Mrs Corrie and Joey doing this annoyed her, and impatiently she wanted to tell them that there was nothing in it, nothing in the things the author wanted to make them believe; that it was fraud, humbug . . . they missed everything. They could not see through it, they read through to the happy ending or the sad ending and took it all seriously.

She struggled in thought to discover why it was she felt that these people did not read books and that she herself did. She felt that she could look at the end, and read here and there a little and know; know something, something they did not know. People thought it was silly, almost wrong to look at the end of a book. But if it spoilt a book, there was something wrong about the book. If it was finished and the interest gone when you know who married who, what was the good of reading at all? It was a sort of trick, a sell. Like a puzzle that was no more fun when you had found it out. There was something more in books than that . . . even Rosa Nouchette Carey and Mrs Hungerford, something that came to you out of the book, any bit of it, a page, even a sentence—and the 'stronger' the author was, the more came. That was why Ouida put those others in the shade, not, not, *not* because her books were improper. It was her, herself somehow. Then you read books to find the author! That was it. That was the difference . . . that was how one was different from most people. . . . Dear Eve; I have just discovered that I don't read books for the story, but as a psychological study of the author . . . she must write that to Eve at once; to-morrow. It was rather awful and strange. It meant never being able to agree with people about books, never liking them for the same reasons as other people. . . . But it was true and exciting. It meant . . . things coming to you out of books, people, not the people in the books, but knowing, absolutely, everything about the author. She clung to the volume in her hand with a sense of wealth. Its very binding, the feeling of it, the sight of the thin serried edges of the closed leaves came to her as having a sacredness . . . and the world was full of books. . . . It did not matter that people went about talking about nice books, interesting books, sad books, 'stories'—they would never be that to her. They were people. More real than actual people. They came nearer. In life everything was so scrappy and mixed up. In a book the author was there in every word.

Why did this strange book come so near, nearer than any

others, so that you *felt* the writing, felt the sentences as if you were writing them yourself? He was a sad pained man, all wrong; bothered and tragic about things, believing in sad black horror. Then why did he come so near? Perhaps because life was sad. Perhaps life was really sad. No; it was somehow the writing, the clearness. That was the thing. He himself must be all right, if he was so clear. Then it was dangerous, dangerous to people like Mrs Corrie and Joey who would attend only to what he said, and not to him . . . sadness or gladness, saying things were sad or glad did not matter; there was something behind all the time, something inside people. That was why it was impossible to pretend to sympathize with people. You don't have to sympathize with authors; you just get at them, neither happy nor sad; like talking, more than talking. Then that was why the people who wrote moral stories were so awful. They were standing behind the pages preaching at you with smarmy voices. . . . Bunyan? . . . He preached to himself too . . . crying out his sins. . . . He did not get between you and himself and point at a moral. An author must show himself. Anyhow, he can't help showing himself. A moral writer only sees the mote in his brother's eye. And you see him seeing it.

A long letter to Eve. . . . Eve would think that she was showing off. But she would be excited and interested too, and would think about it a little. If only she could make Eve see what a book was . . . a dance by the author, a song, a prayer, an important sermon, a message. Books were not stories printed on paper, they were people; the real people; . . . 'I prefer books to people' . . . 'I know now why I prefer books to people.'

'. . . I do wish you 'd tell me more about your extraordinary days. You must have extraordinary days. I do. Perhaps every one has. Only they don't seem to know it!'

. . . This morning, the green common lying under the sun, still and wide and silent; with a little breeze puffing over it; the intense fresh green near the open door of the little Catholic church; the sandy pathway running up into the common, hummocky and twisting and winding, its sand particles glinting in the sun, always there, going on, whoever died or whatever happened, winding amongst happy greenery, in and out amongst the fresh smell of the common. Inside the chapel the incense streaming softly up, the seven little red lamps hanging in the cloud of incense about the altar; the moving of the thick forest of embroidery on the cope of the priest. Funny when he bobbed, but when he just moved quietly, taking a necessary step, all the colour of the forest on his cope moving against the still high wide colours of the chancel. If only any one could express how perfect life is at those moments; every one must know, every one who is looking must know that life is perfectly happy. That is why people go to church; for those moments with the light on all those things in the chancel. It means something. . . . Priests and nuns know it all the time; even when they are unhappy; that is why they can kiss dying people and lepers; they see something else, all the time. Nothing common or unclean. That is why Christ had blazing eyes. Christianity: the sanctification of bread and wine, and lepers and death; the body; the resurrection of the body. Even if there is some confusion and squabbling about Christ there must be something in it if the things that show are so beautiful.

Hard cold vows, of chastity and poverty. That did it. Emptiness, in face of—an unspeakable glory. If one could not, was too weak or proud, 'Verily they have their reward.' Every one got something somehow . . . in hell; thou art there also . . . that shows there is no eternal punishment. Earth is hell, with every one going to heaven.

What is the worldly life? The gay bright shimmering lunch, the many guests, the glitter of the table, mayonnaise red and green and yellow, delicate bright wines; strolling in the woods in the afternoon. . . . Tea, every one telling anecdotes of the afternoon's walk as if it were a sort of competition, great bursts of laughter and abrupt silences and then another story, the moments of laughter were something like those moments in church; whilst there was nothing but laughter in the room

everybody was perfectly happy and good; everybody forgot
everything and ran back somewhere; to the beginning, to the
time when they were first looking at things, without troubling
about anything. But when the laughter ceased, every one ran
away and the rest of their day together showed in a flash, an
awful tunnel that would be filled with the echo of the separate
footsteps unless more laughter could be made, to hide the sad
helpless sounds. Dinner was the noise and laughter of tea-
time grown steadier, a pillow fight with harder whacks and
more time for the strokes, no bitterness, just buffeting and
shouts, and every one laughing the same laugh, as if they were
all in some high secret. They were in some high secret; the
great secret of the worldly life; and if you prevented yourself
from thinking and laughed, they seemed to take you in. That
was the way to live the worldly life. To talk absurdly and
laugh; to be lost in laughter. Why had Mrs Corrie seemed so
vexed? Why had she said suddenly and quietly in the billiard-
room that it seemed rummy to go to Mass and play billiards
in the evening? '*Be* goody if you *are*.' It had spoiled the
day. Mrs Corrie would like her to be goody. But then it was
she who had pushed her down the steps in the afternoon and
called after the actor to take care of her in the woods.

There was something too sad about worldliness and too
difficult about goodness.

Perhaps one had not gone far enough with worldliness. . . .

> Take each fair mask for what it shows itself,
> Nor strive to look beneath it.

That was what she had done drifting about in the wood with
the actor, listening to his pleasant voice. It was an excursion
into pure worldliness. He had never thought for a moment
in his life of the world as anything than what it appeared to be.
He had no suspicion that any one ever did. He had accepted
her as one of the house-party and talked, on and on busily,
about his American tour and his hope of a London engagement,
getting emphatic about his chance, the chanciness of everything. And she had drifted along, delighting in the pleasant
voice sounding through the wood, seeing the wood clear and
steady through the pleasant tone, not caring about chance or

chanciness, but ready to pretend she was interested in them so that the voice might go on; pretending to be interested when he stopped. That was feminine worldliness, pretending to be interested so that pleasant things might go on. Masculine worldliness was refusing to be interested so that it might go on doing things. Feminine worldliness then meant perpetual hard work and cheating and pretence at the door of a hidden garden, a lovely hidden garden. Masculine worldliness meant never being really there; always talking about things that had happened or making plans for things that might happen. There was nothing that could happen that was not in some way the same as anything else. Nobody was ever quite there, realizing.

CHAPTER IV

DURING her second week of giving the children their morning's lessons, Miriam saw finally that it was impossible and would always be impossible to make their two hours of application anything but an irrelevant interval in their lives. They came into the schoolroom with languid reluctance, dreamily indolent from breakfast in bed, fragrant from warm baths. They made no resistance. She sat with the appointed tasks clearly in mind, holding on to the certainty that they were to be done as the only means of getting through the morning. The excitement of taking up everything afresh with her was over and, beyond occasional moments of brightness when she tried to impress a fact or lift them over a difficulty with a jest and they would exchange their glance of secret delight, their curious conspirators' glance of some great certainty shared, they went through their tasks with well-bred preoccupation, sighing deeply now and again and sometimes groaning, with clenched hands pressed between their knees. Their accustomed life of events was close round them, in the garden just beyond the undraped window, on the mat outside the schoolroom door, where at any moment a footstep crossing the landing might fall softly and pause, when their heads would go up in tense listening. 'Rollo!' they would say, waiting for the turning of the handle, holding themselves in for the subdued shoutings they would utter when Mrs Corrie appeared standing in the doorway with a finger on her lips. 'Happy?' she would breathe; 'working like nigger boys?' Unless Miriam looked gravely detached, she would glide in blushing, and passionately caress them. When this happened, sighs and groanings filled the time that remained. Their nearest approach to open rebellion included a tacit appeal to her as a fellow-sufferer to throw up the stupid game. It was quite clear that they did not blame her for their sufferings and they were so much prepared to do the decent thing that her experiment of reading

389

to them regularly, at some convenient half-hour each day, from a book of adventures or fairly tale, not only reconciled them to endure the morning's ordeal, but filled them with a gratitude that astonished her, and the beginnings of a personal regard for her that shook her heart. During the readings, they would lose their air of well-bred detachment and would come near. They would be relaxed and silent; the girl with bent head and brooding defiant curiously smiling and frowning face, the boy gazing at the reader, rapturous. She would sometimes feel against each arm the pressure of a head.

She had felt instinctively and at once that she could not use their lesson hours as opportunities for talking at large on general ideas, as she had done with the children in the Banbury Park school. Those children, the children of tradesmen most of them, could be allowed to take up the beginnings of ideas; 'ideals,' the sense of modern reforms, they could be allowed to discuss anything from any point of view and take up attitudes and have opinions. The opportunity for discussion and for encouraging a definite attitude towards life was much greater in this quiet room with only the two children; but it would have been mean, Miriam felt, to take advantage of this opportunity; to be anything but strictly neutral and wary of generalizations. It would have been so easy. Probably a really 'conscientious' woman would have done it, have 'influenced' them, given the girl a bias in the direction of some life of devotion, hospital nursing or slum missionary work, and have filled the boy with ideas as to the essential superiority of 'Radicals.' Their minds were so soft and untouched. . . . It ended in a conspiracy, they all sat masquerading, and finished their morning exhausted and relieved. The children knew the lessons tortured her and made her ill at ease, and they were puzzled without disapproving. Through it all she felt their gratitude to her for not being 'simple,' like Bunnikin.

There was to be another week-end. Again there would be the sense of being a visitor amongst other visitors; visitor was not the word; there was a French word which described the thing, *convive, les convives* . . . people sitting easily about a table with flushed faces . . . someone standing drunkenly up with eyes blazing with friendliness and a raised wineglass . . . women and wine, the roses of Heliogabalus; but he was a Greek and dreadful in some way, *convives* were Latin, Roman; fountains, water flowing over marble, white-robed strong-faced people reclining on marble couches, feasting . . . taking each fair mask for what it shows itself; that was what this kind of wealthy English people did, perhaps what all wealthy people did . . . the maimed, the halt, the blind, *compel* them to come in . . . but that was after the others had refused. The thing that made you feel jolliest and strongest was to forget the maimed, to *be* a fair mask, to keep everything else out and be a little circle of people knowing that everything was kept out. Suppose a skeleton walked in? Offer it a glass of wine. People have no right to be skeletons, or, if they are to, make a fuss about it. These people would be all the brighter if they happened to have neuralgia; some strong pain or emotion made you able to do things. Taking each fair mask was a fine grown-up game. Perhaps it could be kept up to the end? Perhaps *that* was the meaning of the man playing cards on his death-bed. Defying God. That was what Satan did. He was brave; defying a tyrant . . . 'nothing to do but curse God and die.' Who said that? there was something silly about it; giving in, not real defiance. It didn't settle anything; if the new ideas were true; the thing went on. The love of God was like the love of a mother; always forgiving you, ready to die for you, always waiting for you to be good. Why? It was mean. The things one wanted one could not have if one were just tame and good. . . . It is morbid to think about being good; better the fair mask —anything. But it did not make people happy. These people were not happy. They were not real.

Spring; everywhere, inside and outside the house. The spring outside had a meaning here. It came in through the windows without obstruction and passed into everything. At home, it had sent one nearly mad with joy and anticipation and passed and left you looking for it for the rest of the year; in Germany it had brought music and wild joy—the secret had passed from eye to eye; all the girls had known it. At Wordsworth House it had stood far away, like a picture in a dream, something that could be seen from windows, and found for a moment in the park, but powerless to get into the house. Here it came in; you could not forget it for a moment; and it was a background for something more wonderful than itself; something that made it wonderful; something there were no words for; voices, movements from room to room, strange food, the soft chink of Venetian glass, amber wine, the light drowned in wine, through the window a sharp gleam on things that reflected, day and night, into everything, even into one's thoughts. Why was the spring suddenly so real? Why was it that you could stand as it were in a shaft of it all the time, feeling in your breathing, hearing in your voice the sound of the spring, the blood in your fingertips seeming like the roses that they would touch soon in the garden?

How ignorant the man was who said, 'each fair mask for what it shows itself.' Life is not a mask, it *is* fair; the gold in one's hair is real.

Friday brought an atmosphere of expectation. Mr Kronen, an old friend of the Corries, was coming down, with a new Mrs Kronen.

By the early afternoon the house was full of fragrance; coming downstairs dressed for an errand in the little town two miles away, Miriam saw the hall all pink and saffron with azaleas. Coming across the hall, she found a scent in the air that did not come from the azaleas, a sweet familiar syrupy distillation . . . the blaze of childhood's garden was round her again, bright magic flowers in the sunlight, magic flowers, still there, nearer to her than ever in this happy house; she could almost hear the humming of the bees, and flung back the bead curtain with unseeing eyes, half expecting some doorway to open on the remembered garden; the scent was overpowering . . . the drawing-room was cool and silent with closed windows and drawn blinds; bowls of roses stood in every available place; she tiptoed about in the room gathering their scent.

As she opened the hall door, Mrs Corrie's voice startled her from the dining-room.

Going into the dining-room she found her with a flushed face and excited eyes and the children dancing round her. 'Another tin! One more tin!' they exclaimed, plucking at Miriam. From the billiard-room came the smell of fresh varnish. Wiggerson was on her knees near the door.

'She's done some stupid thing,' thought Miriam, looking at Mrs Corrie's excited, unconscious face with sudden anxiety; 'some womanish overdoing it, wanting to do too much and spoiling everything.' She felt as if she were representing Mr Corrie.

'Will it be dry in time?' she asked, half angrily, scarcely knowing what she said, in the midst of Mrs Corrie's apologetic petition that she would bring a tin of oak stain back with her.

'Lordy, don't you think so?' whispered Mrs Corrie, only half dismayed.

Miriam had not patience to follow her as she went to survey the floor ruefully chanting, 'Oh, Wiggerson, Wiggerson.'

'Anyhow I'm sure it oughtn't to have any more on as late as when I come back,' she scolded boldly. How annoyed Mr Corrie would be. . . .

As she was going down the quiet road past the high oak garden palings of the nearest house she heard the bumping and scrabbling of a heavy body against the palings, and a dog leapt into the road almost at her feet, making the dust fly. It was an Irish terrier. It smiled and barked a little, waiting, looking up into her face and up and down the road. 'It thought it knew me,' she pondered; 'it mistook me for someone else.' She patted his head and went forward thinking of the joyful scrabbling, its headlong determination. The dog jerked back its head with a wide smile, tore down the road and came back leaping and smiling. Something disappeared from the vista of the roadway as the dog rushed along it nosing after scents, looking round now and again, and now and again rushing back to greet her. It brought back the sense of the house and the strange gay life she had just left to go on her errand to the little unknown town. It wore a smart collar; it belonged to that life. People in it were never alone; when they went out there was always a dog with them. 'It thinks I'm one of them.' But it liked the wild; when they came out on to the common it rushed up a sandy pathway and disappeared amongst the gorse bushes. For a while Miriam hoped it would come back and kept looking about for it; then she gave it up and went ahead with the commons drifting slowly by on either side; she wished that the action of walking were not so jerky, that the expanses on either side might pass more smoothly and easily by; 'that's why people drive,' she thought; 'you can only really see the country when you are not moving yourself.' Standing still for a moment she looked across the open stretch to her left and smiled at it and went on again, walking more quickly; the soft beauty that had retreated to the horizon when the dog was with her was spreading back again across the whole expanse and coming towards her; she hurried on singing softly at random, 'Scorn such a *foe* . . . though I could fell thee at a blow, though I-i, cou-uld fe-ell thee-ee a-at a-a *blow*' . . . people walking and thinking and fussing, people driving somewhere in victorias were always coming along the road, to them it was a sort of suburb, quite ordinary, the bit near home. But it was big enough to be full of waves and waves of something real, something cool and true and unchanging. Had anybody seen it, did the people who lived there know it? Did anybody know this strange thing? She almost ran; *my* 'commons,' she said. 'I know how beautiful you are; if only I knew whether you know that I know. I know, I know,' she said, 'I shan't forget you.' 'True, true till death; bear it, oh wind, on thy lightning breath.'

The sun was very warm; before she reached the end of the

long road, the sandy pathways were beginning to glare. There
was the river and the little bridge and the first shop just beyond
it, where her purchase was to be made. Its woodwork was
very bright white; it had a seaside look. She stood still on the
slight ascent of the bridge, mopping her face and preparing to
represent Mrs Corrie in the shop. Scrambling up the shallow
bank from the common came the yellow dog. 'Oh, hooray—
you duck,' she breathed, patting the warm stubbly head and
listening to his breathless snortings. A piano-organ broke into
loud music in the little street. It was not a mysterious little
town, there was nothing of the village about it. The white
framed windows held things you would see in a Regent Street
confectioner's; it was a special shop for the kind of people who
lived here. Miriam felt for her three and six and asked for her
pound of coffee creams with a bored air, wishing she knew the
dog's name so that she could claim him familiarly. She contented herself with telling him to lie down in an angry whisper
repeatedly, as the creams were being weighed. He stood
panting and gazing at her, wagging his stump. ''Ullo, Bushy,'
said the shopwoman languidly; the dog faced round panting
more loudly. 'There you are, Bush,' she said, as the scales
balanced, and flung the dog a chocolate wafer which he caught
with a snap. Miriam gazed vaguely at the unfamiliar spectacle,
angrily feeling that the shopwoman was observing her. 'You're
not going to take him through the town?' said the shopwoman
severely.

'Oh, no,' said Miriam nervously.

'He's the worst fighter in the parish; they never bring him
into the town, unless it's the groom sometimes.'

'Thank you,' said Miriam, taking her bag of coffee creams.
'Dogs *are* a nuisance, aren't they?' she added in an emphatically sympathetic tone, getting away through the swing door
almost hating the yellow body that squeezed through at her
side and stood eagerly facing towards the market-place, waiting
for her movements.

She hurried up over the bridge calling to the dog without
looking round, listening fearfully for sounds of conflict with a
brown collie she had caught sight of standing with head high

and ears pricked, twenty yards down the street. The piano-
organ jingled angrily. The dog came thoughtfully trotting
over the bridge and ambled off across the common—safe. He
might have been killed, or killed another dog; how cruel dogs
were, without knowing better. She looked to the common,
asking consolation for her beating heart. The bag of creams
was safe and heavy in her hand, the dog had gone, the little
town was behind; it had hurt her; it was spoiled; she would
never like it. It had done nothing but remind her that she
was a helpless dingy little governess. She toiled along, feeling
dreadfully tired; the sounds of her boot soles on the firm,
sand-powdered road mocked her, telling her she must go on.
If she could be quite sure of finding a kind woman, not a hard-
featured woman with black and grey hair, like the shopwoman,
but kind, knowing and understanding everything, in a large
print apron with her sleeves rolled up to the elbows, living in a
large cottage with a family, who would look at her and smile a
quiet short certain smile, as if she had been waiting for her,
and take her in and let her help and stay there for ever, she
would put down the bag of coffee creams on the edge of the
common and go straight across it to her; but there would not
be a woman like that here; all that the women round here
would think about her would be to wonder which of the
families she belonged to. If a victoria came along and in it a
delicate, lonely old gentleman who had a large empty house with
deep quiet rooms and a large sunny garden with high walls, and
wanted someone to be about there, singing and happy till he
died, she would go. He would drive away with her and shut
her up in the quiet beautiful house, protecting her and keeping
people off, and she would sing all day in the garden and the
house and play to him and read sometimes aloud, and he would
forget he was old and ill, and they would share the great secret,
dying of happiness. Die of happiness. People ought to be
able to die of happiness if they were able to admit how happy
they were. If they admitted it aloud, they would pass straight
out of their bodies, alive; unhappiness was the same as death,
not suffering; but letting suffering make you unhappy—curse
God and die, curse life, that was letting life beat you; letting

God beat you. God did not want that. No one admitted it. No one seemed to know anything about it. People just went on fussing.

The violent beating of her heart died down. The sun was behind her; the commons glowed. She must have been looking at them for some time because she could close her eyes and see exactly how they looked, all alive in steady colour, gleaming and fresh. The thumping and trilling of the distant piano-organ offered itself equally to everybody. It knew the secret and twirled and swept all the fussing away into a tune. Quietly the clock of the church in the little town struck four. She would be late for tea. The children would have tea with Mrs Corrie. Wiggerson would make a fresh pot for her when she got in. There would be a little tray in her quiet room, a cup and saucer, the little sprigged silk tea-cosy, the *Human Document*. It would be the beginning of the week-end. It would link her up again with the early afternoon, the rose-filled drawing-room, the excited dining-room, the smell of varnish from the billiard-room floor.

Mrs Corrie and the children were dancing in a lingering patch of sunlight at the far end of the lawn as Miriam came up the drive with her chocolates. They waved and shouted to her, trumpeting questions through their hands. She held up the bag. 'Go and have *tea*, you poor soul,' sang Mrs Corrie. How excited they were. In the flower-filled hall, Stokes, muttering excitedly to herself, was lighting the fire. The crackling of wood came from the dining-room.

Wiggerson was swishing about in the dining-room clearing away tea.

Sitting in her low basket chair with her dismantled tea-tray at her side and a picture in her mind of the new Mrs Kronen coming down from London in the train in bright new clothes and a dust-cloak, Miriam was startled by hearing frightened footsteps rush across the landing and a frightened voice calling for Wiggerson.

'Something's happened,' she told herself angrily, 'it always does when everybody's so excited—"tel qui rit vendredi, dimanche pleurera."'

Opening the door, she found the landing empty and quiet, the setting sun streamed across its coloured spaces, the flowers blazed as if they were standing in a garden. . . . Joey always went for walks if she were feeling thick and fat, she always went for a long walk; in coats with skirts to match; a costume; never a jacket, with a different skirt . . . the long cool passage leading away to the invisible door of Mr Corrie's room was full of wreathing smoke. Wiggerson rushed across the landing along the passage, followed by Mrs Corrie, with her head up and her handkerchief to her nose and all her figure tense and angular and strong. Both had passed silently; but there were shriekings on the stairs and the children came at Miriam with cries and screams. 'Rollo 'll be *killed*!'; 'Go to her!' 'Go and save vem!' the children shrieked, and leaped up and down in front of her. The boy's white features worked as if they must dislocate; his eyes were black with terror; he wrung his hands. Sybil's face, scarlet and shapeless and streaming with tears, blazed wrath at Miriam through her green eyes. 'Be quiet,' Miriam said in loud tones. 'I shall do nothing till you are quiet.' With a shriek the girl lashed at her with the dog-whip. 'Save vem, *save* vem!' shrieked the boy, twisting his arms in the air. 'Will you both be quiet *instantly*?' shouted Miriam, as the blood rose to her head, catching and holding the boy. Both children howled and choked; Sybil flung herself forward howling, and Miriam felt her teeth in her wrist. The smoke came pouring out of the little hidden room, coiling itself against the air of the passage like some fascinating silent inevitable grimace. Wiggerson's figure, flying through it, stirred it strangely, but it closed behind her and billowed horribly out towards Mrs Corrie standing just clear of its advance with her handkerchief pressed to her face, quiet, not calling to Wiggerson, waiting where she had disappeared. Miriam could not move. Sybil's body hung fastened to her own with entwining limbs . . . 'a fight in the jungle,' a tiger flung fixed like a leech against the breast of a screaming elephant . . . the boy had the whip and was slashing at her legs through her thin dress and uttering piercing shrieks.

'Stokes is an idjut,' said Mrs Corrie, going gaily downstairs with the two exhausted white-faced children, followed by Wiggerson flitting along with bloodshot, blinking eyes.

Stokes, sullenly brooding, lighting Mr Corrie's fire without putting back the register.   What was it that made Stokes sullen and brooding so that the accident had happened and the smoke had come?   Stokes had seen something, someone, like the fearful oncoming curving stare of the smoke.   Mrs Corrie and Wiggerson did not brood like that.   They laughed and wept and snatched things out of danger.   They had thin faces.   Mrs Corrie was alone, like an aspen shaking its leaves in windless air. She knew she was alone.   Wiggerson . . . Wiggerson was . . . ? Making her toilet in the spring sunset, Miriam saw all the time Wiggerson's tall body hurtling about in her small pantry, quickly selecting and packing things on a tray — her eyes glancing swiftly downwards as her foot caught, the swift bending of body, the rip, rip as she tore the braiding from her skirt, her intent face as she threw it from her and swept sinuously upright, her undisturbed hands once more at their swift work.

What a strange photograph . . . a woman in Grecian drapery seated on a stonework chair with a small harp on her knees, one hand limply tweaking the strings of her harp; her head thrown back, her eyes, hard and bright, staring up into the sky, 'Inspiration' printed in ink on the white margin under the photograph.   It was an Englishwoman, a large stiff square body, a coil of carefully crimped hair and a curled fringe, pre-tending.   There were people who would say, 'What a pretty photograph,' and mean it . . . the draperies and the attitude. How easy it was to take people in, just by acting.   Not the real people. There were real people. Where were they? That horrid thing could get itself on to Mrs Corrie's drawing-room table, and sit there unbroken. All women were inspired in a way. It was true enough. But it was a secret. Men ought not to be told. They must find it out for themselves. To dress up and try to make it something to attract somebody. She was not a woman, she was a *woman* . . . oh, curse it all. But men liked actresses. They liked being fooled.

Miriam looked closely at the photograph with hatred in her eyes. Why not the stone steps and the chair and the sense of sunlight; sunlit air? That would be enough. 'You get in the way of the air, you *thing*,' she muttered, and the woman's helpless unconscious sandalled feet reproached her. Voices were shouting to each other on the upper landing. It was Mrs Kronen's photograph, of course. Miriam moved quickly away, ashamed of having stared. But it was too late; she had done a horrid thing again. She saw, as if it were in the room with her, the affair of the taking of the photograph, a cross face coming down from its pose to argue with the photographer, and then flung upwards again, waiting. And she had put or let someone put it, in a frame, at once, on a strange drawing-room table. Perhaps her husband had put it there. But if he valued it he would hide and shelter it. . . . When we meet, she will know I have stared at her photograph.

Mrs Kronen came suddenly in with Mrs Corrie, talking in a rich deep thick voice that moved, with large intervals, up and down a long scale and yet produced a curious effect of toneless flatness, just as if she were speaking a narrow nasal Cockney. There was a Cockney sound somewhere in her voice. She began at once loudly praising everything in the room, hardly pausing when Miriam was introduced to her, and giving no sign of having seen her. If I were alone with her, thought Miriam, I should want to say ''Ullo, 'ow's yourself?' and grin. It would be the only thing one could genuinely do. Mrs. Corrie almost giggled at the end of each of Mrs Kronen's exclamations, but she was very gay and animated and so was Mr Corrie when he came in with Mr Kronen. They all went in to dinner talking and laughing loudly. And they went on laughing and joking and talking loudly against each other through dinner.

Mr and Mrs Corrie looked thin and small and very young. Once or twice they laughed at the same moment and glanced at each other. Mr Corrie's face was flushed. Mr and Mrs Kronen looked like brother and sister—only that she said South Africa as if it were a phrase in a tragic recitative from an oratorio and he as if it were something he had behind him that gave him a sort of advantage over every one. It seemed to be all he had. They had both been in South Africa, travelling in bullock wagons blinded by the fierce light and choked with sand. It seemed to linger in the curious brickish look of their complexions and the hard yellow of their hair. The talk about South Africa lasted all dinner-time. It seemed to interest Mr Corrie. His eyes gleamed strangely as he talked about I.D.B.'s. Everybody at the table said, 'Illicit dahmond bah' at least once, with a little thrill of the face. Why was it illicit to buy diamonds?—strange people out there in the glare, buying gleaming stones from miners and this curious feeling about it all round the table, everybody with hot glinting excited eyes—and somebody, some man, a business man who had handed round diamonds, like chocolates, to his friends in his box at the opera, a Stock Exchange man in a frock-coat throwing himself into the sea somewhere between England and South Africa—ah, what a pity, worried to death, with an excited head. He wanted diamonds. And when Mr Corrie handed Mrs Kronen a dish of fruit and said, 'A banana? A bite of a barnato?' they all laughed, so comfortably. Something illicit seemed to creep into the very pictures and flow over the walls. The poor man's body falling desperately into the sea. He could not endure his own excited eyes.

Early on Monday morning Miriam heard Mrs Kronen singing in the bathroom. She tried not to listen and listened. The bold sound had come in through her open door when Stokes brought her breakfast tray. With it had come the smell of a downstairs breakfast, coffee, a curious fresh, sustaining odour of coffee and freshly frying rashers. There was coffee on her own tray this morning and a letter addressed to her in a bold unknown hand. She sipped her coffee at once and put the overwhelming letter aside on her blue coverlet. It was an overweight, something thrown in on the surface of the tide on which she had awakened in the soft fresh harmonies of rose and blue of her curtained room. It could wait. It had come out of the world for her; but she felt independent of it. It did not disturb her. Its overwhelming quality was in the fact that she had called it to her out of the world. It was as if she had herself addressed the large bold envelope. She left it. Her sipped coffee steered her into the tide of the downstairs life. There was breakfast downstairs, steaming coffee and entrée dishes for Mr Corrie and the Kronens, and they were all going off by the early train.

'C'est si bon,' sang Mrs Kronen in a deep baritone, as Miriam drank her coffee; 'de con-fon-dre en un, deu-eux bai-sers.' She sang it out through the quiet upstairs rooms, she met with it the bustle of preparation downstairs. It was a world she lived in that made her able to carry off these things without being disturbed by them, a rosy secret world in which she lived secure. A richness at the heart of things. She was there. She possessed it with her large strong brick-red and rose-white frame and her strong yellow hair. Did she, really? At any rate she wanted to suggest that she did—that that secret richness was the heart of things. She flung out boldly that it was and that she was there, but a sort of soft horrible slurring flatness in her voice suggested evil, as if a sort of restless acceptance of something evil was the price of her carelessness. Perhaps that was how things were. Perhaps that was part of taking each fair mask for what it shows itself. She made every one else seem cloudy and shrivelled and dim. Miriam took up the stupendous envelope and held its solid weight in her hand as Mrs Kronen sang on. 'All right,' she said, and smiled at it, feeling daring and strong. Its arrival would have been quite different if Mrs Kronen had not been there; this curious powerful independent morning in the rose-blue room

would not have happened in the same way without Mrs
Kronen. . . . Live, don't worry. . . . I've always been
worrying and bothering. I'm going to be like Mrs Kronen;
but quite different, because she hasn't the least idea how
beautiful things really are. She doesn't know that everyone is living a beautiful strange life that has never been lived
before. If she did she would not be ashamed of herself.
Miriam gave a great sigh and smiled.

Her breakfast was a feast. Sitting back under the softly
tinted canopy with the soft folds of the bed curtains hanging
near either side she stared at the bright light pouring in through
the lattices. Her room was a great square of happy light . . .
happy, happy. She gathered up all the sadness she had ever
known and flung it from her. All the dark things of the past
flashed with a strange beauty as she flung them out. The
light had been there all the time; but she had known it only at
moments. Now she knew what she wanted. Bright mornings, beautiful bright rooms, a wilderness of beauty all round
her all the time—at any cost. Any life that had not these things
she would refuse. . . . Roses in her blood and gold in her hair
. . . it was something belonging to them, something that made
them gleam. It was her right; even if they gleamed only for
her. They gleamed, she knew it. Youth, the glory of youth.
So strong. She had got herself into this beautiful life, found
her way to it; she would stay in it for ever, work in it, make
money and when she was old, have soft pink curtains and
fragrant things to remind her, as long as she could lift her hand.
No more ugliness, no more schools or mean little houses.
Luxuries, beautiful gleaming things . . . a secret happy life.

She smiled securely, with her eyes, the strange happy smile
that had come in the brougham. . . .

How strong Mrs Kronen was. . . . How huge and strong
she had looked standing in the hall while Mr Corrie said cruel
laughing little things about the billiard-room floor. . . .
'She'll paint Madonna lilies on the table next.' . . . Mrs

Kronen saying nothing, smiling more and more without moving her face, growing bigger and stronger and taller as Mr Corrie grumbled and Mr Kronen fidgeted, cross and disappointed by the hall fire, and then suddenly lifting her head and singing, a great flourish of clear strong notes filling the hall and pealing up through the house as she swept into the drawing-room.

Singing song after song to her own loud accompaniment, great emphatic sweeps of song, so that every one came and sat about in the room listening and waiting, the men staring at the back of her head as she sat at the piano. Waiting, for music——they did not know they were waiting for music, waiting for her to stop getting between them and the music. They admired her, her magnificent singing and waited, unsatisfied, in the sweetness of the lamp-lit, flower-filled room that her music did not touch. She sang on and on and they all grew smaller and smaller in the great sea of sound, more and more hopelessly waiting.

And Mrs Corrie had sat deep in her large chair, dead and drowned. Dead because of something she had never known. Dead in ignorance and living bravely on—her sweet thin voice rising above the gloom where she lay hid—a gloom where there were no thoughts. Nearly all women were like that, living in a gloom where there were no thoughts. If any one could persuade her that she was alive, she would do nothing but rush about and dance and sing . . . how irritating that would be . . . making men smile and trot about and look silly . . . no room for ideas; except in smoking-rooms—and—laboratories. . . . She was a good woman; a God woman; the sweetness of her bones and her thin sweet voice of tears and laughter were of God. Every one knew that and worshipped her. Men's ideas were devilish; clever and mean. . . . Was God a woman? Was God really irritating? No one could endure God really. . . . Men could not. . . . Women were of God in some way. That is what men could never forgive; the superiority of women. . . . 'Perhaps I can't stand women because I'm a sort of horrid man.'

Mrs Kronen was a sort of man too. She was not perplexed.

But she was a woman too—because she was not mean and petty and fussy as men are . . . sitting tall and square at the piano with the square tall form of her husband standing ready to turn the pages—her strong baritone voice rolling out, 'Ai-me-moi . . . car ton charme-est étrange . . . et-je-t'ai-me.'

Recalling the song, as she sat back in the alcove of her bed, motionless, keeping the brightness of her room at its first intensity, Miriam remembered that it had brought her a moment when the flower-filled drawing-room had seemed to be lit, from within herself, a sudden light that had kept her very still and made the bowls of roses blaze with deepening colours. In her mind she had seen garden beyond garden of roses, sunlit, brighter and brighter, and had made a rapturous prayer. She remembered the words . . . God. . . . I'm not afraid of you. Look at the gardens . . . and something had smiled through the lit gardens exultantly, and Mrs Kronen's voice had raged through the room like a storm, 'Ai-me-moi! . . .' and Mr Corrie's eyes were strange and hard with shadows. . . . He knew, in some strange way, men knew there were gardens everywhere, not always visible. Women did not seem to know. . . .

The letter on her tray was a sort of response to her prayer.

CHAPTER V

IT was quite a long letter—signed with a large 'Bob' set cross-wise. It began by asking her advice about a wedding present for Harriett and ended with the suggestion that she should meet him and help him to make a suitable selection. It was written from the British Chess Club, to her, because Bob Greville wanted to see her. Harriett's wedding present was only an excuse. She flung the envelope and the two sheets of notepaper, spread loose, on her blue coverlet and smiled into her cup as she finished her coffee. Old Bob did not know that he had clad her in armour. He wanted to meet her alone. They two people were to meet and talk, without any reason, because they wanted to. But what could she have to say to any one who thought that *Mrs Caudle's Curtain Lectures*, even a nice edition bound in calf, or *How to be Happy though Married*, suitable for a wedding present for Harriett, or for anybody? Still, they might write to each other. It was right that letters, secret letters, should be brought into her blue room in the morning with her breakfast. She dropped out of bed smiling, and sniffed at the roses she had worn the day before, standing in a glass on her washstand, freshened, half faded, half fresh, intoxicating as she bent over them. She dressed, without drawing back her curtains, in the soft rose-blue light, singing Mrs Kronen's song in an undertone.

At eleven o'clock, Mrs Corrie swept into the schoolroom. Miriam looked easily up at her from the dreamy thicket where she and the children had spent their hour, united and content, speaking in undertones, getting easily through books that had seemed tiresome and indifferent the day before. She had felt the play of her mind on theirs and their steady, adult response. They had joined as conspirators in this mad contemptible business of mastering the trick of the text-book, each dreaming the while his own dream.

'You darlings,' cried Mrs Corrie, 'how sweet you all look!' They raised drunken eyes and beamed drowsily at her. 'Give them a holiday,' said Mrs Corrie, raising her hands over the table like a conductor about to start an orchestra. 'Give them a holiday—a picnic—and come and buy hats!'

In a moment the room was an uproar of capering figures. 'Hats! A new hat for Rollo! Heaps of cash! I've got heaps of cash!'

Miriam blinked from her thicket. This was anarchy; she felt herself sliding. But they were so old. All so old and experienced. She so young, by so far the youngest of the four.

Mrs Corrie sat back in the victoria, her face alight under the cream lace veil she had twisted round her soft winter hat, and talked in quiet clipped phrases: soft shouts. They were driving swiftly through the fresh warmth of the April midday.

They were off for the afternoon. The commons gleamed a prelude. Miriam saw that Mrs Corrie did not notice them nor think of sweeping back across them later on through the afternoon air and seeing them move and gleam in the afternoon light. She did not think of the bright shops, the strangely dyed artificial flowers with their curious fascinating smell interwoven with the strange warm smell of velvet and chenille and straw. . . . Miriam had once bought a hat in a shop in Kensington. As long as it lasted it had kept for her, whenever she looked at its softly dyed curiously plaited straw, something of the exciting fascination of the shop, the curious faint flat odours of millinery, the peculiar dim warm smell of silks and velvets—silk, China and Japan, silkworms weaving shining threads in the dark. Even when it had become associated with outings and events and shabby with exposure, it remained, each time she took it afresh from its box of wrappings, a mysterious sacred thing; and the soft blending of its colours, the coiled restraint of its shape, the texture of its snuggled trimmings were a support, refreshing her thoughts. She had never known any one who went regularly to good hat shops; the sense of them as a part of life was linked only with Mrs Kronen—Mrs Kronen's little close toque made of delicately shaded velvet violets and lined with satin, her silky peacock-blue straw shining with rich filmy tones, its mass of dull shot blue-green ribbon and the soft rose pink of its velvet roses. These hats had excited Mrs Corrie; the hats and the sand-coloured silk dust cloak explained her cheque and her sudden happiness. But they only made her want to buy hats. The going and the shops were nothing to her. She talked about the Kronens as they drove, speaking as though she wanted Miriam to hear without answering. 'She knows Mrs Kronen fascinates me,' thought Miriam.

'Ain't they a pair, lordy . . . him divorced and her divorced, and then marryin' each other. Ain't it scandalous, eh?'

People like the Corries disapproved of people like the Kronens, but had them to stay with them and were excited about their clothes. Miriam returned to listen to the singing of her spirit; it would sing until they got to the station. As she listened she held firmly clasped the letter she had addressed to the British Chess Club to say she would be nowhere near London until the weddings. 'She doesn't care a rap about him—not a teeny rap . . . she's a wise lady . . . dollars— that's the thing,' whispered Mrs Corrie gaily. What does she want me to say? thought Miriam. What would she say if I pretended to agree?

Should she tell her about the weddings? Perhaps not. It would be time enough, she reflected rapidly, when she had to ask permission to go home for them. Mrs Corrie had not asked her a single question about things at home, and if she were to say, 'We used to live in a big house and my father lost nearly all his money and we live now in a tiny villa and two of my sisters are to be married,' it would break into this strange easy new life. It would break the charm and not bring her any nearer to Mrs Corrie. And Mrs Corrie would not really under- stand about the home troubles. Mrs Corrie had always been lonely and sad, inside. She had been an orphan, but brought up by a wealthy uncle and always living in wealth and now she seemed to think about nothing but the children and the house and the garden—hating theatres and dances and never going to them or paying visits or seeing the wonder of anything. She would only say, 'Don't you marry yourself off, young lady; marriage is a fraud. You wait for a wealthy one.' Whatever one said to her, whatever joy one showed her, would lead to that.

But the two weddings hovered about the commons. They were a great possession. Nothing to worry about in them. Gerald and Bennett, who had managed everything since the smash, would manage them. Sarah and Harriet would be married from the little villa and would be Mrs Brodie and Mrs Ducayne just like anybody else. So safe. And she herself, free, getting interesting letters, going up to town with Mrs Corrie, no worry, spring hats and the commons and garden waiting for them. She was sure she did not want to see the commons over-burdened by the idea of her own wedding. Two was enough for the present. Of course, some day— someone, somewhere, wonderful and different from every one else. Cash—no, not business and cigars and offices . . . the City, horrible bloated men with shapeless figures, horrible chemists' shops advertising pick-me-ups . . . a cottage—a cottage. Why did people laugh at love in a cottage? The outsides of cottages were the best part, every one said. They were dark inside; but why not? A lamp; and outside the garden and the light.

'She's had all *kinds* of operations,' mused Mrs Corrie.

'*Really ?*'

'Deadly awful. In nursing homes. She'll never have any kiddies.'

Were there cold shadows on everything, everywhere?

She turned a pleading face to Mrs Corrie. They were driving into the station yard.

'It's true, true, true,' laughed Mrs Corrie. 'She doesn't care, she doesn't want any. They're all like that, that sort.'

Miriam mused intensely. She felt Mrs Kronen ought to be there to answer. She had some secret Mrs Corrie did not possess. Mrs Corrie looked suddenly small and mild and funny. Why did she think it dreadful that Mrs Kronen should have no children? There was nothing wonderful in having children. It was better to sing, She was perfectly sure that she herself did not want children. . . . 'Superior women don't marry,' she said, 'sir she said, sir she said, su, per, *i*, or women'—but that meant blue-stockings.

'I don't want a silly hat,' said Mrs Corrie, as their hansom drew up in bright sunlight outside a milliner's at the southern end of Regent Street. 'Let's buy a real lovely teapot or a Bartolozzi or somethin'. What fun to go home with somethin' real nice. Eh? A real real beauty Dresden teapot,' she chanted, floating into the dimness of the shop where large hats standing on long straight stands flared softly like blossoms in the twilight.

She swept about, in her flowing lace-trimmed twine-coloured overcoat, on the green velvet carpet, or stood ruthlessly trying on a hat, pressing its wire frame to fit her head, crushing her fingers into tucked tulle, talking and trying and discarding, until the collection was exhausted. Miriam sat angry and admiring, wondering at the subdued helplessness of the satin-clad assistant, sorry for the discarded hats lying carelessly about, their glory dimmed. All the hats, whatever their shape or colour, seemed to her to decorate the bronze head and the twine-coloured coat. The little toques gave slenderness and willowy height, and the large flowered ribboned hats, the moment a veil draped the boniness of the face, made, Miriam felt, an entrancing picturesqueness. With each hat, Mrs Corrie addressed the large mirror calling herself a freak, a sketch, a nightmare, a real, real fogey.

The process seemed endless and Miriam sat at last scourging herself with angry questions. 'Why doesn't she decide,' she found herself repeating almost aloud, her hot tired eyes turning for relief to the soft guipure-edged tussore curtain screening the lower part of the window, 'what kind of hat she really wants and then look at the few most like it and perhaps have one altered? . . .' 'It's so awfully silly not to have a plan.

She 'll go on simply for ever.' But the soft curtain running so evenly along its smooth clean brass rod was restful, and plan or no plan the trouble would presently come to an end and there would be no discomforts to face when it was over— no vulgar bun-shops, no struggling on to a penny bus with your ride perhaps spoiled by a dreadful neighbour, but Regent Street in the bright sun, a hansom, a smart obliging driver with a buttonhole, skimming along to tea somewhere, the first-class journey home, the carriage at the station, the green commons.

'Perhaps,' said the assistant at last in a cheerful suggestive furious voice, flinging aside with just Mrs Corrie's cheerful abandon a large cream lace hat with a soft fresh mass of tiny banksia roses under its left brim. 'Perhaps moddom will allow me to make her a shape and trim it to her own design.'

Mrs Corrie stood arrested in the middle of the green velvet floor. Wearily Miriam faced the possibility of the development of this fresh opportunity for going on for ever.

'Wouldn't that be lovely?' said Mrs Corrie, turning to her enthusiastically.

'Yes,' said Miriam eagerly. Both women were facing her and she felt that anything would be better than their united contemplation of her brown stuff dress with its square sleeves and her brown straw hat with black ribbon and its yellow paper buttercups.

'Can't be did though,' said Mrs Corrie in a cold level voice, turning swiftly back to the hats massed in a confused heap on the mahogany slab. Standing over them and tweaking at one and another as she spoke, she made a quiet little speech, indicating that such and such might do for the garden and such others for driving, some dozen altogether she finally ordered to be sent at once to an address in Brook Street where she would make her final selection whilst the messenger waited. 'Have you got the address all right?' she wound up; 'so kind of you.' 'Come along, you poor thing, you look worn out,' she cried to Miriam, without looking at her, as she swept from the shop. She waved her sunshade at a passing hansom and as it drew sharply up with an exciting clatter at the kerb she grasped Miriam's arm, 'Shall we try Perrin's? It 's only three

doors up.' Miriam glanced along and caught a glimpse of
another hat shop. 'Do you really want to?' she suggested
reluctantly. 'No! No! not a bit, old spoil-sport! Chum
yong, jump in,' laughed Mrs Corrie.

'Oh, if you really want to,' began Miriam, but Mrs Corrie,
singing out the address to the driver, was putting her into the
cab and showing her how to make an easy passage for the one
who gets last into a hansom by slipping into the near corner.
Her appreciation of this little manœuvre helped her over her
contrition and she responded with gay insincerity to Mrs
Corrie's assurance of the fun they would have over the hats
at Mrs Kronen's. . . . Tea at Mrs Kronen's, then. How
strange and alarming . . . but she felt too tired to sustain a
tête-à-tête at a smart tea shop. 'After tea we'll drop into a
china shop and get somethin' real nice,' said Mrs Corrie
excitedly, as they bowled up Regent Street.

They found Mrs Kronen in a mauve and white drawing-
room, reclining on a mauve and white striped settee in a pale
mauve tea-gown. On a large low table, a frail mauve tea
service stood ready, and Mrs Kronen rose tall to welcome them,
dropping on to the mauve carpet a little volume bound in pale
green velvet. On a second low table were strawberries in a
shallow wide bowl, a squat jug brimming with cream, dark
wedding cake hiding a pewter plate, a silken bag unloosed,
showing marvellous large various sweetmeats heavy against its
silk lining. As Mrs Kronen slurred her fingers across Miriam's
hand she ordered the manservant who had dipped and gathered
up the green velvet volume to ask for the tea-cakes.

Then this was 'Society.' To come so easily up from the
Corries' beautiful home, via the West End hat shop, to this
wonderful West End flat and eat strawberries in April. . . .
If only the home people could see. Her fatigue vanished.

Secure from Mrs Kronen's notice, she sat in a mauve and white striped chair and contemplated her surroundings.

While they were waiting for the tea-cakes, Mrs Kronen trailed about the mauve floor reciting her impressions of the weather. 'So lovely,' she intoned in her curious half-Cockney. 'I almost—went—out. But I haven't. I—haven't—stirred. It is lovely inside on this sort of spring day—the *light*.'

She paused and swept about. There *is* something about her, thought Miriam. It's true, the light inside on a clear spring day. . . . I never thought of that. It is somehow spring in here in the middle of London in some real way. Her blood leaped and sang as it had done driving across the commons; but even more sweetly and keenly. It wouldn't be, in a dingy room, even in the country. . . . It's an essence—something you feel in the right surroundings. . . . What chances these people have! They get the most out of everything. Get everything in advance and over and over again. They can go into the country any minute, as well as have clear light rooms. Nothing is ever grubby. And London there, all round; London . . . London was a soft, sea-like sound; a sound shutting in the spring. The spring gleamed and thrilled through everything in the pure bright room. . . . She hoped Mrs Kronen would say no more about the light. Light, light, light. As the manservant brewed the tea, the silver teapot shone in the light as he moved it—silver and strange black splashes of light—caught and moving in the room. Drawing off her gloves, she felt as if she could touch the flowing light. . . . Flowing in out of the dawn, moving and flowing and brooding and changing all day, in rooms. Mrs Kronen was back on her settee sitting upright in her mauve gown, all strong soft curves. 'That play of *Wilde*'s . . .' she said. Miriam shook at the name. 'You ought not to miss it. He—has—such—*genius*.' *Wilde* . . . *Wilde* . . . a play in the spring—someone named Wilde. Wild spring. That was genius. There was something in the name. . . . 'Never go to the theatre; never, never, never,' Mrs Corrie was saying, 'too much of a bore.' Genius . . . genius is an infinite capacity for taking pains. Capacity. A silly definition; like a proverb—

made up by somebody who wanted to explain. . . . Wylde,
Wilde. . . . Spring. . . . Genius.

The little feast was over and Mrs Kronen was puffing at a
cigarette, when the hats were announced. As the fine incense
reached her, Miriam regretted that she had not confessed to
being a smoker. The suggestion of tobacco brought the
charm of the afternoon to its height. When the magic of the
scented cloud drew her eyes to Mrs Kronen's face, it was
almost intolerable in its keenness. She gazed, wondering
whether Mrs Kronen felt so nearly wild with happiness as she
did herself. . . . Life what are you—what is life? she almost
said aloud. The face was uplifted as it had been in the
photograph, but with all the colour, the firm bows of gold hair,
the colour in the face and strong white pillar of neck, the eyes
closed instead of staring upwards and the rather full mouth
flattened and drooping with its weight into a sort of tragic
shapeliness—like some martyr . . . that picture by Rossetti,
Beata Beatrix, thought Miriam . . . perfect reality. She
liked Mrs Kronen for smoking like that. She was not doing
it for show. She would have smoked in the same way if she
had been alone. She probably wished she was, as Mrs Corrie
did not smoke. How she must have hated missing her smokes
at Newlands, unless she had smoked in her room.
'It's—a—mis-take,' said Mrs Kronen incredulously, in
response to the man's announcement of the arrival of the
hats. She waved her cigarette 'imperiously,' thought Miriam,
'how she enjoys showing off' . . . to and fro in time with
her words. Mrs Corrie rose laughing and explaining and
apologizing. Waving her cigarette about once more, Mrs
Kronen ordered the hats to be brought in and her maid to be
summoned, but retained her expression of vexed incredulity.
She's simply longing for us to be off now, thought Miriam,
and changed her opinion a few moments later when Mrs
Kronen, assuming on the settee the reclining position in which
they had found her when they came in, disposed one by one of

the hats, as Mrs Corrie and the maid freed them from their boxes and wrappings, with a little flourish of the cigarette and a few slow words. . . . 'Im-poss-i-ble; not-in-key-with-your-lines; slightly *too ingénue*,' etc.: to three or four she gave a grudging approval, whereupon Mrs Corrie, who was laughing and pouncing from box to box, would stand upright and pace, holding the favoured hat rakishly on her head. The selection was soon made and Miriam, whose weariness had returned with the millinery, was sent off to instruct the messenger that three hats had been selected and a bill might be sent to Brook Street in the morning.

As she was treating with the messenger in the little mauve and white hall, Mrs Corrie came out and tapped her on the shoulder. Turning, Miriam found her smiling and mysterious. 'We're going by the 5.30,' she whispered. 'Would you like to go for a walk for half an hour and come back *here*?'

'*Rather!*' said Miriam heartily, with a break in her voice and feeling utterly crushed. The beautiful clear room. She loved it and belonged to it. She was turned out. 'All right,' smiled Mrs Corrie encouragingly and disappeared. Under the eyes of the messenger, and the servants who were coming out of the boudoir laden with hat boxes, she got herself out through the door.

CHAPTER VI

THE West End street . . . grey buildings rising on either side, angles sharp against the sky . . . softened angles of buildings against other buildings . . . high moulded angles soft as crumb, with deep undershadows . . . creepers fraying from balconies . . . strips of window blossoms across the buildings, scarlet, yellow, high up; a confusion of lavender and white pouching out along the dipping sill . . . a wash of green creeper up a white painted house-front . . . patches of shadow and bright light. . . . Sounds of visible near things streaked and scored with broken light as they moved, led off into untraced distant sounds . . . chiming together.

Wide golden streaming Regent Street was quite near. Some near narrow street would lead into it.

Flags of pavement flowing—smooth clean grey squares and oblongs, faintly polished, shaping and drawing away—sliding into each other. . . . I am part of the dense smooth clean paving stone . . . sunlit; gleaming under dark winter rain; shining under warm sunlit rain, sending up a fresh stony smell . . . always there . . . dark and light . . . dawn, stealing . . .

Life streamed up from the close dense stone. With every footstep she felt she could fly.

The little dignified high-built cut-through street, with its sudden walled-in church, swept round and opened into brightness and a clamour of central sounds ringing harshly up into the sky.

The pavement of heaven.

416

To walk along the radiant pavement of sunlit Regent Street, for ever.

She sped along looking at nothing. Shops passed by, bright endless caverns screened with glass . . . the bright teeth of a grand piano running along the edge of a darkness, a cataract of light pouring down its raised lid; forests of hats; dresses, shining against darkness, bright headless crumpling stalks; sly, silky, ominous furs; metals, cold and clanging, brandishing the light; close prickling fire of jewels . . . strange people who bought these things, touched and bought them.

She pulled up sharply in front of a window. The pavement round it was clear, allowing her to stand rooted where she had been walking, in the middle of the pavement, in the midst of the pavement, in the midst of the tide flowing from the clear window, a soft fresh tide of sunlit colours . . . clear green glass shelves laden with shapes of fluted glass, glinting transparencies of mauve and amber and green, rose-pearl and milky blue, welded to a flowing tide, freshening and flowing through her blood, a sea rising and falling with her breathing.

The edge had gone from the keenness of the light. The street was a happy, sunny, simple street—small. She was vast. She could gather up the buildings in her arms and push them away, clearing the sky . . . a strange darkling, and she would sleep. She felt drowsy, a drowsiness in her brain and limbs and great strength, and hunger.

A clock told her she had been away from Brook Street ten minutes. Twenty minutes to spare. What should she do with her strength? Talk to someone or write . . . Bob;

where was Bob? Somewhere in the West End. She would
write from the West End a note to him in the West End.

There were no cheap shops in Regent Street. She looked
about. Across the way a little side street, showing a small
newspaper shop, offered help.

She hurried with clenched hands down the little mean street
ready to give up her scheme at the first sight of an unfriendly
eye. 'We went through those *awful* side streets off the West
End; I was *terrified*; I didn't know *where* he was driving us,'
Mrs Poole had said, about a cabman driving to the theatre . . .
and her face as she sat in her thick pink dress by the dining-
room fire had been cunning and mean and full of terror. The
small shop appeared close at hand, there were newspaper
posters propped outside it and its window was full of fly-blown
pipes, toilet requisites, stationery and odd-looking books.
'Letters may be left here,' said a dirty square of cardboard in
the corner of the window. 'That's all right,' thought Miriam,
'it's a sort of agency.' She plunged into the gloomy interior.
'*Yes!*' shouted a tall stout man with a red coarse face, coming
forward as if she had asked something that had made him
angry. 'I want some notepaper, just a little, the smallest
quantity you have, and an envelope,' said Miriam, quivering
and panic-stricken in the hostile atmosphere. The man
turned and whisked a small packet off a shelf, throwing it down
on the counter before her. 'One penny!' he bellowed as she
took it up. 'Oh, thank you,' murmured Miriam ingratiatingly,
putting down twopence. 'Do you sell pencils?' The man's
great fingers seemed an endless time wrenching a small metal-
sheathed pencil from its card. The street outside would have
closed in and swallowed her up for ever if she did not quickly
get away.

'Dear Mr Greville,' she wrote in a clear bold hand. . . . He
won't expect me to have that kind of handwriting, like his own,
but stronger. He'll admire it on the page and then hear a
man's voice, pater's voice talking behind it and not like it.

Me. He'll be a little afraid of it. She felt her hard self
standing there as she wrote, and shifted her feet a little, raising
one heel from the ground, trying to feminize her attitude; but
her hat was hard against her forehead, her clothes would not
flow. . . . 'Just imagine that I am in town—I could have
helped you with your shopping if I had known I was
coming. . . .' The first page was half filled. She glanced
at her neighbours, a woman on one side and a man on the
other, both bending over telegram forms in a careless preoccupied way—wealthy, with expensive clothes with West
End lines. . . . Regent Street was Salviati's. It was Liberty's
and a music shop and the shop with the chickens. But most
of all it was Salviati's. She feared the officials behind the
long grating could see by the expression of her shoulders
that she was a scrubby person who was breaking the rules
by using one of the little compartments, with its generosity of
ink and pen and blotting-paper, for letter writing. Someone
was standing impatiently just behind her, waiting for her place.
'Telle est la vie,' she concluded with a flourish, 'yours sin-
cerely,' and addressed the envelope in almost illegible scrawls.
Guiltily she bought a stamp and dropped the letter with a
darkening sense of guilt into the box. It fell with a little
muffled plop that resounded through her as she hurried away
towards Brook Street. She walked quickly, to make everything surrounding her move more quickly. London revelled
and clamoured softly all round her; she strode her swiftest,
heightening its clamorous joy. The West End people, their
clothes, their carriages and hansoms, their clean bright spring-
filled houses, their restaurants and the theatres waiting for
them this evening, their easy way with each other, the mysterious something behind their faces, was hers. She, too, now
had a mysterious secret face—a West End life of her own. . . .

CHAPTER VII

THE next morning there was a letter from Bob containing a page of description of his dull afternoon at his club, within half a mile of her. 'Let me know, my dear girl,' it went on, 'whenever you escape from your jailers, and do not suffer the thought of old Bob's making himself responsible for all the telegrams you may send, to cloud your joyous young independence.'

Miriam recoiled from the thought of a dull bored man looking to her for enlivenment of the moving coloured wonder of London, and felt that Mr and Mrs Corrie were anything but jailers. She was not sorry that she had missed the opportunity of seeing him. 'Meanwhile write and tell me your thoughts,' was the only sentence that had appealed to her in the letter; but she was sure she could not whole-heartedly offer her thoughts as entertainment to a man who spent his time feeling dull in a club. He's . . . blasé, that's it, she reflected. Perhaps it would be better not to write again. He's not my sort a bit, she pondered, with a sudden dim sense of his view of her as a dear girl. But she knew she wanted to retain him to decorate her breakfast tray with letters.

The following day Mrs Corrie decided that she did not want to keep the hats. She would spend the money intended for them on sketching lessons. An artist should come once a week and teach them all to paint, from Nature. This decision excited Miriam deeply, putting everything else out of her mind. It promised the satisfaction of   desire she had cherished with bitter hopelessness ever since her schooldays, when every Friday had brought the necessity of choking down her longing to join the little crowd of girls who took 'extras' and filed carelessly in to spend a magic afternoon amongst easels and casts in the large room. The old longing came leaping back higher than it had ever done before, making a curious eager smouldering in her chest—as Mrs Corrie talked. An old sketch-book was brought out and Mrs Corrie spent the morning making drawings of the heads of the children as they sat at lessons. The book was almost full of drawings of the children's heads. Besides the heads there were rough sketches of people Miriam did not know. The first half-dozen pages were covered with small outlines, hands, feet, eyes, thumbs; a few lines suggesting a body. These pages seemed full of life. But the sketches of the children and the unknown people, sitting posed, in profile, looking up, looking down, full face, quarter face, three-quarters, depressed her. Learning to draw did not seem worth while if this was the result. The early pages haunted her memory as she sat over the children's lessons. Feet, strange things stepping out, going through the world, running, dancing; the silent feet of people sitting in chairs pondering affairs of state. Eyes, looking at everything; looking at the astonishingness of everything.

'That's the half-crown Mrs Corrie gave me for the cabman, and the shilling for my tea,' said Miriam, handing the coins to her companion as they bowled over Waterloo Bridge. Sea-gulls were rising and dipping about the rim of the bridge and the sunlight lay upon the water and shimmered and flashed along the forms of the sea-gulls as they hovered and wheeled in the clear air. Miriam glanced at them through the little side window of the hansom with a remote keen part of her consciousness . . . light, flashing from the moving wing of a sea-gull, the blue water, the brilliant sky, the bite of sun-scorched air upon her cheek, the sound about her like the sound of the sea. . . . As she turned back to the shaded enclosure of the hansom, these things shrivelled and vanished and left her dumb, helplessly poised between two worlds. This shabby part of London and the seaside bridge could make no terms with the man at her side, his soft grey suit, his soft grey felt hat, the graceful crook of his crossed knees, his gleaming spats, the glitter of the light upon patent leather shoes. He was gazing out ahead, with the look with which he had looked across Australia in his gold-digging days, weary until he got back to the West End, not talking because the cab made such a noise crossing the bridge. It was stupid of her to peer out of the window and get away to her own world like that. Nothing that we can ever say to each other can possibly interest us, she reflected. Why am I here? Her coins reassured her.

'Don't think about pence, dear girl,' he said, in a voice that quavered a little against the noise of the cab, 'when you 're with old Bob.' Without looking at her he gently closed her hand over the money.

'All right,' she shouted, 'we 'll see, later on!'

The cab swept round into a street and the noise abated.

'When we 've dropped those famous hats and rung the bell and run away, we 'll go on to Bumpus's and choose our book,' he said, as if asserting themselves and their errand against the confusion through which they were driving.

Mrs Caudle's Curtain Lectures, thought Miriam, glancing with loathing at the pointed corner of the collar that stuck out across the three firm little folds under the clean-shaven chin. . . . How funny I am. I suppose I shall get through the afternoon somehow. We shall go to the bookshop and then have tea, and then it will be time to go back.

'The cabman is to take the hats into the shop and leave them. Isn't it extraordinary?'

Bob laughed with a little fling of his head.

'The vagaries of the Fair, dear girl,' he said presently, in a soft blurred tone.

That 's one of his phrases, thought Miriam—that 's old-fashioned politeness; courtliness. Behind it he 's got some sort of mannish thought . . . 'the unaccountability of women' . . . 'who can understand a woman?—she doesn't even under-stand herself'—thought he 'd given up trying to make out. He 's gone through life and got his own impressions; all utterly wrong . . . talking about women, with an air of wisdom, to young men like Gerald . . . my dear boy, a woman never knows her own mind. How utterly detestable mannishness is; so mighty and strong and comforting when you have been mewed up with women all your life, and then suddenly, in a second, far away, utterly imbecile and aggravating, with a superior self-satisfied smile because a woman says one thing one minute and another the next. Men ought to be horse-whipped, all the grown men, all who have ever had that self-satisfied smile, all, all, horse-whipped until they apologize on their knees.

They sat in a curious oak settee, like a high-backed church pew. The waitress had cleared away the tea things and brought cigarettes, large flat Turkish cigarettes. Responding to her companion's elaborate apologetic petition for permission to smoke, it did not occur to Miriam to confess that she herself occasionally smoked. She forgot the fact in the completeness of her contentment. On the square oak table in front of them was a bowl of garden anemones, mauve and scarlet with black centres, flaring richly in the soft light coming through the green-tented diamond panes of a little low square deep-silled window. On either side of the window, short red curtains were drawn back and hung in straight, close folds . . . scarlet geraniums . . . against the creamy plaster wall. Bowls of flowers stood on other tables placed without crowding or confusion about the room, and there was another green window with red curtains near a far-off corner. There were no other customers for the greater part of their time and, when the waitress was not in the room, it was still; a softly shaded stillness. Bob's low blurred voice had gone on and on undisturbingly, no questions about her life or her plans, just jokes, about the tea-service and everything they had had, making her laugh. Whenever she laughed, he laughed delightedly. All the time her eyes had wandered from the brilliant anemones across to the soft green window with its scarlet curtains.

CHAPTER VIII

WHEN May came, life lay round Miriam without a flaw. She seemed to have reached the summit of a hill up which she had been climbing ever since she came to Newlands. The weeks had been green lanes of experience, fresh and scented and balmy and free from lurking fears. Now the landscape lay open before her eyes, clear from horizon to horizon, sunlit and flawless, past and future. The present, within her hands, brought her, whenever she paused to consider it, to the tips of her toes, as if its pressure lifted her. She would push it off, smiling—turning and shutting herself away from it, with laughter and closed eyes. She found herself deeper in the airy flood and, drawing breath, swam forward.

The old troubles, the things she had known from the beginning, the general shadow that lay over the family life and closed punctually in whenever the sun began to shine, her own personal thoughts, the impossibility of living with people, poverty, disease, death in a dark corner, had moved and changed, melted and flowed away.

The family shadow had shrunk long ago, back in the winter months they had spent in Bennett's little bachelor villa, to a small black cloud of disgrace hanging over her father. At the time of its appearance, when the extent of his embarrassment was exactly known, she had sunk for a while under the conviction that the rest of her life must be spent in a vain attempt to pay off his debts. Her mind revolved round the problem hopelessly. . . . Even if she went on the stage she could not make enough to pay off one of his creditors. Most women who went on the stage, Gerald had said, made practically nothing, and the successful ones had to spend enormous sums in bribery whilst they were making their way—even the orchestra expected to be flattered and bribed. She would have to go on being a resident governess, keeping ten pounds a year for dress

424

and paying over the rest of her salary. Her bitter rebellion
against this prospect was reinforced by the creditors' refusal
to make her father a bankrupt. The refusal brought her a
picture of the creditors, men 'on the Stock Exchange,' sitting
in a circle, in frock-coats, talking over her father's affairs. She
winced, her blood came scorching against her skin. She confronted them, 'Stop!' she shouted, 'stop *talking*—you smug
ugly men! You shall be paid. Stop! Go away. . . .' But
Gerald had said, 'They *like* the old boy . . . it won't hurt
them . . . they're all *made* of money.' They liked him.
They would be kind. What right had they to be 'kind'?
They would be kind to her, too. They would smile at her plan
of restitution and put it on one side. And yet secretly she
knew that each one of them would like to be paid and was vexed
and angry at losing money, just as she was angry at having
to sacrifice her life to them. She would not sacrifice her life, but
if ever she found herself wealthy she would find out their
names and pay them secretly. Probably that would be never.

Disgrace had closed round her, stifling. 'It's *us*—we're
doomed,' she thought, feeling the stigma of her family in her
flesh. 'If I go on after this, holding up my head, I shall be a
liar and a cheat. It will show in my face and in my walk, always.'
She bowed her head. 'I want to live,' murmured something.
'I want to live, even if I slink through life. I will. I don't
care, inside. I shall always have myself to be with.'

Something that was not touched, that sang far away down
inside the gloom, that cared nothing for the creditors and could
get away down and down into the twilight, far away from the
everlasting accusations of humanity. . . . The disgrace sat
only in the muscles of her face, in her muscles, the stuff of her
that had defied and fought and been laughed at and beaten. It
would not get deeper. Deeper down was something cool and
fresh—endless garden. In happiness it came up and made
everything in the world into a garden. Sorrow blotted it over,
but it was always there, waiting and looking on. It had looked
on in Germany and had loved the music and the words and the
happiness of the German girls; and at Banbury Park, giving
her no peace until she got away.

And now it had come to the surface and was with her all the time. Away in the distance, filling in the horizon, was the home life. Beyond the horizon, gone away for ever into some outer darkness, were her old ideas of trouble, disease and death. Once they had been always quite near at hand, always ready to strike, laying cold hands on everything. They would return, but they would be changed. No need to fear them any more. She had seen them change. And when at last they came back, when there was nothing else left in front of her, they would still be changing. 'Get along, old ghosts,' she said, and they seemed friendly and smiling. Her father and mother, whose failure and death she had foreseen as a child with sudden bitter tears, were going on now step by step towards these ghostly things in the small bright lamplit villa in Gunnersbury. She had watched them there during the winter months before she came to Newlands. They had some secret together and did not feel the darkness. Their eyes were careless and bright. Startled, she had heard them laugh together as they talked in their room. Often their eyes were preoccupied, as if they were looking at a picture. She had laughed aloud at the thought, whenever there had been any excuse, and they had always looked at her when she laughed her gay laugh. Had they understood? Did they know that it was themselves laughing in her? Families ought to laugh together, whenever there is any excuse. She felt that her own grown-up laughter was the end of all the dreadful years. And three weeks ahead were the two weddings. The letters from home gleamed with descriptions of the increasing store of presents and new-made clothing. Miriam felt that they were her own; she would see them all at the last best moment when they were complete. She would have all that, and all her pride in the outgoing lives of Sarah and Harriett, that were like two sunlit streams. And meanwhile here within her hands was Newlands. Three weeks of days and nights of untroubled beauty. Interminable.

The roses were in bud. Every day she managed to visit them at least once, running out alone into the garden at twilight and coming back rich with the sense of the twilit green garden and the increasing stripes of colour between the tight shining green sheaths.

There had been no more talk of painting lessons. The idea had died in Mrs Corrie's mind the day after it had been born, and a strange interest, something dreadful that was happening in London, had taken its place. It seemed to absorb her completely and to spread a strange curious excitement throughout the house. She sent a servant every afternoon up to the station for an evening newspaper. The pink papers disappeared, but she was perpetually making allusions to their strange secret in a way that told Miriam she wanted to impart it, and that irritated without really arousing her interest. She felt that anything that was being fussed over in pink evening papers was probably really nothing at all. She could not believe that anything that had such a strange effect on Mrs Corrie could really interest her. But she longed to know exactly what the mysterious thing was. If it was simply a divorce case, Mrs Corrie would have told her about it, dropping out the whole story abstractedly in one of her little shocked sentences, and immediately going on to speak of something else. She did not want to hear anything more about divorce; all her interested curiosity in divorced people had been dispersed by her contact with the Kronens. They had both been divorced and their lives were broken and muddly and they were not sure of themselves. Mrs Kronen was strong and alone. But she was alone and would always be. If it were a murder, everybody would talk about it openly. It must be something worse than a murder or a divorce. She felt she must know, must make Mrs Corrie tell her and knew at the same time that she did not want to be distracted from the pure solid glory of the weeks by sharing a horrible secret. The thing kept Mrs Corrie occupied and interested and left her free to live undisturbed. It was a barrier between them. And yet . . . something that a human being had done that was worse than a murder or a divorce.

'Is it a divorce?' she said suddenly and insincerely one afternoon coming upon Mrs Corrie scanning the newly arrived newspaper in the garden.

'Lordy no,' laughed Mrs Corrie self-consciously, scrumpling the paper under her arm.

'What is it?' said Miriam, shaking and flushing. 'Don't tell me, don't tell me,' cried her mind, 'don't mention it, you don't know yourself what it is. Nobody knows what anything is.'

'I couldn't tell you!' cried Mrs Corrie.

'Why *not*?' laughed Miriam.

'It's too awful,' giggled Mrs Corrie.

'Oh, you must tell me now you've begun.'

'It's the most awful thing there is. It's in the Bible,' said Mrs Corrie, and fled into the house.

Little cities burning and flaring in a great plain until everything was consumed. Everything beginning again—clean. Would London be visited by destruction? Humanity was as bad now as in Bible days. It made one feel cold and sick. In the midst of the beauty and happiness of England—awful things, the worst things there were. What awful faces those people must have. It would be dreadful to see them.

At the week-end the house seemed full of little groups of conspirators, talking in corners, full of secret glee . . . someone describing a room, drawn curtains and candlelight at midday . . . wonderful . . . and laughing. Why did they laugh? A candle-lit room in the midst of bright day . . . wonderful, like a shrine.

The low-toned talk went on, in Mr Corrie's little study behind the half-closed door, in corners of the hall. Names were mentioned—the name of the man who wrote the plays, Mrs Kronen's 'genius.' Miriam could only recall when she was alone that it was a woodland springtime name. It comforted her to think that this name was concerned in the horrible mystery. Her sympathies veered vaguely out towards the patch of disgrace in London and her interest died down.

The general preoccupation and excitement seemed to destroy her link with the household. As soon as the children's tea was over she felt herself free. A strange tall woman came to stay in the house, trailing about in long jewelled dresses with a slight limp; Miss Tower, Mrs Corrie called her Jin. But the name did not belong to her. Miriam could not think of any name that would belong to her . . . talking to Mrs. Corrie at lunch with amused eyes and expressionless, small fine features, of some illness that might kill her in eight or ten years, of her friends, talking about her men friends as if they were boys to be cried over. 'Why don't you marry him?' Mrs Corrie would say of one or another. How happy the man would be, thought Miriam, gazing into the strange eyes and daring her to marry any one and alter the eyes. Miss Tower spoke to her now and again as if she had known her all her life. One day after lunch she suddenly said, 'You ought to smile more often—you've got pretty teeth; but you forget about them. Don't forget about them'; and one evening she came into her room just as she was beginning to undress and stood by the fire and said, 'Your evening dresses are all wrong. You should have them cut higher, above the collar-bone—or much lower—don't forget. Don't forget, you could be charming.'

Mrs Corrie came in herself the next evening and gave Miriam a full-length cabinet photograph of herself, suddenly. Afterwards she heard her saying to Jin on the landing, 'Let the poor thing rest when she can,' and they both went into Jin's room.

Every day, as soon as the children's tea was over, she fled to her room. The memory of Mrs Corrie's little sketch-book had haunted her for days. She had bought a block and brushes, a small box of paints and a book on painting in water colours. For days she painted, secure in the feeling of Mrs Corrie and

Jin occupied with each other. She filled sheet after sheet with swift efforts to recall Brighton skies—sunset, the red mass of the sun, the profile of the cliffs, the sky clear or full of heavy cloud, the darkness of the afternoon sea streaked by a path of gold, bird-specks, above the cliffs above the sea. The painting was thick and confused, the objects blurred and ran into each other, the image of each recalled object came close before her eyes, shaking her with its sharp reality, her heart and hand shook as she contemplated it, and her body thrilled as she swept her brushes about. She found herself breathing heavily and deeply, sure each time of registering what she saw, sweeping rapidly on until the filled paper confronted her, a confused mass of shapeless images, leaving her angry and cold. Each day what she had done the day before thrilled her afresh and drove her on, and the time she spent in contemplation and hope became the heart of the days as April wore on.

On the last day of Jin Tower's visit, Miriam came in from the garden upon Mrs Corrie sitting in the hall with her guest. Jin was going and was sorry that she was going. But Miriam saw that her gladness was as great as her sorrow. It always would be. Whatever happened to her. Mrs Corrie was sitting at her side, bent from the waist with her arms stretched out and hands clasped beyond her knees. Miriam was amazed to see how much Mrs Corrie had been talking, and that she was treating Jin's departure as if it were a small crisis. There was a touch of soft heat and fussiness in the air. Mrs Corrie's features were discomposed. They both glanced at her as she came across the hall and she smiled, awkwardly, and half paused. Her mind was turned towards her vision of a great cliff in profile against a still sky with a deep sea brimming to its feet in a placid afterglow; the garden with its lawn and trees, its bushiness and its buttons of bright rosebuds had seemed small and troubled and talkative in comparison. In her slight pause she offered them her vision, but knew as she went on upstairs that her attitude had said, 'I am the paid governess.

You must not talk to me as you would to each other; I am an inferior and can never be an intimate.' She was glad that Jin had left off coming to her room. She did not want intimacy with any one if it meant that strained fussiness in the hall. Meeting Mrs Corrie later on the landing she asked, with a sudden sense of inspiration, whether she might have her meal in her room, adding in an insincere effort at explanation that she wanted to do some reading up for the children. Mrs Corrie agreed with an alacrity that gave her a vision of possible freedom ahead and a shock of apprehension. Perhaps she had not succeeded even so far as she thought in living the Newlands social life. She spent the evening writing to Eve, asking her if she remembered sea scenes at Weymouth and Brighton, pushing on and on weighed down by a sense of the urgency of finding out whether, to Eve, the registration of impressions was a thing that she must either do or lose hold of something essential. She felt that Eve would somehow admire her own stormy emphasis but would not really understand how much it meant to her. She remembered Eve's comparison of the country round the Greens' house to Leader landscapes—pictures, and how delightful it had seemed to her that she had such things all round her to look at. But her thoughts of the great brow and downward sweep of cliff and the sea coming up to it was not a picture, it was a thing; her cheeks flared as she searched for a word—it was an experience, perhaps the most important thing in life—far in away from any 'glad mask,' a thing belonging to that strange inner life and independent of everybody. Perhaps it was a betrayal, a sort of fat noisy gossiping to speak of it, even to Eve. 'You 'll think I 'm *mad*,' she concluded, 'but I 'm not.'

When the letter was finished, the Newlands life seemed very remote. She felt a touch of the half-numb half-feverish stupor that had been her daily mood at Banbury Park. She would go on teaching the Corrie children, but her evenings in future would be divided between unsuccessful efforts to put down her flaming or peaceful sunset scenes and to explain their importance to Eve.

CHAPTER IX

BUT the next evening, when Mr Corrie came down for the week-end with a party of guests, Mrs Corrie appeared with swift suddenness in Miriam's room and glanced at her morning dress.

'I say, missy, you 'll have to hurry up.'

'Oh, I didn't dress . . . the house is full of strangers.'

'No, it isn't; there 's Mélie and Tom . . . Tommy and Mélie.'

'Yes, but I know there are crowds.'

She did not want to meet the Cravens again, and the strangers would turn out to be some sort of people saying certain sorts of things over and over again, and if she went down she would not be able to get away as soon as she knew all about them. She would be fixed; obliged to listen. When any one spoke to her, grimacing as the patronized governess, or saying what she thought and being hated for it.

'Crowds,' she repeated, as Mrs Corrie placed a large lump in the centre of the blaze.

They had her here, in this beautiful room and looked after her comfort as if she were a guest.

'Nonsensy-nonsense. You *must* come down and see the fun.' Miriam glanced at her empty table. In the drawer hidden underneath the table-cover were her block and paints. Presently she could, if she held firm, be alone, in a grey space inside this alien room, cold and lonely and with the beginning of something . . . dark painful beginning of something that could not come if people were there. . . . Downstairs, warmth and revelry.

'You *must* come down and see the fun,' said Mrs Corrie, getting up from the fire and trailing across the room with bent head. 'A nun—a nun in amber satin,' thought Miriam, surveying her back.

432

'*Want* you to come down,' said Mrs Corrie plaintively from the door. Cold air came in from the landing; the warmth of the room stirred to a strange vitality, the light glowed clearer within its ruby globe. The silvery clatter of entrée dishes came up from the hall.

'All right,' said Miriam, turning exultantly to the chest of drawers.

'A victory over myself or some sort of treachery?' . . . The long drawer which held her evening things seemed full of wonders. She dragged out a little home-made smocked blouse of pale blue nun's veiling that had seemed too dowdy for Newlands and put it on over her morning skirt. It shone upon her. Rapidly washing her hands, away from the glamour of the looking-glass, she mentally took stock of her hair, untouched since the morning, the amateur blouse, its crude clear blue hard against the harsh black skirt. Back again at the dressing-table as she dried her hands she found the miracle renewed. The figure that confronted her in the mirror was wrapped in some strange harmonizing radiance. She looked at it for a moment as she would have looked at an unknown picture, in tranquil disinterested contemplation. The sound of the gong came softly into the room, bringing her no apprehensive contraction of nerves. She wove its lingering note into the imagined tinkling of an old melody from a wooden musical-box. Opening the door before turning out her gas she found a small bunch of hothouse lilies of the valley left on the writing-table. . . . Mrs Corrie—'you must come.'

Tucking them into her belt she went slowly downstairs, confused by a picture coming between her and her surroundings like a filmy lantern slide, of Portland Bill lying on a smooth sea in a clear afterglow. . . .

'Quite a madonna,' said Mrs Staple-Craven querulously. She sat low in her chair, her round gold head on its short stalk standing firmly up from billowy frills of green silk . . . 'a fat water-lily,' mused Miriam, and went wandering through the great steamy glass-houses at Kew, while the names that had been murmured during the introductions echoed irrelevantly in her brain.

'She *must* wear her host's colours sometimes,' said Mr Corrie quickly and gently.

Miriam glanced her surprise and smiled shyly in response to his smile. It was as if the faint radiance that she felt all round her had been outlined by a flashing blade. Mrs Craven might go on resenting it; she could not touch it again. It steadied and concentrated; flowing from some inexhaustible inner centre, it did not get beyond the circle outlined by the flashing blade, but flowed back on her and out again and back until it seemed as if it must lift her to her feet. Her eyes caught the clear brow and smooth innocently sleeked dark hair of a man at the other end of the table. Under the fine level brows was a loudly talking, busily eating face—all the noise of the world, and the brooding grieving unconscious brow above it. Every one was talking. She glanced. The women showed no foreheads; but their faces were not noisy; they were like the brows of the men, except Mrs Craven's. Her silent face was mouthing and complaining aloud all the time.

'Old Felix has secured himself the best partner,' Miriam heard someone mutter as she made her fluke, a resounding little cannon and pocket in one stroke. Wandering after her ball she fought against the suggesting voice. It had come from one of the men moving about in the gloom surrounding the radiance cast by the green-shaded lamps upon the long green table. Faces moving in the upper darkness were indistinguishable. The white patch of Mrs Corrie's face gleamed from the settee as she sat bent forward with her hands clasped in front of her knees. Beyond her, sitting back under the shadow of the mantelpiece and the marking board, was Mrs Craven, a faint mass of soft green and mealy white. All the other forms were standing or moving in the gloom; standing watchful and silent, the gleaming stems of their cues held in rest, shifting and moving and strolling with uncolliding ordered movements and little murmurs of commentary after the little drama—the sudden snap of the stroke breaking the stillness, the faint thundering roll of the single ball, the click of the concussion, the gentle angular explosion of pieces into a new relation and the breaking of the varying triangle as a ball rolled to its hidden destination, held by all the eyes in the room until its rumbling pilgrimage ended out of sight in a soft thud. It was pure joy to Miriam to wander round the table after her ball, sheltered in the gloom, through an endless 'grand chain' of undifferentiated figures that passed and repassed without awkwardness or the need for forced exchange; held together and separated by the ceremony of the game. Comments came after each stroke, words and sentences, sped and smoothed and polished by the gloom, like the easy talking of friends in a deep twilight; but between each stroke were vast intervals of un-troubled silent intercourse. The competition of the men, the sense of the desire to win, that rose and strained in the room could not spoil this communion. After a stroke, pondering the balls while the room and the radiance and the darkness moved and flowed and the dim figures settled to a fresh miracle of grouping, it was joy to lean along the board to her ball, keeping punctual appointment with her partner whose jaunty little figure would appear in supporting opposition under the bright light, drawing at his cigarette with a puckering half-smile, awaiting her suggestion and ready with counsel. Doing her best to measure angles and regulate the force of her blow she struck careless little lifting strokes that made her feel as if she danced, and managed three more cannons and a pocket before her little break came to an end.

'It must be jolly to smoke in the in-between times,' said Miriam, standing about at a loss during a long break by one of her opponents.

'Yes, you ought to learn to smoke,' responded Mr Corrie judicially. The quiet smile—the serene offer of companionship, the whole room troubled with the sense of the two parties, the men with whom she was linked in the joyous forward-going strife of the game and the women on the sofa, suddenly grown monstrous in their opposition of clothes and kindliness and the fuss of distracting personal insincerities of voice and speech, attempting to judge and condemn the roomful of quiet players, shouting aloud to her that she was a fool to be drawn in to talking to men seriously on their own level, a fool to parade about as if she really enjoyed their silly game. 'I hate women and they 've got to know it,' she retorted with all her strength, hitting blindly out towards the sofa, feeling all the contrivances of toilet and coiffure fall in meaningless horrible detail under her blows.

'I do smoke,' she said, leaving her partner's side and going boldly to the sofa corner. 'Ragbags, bundles of pretence,' she thought, as she confronted the women. They glanced up with cunning eyes. They looked small and cringing. She rushed on, sweeping them aside. . . . Who had made them so small and cheated and for all their smiles so angry? What was it they wanted? What was it women wanted that always made them so angry?

'Would you mind if I *smoked*?' she asked in a clear gay tone, cutting herself from Mrs Corrie with a wrench as she faced her glittering frightened eyes.

'Of *course* not, my dear lady—I don't mind, if *you* don't,' she said, tweaking affectionately at Miriam's skirt. 'Ain't she a gay dog, Mélie, ain't she a gay dog!'

'It 's a pleasure to see you smoke,' murmured Mr Corrie fervently, 'you 're the first woman I 've seen smoke *con amore*.'

Contemplating the little screwed-up appreciative smile on the features of her partner, bunched to the lighting of his own cigarette, Miriam discharged a double stream of smoke violently through her nostrils—breaking out at last a public defiance of the freemasonry of women. 'I suppose I 'm a new woman— I 've said I am now, anyhow,' she reflected, wondering in the background of her determination how she would reconcile the role with her work as a children's governess. 'I 'm not in their crowd, anyhow; I despise their silly secret,' she pursued, feeling out ahead towards some lonely solution of her difficulty that seemed to come shapelessly towards her, but surely—the happy weariness of conquest gave her a sense of some unknown strength in her.

For the rest of the evening the group in the sofa-corner presented her a frontage of fawning and flattery.

Coming down with the children to lunch the next day, Miriam found the room dark and chill in the bright midday. It was as if it were empty. But if it had been empty it would have been beautiful in the still light, and tranquil. There was a dark cruel tide in the room, she sought in vain for a foothold. A loud busy voice was talking from Mr Corrie's place at the head of the table. Mr Staple-Craven, busy with cold words to hide the truth. He paused as the nursery trio came in and settled at the table, and then shouted softly and suddenly at Mrs Corrie, 'What's Corrie having?'

'Biscuits,' chirped Mrs Corrie eagerly, 'biscuits and sally, in the study.' She sat forward, gathering herself to disperse the gloom. But Mrs Craven's deep voice drowned her unspoken gaieties . . . ah—he's not gone away, thought Miriam rapidly, he's in the house. . . .

'Best thing for biliousness,' gonged Mrs Craven, and Mr Craven busily resumed.

'It's only the fisherman who knows anything, anything whatever about the silver stream. Necessarily. Necessarily. It is the—the *concentration*, the—the *absorption* of the passion that enables him to see. Er, the fisherman, the poet-tantamount; exchangeable terms. Fishing is, indeed one might say——'

The men of the party were devouring their food with the air of people just about to separate to fulfil urgent engagements. They bent and gobbled busily and cast smouldering glances about the table, as if with their eyes they would suggest important mysteries brooding above their animated muzzles.

Miriam's stricken eyes sought their foreheads for relief. Smooth brows and neatly brushed hair above; but the smooth motionless brows were ramparts of hate; pure murderous hate. That's men, she said, with a sudden flash of certainty, that's men as they are, when they are opposed, when they are real. All the rest is pretence. Her thoughts flashed forward to a final clear issue of opposition, with a husband. Just a cold blank hating forehead and neatly brushed hair above it. If a man doesn't understand or doesn't agree he's just a blank bony conceitedly thinking, absolutely condemning forehead, a face below, going on eating—and going off somewhere. Men are all hard angry bones; always thinking something, only one thing at a time and unless that is agreed to, they murder. My husband shan't kill me. . . . I'll shatter his conceited brow— *make* him see . . . two sides to every question . . . a million sides . . . no questions, only sides . . . always changing. Men argue, think they prove things; their foreheads recover— cool and calm. Damn them all—all men.

'Fee ought to be out here,' said Mrs Corrie, moving her basket chair to face away from the sun.

The garden blazed in the fresh warm air. But there was no happiness in it. Everything was lost and astray. The house-party had dispersed and disappeared. Mrs Corrie sat and strolled about the garden, joyless, as if weighed down by some immovable oppression. If Mr Corrie were to come out and sit there too it would be worse. It was curious to think that the garden was his at all. He would come feebly out, looking ill, and they would all sit, uneasy and afraid. But Mrs Corrie wanted him to come out, knew he ought to be there. It was she who had thought of it. It was intolerable to think of his coming. Yet he had been 'crazy mad' about her for five years. Five years and then this. Whose fault was it? His or hers? Or was marriage always like that? Perhaps that was why she and Mrs Craven had laughed when they were asked whether marriage was a failure. Mrs Craven had no children. Nothing to think about but stars and spirits and her food and baths and little silk dresses, and Mr Craven treated her as if she were a child he had got tired of petting. She did not even go fishing with him. She was lying down in her room and tea would be taken up to her. At least she thought of herself and seemed to enjoy life. But she was getting fatter and fatter. Mrs Corrie did not want anything for herself, except for the fun of getting things. She cared only for the children, and when they grew up they would have nothing to talk to her about. Sybil would have thoughts behind her ugly strong face. She would tell them to no one. The boy would adore her, until his wife, whom also he would adore, came between them. So there was nothing for women in marriage and children. Because they had no thoughts. Their husbands grew to hate them because they had no thoughts. But if a woman had thoughts a man would not be 'silly' about her for five years. And Mrs Corrie had her garden. She would always have that, when he was not there.

'If you were to go and ask him,' said Mrs Corrie, brushing out her dress with her hands, 'he 'd come out.'

'*Me!*' said Miriam in amazement.

'Yes, go on, my dear, you see; he 'll come.'

'But perhaps he doesn't want to,' said Miriam, suddenly feeling that she was playing a familiar part in a novel and wanting to feel quite sure she was reading her role aright.

'You go and try,' laughed Mrs Corrie gently. '*Make* him come out.'

'I 'll tell him you wish him to come,' said Miriam gravely, getting to her feet. 'All *right*,' she thought, 'if I have more influence over him than you it 's not my fault, not anybody's fault; but how horrid you must feel.'

Her trembling fingers gave a frightened fumbling tap at the study door. 'Come in,' said Mr Corrie officially, and coughed a loose, wheezy cough. He was sitting by the fire in one of the huge arm-chairs and didn't look up as she entered. She stood with the door half closed behind her, fighting against her fear and the cold heavy impression of his dull grey dressing-gown and the grey rug over his knees.

'It 's so lovely in the garden,' she said, fervently fixing her eyes on the small white face, a little puffy under its grizzled hair. He looked stiffly in her direction.

'The sun is so warm,' she went on hurriedly. 'Mrs Corrie thought——' she stopped. Of course the man was too ill to be worried. For an eternity she stood, waiting. Mr Corrie coughed his little cough and turned again to the fire. If only she could sit down in the other chair, saying nothing and just be there. He looked so unspeakably desolate. He hated being there, not able to play or work.

'I hate being ill,' she said at last, 'it always seems such waste of time.' She knew she had borrowed that from someone and that it would only increase the man's impatience. 'I always have to act and play parts,' she thought angrily—and called impatiently to her everyday vision of him to dispel the obstructive figure in the arm-chair.

'Umph,' said Mr Corrie judicially.

'You could have a chair,' she ventured, 'and just sit quietly.'

'No thanks, I 'm not coming out.' He turned a kind face in her direction without meeting her eyes.

'You have such a nice room,' said Miriam vaguely, getting to the door.

'Do you like it?' It was his everyday voice, and Miriam stopped at the door without turning.

'It 's so absolutely your own,' she said.

Mr Corrie laughed. 'That 's a strange definition of charm.'

'I didn't say charming. I said your own.'

Mr Corrie laughed out. 'Because it 's mine it 's nice, but it is, for the same reason, not charming.'

'You 're tying me up into something I haven't said. There 's a fallacy in what you have just said, somewhere.'

'You 'll never be tied up in anything, mademoiselle—you 'll tie other people up. But there was no fallacy.'

'No verbal fallacy,' said Miriam eagerly, 'a fallacy of intention, deliberate misreading.'

'No wonder you think the sun would do me good.'

'How do you mean?'

'I 'm such a miscreant.'

'Oh no, you 're not,' said Miriam comfortingly, turning round. 'I don't want you to come out'—she advanced boldly and stirred the fire. 'I always like to be alone when I 'm ill.'

'That's better,' said Mr Corrie.

'Good-bye,' breathed Miriam, getting rapidly to the door
. . . poor wretched man . . . wanting quiet kindness.

'Thank you; good-bye,' said Mr Corrie gently.

'Then you'd say, Corrie,' said Mr Staple-Craven, as they
all sat down to dinner on Sunday evening . . . now comes
flattery, thought Miriam calmly—nothing mattered, the curtains were back, the light not yet gone from the garden and
birds were fluting and chirruping out there on the lawn where
she had played tennis all the afternoon—at home there was the
same light in the little garden and Sarah and Harriett were there in
happiness, she would see them soon and meantime, the wonder,
the fresh rosebuds, this year's, under the clear soft lamplight.

'You'd say that no one was to blame for the accident.'

'The cause of the accident was undoubtedly the signalman's
sudden attack of illness.'

Pause. 'It sounds,' thought Miriam, 'as if he were reading
from the Book of Judgment. It isn't true either. Perhaps a
judgment can never be true.' She pondered to the singing of
her blood.

'In other words,' said one of the younger men, in a narrow
nasal sneering clever voice, 'it was a purely accidental accident.'

'Purely,' gurgled Mr Corrie, in a low, pleased tone.

'They think they're really beginning,' mused Miriam,
rousing herself.

'A genuine accident within the meaning of the act,' blared
Mr Craven.

'An actident,' murmured Mr Corrie.

'In that case,' said another man, 'I mean since the man was
discovered ill, not drunk, by a doctor in his box, all the elaborate
legal proceedings would appear to be rather—superfluous.'

'Not at all, not at all,' said Mr Corrie testily.

Miriam listened gladly to the anger in his voice, watching
the faint movement of the window curtains and waiting for the
justification of the law.

'The thing must be subject to a detailed inquiry before the man can be cleared.'

'He might have felt ill before he took up his duties—you 'd hardly get him to admit that.'

'Lawyers can get people to admit anything,' said Mr Craven cheerfully, and broke the silence that followed his sally by a hooting monotonous recitative which he delivered, swaying right and left from his hips, 'that is to say—they, by bene-ficently pursuing unexpected—quite *unexpected* bypaths—suddenly confront—their—their examinees—with the truth—the Truth.'

'It 's quite a good point to suggest that the chap felt ill earlier in the day—that 's one of the things you 'd have to find out. You 'd have, at any rate, to know all the circumstances of the seizure.'

'Indigestible food,' said Miriam, 'or badly cooked food.'

'Ah,' said Mr Corrie, his face clearing, 'that 's an excellent refinement.'

'In that case the cause of the accident would be the cook.'

Mr Corrie laughed delightedly.

'I don't say that because I 'm interested, but because I wanted to take sides with him,' thought Miriam, 'the others know that and resent it and now I 'm interested.'

'Perhaps,' she said, feeling anxiously about the incriminated cook, 'the real cause then would be a fault in her upbringing, I mean he may have lately married a young woman whose mother had not taught her cooking.'

'Oh, you can't go back further than the cook,' said Mr Corrie finally.

'But the cause,' she persisted, in a low, anxious voice, 'is the sum total of *all* the circumstances.'

'No, no,' said Mr Corrie impenetrably, with a hard face — 'you can't take the thing back into the mists of the past.'

He dropped her and took up a lead coming from a man at the other end of the table.

'Oh,' thought Miriam coldly, appraising him with a glance, the slightly hollow temples, the small skull, a little flattened, the lack of height in the straight forehead, why had she not noticed that before?—the general stinginess of the head balancing the soft keen eyes and whimsical mouth—'that's you; you won't, you can't look at anything from the point of view of life as a whole'—she shivered and drew away from the whole spectacle and pageant of Newlands' life. It all had this behind it, a man, able to do and decide things who looked about like a ferret for small clever things, causes, immediate near causes that appeared to explain, and explained nothing and had nothing to do with anything. Her hot brain whirled back—signalmen, in bad little houses with bad cooking—tinned foods—they're a link—they bring all sorts of things into their signal boxes. They ought to bring the fewest possible dangerous things. Something ought to be done.

Lawyers were quite happy, pleased with themselves if they made some one person guilty—put their finger on him. 'Can't go back into the mists of the past . . . you *didn't understand*, you're not capable of understanding any real *movements* of thought. I always knew it. You think—in propositions. Can't go back. Of course you can go back, and round and up and everywhere. Things as a whole . . . you understand nothing. We've done. That's you. Mr Corrie—a leading Q.C. Heavens.'

In that moment Miriam felt that she left Newlands for ever. She glanced at Mrs Corrie and Mrs Craven—bright beautiful coloured birds, fading slowly year by year in the stifling atmosphere, the hard brutal laughing complacent atmosphere of men's minds . . . men's minds, staring at things, ignorantly, knowing 'everything' in an irritating way and yet *ignorant*.

CHAPTER X

COMING home at ten o'clock in the morning, Miriam found the
little villa standing quiet and empty in the sunshine. The
sound of her coming down the empty tree-lined roadway had
brought no face to either of the open windows. She stood on
the short fresh grass in the small front garden looking up at the
empty quiet windows. During her absence the dark winter
villa had changed. It had become home. The little red
brick façade glowed as she looked up at it. It belonged to her
family. All through the spring weather they had been living
behind the small bright house-front. It was they who had set
those windows open and left them standing open to the spring
air. They had gone out, of course; all of them; to be busy about
the weddings. But inside was a place for her; things ready; a
bed prepared where she would lie to-night in the darkness.
The sun would come up to-morrow and be again on this green
grass. She would come out on the grass in the morning.

The sounds of her knocking and ringing echoed through the
house with a summery resonance. All the inside doors were
standing open. Footsteps came and the door opened upon
Mary. She had forgotten Mary, and stood looking at her.
Mary stood in her lilac print dress and little mob cap, filling
the doorway in the full sunlight. She had shone through all
the years in the grey basement kitchens at Barnes. Miriam had
never before seen her face to face in the sunlight, her tawny red
Somersetshire hair; the tawny freckles on the soft rose of her
face; the red in her shy warm eyes. They both stood gazing.
The strong sweet curve of Mary's bony chin moved her
thoughtful mouth. 'How nice you do look, Miss Mirry.'
Miriam took her by the arm and trundled her into the house.
They moved into the little dining-room filled with a blaze of
sunlight and smelling of leather and tobacco and fresh brown
paper and string and into the dim small drawing-room at the

back. The tiny greenhouse plastered on its hindermost wall was full of growing things. Mary dropped phrases, offering Miriam her share of the things that had happened while she had been away. She listened deferentially, her heart rising high. After all these years she and Mary were confessing their love for each other.

She went down the road with a bale of art muslin over her shoulder and carrying a small bronze table-lamp with a pink silk shade. The bright bunchy green heads of the little lopped acacia trees bobbed against their background of red brick villa as she walked . . . little moving green lampshades for Harriett's life; they were like Harriett; like her delicate laughter and absurdity. The sounds of the footsteps of passers-by made her rejoice more keenly in her burdens. She felt herself a procession of sacred emblems, in the sunshine. The sunshine streamed about her from an immense height of blue sky. The sky had never been so high as it was above Harriett's green acacias. It had gone soaring up to-day for them all; their sky.

That eldest Wheeler girl, going off to India, to marry a divorced man. Julia seemed to think it did not matter if she were happy. How could she be happy? . . . Coming home from the *Second Mrs Tanqueray* Bennett had asked Sarah if she would have married a man with a past . . . it was not only that his studies had kept him straight. It was himself . . . and Gerald too. It was . . . there were two kinds of men. You could tell them at a glance. Life was clean and fresh for Sarah and Harriett. . . . There were two kinds of people. Most of the people who were going about ought to be shut up, somehow, in prison.

Eve came into the little room with her arms full of Japanese anemones. Behind her came a tall man with red-brown hair, a stout fresh face and beautifully cut clothes. Miriam bowed him a greeting without waiting for an introduction and went on arranging her festoons of art muslin about the white wooden mantelpiece. He was carrying a trayful of little fluted green glasses each half filled with water. He came into the room on a holiday—a little interval in his man's life—delighted to be arranging the tray of glasses; half contemptuous and very happy. Pleased and surprised at himself and ready for miracles. He was not married—but he was a marrying man—a ladies' man—a man of the world—something like Bob Greville—with the same sort of attitude towards women. . . . 'The vagaries of the Fair' . . . a special manner for women and a clubby life of his own, with men. Women meant sex to him, the reproduction of the species, my dear chap, and his comforts and a little music on Sunday afternoon. He loved his mother, that was certain, Miriam felt, from something in his voice, and respected all mothers; the sort of man who would 'look after' a woman properly, but would never know anything about her. And there was something in himself that he knew nothing about. Some woman would live with him in loneliness, maddened, waiting for that something to speak. Secretly he would be half contemptuous, half afraid of her and would keep on always with that mocking, obsequious, patronizing manner. Horrible—and so easy to deceive, and yet cruel to deceive. *Hit* him . . . hit him awake. He put down the tray of glasses near the heap of anemones that Eve had flung on the table and inquired whether they were to put one bloom in each glass. . . . He had a secret, indulgent life of his own. Did he imagine that no one knew? . . . Eve giggled and tittered . . . this new giggling way of Eve's . . . perhaps it was the way the Greens treated young men; arch and silly, like the girls at the tennis club. He must see through it. He was not in the least like the tennis club young men, most of whom needed to be giggled at before they could be anything but just sneery and silly.

But it was fascinating, like something in a novel come true; the latest tableau in all the wedding tableaux; their own. Bennett and Gerald had swept the lonely Henderson family into this.

One was going to be a sister-in-law for certain, to-morrow. . . .
Held up by this dignity, Miriam concentrated on her folds and
loops, adjusting and pinning with her back to the room,
listening to the sparring and giggling, the sounds of the tinkling
glasses—the scissors snipping and dropping with a rattle on to
the table, the soft flurring of shifted blossoms. The moment
was coming. The man was being impudently patronizing to
Eve, but really talking at her, trying to make her turn round.
She did not want him. There was something . . . some
quality in men that this kind of man did not possess . . . something she knew . . . who? It was somewhere, but not in him.
Still, his being there gave an edge to her freedom and happiness.
She owed him some kind of truth . . . some blow or shock.
Holding her last festoon in place she consulted some jumbled
memory and found a phrase: 'Will you people leave off
squabbling and just see if this is all right before I nail it up?'
She spoke in a cool even tone that filled the room. It startled
her, making her feel sad, small and guilty. Still with her
back to the room, she waited during the moment of silence
that followed her words. 'It's simply lovely, Mirry,' said
Eve. Had she been more vulgar than Eve? She knew her
decoration was all right and did not want an opinion. She
wanted to crush the man's behaviour, trample on it and fling
it out of the room. Eve was sweeter and more lovable than
she. Mother said it was natural and right to laugh and
joke with young men. No . . . no . . . no. . . .

She glanced, asking Eve to hold the corner while she went
for the hammer and nails. Eve came eagerly forward. The
man was standing upright and motionless by the table, looking quietly at her as she stood back for Eve to substitute
a supporting hand. 'Er—let me do that,' he said gravely
—'or go for the hammer.' He was at the door: 'Oh—
thanks,' said Miriam, in a hard tone; 'you will find it in
the kitchen.'

Eve remained holding the muslin with downcast face and
conscious lips. Seizing a vase of anemones Miriam put it on
the marble, bunching up the muslin to hide the vase.

'This is their smoking-room,' she said, her voice praying for tolerance. Eve beamed sadly and gladly. 'Yes—isn't it jolly?' Joining hands they waltzed about the room. Eve did not really mind; she fought, but there was something in her that did not mind.

Through the french windows of the new drawing-room Miriam saw a group of figures moving towards the end of the garden. In a moment they would have reached the low brick wall at the end of the garden. They might stand talking there with their heads outlined against the green painted trellis-work that ran along the top of the wall, or they might walk back towards the house and see her at the window.

She hid herself from view. The room closed round her. She could not sit down on one of the new chairs. The room was too full. Things were speaking to her. Their challenge had sent her to the window when she came into the room. It had made her feel like a trespasser. Now she was caught. She stood breathing in curious odours; faint odours of new wood and fresh upholstery, and the strange strong subdued emanation coming from the black grand piano, a mingling of the smell of aromatic wood with the hard raw bitter tang of metal and the muffled woolly pungency of new felting.

The whole of the floor space, up to the edge of the skirting, was filled by a soft thick rich carpet of clear green with a border and centre-piece of large soft fresh pink full-blown roses. Standing about on it were a set of little delicate shiny black chairs, with seats covered with silken stripings of pink and green, two great padded easy-chairs, deep cushioned and low-seated, and three little polished black tables of different shapes. A black overmantel with shelves and side brackets, holding fluted white bowls, framed a long strip of deeply bevelled mirror. The wooden mantelpiece was draped at the sides like the high french windows with soft straight hanging green silk curtains. At the windows, long creamy net curtains hung, pulled in narrow straight folds just within the silk ones.

The walls swept up, dimly striped with rose and green, the green misty and changeful, glossy or dull as you moved. And, on the widest spaced wall, dreadful presences . . . two long narrow dark-framed pictures, safe and far-off and dreamy in shop windows, but now, shut in here, suddenly full of sad heavy dreadful meaning. A girl, listening to the words she had waited for, not seeing the youth who is gazing at her, not even thinking of him, but seeing suddenly everything opening far far away, and leaving him, going on alone, to things he will never see, joining the lonely women of the past, feeling her old self still there, wanting every one to know that she was still there, and cut off, for ever. There was something ahead; but she could not take him with her. He would see it now and again, in her face, but would never understand. And the other picture; the girl grown into a woman; just married, her face veiled forever, her eyes closed; sinking into the tide, his strong frame near her the only reality; blindly trying to get back to him across the tide of separation.

Their child will come—throwing even the support of him off and away, making her monstrous . . . and then born into life between them, forever, 'drawing them together,' showing they were separate; between them, for ever. There was no getting away from that.

The strange strong crude odours breathing quietly out from the open lid of the new piano seemed to support them, to make them more mockingly inexorable.

The smell of the piano would go on being there while inexorable things happened.

Voices were sounding in the garden. . . .

Hanging on either side of the mantelpiece were two more pictures—square green garden scenes. . . . There was relief in the deeps of the gardens and in under the huge spreading trees that nearly filled the sky. There were tiresome people fussing in the foreground. . . . Marcus Stone people—having scenes—not noticing the garden; getting in the way of the garden. But the garden was there, blazing, filled with some particular time of day, always being filled with different times of day.

There would be in-between times for Harriett—her own times. Times when she would be at peace in this room near the garden. Away from the kitchen and strange-eyed servants, and from the stern brown and yellow pig-skin dining-room. In here she would have fragrant little teas; and talk as if none of those other things existed. There were figures standing at the french window.

She opened the window upon Harriett and Gerald. Standing a little aloof from them was a man. As Harriett spoke to her Miriam met his strange eyes wide and dark, unseeing; no, glaring at things that did not interest him . . . desperate, playing a part. His thin squarish frame hung loosely, whipped and beaten, within his dark clothes.

His eyes passed expressionlessly from her face to Harriett.

A great gust of laughter sounded from the open kitchen window away to the left, screened by a trellis over which the lavish trailings of a creeper made a bright green curtain. It was Bennett's voice. He had just accomplished something or other.

'Ullo,' said Harriett. The strange man was holding his lower lip in with his teeth, as if in horror or pain. . . . They stood in a row on the gravel.

'Let me introduce Mr Grove,' said Harriett, with a shy movement of her head and shoulders, keeping her hands clasped. Her face was all broken up. She could either laugh or cry. But there was something, a sort of light, chiselling, holding everything back.

Miriam bowed. 'What 's Bennett doing?' she said hurriedly.

'The last time *I* saw him he was standing on the kitchen table fighting with the gas bracket,' said Gerald.

The sallow man drew in his breath sharply and stood aside, staring down the garden. Miriam glanced at him, wondering. He was not criticizing Gerald. It was something else.

'I say, Mirry, what did you do to old Tremayne this morning?' went on Gerald.

'What do you mean?' said Miriam interested. This was the novel going on. . . .

She must read it through even at this strange moment . . . this moment was the right setting to read, through Gerald, that little exciting faraway finished thing of the morning, to know that it had been right. She felt decked. Gerald stood confronting her and spoke low, fingering the anemones in her belt. The others were talking. Harriett in high short laughing sentences, the man gasping and moaning his replies, making jerky movements. He was not considering his words, but looking for the right, appropriate things to say. Miriam rejoiced over him as she smiled encouragingly at Gerald.

'Well, my dear, he wanted to know—*who* you were; and he swears he's going to be engaged to you before the year is out.'

'What abominable cheek,' said Miriam, flushing with delight. Then she had taken the right line. How easy. This was how things happened.

'No, my dear, he didn't mean to be cheeky.'

'I call it the most abominable cheek.'

'No you don't'; Gerald was looking at her with fatherly solicitude. 'That's what he said anyhow—and he meant it. Ask Harry.'

'Frivolous young man.'

'Well, he's an awful flirt, I warn you; but he's struck this time—all of a heap . . . came and raved about you the minute he'd seen you, and when he heard you were Harry's sister that's what he said.'

'I'm sure I'm awfully obliged to his majesty.'

Gerald laughed and turned, looking for Harriett and moving to her. Miriam caught at a vision of the well-appointed man, a year . . . a home full of fresh new things, no more need to make money; a stylish, contented, devoted sort of man, who knew nothing about one. It would be a fraud, unfair to him . . . so easy to pretend to admire him . . . well, there it was . . . an offer of freedom . . . that was admirable, in almost

any man, the power to lift one out into freedom. He wanted
to lift her out—her, not any other woman. It was rather
wonderful, and appealing. She hung over his moment of
certainty in pride and triumph. But there was something
wrong somewhere; though she felt that someone had placed a
jewel in her hair. Gerald had drawn Harriett through the
doorway into the drawing-room. The sunlight followed
them. They looked solid and powerful. The strange terrors
of the room were challenged by their sunlit figures.

Moving to the side of Gerald's strange friend, Miriam said
something about the garden in a determined manner. He
drew a sawing breath without answering. They walked down
the short garden. It moved about them in an intensity of
afternoon colour. He did not know it was there; there was
something between him and the little coloured garden. He
walked with bent head, his head dipping from his shoulders
with a little bob at each step. Miriam wanted to make him
feel the garden moving round them; either she must do that
or ask him why he was suffering. He walked responsively, as
if they were talking. He was feeling some sort of reprieve . . .
perhaps the afternoon had bored him. They had turned and
were walking back towards the house. If they reached it
without speaking, they would not have courage to go down
the garden again. She could not relinquish the strange painful comradeship so soon. They must go on expressing their
relief at being together; anything she might say would destroy
that. She wanted to take him by the arm and groan . . . on
Harriett's wedding-eve, and when she was feeling so happy
and triumphant. . . .

'Have you known Gerald long?' she said, as they reached
the house. He turned sharply to face the garden again.

'Oh, for a very great number of years,' he said quickly, 'a—
very—great—number.' His voiçe was the voice of the ritua-
listic curate at All Saints. He sighed impatiently. What was
it he was waiting for her to say? Nothing perhaps. This

busy walking was a way of fi.. ishing his visit without having to try to talk to anybody.

'How different people are,' she said airily.

'I'm very different,' he said, with his rasping, indrawn breath. A darkness coming from him enfolded her.

'Are you?' she said insincerely. Her eyes consulted the flowered border. She saw it as he saw it, just a flowered border, meaningless.

'You cannot possibly imagine what I am.'

Her mind leapt out to the moving garden, recapturing it scornfully. He is conceited about his difficulties and differences. He doesn't think about mine. But he couldn't talk like this, unless he knew I were different. He knows it, but is not thinking about me.

'Don't you think people are all alike, really?' she said impatiently.

'Our common humanity,' he answered bitingly.

She had lost a thread. They were divided. She felt stiffly about for a conventional phrase.

'I expect that most men are the average manly man with the average manly faults.' She had read that somewhere. It was sly and wrong, written by somebody who wanted to flatter.

'It is wonderful, *wonderful* that you should say that to me.' He stared at the grass with angry eyes. His mouth smiled. His teeth were large and even. They seemed to smile by themselves. The dark, flexible lips curled about them in an unwilling grimace.

'He's in some horrible pit,' thought Miriam, shrinking from the sight of the desolate garden.

'What are you going to do in life?' she said suddenly.

During the long silent interval she had felt a growing longing to hurt him in some way.

'If I had my will—if—I had my will—I should escape from the world.'

'What would you do?'

'I should join a brotherhood.'

'Oh. . . .'

'That is the life I should choose.'

'Do you see how unfair everything is?'

'Um?'

'If a woman joins an order she must confess to a man.'

'Yes,' he said indifferently. . . . 'I can't carry out my wish, I can't carry out my dearest wish.'

'You have a dearest wish; that is a good deal.'

She ought to ask him why not and what he was going to do. But what did it matter? He was going unwillingly along some dreary path. There was some weak helplessness about him. He would always have a grievance and be sorry for himself . . . self-pity. She remained silent.

'I'm training for the Bar,' he murmured, staring away across the neighbouring gardens.

'Why—in Heaven's name?'

'I have no choice.'

'But it's absurd. You are almost a priest.'

'The Bar. That is my bourne.'

'Lawyers are the most ignorant, awful people.'

'I cannot claim superiority.' He laughed bitterly.

'But you can; you are. You can never be a lawyer.'

'It is necessary to do one's duty. Occupation does not matter.'

'There you are; you're a Jesuit already,' said Miriam angrily, seeing the figure at her side shrouded in a habit, wrapped in tranquillity, pacing along a cloister, lost to her. But if he stayed in the world and became a lawyer he would be equally lost to her.

'I have been . . . *mad*,' he muttered; 'a madman . . . nothing but the cloister can give me peace—nothing but the cloister.'

'I don't know. It seems like running away.'

'Running towards, running towards——'

Can't you be at peace now, in this garden? ran her thoughts. I don't condemn you for anything. Why can't we stop worrying at things and be at peace? If I were beautiful I could make you be at peace—perhaps. But it would be a trick. Only real religion can help you. I can't do anything. You are religious. I must keep still and quiet. . . .

If some cleansing fire could come and consume them both
. . . flaring into the garden and consuming them both, together.
Neither of them were wanted in the world. No one would
ever want either of them. Then why could they not want
each other? He did not wish it. Salvation. He wanted
salvation—for himself.

'My people must be considered first,' he said speculatively.

'*They* want you to be a barrister. That's the last reason in
the world that would affect *me*.'

He glanced at her with far-off speculative eyes, his upper lip
drawn terribly back from his teeth.

'He is thinking I am a hard, unfeminine, ill-bred woman.'

'I do it as an atonement.'

The word rang in the garden . . . the low tone of a bell.
Her thoughts leaned towards the strength at her side.

'Oh, that's grand,' she said hastily, and fluted quickly on,
wondering where the inspiration had come from: 'Luther said
it's much more difficult to live in the world than in a cell.'

'I am glad I have met you, glad I have met you,' he said, in
a clear light tone.

She felt she knew the quality of the family voice, the way he
had spoken as a lad, before his troubles came, his own voice
easy and sincere. The flowers shone firm and steady on their
stalks.

She laughed and rushed on into cheerful words, but his
harsh voice drowned hers. 'You have put my life in a nutshell.'

'How uncomfortable for you,' she giggled excitedly.

He laughed with a dip of the head obsequiously. There was
a catch of mirth in his tone.

Miriam laughed and laughed, laughing out fully in relief.
He turned towards her a young lit face, protesting and insisting.
She wanted to wash it, with soap, to clear away a faint greasi-
ness and do something with the lank, despairing hair.

'You have come at the right instant, and shown me wisdom.
You are wonderful.'

She recoiled. She did not really want to help him. She
wanted to attract his attention to her. She had done it and he

did not know it. Horrible. They were both caught in
something. She had wanted to be caught, together with this
agonizing priestliness. But it was a trick. Perhaps they
hated each other now.

'It is jolly to talk about things,' she said, as the blood surged
into her face.

He was grave again and did not answer.

'People don't talk about things nearly enough,' she pursued.

'I saw Miriam through the window, *deep* in conversation
with a most interesting young man.'

'Have those people written about the bouquets?' said
Miriam irritably. . . . Then mother had moved about the new
house, and was looking through those drawing-room windows
this afternoon. She had looked about the house with someone else, saying all the wrong things, admiring things in the
wrong way, impressed in the wrong way, having no thoughts,
and no one with her to tell her what to think. . . .

She flashed a passionate glance towards the clear weak
flexible voice, half seeing the flushed face . . . you 're not
upset about the weddings—'Miriam's scandalous goings-on
the whole day long,' said somebody—because you 've got me.
You don't know me. You wouldn't like me if you did. You
don't know him. He doesn't know you. But I know you,
that 's the difference. . . .

'I 've just thought something out,' she said aloud, her voice
drowned by two or three voices and the sound of things being
served and handed about the supper-table. They were trying
to draw her—still talking about the young men and her 'goings-
on.' They did not know how far away she was and how secure
she felt. She laughed towards her mother and smiled at her
until she made her blush. Ah, she thought proudly, it 's I
who am your husband. Why have I not been with you all
your life? . . . all the times you were alone; I know them all.
No one else knows them.

'I say,' she insisted, 'what about the bouquets?'

Mrs Henderson raised her eyebrows helplessly and smiled, disclaiming.

'Hasn't anybody done anything?' roared Miriam.

Mary came in with a dish of fruit. Everyone went on so placidly. . . . She thought of the perfect set of her white silk bridesmaid's dress, its freshness, its clear apple green pipings, the little green leaves and fresh pink cluster roses on the white chip hat. If the shower-bouquets did not come, it would be simply ghastly. And everybody went on chattering.

She leaned anxiously across the table to Harriett.

'Oo—what's up?' asked Harriett.

Conversation had dropped. Miriam sat up to fling out her grievances.

'Well—just this. I'm told Gerald said the people would send a line to say it was all right, and they haven't written, and so far as I can make out nothing's been done.'

'Bouquets would appear to be one of the essentials of the ceremony,' hooted Mr Henderson.

'Well, of course,' retorted Miriam savagely, 'if you *have* a dress wedding at all. That's the point.'

'Quite so, my dear, quite so. I was unaware that you were depending on a message.'

'I'm not anxious. It's simply silly, that's all.'

'It'll be all right,' suggested Harriett, looking into space. 'They'd have written.'

'Well, it's *your* old bouquet, principally.'

'Me. With a bouquet. Hoo——'

'Peace I give unto you, My peace I give unto you. Not as the world giveth, give I unto you——'

Christ said that. But peace came from God—the peace of God that passeth all understanding. How could Christ give that? He put Himself between God and man. Why could not people get at God direct? He was somewhere.

The steam was disappearing out of the window; the row of objects ranged along the far side of the bath grew clear. Miriam

looked at them, seeking escape from the problem—the upright
hand-glass, the brush bag propped against it, the small bottle
of Jockey Club, the little pink box of French face powder—
perhaps one day she would learn to use powder without looking
like a pierrot—how nice to have a thick white skin that never
changed and took powder like a soft bloom.

But as long as the powder-box were there it would be impossible to reach that state of peace and freedom that Thomas
à Kempis meant. 'To Miriam, from her friend, Harriett A.
Perne.' Had Miss Haddie found anything of it? No—she
was horribly afraid of God and turned to Christ as a sort of
protecting lover to be flattered and to lean upon. . . .

There were so many exquisite and wise things in the book;
the language was so beautiful. But somehow there was a
whining going all through it . . . fretfulness. Anger too—'I
had rather feel compunction than know the definition thereof.'
Why not both? He was talking at someone in that sentence.

The Kingdom of Heaven is *within* you. But even Christ went
about sad, trying to get people to do some sort of trick that He
said was necessary before they could find God—something to
do with Himself. There was something wrong about that.

If one were perfectly still, the sense of God was there.

Supposing every one could be got to stay perfectly still,
until they died . . . like that woman in the book who was
dying so happily of starvation . . . and then the friend came
fussing in with soup. . . .

Things were astounding enough; enough to make you die
of astonishment, if you did nothing at all. Being *alive*. If
one could realize that clearly enough, one *would* die.

Everything every one did was just a distraction from
astonishment.

It could only be done in a convent. . . . It cost money to
get into a convent, except as a servant. If you were a servant
you could not stay day and night in your cell—watching the
light and darkness until you died. . . . Perhaps in women's
convents they would not let you anyhow.

Why did men always have more freedom? . . . His head
had a listening look. His eyes were waiting desperately, seeing

nothing of the things in the world . . . he wanted to stay still until the voice of things grew so clear and near that one could give a great cry and fall dead . . . a long long cry. . . . Your hot heart, all of you, pouring out, getting free. Perhaps that happened to people when they were happy. They cried out to each other and were free—lost in another person. Whoso would save his soul . . . but then they grew strange and apart. . . . Marriage was a sort of inferior condition . . . an imitation of something else. . . . Ho-o-zan-na-in-the-Hi . . . i . . . est . . . the top note rang up and stayed right up, in the rafters of the church.

'Did you ever notice how white the insides of your wrists are?' Why did Bob seem so serious? . . . What a bother, what a bother.

It is a good thing to be plain . . . 'the tragedy of beauty; woman's greatest curse.' . . . Andromeda on a rock with her hair blowing over her face. . . .

She was afraid to look at the monster coming out of the sea. If she had looked at it, it would not have dared to come near her. Because Perseus looked and rescued her, she would have to be grateful to him all her life and smile and be Mrs Perseus. One day they would quarrel and he would never think her beautiful again. . . .

Adam had not faced the devil. He was stupid first, and afterwards a coward and a cad . . . 'the divine curiosity of Eve. . . .' Some parson had said that. . . . Perhaps men would turn round one day and see, what they were like. Eve had not been unkind to the devil; only Adam and God. All the men in the world, and their God, ought to apologize to women. . . .

To hold back and keep free . . . and real. Impossible to be real unless you were quite free. . . . Two married in one family was enough. Eve would marry, too.

But money.

The chair-bed creaked as she knelt up and turned out the gas. 'I love you' . . . just a quiet manly voice . . . perhaps one would forget everything, all the horrors and mysteries . . . because there would be somewhere then always to be, to rest,

and feel sure. If only . . . just to sit hand in hand . . .
watching snowflakes . . . to sit in the lamplight, quite quiet.

Pictures came in the darkness . . . lamplit rooms, gardens,
a presence, understanding.

Voices were sounding in the next room. Something being
argued. A voice level and reassuring; going up now and again
into a hateful amused falsetto. Miriam refused to listen. She
had never been so near before. Of course they talked in their
room. They had talked all their lives; an endless conversation;
he laying down the law . . . no end to it . . . the movement
of his beard as he spoke, the red lips shining through the fair
moustache . . . splash baths and no soap; soap is not a
cleansing agent . . . he had a ruddy skin . . . healthy.

A tearful, uncertain voice. . . .

'Don't, mother . . . don't, don't . . . he can't understand.
. . . Come to me! Come in here. . . . Well, well! . . .'
A loud clear tone moving near the door, 'Leave it all to nature,
my dear. . . .'

They 're talking about Sally and Harriett. . . . He is *amused*
. . . like when he says 'the marriage service begins with
"dearly beloved" and ends with "amazement." . . .'

She turned about, straining away from the wall and burying
her head in her pillow. Something seemed to shriek within
her, throwing him off, destroying, flinging him away. Never
again anything but contempt. . . .

She lay weak and shivering in the uncomfortable little bed.
Her heart was thudding in her throat and in her hands . . .
beloved . . . beloved . . . a voice, singing:

> So ear—ly *in* the mor—ning,
> My beloved—my beloved.

Silence, darkness and silence.

Waking in the darkness, she heard the fluttering of leafage
in the garden and lay still and cool listening and smiling. That

went on . . . flutter, flutter, in the breeze. It was enough
. . . and things happened, as well, in the far far off things
called 'days.'

A fearful clamour—bright sunlight; something sticking sideways through the partly opened door—a tin trumpet. It
disappeared with a flash as she leapt out of bed. The idea of
Harriett being up first!

Harriett stood on the landing in petticoat and embroidered
camisole, her hair neatly pinned, her face glowing and fresh.

'Gerrup,' she said at once.

'You *up*! You oughtn't to be. I'm going to get your
breakfast. You mustn't dress yourself. . . .'

'Rot! You hurry up, old silly; breakfast's nearly ready.'

She ran upstairs tootling her trumpet. 'Hurry up,' she said,
from the top of the stairs, with a friendly grin.

Miriam shouted convivially and retired into her crowded
sunlit bathroom, turning on both bath taps so that she might
sing aloud. Harriett had made the day strong . . . silver
bright and clean and clear. Harriett was like a clear blade.
She splashed into the cold water gasping and singing. Two
o'clock—ages yet before the weddings. There was a smell of
bacon frying. They would all have breakfast together. She
could smile at Harriett. They had grown up together and
could admit it, because Harriett was going away. But not for
ages. She flew through her toilet; the little garden was
blazing. It was a fine hot day.

Bennett and Gerald had turned strained pale faces to meet
the brides as they came up the aisle. Now, Bennett's broad
white forehead seemed to give out a radiance. It had been
fearful to stand behind Harriett through the service listening to
the bland hollow voice of the vicar and the four unfamiliar low
voices responding, and taking the long glove smooth and warm

from Harriett's hand, her rustling heavy-scented bouquet. At the sight of Bennett's grave radiant face the fear deepened and changed. Marriage was a reality . . . fearful, searching reality; it changed people's expressions. Hard behind came Gerald and Harriett; Gerald's long face still pale, his loosely knit figure carried along by her tense little frame as she walked, a little firm straight figure of satin, her veil thrown back from her little snub face, her face held firmly; steady and old with its solid babyish curves and its brave stricken eyes: old and stricken; that was how Sarah had looked too. No radiance on the faces of Sarah and Harriett.

The Wedding March was pealing out from the chancel, a great tide of sound blaring down through the church and echoing back from the west window, near the door where they would all go out, in a moment, out into the world. On they went; how swift it all was. . . . Sarah and Harriett, rescued from poverty and fear . . . mother's wedding on a May morning long ago . . . in the little village church . . . to walk out of church into the open country; in the morning; a bride. There were no brides in London.

Now to fall in behind Eve and Mr Tremayne. Mr Grove walked clumsily. His arm brushed against the shower bouquet.

The upturned faces of the pink carnations were fresh and sweet; for nothing. To-morrow they would be dead. Harriett's bouquet, dead too . . . a wonderful dead bouquet that meant life. 'Where are you, my friend, my own friend?'

A wedding seemed to make everybody happy. The people moving in Harriett's new rooms were happy. Old people were new and young. They laughed. . . . The sad dark man, following with his tray of glasses as she went from guest to guest with Harriett's champagne-cup, had laughed again and again. . . .

The voices of the grey-clad bridegrooms rang about the rooms, full of quiet relieved laughter. The outlines of their well-cut grey clothes were softly pencilled with a radiance of marriage. Round about Sarah and Eve was a great radiance. Light streamed from their satin dresses. But they were untouched. Silent and untouched and far away. What should these strange men ever know of them; coming and going?

She found herself standing elbow to elbow with Harriett. Warm currents came to her from Harriett's body; she moved her elbow against Harriett's to draw her attention. Harriett turned a scorched cheek and a dilated unseeing eye. Their hands dropped and met. Miriam felt the quivering of firm, strong fingers and the warm metal of rings. She grasped the matronly hand with the whole strength of her own. Harriett must remember . . . all this wedding was nothing. . . . She was Harriett . . . not the Mrs Ducayne Bob Greville had just been talking to about Curtain Lectures and the Rascality of the Genus Homo . . . she must remember all the years of being together, years of nights side by side . . . night turning to day for both of them, at the same moment. She gave her hand a little shake. Harriett made a little skipping movement and grinned her own ironic grin. It was all right. They were quite alone and irreverent; they two; the festive crowd was playing a game for their amusement. They laughed without a sound, as they had so often done in church. The air that encircled them was the air of their childhood.

Gerald's voice sounded near. It made no break in their union though Harriett welcomed it, clearing her throat with a businesslike cough.

'Time you changed, Mrs La Reine,' said Gerald, in a frightened friendly voice.

'Oh, lor', is it?' . . . that kindliness was only in Harriett's voice when she had hurt someone.

. . . The edge of Gerald's voice, kind to every one, would always be broken when he spoke to Harriett. She would

always be this young absurd Harriett to him, always. He
would go on fastening her boots for her, tenderly, and go
happily about his hobbies. She would never hear him call
her 'my dear.' That old-fashioned, mock-polite insolence of
men . . . paterfamilias.

The four of them were together in a room again, fastening
and hooking and adjusting; standing about before mirrors.
We 've all grown up together . . . we can admit it now . . .
we 're admitting it. Everything clear, back to the beginning;
happy and good. The room was still, with the hush of its
fresh draperies, hemming them in. Beautiful immortal forms
moved in the room, reaping . . . voices, steady and secure,
said nothing but the necessary things, borne down with wealth,
all the wealth there was . . . all the laughter and certainty.
Immortality. Nothing could die. They saw and knew everything. Each tone was a confession and a song of truth. They
need never meet and speak again. They had known. The
voices of Sarah and Harriett would go on . . . marked with
fresh things. . . . Her own and Eve's would remain, separate,
to grow broken and false and unrecognizable in the awful
struggle for money. No matter. The low, secure, untroubled
tone of a woman's voice. There was nothing like it on earth.
. . . If you had once heard it . . . in your own voice, and the
voice of another woman responding . . . everything was there.

Was there any one who fully realized how amazing it was . . .
a human tone. Perhaps every one did, really, most people
without knowing it. A few knew. Perhaps that was what
kept life going.

In a few minutes they would go. They avoided each other's
eyes. Miriam began to be afraid Eve would say something

cheerful, or sing a snatch of song, desecrating the singing that was there, the deep eternal singing in each casual tone.

Gerald's whistle came up from the front garden.

Miriam opened the door. Bennett's voice came from the hall, calling for Sarah.

'Your skirt sets simply perfectly, Sally.' . . . Sarah was at the door in her neat soft dark blue travelling dress, and a soft blue straw hat with striped ribbon bands and bows, hurrying forward, her gold hair shining under her hat; seeing nothing but the open door downstairs and Bennett waiting.

The garden and pathway was thronged with bright-coloured guests. Miriam found herself standing with Gerald on the kerb, waiting for Harriett to finish her farewells. He crushed her arm against his side. 'Good Lord, Mirry, ain't I glad it's all over.'

Sarah was stepping into the shelter of the first of the two waiting carriages. Her face was clear with relief. Bennett followed, dressed, like her, in dark blue. On the step he spoke abruptly, something about a small portmanteau. Sarah's voice sounded from inside. Miriam had never heard her speak with such cool unconcern. Perhaps she had never known Sarah. Sarah was herself now, for the first time free and unconcerned. What freedom! Cool and unconcerned. The door shut with a bang. They had forgotten every one. They were going to forget to wave. Every one had watched them. But they did not think of that. They saw green Devonshire ahead, and their little house waiting in the Upper Richmond Road, with work for them both, work they could both do well, with all their might, when they came back. Someone shouted. Rice was being showered. People were running down the road, showering rice. The road and pathway were bright with happy marriage, all the world linked in happy marriages.

The second carriage swept round the bend of the road with a yellow silk slipper swinging in the rear. Miriam struggled for breath through tears. Gerald and Harriett had taken the old life away with them in their carriage. Harriett had taken it, and gone. But she knew. She would bring it back with her. They would come back. Harriett would never forget. Nothing could change or frighten her. She would come back the same, in her new dresses, laughing.

A fat voice . . . Mrs Bywater . . . 'proud of your gails, Mrs Henderson' . . . fat flattering voice. The brightness had gone from the houses and the roadway . . . unreal people were moving about with absurd things on their heads. Brides-maids in cold white dresses, moving in pounces, as people spoke to them . . . the Hendon girls. . . . What bad complexions Harriett's school friends had. Why were they all dark? Why did Harriett like them? Who was Harriett? Why did she have dark, sallow friends? Oh . . . this dark face, near and familiar . . . saying something—eyes looking at nothing; haunted eyes looking at nothing, very dear and familiar . . . relief . . . the sky seems to lift again; kind, harmless, bitter features, coming near and speaking.

'I am obliged to go——' rasping voice, curious sawing breath. . . .

'Oh yes. . . .' Perhaps there will be a thunderstorm or something—something will happen.

'We shall meet again.'

'Yes—oh, yes.'

There was no reason to feel nervous, at any rate for a night or two. Burglars who wanted the presents would take some time to find out that there was only one young lady in the house and a little servant sleeping in a top room. It was all right. No need to put the dinner-bell on the dressing-table. Next week the middle-aged servant would have arrived. Would she mind being alone with the presents and the little maid? The only way to feel quite secure at night would be to marry . . . how awful . . . either you marry and are never alone or you risk being alone and afraid . . . to marry for safety . . . perhaps some women did. No wonder . . . and not to turn into a silly scared nervous old maid . . . how tiresome, one thing or the other . . . no choice.

She laid her head on the pillow. Thank Heaven I 'm here and not at home . . . out of it. . . . 'I 'll come round, first thing, to cut up the cake'—that would be jolly too. But here . . . with all these new things, magical and easy, secure with Gerald and Harriett, chosen to embark on their new life with them. . . . 'You chuck your job, my dear, and stay with us for a bit.' They would like it. That was so jolly. Absurd free days with Harriett; tea in the garden, theatres; people coming, Mr Tremayne and Mr Grove. . . .

But there was something, some thought sweeping round all these things, something else, sweeping round outside the weddings and the joy of being at home, making all these things extra, like things thrown in, jolly and perfect and surprising, but thrown in with something else that was her own, some-thing hovering around and above, in and out the whole day, keeping her apart. This morning the weddings had seemed the end of everything. They were over, Harriett's and Sarah's lives going forward and her own share in them, and home still there too, three things instead of one, easily hers. And yet they did not concern her. It would be a sham to pretend they did, with this other thing haunting—to go on from thing to thing, living with people and for them as if there were nothing else, as people seemed to do, one thing happening after another all the time. Sham.

Harriett and Sarah had rushed out into life. They had changed everything. Things did not seem to matter, now that they had achieved all that. Harriett would take the first shock of life for her. Curiosities could come to an end. It did not seem to matter. That was all at peace, through Harriett. Life had come into the family, leaving her free. . . .

Was she free ? That strange, dark priestliness. If he called to her, if he really called. . . . But he called in a dark dreadful way . . . and yet mysteriously linked to something in her. She could not give the help he needed. She would fail. Over their lives would shine, far away, visible to both of them, the radiance of heaven. They both wanted to be good; redemption from sin. They both believed these things. But he was weak, weak . . . and she not strong enough to help. And there was that other thing beckoning, far from this suburban life and quite as far from him, away, up in London, down at Newlands, a brightness. . . .

She looked through the darkness at the harmony of soft tones and draperies at distant Newlands . . . etchings; the strange effect of etchings . . . there were no etchings in the suburbs . . . curious, close, strong lines that rested you and had a meaning and expression even though you did not understand the subject. There were so many things to take you away from people. In the suburbs people were everything, and there was nothing in them. They did not understand anything; but going on. They were helpless and without thoughts; amongst their furniture. They did not even have busts of Beethoven. At Newlands people might be dead, the women in bright hard deaths or deaths of cold, cruel deceitfulness, the men tiny insects of selfishness, but there were things that made up for everything, full and satisfying.

And Salviati's window. . . .

She must hold on to these things. Life without them would be impossible.

It was—Style . . . or something. *Le style c'est l'homme.* That meant something. It was the same with clothes. . . . Suburban people could be fashionable, never stylish. And manners. . . . They were fussily kind and nice to each other; as if life were pitiful . . . *life* . . . pitiful. They all pitied, and despised each other.

The night was vast with all the other things. No need to sleep. To lie happy and strong in the sense of them, was better than sleep. In a few hours the little suburban day would come . . . everything gleaming with the light of the big things beyond. One could go through it in a drowse of strength, full of laughter . . . laughter to the brim, all one's limbs strong and heavy with laughter.

Bob Greville had gone jingling down the road in a hansom—
grey holland blinds and a pink rosebud in the driver's buttonhole. Why had he come? Going in and out of the weddings
a pale grey white-spatted guest, talking to every one . . . a
preoccupied piece of the West End. Large club windows
looking out on sunlit Piccadilly; a glimpse of the haze of the
Green Park. Weddings must be laughable to him with his
Mrs Caudle's Curtain Lectures ideas. His wife was dead. She
had been fearfully ill suddenly on their wedding tour . . . at
'Law*zanne*.' That was the wrong way to pronounce Lau-
sanne. And that wrong way of pronouncing was somehow
part of his way of thinking about her. He seemed to remember
nothing but her getting ill, and spoke with a sort of laughing,
contemptuous *fear*. Men.

But in some way he was connected with that strange thing
outside the everyday things.

How stupid of Eve to be vexed because she was told there
was no need to scrawl the addresses of the little cake boxes
right across the labels. Impossible now to ask her to come
and play song accompaniments. Besides, she was tired. Eve
was tired because she did not really know how glorious life
was. In her life with the Greens in Wiltshire there was
nothing besides the Greens but the beautiful landscape. And
the landscape seen from the Greens's windows must look commercial, in the end. Eve was evidently beginning to tire of it.
And they had worked so hard all the morning cutting up the
cake. Eve did not know that towards the end of the morning
she had thought of singing after lunch . . . feeling so strong
and wanting to make a noise. Bohm's songs. It was better
really to sing to one's own accompaniment; only there was no
one to listen. . . .

Und wenn i dann mal wie-ie-d-er *komm.*

a German girl, her face *strahlend mit Freude—radiant* with joy
. . . but *strahlend* was more than radiant . . . streaming—

like sunlight—shafts of sunlight. German women were not self-conscious. They were full of joy and sorrow. Perhaps *happier* than any other women. Their mountains and woods and villages and towns were beautiful with joy. They did not care what men thought or said. They were happy in their beautiful country in their own way. Germany . . . all washed with poetry and music and song. 'Freue dich des Lebens.' *Freue . . . Freue dich . . .* the words were like the rush of wings . . . the flutter of a fresh skirt round happy hurrying feet.

'What a melancholy ditty, chick.'

Miriam laughed and dropped into the accompaniment of Schubert's *Ave Maria*. 'Listen, mother . . . there was a monk who sang this so beautifully in a church that he had to be stopped.' She played through the *Ave Maria* and looked round. Mrs Henderson was sitting stiffly in a stiff straight chair with her hands twisted in her lap. 'Oh bother,' thought Miriam, 'she's feeling hysterical . . . and it's my turn this time. What on earth shall I do?' The word had come up through the years. Sarah had seen 'attacks of hysteria. . . .' Was she going to have one now . . . laugh and cry and say dreadful things and then be utterly exhausted? Good Lord, how fearful. And what was the good? She 'couldn't help it.' That was why you had to be firm with hysterical people. But there was no need, now. Everything was better. Two of them married; the boys ready to look after everything. It was simply irritating . . . and the sun just coming round into the green of the conservatory. . . .

She sat impatient, feeling young and strong and solid with joy, on the piano stool. Couldn't mother see her, sitting there in a sort of blaze of happy strength? She swung impatiently round to the keyboard and glanced at the open album. There was silence in the room. Her heart beat anxiously . . . some German printer had printed those notes . . . in pain and illness perhaps—but pain and illness in *Germany*, not in this

dreadful little room where despair was shut in. . . . *Comus*,
The Seven Ages of Man, *The Arctic Regions*, beautiful bindings
on the little old inlaid table, things belonging to those sunny
beginnings and ending with that awful agonized figure, sitting
there silent. She cleared her throat and stretched a hand out
over the notes of a chord without striking it. Something was
gaining on her. Something awful and horrible.

'Play something cheerful, chickie,' said her mother, in a
dreadful deep trembling voice. Suddenly Miriam knew, in
horror, that the voice wanted to scream, to bellow. Bellow
. . . that huge, tall woman striding about on the common at
Worthing . . . bellowing . . . mad—madness. She summoned,
desperately, something in herself, and played a thing she disliked, wondering why she chose it. Her hands played carefully, holding to the rhythm, carefully avoiding pressure and
emphasis. Nothing could happen as long as she could keep
on playing like that. It made the music seem like a third
person in the room. It was a new way of playing. She would
try it again when she was alone. It made the piece wonderful
. . . traceries of tone shaping themselves one after another,
intertwining, and stopping against the air . . . tendrils on a
sunlit wall. . . . She had a clear conviction of manhood . . .
that strange hard feeling that was always twining between her
and the things people wanted her to do and to be. Manhood
with something behind it that understood. This time it was
welcome. It served. She asserted it, sadly feeling it mould
the lines of her face.

The end of the piece was swift and tuneful and stormy, the
only part she had cared for hitherto. For a moment she was
tempted to dash into it . . . her hands were so able and strong,
so near to mastery of the piano after that curious careful playing. But it would be cruel. She passed on to the final chords
—broad and even and simple. They suggested quiet music
going on, playing itself in the room. Getting up beaming and
shy and embarrassed she did not dare to look at the waiting

figure, and looked busily into the dark interiors of the bowls and vases along the mantelpiece. . . . There was something in the waiting figure that did not want to scream. Something exactly like herself. . . . At the bottom of one of the deep bowls was a curling-pin. She giggled, catching her breath.

Mrs Henderson glanced up at her and looked away, looking about the room. That's naughty, thought Miriam. She's not trying; she's being naughty and tiresome. Perhaps she's angry with me, and thinks I mean she must just go on enduring.

'I can't correct a misprint with a curling-pin.'

Mother believed in the misprint. . . . Talk on about misprints . . . why was it necessary to be insincere if one wanted to make anything happen? But anything was better than saying, What is the matter? That would be just as insincere, and impudent too.

'These cheap things are always so badly printed.'

'Oh!' . . . Mother's polite tone, trying to be interested. That was all she'd had for years. All she'd ever had, from him. Miriam sat down conversationally, in a long chair. She felt a numb sleepiness coming over her, and stretched all her muscles lazily, to their full limit . . . mother, just mother in the room, perfect ease and security . . . and relaxed with a long yawn, feeling serenely awake. The little figure ceased to be horrible.

'My life has been so useless,' said Mrs Henderson suddenly.

Here it was . . . a jolt . . . an awful physical shock, jarring her body. . . . She braced herself and spoke quickly and blindly . . . a network of feeling vibrated all over to and fro, painfully.

'It only seems so to you,' she said, in a voice muffled by the beating of her heart. Anything might happen—she had no power. . . . Mother—almost killed by things she could not control, having done her duty all her life . . . doing thing after thing had not satisfied her . . . being happy and brave had not satisfied her. There was something she had always wanted, for herself . . . even mother. . . .

Mrs Henderson shuddered and sighed. Her pose relaxed a little.

'I might have done something for the poor.'

'Oh, yes? What things?' She had lived in a nightmare of ways and means, helpless. . . .

'I might have made clothes, sometimes. . . .'

'That worries you, so that you can hardly bear it.'

'Yes.'

'It needn't. I don't mean the poor need not be helped. But you needn't have that feeling.'

'You understand it?'

'I feel it this moment, as you feel it.'

'Well?'

'You needn't.'

Miriam held back her thoughts. Nothing mattered but to sit there holding back thought and feeling and argument, if only she could without getting angry. . . . There was something here, something decisive. This was what she had been born for, if only she could hold on. She felt very old. No more happiness . . . the little house they sat in was a mockery, a fiendish contrivance to hide agony. There was nothing in these little houses in themselves, just indifference hiding miseries.

She sat forward conversationally. A rain of tears was coming down her companion's cheeks. To hold on . . . hold on . . . not to think or feel glad or sorry . . . it would be impudent to feel anything . . . to hold on if the tears went on for an hour . . . treating them as if they were part of a conversation.

'You understand me?'

'Of course.'

'You are the only one.'

The relieved voice . . . steady, as she had known it correcting her in her babyhood.

'I should be better if I could be more with you . . .' oh Lord . . . impossible.

'You must be with me as much as you like.'

That was the thing. That was what must be done somehow.

'Mother! would you mind if I smoked a cigarette?'

It was suddenly possible, the unheard-of, unconfessed . . . suddenly easy and possible.

'My dearest child!' Mrs Henderson's flushed face crimsoned unresistingly. She was shocked and ashamed and half delighted. Miriam gazed boldly, admiring and adoring. She felt she had embarked on her first real flirtation, and blessed the impulse that had that morning transferred cigarettes and matches from her handbag to her hanging pocket, as a protection against suburban influence and a foretaste of her appointment with Bob. She lit a cigarette with downcast lids and a wicked smile, throwing a triumphant possessive glance at her mother as it drew. The cigarette was divine. It was divine to smoke like this, countenanced and beloved—scandalous and beloved.

Miriam ran all the way to the station. The gardens on either side of Gipsy Lane were full of flowering shrubs massed up against laburnum and red may trees in flower . . . fresh clean colours, pink and lilac and yellow and everywhere new bright fresh green . . . May. She flung herself into an empty carriage of the three o'clock Vauxhall and Waterloo train, her eyes filled with the maze of garden freshness, and was carried off along the edge of the common, streaming blazing green in the full sunlight, dotted with gorse. Bob would not have to wait at Waterloo. . . . Further down the line, towards Kew, was the mile of orchards, close on either side of the line, thick with bloom. . . . Walls and houses began to appear. She took her eyes from the window, and the gardens and the common and the imagined orchards passed before her eyes in the dusty enclosure. As she gazed they seemed to pass through her, the freshness of the blossoms backed by fresh greenery was a feeling, cool and fresh in her blood. The growing intensity of this feeling stirred her to movement and consciousness of the dust-filmed carriage, the smell of dust. Still again, the sight of the spring flowing from her eyes, into them, out through them, breathing with her breath, the feeling of spring in the soft beating from head to foot of her blood, was all there was, anywhere, out to the limits of space. The dusty carriage

was a speck in the great fresh tide, and the vision of Eve,
drifting in the carriage, in the corner, opposite, with pale
frightened face, saying the things she had said just now, was
no longer terrifying, though each thing she said came clearly,
a separate digging blow.

. . . 'Dr Ryman is giving her bromide . . . she can't sleep
without it.' Sleeplessness, insomnia . . . she can't see the
spring . . . why not? And forget about herself.

'It's nerves. He says we must behave as if there was
nothing wrong with her. There *is* nothing wrong but nerves.'

That fevered frame, the burning hands and burning eyes
looking at everything in the wrong way, the brain seeking
about, thinking first this and then that . . . nerves; and fat
Dr Ryman giving bromide . . . awful little bottles of bromide
coming to the house wrapped up in white paper. And every
one satisfied. 'She's in Dr Ryman's hands. Dr Ryman is
treating her.' Mrs Poole said Dr Ryman was a very able man.
What did she mean? How did she know? Suburban faces;
satisfied. 'In the doctor's hands.' A large square house, a
square garden, high walls, a delicate wife always being ill,
always going to that place in Germany—how did he know,
going about in a brougham—and he had gout . . . how did
he know more than any one else? . . . bottles of bromide,
visits, bills, and mother going patiently on, trusting and feeling
unhelped. Going on. People went . . . mad. If she could
not sleep she would go . . . *mad*. . . . And every one be-
having as if nothing were wrong.

And the vicar! Praying in the dining-room. Sarah had
heard. . . . The vicar, kneeling on the Turkey carpet . . .
praying. Couldn't God see her, on the carpet, praying and
trying? And the vicar went away. And things were the
same and that night she could not sleep, just the same. Of
course not. Nothing was changed. It was all going on for
her in some hot, wrong, shut-up way. Bromide and prayers.

And she blamed herself. If only she would not blame

herself. 'He 's one in a thousand . . . if only I could be as
calm and cool as he is.' Why not be calm and cool? She had
gone too far . . . 'the end of my tether' . . . mother, a clever
phrase like that, where had she got it? It was true. Her
suffering had taught her to find that awful phrase. She feared
her room, 'loathed' it. She, always gently scolding exaggeration, used and meant that violent word.

Money. That was why nothing had been done. 'The
doctor' had to be afforded as she was so ill, but nothing had
been done. Borrow from the boys to take her away. 'A
bright place and a cool breeze.' She dreamed of things—
faraway impossible things. Had she told the others she wanted
them? They must be told. To-morrow she should know
she was going away. Nothing else in life mattered. Someone must pay, any one. Newlands must go. To-morrow and
every day till they went away she should come round to Harriett's new house. Something for her to do every day.

The little bonneted figure . . . happy, shocked, smiling. To
go about with her, telling her everything, dreadful things.
The two of them going about and talking and not talking, and
going about.

Miriam moved uneasily to the mantelpiece. An unlit fire
was laid neatly in the grate. A ray of sunlight struck the black
bars of the grate; false uneasy sunlight. Two strange, round-
bowled, long-necked vases stood on the mantelpiece amongst
the litter of Bob's belongings. Dull blue and green enamel-
lings moving on a dark almost black background . . . strange
fine little threads of gold. . . . She peered at them.

'My dear girl, do you like my vases?' Bob came and stood
at her side.

'Yes—they 're funny and queer. I like them.'

'They 're clawzonny—Japanese clawzonny.' He took one

of them up and tapped it with his nail. It gave out a curious dull metallic ring. Miriam passed her finger over the enamelled surface. It was softly smooth and with no chill about it; as if the enamel were alive. She marvelled at the workmanship, wondering how the gold wires were introduced. They gleamed, veining over the curves of the vase.

Her uneasiness had gone. While they were looking at the vases it did not seem to matter that she had consented, defying the whole world, to come and see Bob's bachelor chambers. She did not like them and wanted to be gone. The curious dingy dustiness oppressed her, and there was an emptiness. Fancy having breakfast in a room like this. Who looked after a man's washing when he lived alone? There must be some dreadful sort of charwoman who came, and Bob had to speak kindly to her in his weary old voice, and go on day after day being here. But the vases stood there alive and beautiful and he liked them. She turned to see his liking in his face. As she turned his arm came round her shoulders and the angle of his shoulder softly touched her head. Behind her head there was a point of perfect rest; comfort, perfect. Australia; a young man in shirt-sleeves, toiling and dreaming. Was that there still in his face?

'Are you happy, dear girl? Do you like being with old Bob in his den?'

He came nearer and spoke with a soft husky whisper.

'Let me go,' said Miriam wearily, longing to rest, longing for the stairs they had come up and the open street in the sunshine and freedom.

She moved away and gathered up her gloves and scarf.

CHAPTER XI

MIRIAM sat with her mother near the bandstand. They faced the length of the esplanade with the row of houses that held their lodgings to their right and the sea away to the left. She had found that it was better to sit facing a moving vista; forms passing by too near to be looked at and people moving in the distance too far away to suggest anything. The bandstand had filled. The town-clock struck eleven. Presently the band would begin to play. Any minute now. It had begun. The introduction to its dreamiest waltz was murmuring in a conversational undertone. The stare of the esplanade rippled and broke. The idling visitors became vivid blottings. The house-rows stood out in lines and angles. The short solemn symphony was over. Full and soft and mellow, the euphonium began the beat of the waltz. It beat gently within the wooden kiosk. The fluted melody went out across the sea. The sparkling ripples rocked gently against the melody. A rousing theme would have been more welcome to the suffering at her side. She waited for the loud gay jerky tripping of the second movement. When it crashed brassily out the scene grew vivid. The air seemed to move; freshness of air and sea coming from the busy noise of the kiosk. The restless fingers ceased straying and plucking. The suffering had shifted. The night was over. When the waltz was over, they would be able to talk a little. There would be something . . . a goat-chaise; a pug with a solemn, injured face. Until the waltz came to an end, she turned towards the sea, wandering out over the gleaming ripples, hearing their soft sound, snuffing freshness, seeing the water just below her eyes, transparent green and blue and mauve, salt-filmed.

The big old woman's voice grated on about Poole's Miriorama. She had been a seven-mile walk before lunch and meant to go to Poole's Miriorama. She knew everything there was in it and went to it every summer, and for long walks, and washed lace in her room and borrowed an iron from Miss Meldrum. No one listened and her deep voice drowned all the sounds at the table. She only stopped at the beginning of a mouthful, or to clear her throat with a long harsh grating sound. She did not know that there was nothing wonderful about Poole's Miriorama or about walking every morning to the end of the parade and back. She did not know that there were wonderful things. She was like her father . . . she was mad. Miss Meldrum listened and answered without attending. The other people sat politely round the table and passed things with a great deal of stiff politeness. One or two of them talked suddenly, with raised voices. The others exclaimed. They were all in agreement . . . a young woman with a baritone voice . . . a frog, white, keeping alive in coal for hundreds of years . . . my cousin has crossed the Atlantic six times. . . . Nothing of any kind would ever stop them. They would never wait to know they were alive. They were mad. They would die mad. Of diseases with names. Even Miss Meldrum did not quite know. When she talked she was as mad as they were. When she was alone in her room and not thinking about ways and means, she read books of devotion and cried. If she had had a home and a family she would have urged her sons and daughters to get on and beat other people. . . . But she knew mother was different. All of them knew it in some way. They spoke to her now and again with deference, their faces flickering with beauty. They knew she was beautiful. Sunny and sweet and good, sitting there in her faded dress, her face shining with exhaustion.

They walked down the length of the pier, through the stiff breeze, arm in arm. The pavilion was gaslit, ready for the entertainment.

'Would you rather stay outside this afternoon?'

'No. Perhaps the entertainment may cheer me.'

There was a pink paper with their tickets: 'The South Coast Entertainment Company' . . . that was better than the usual concert. The inside of the pavilion was like the lunch table . . . the same people. But there was a yellow curtain across the platform. Mother could look at that. It was quite near them. It would take off the effect of the audience of people she envied. The cool sound of the waves flumping and washing against the pier came in through the open doors with a hollow echo. They were settled and safe for the afternoon. For two hours there would be nothing but the things behind the curtain. Then there would be tea. Mother had felt the yellow curtain. She was holding the pink programme at a distance trying to read it. Miriam glanced. The sight of the cheap black printing on the thin pink paper threatened the spell of the yellow curtain. She must manage to avoid reading it. She crossed her knees and stared at the curtain, yawning and scolding, with an affected manliness, about the forgotten spectacles. They squabbled and laughed. The flump-wash of the waves had a cheerful sunlit sound. Mrs Henderson made a brisk little movement of settling herself to attend. The doors were being closed. The sound of the waves was muffled. They were beating and washing outside in the sunlight. The gaslit interior was a pier pavilion. It was like the inside of a bathing-machine, gloomy, cool, sodden with sea-damp, a happy caravan. Outside was the blaze of the open day, pale and blinding. When they went out into it it would be a bright unlimited jewel, getting brighter and brighter, all its colours fresher and deeper until it turned to clear deep live opal and softened down and down to darkness dotted with little pin-like jewellings of light along the esplanade; the dark luminous waves washing against the black beach until dawn. . . . The curtain was drawing away from a painted spring scene . . . the fresh green of trees feathered up into a blue sky. There were boughs of apple-blossom. Bright green grass sprouted along the edge of a pathway. A woman floundered in from the side in a pink silk evening dress. She stood in the centre of the scene preparing to sing, rearing her gold-wigged head and smiling at the audience. Perhaps the players were not ready. It was a solo. She would get through it and then the play would begin. She smiled promisingly. She had bright large teeth and the kind of mouth that would say 'chahld' for 'child.' The orchestra played a few bars. She took a deep breath. 'Bring back—the yahs—that are—DEAD!' she screamed violently.

She was followed by two men in shabby tennis flannels, with little hard glazed tarpaulin hats, who asked each other riddles. Their jerky broken voices fell into cold space and echoed about the shabby pavilion. The scattered audience sat silent and still, listening for the voices . . . cabmen wrangling in a gutter. The green scene stared stiffly—harsh cardboard, thin harsh paint. The imagined scene moving and flowing in front of it was going on somewhere out in the world. The muffled waves sounded near and clear. The sunlight was dancing on them. When the men had scrambled away and the applause had died down, the sound of the waves brought dancing gliding figures across the stage, waving balancing arms and unconscious feet gliding and dreaming. A man was standing in the middle of the platform with a roll of music— bald-headed and grave and important. The orchestra played the overture to *The Harbour Bar*. But whilst he unrolled his music and cleared his throat his angry voice filled the pavilion: 'it's all your own fault . . . you get talking and gossiping and filling yer head with a lot of nonsense . . . now you needn't begin it all over again twisting and turning everything I say.' And no sound in the room but the sound of eating. His singing was pompous anger, appetite. Shame shone from his rim of hair. He was ashamed, but did not know that he showed it.

They could always walk home along the smooth grey warm esplanade to tea in an easy silence. The light blossoming from the horizon behind them was enough. Everything ahead dreamed in it, at peace. Visitors were streaming homewards along the parade, lit like flowers. Along the edge of the tide

the town children were paddling and shouting.   After tea they
would come out into the sheltering twilight, at peace, and stroll
up and down until it was time to go to the flying performance
of *The Pawnbroker's Daughter*.

They were late for tea and had it by themselves at a table
in the window of the little smoking-room looking out on the
garden.   Miss Meldrum called cheerily down through the
house to tell them, when they came in.   They went into the
little unknown room and the cook brought up a small silver
teapot and a bright cosy.   Outside was the stretch of lawn
where the group had been taken in the morning, last year.   It
had been a seaside town lawn, shabby and brown, with the
town behind it; unnoticed because the fresh open sea and sky
were waiting on the other side of the house . . . seaside town
gardens were not gardens . . . the small squares of greenery
were helpless against the bright sea . . . and even against shabby
rooms, when the sun came into the rooms off the sea . . . sea-
rooms. . . .   The little smoking-room was screened by the
shade of a tree against whose solid trunk half of the french
window was thrown back.
When the cook shut the door of the little room the house
disappeared.   The front rooms bathed in bright light and
hot with the afternoon heat, the wide afterglow along the front,
the vast open lid of the sky, were in another world. . . .
Miriam pushed back the other half of the window and they
sat down in a green twilight on the edge of the garden.   If
others had been there Mrs Henderson would have remarked
on the pleasantness of the situation and tried to respond to it
and been dreadfully downcast at her failure, and brave.   Miriam
held her breath as they settled themselves.   No remark came.
The secret was safe.   When she lifted the cosy the little teapot shone silver-white in the strange light.   A thick grey
screen of sky must be there, above the trees, for the garden
was an intensity of deep brilliance, deep bright green, and
calceolarias and geraniums and lobelias, shining in a brilliant

gloom. It was not a seaside garden . . . it was a garden . . . all gardens. They took their meal quietly and slowly, speaking in low tones. The silent motionless brilliance was a guest at their feast. The meal-time, so terrible in the hopelessness of home, such an effort in the mocking glare of the boarding-house, was a great adventure. Mrs Henderson ate almost half as much as Miriam, serenely. Miriam felt that a new world might be opening.

'The storm has cleared the air wonderfully.'

'Yes; isn't it a blessing.'

'Perhaps I shan't want the beef-tea to-night.' Miriam hung up her dress in the cupboard, listening to the serene tone. The dreadful candle was flickering in the night-filled room, but mother was quietly making a supreme effort.

'I don't expect you will'; she said casually from the cup-board, 'it's ready if you should want it. But you won't want it.'

'It *is* jolly and fresh,' she said a moment later from the window, holding back the blind. Perhaps in a few days it would be the real jolly seaside and she would be young again, staying there alone with mother, just ridiculous and absurd and frantically happy, mother getting better and better, turning into the fat happy little thing she ought to be, and they would get to know people and mother would have to look after her, and love her high spirits, and admire and scold her and be shocked, as she used to be. They might even bathe. It would be heavenly to be really at the seaside with just mother. They would be idiotic.

Mrs Henderson lay very still as Miriam painted the acid above the unseen nerve centres, and composed herself after-wards quietly without speaking. The air was fresh in the room. The fumes of the acid did not seem so dreadful to-night.

The pawnbroker's daughter was with them in the room, cheering them. The gay young man had found out somehow, through her, that 'goodness and truth' were the heart of his life. She had not told him. It was he who had found it out. He had found the words and she did not want him to say them. But it was a new life for them both, a new life for him and happiness for her even if he did not come back, if she could forget the words.

Putting out the candle at her bedside suddenly and quietly with the match-box to avoid the dreadful puff that would tell her mother of night, Miriam lay down. The extinguished light splintered in the darkness before her eyes. The room seemed suddenly hot. Her limbs ached, her nerves blazed with fatigue. She had never felt this kind of tiredness before. She lay still in the darkness with open eyes. Mrs Henderson was breathing quietly, as if in a heavy sleep. She was not asleep but she was trying to sleep. Miriam lay watching the pawnbroker's daughter in the little room at the back of the shop, in the shop, back again in the little room, coming and going. There was a shining on her face and on her hair. Miriam watched until she fell asleep.

She dreamed she was in the small music-room in the old Putney school, hovering invisible. Lilla was practising alone at the piano. Sounds of the girls playing rounders came up from the garden. Lilla was sitting in her brown merino dress, her black curls shut down like a little cowl over her head and neck. Her bent profile was stern and manly, her eyes and her bare white forehead manly and unconscious. Her lissome brown hands played steadily and vigorously. Miriam listened incredulous at the certainty with which she played out her sadness and her belief. It shocked her that Lilla should know so deeply and express her lonely knowledge so ardently. Her gold-flecked brown eyes, that commonly laughed at everything, except the problem of free-will, and refused questions, had as much sorrow and certainty as she had herself. She and Lilla were one person, the same person. Deep down in every one was sorrow and certainty. A faint resentment filled her. She turned away to go down into the garden. The scene slid into the large music-room. It was full of seated forms. Lilla was at the piano, her foot on the low pedal, her hands raised for a crashing chord. They came down, collapsing faintly on a blur of wrong notes. Miriam rejoiced in her heart. What a fiend I am . . . what a fiend, she murmured, her heart hammering condemnation. Someone was sighing harshly; to be heard; in the darkness; not far off; fully conscious she glanced at the blind. It was dark. The moon was not round. It was about midnight. Her face and eyes felt thick with sleep. The air was rich with sleep. Her body was heavy with a richness of sleep and fatigue. In a moment she could be gone again. . . . 'Shall I get the beef-tea, mother?' . . . she heard herself say in a thin wideawake voice. 'Oh no, my dear,' sounded another voice patiently. Rearing her numb consciousness against a delicious tide of oncoming sleep, she threw off the bed-clothes and stumbled to the floor. 'You can't go on like this night after night, my dear,' 'Yes I can,' said Miriam in a tremulous faint tone. The sleepless even voice reverberated again in the unbroken sleeplessness of the room. 'It's no use . . . I am cumbering the ground.' The words struck, sending a heat of anger and resentment through Miriam's shivering form. She spoke sharply, groping for the matches.

Hurrying across the cold stone floor of the kitchen, she lit the gas from her candle. Beetles ran away into corners, crackling sickeningly under the fender. A mouse darted along the dresser. She braced herself to the sight of the familiar saucepan, Miss Meldrum's good beef-tea, brown against the white enamel—helpless. . . . Waiting for the beef-tea to get hot, she ate a biscuit. There was help somewhere. All those people sleeping quietly upstairs. If she asked them to help, they would be surprised and kind. They would suggest rousing her and getting her to make efforts. They would speak in rallying voices, like Dr Ryman and Mrs Skrine. For a day or two it would be better and then much worse and she would have to go away. Where? It would be the same everywhere. There was no one in the world who could help. There was something . . . if she could leave off worrying. But that had been pater's advice, all his life, and it had not helped. It was something more than leaving off . . . it was something real. It was not affection and sympathy. Eve gave them; so easily, but they were not big enough. They did not come near enough. There was something crafty and worldly about them. They made a sort of prison. There was something true and real somewhere. Mother knew it. She had learned how useless even the good kind people were, and was alone, battling to get at something. If only she could get at it and rest in it. It was there, everywhere. It was here in the kitchen, in the steam rising from the hot beef-tea. A moon-ray came through the barred window as she turned down the gas. It was clear in the eye of the moon-ray; a real thing.

Some instinct led away from the New Testament. It seemed impossible to-night. Without consulting her listener, Miriam read a psalm. Mrs Henderson put down her cup and asked her to read it again. She read and fluttered pages quietly to tell the listener that in a moment there would be some more. Mrs Henderson waited, saying nothing. She always sighed regretfully over the gospels and St Paul, though she asked for them and seemed to think she ought to read them. They were so dreadful; the gospels full of social incidents and reproachfulness. They seemed to reproach every one and to hint at a secret that no one possessed . . . the epistles did nothing but nag and threaten and probe. St Paul rhapsodized sometimes . . . but in a superior way . . . patronizing; as if no one but himself knew anything. . . .

'How beautiful upon the mountains are the feet of those who bring' she read evenly and slowly. Mrs Henderson sighed quietly. . . . 'That's Isaiah, mother. . . . Isaiah is a beautiful name.' . . . She read on. Something had shifted. There was something in the room. . . . If she could go droning on and on in an even tone, it would be there more and more. She read on till the words flowed together and her droning voice was thick with sleep. The town clock struck two. A quiet voice from the other bed brought the reading to an end. Sleep was in the room now. She felt sure of it. She lay down leaving the candle alight and holding her eyes open. As long as the candle was alight the substance of her reading remained. When it was out there would be the challenge of silence again in the darkness . . . perhaps not; perhaps it would still be there when the little hot point of light had gone. There was a soft sound somewhere . . . the sea. The tide was up, washing softly. That would do. The sound of it would be clearer when the light was out . . . drowsy, lazy, just moving, washing the edge of the beach . . . cool, fresh. Leaning over she dabbed the candle noiselessly and sank back asleep before her head reached the pillow.

In the room yellow with daylight a voice was muttering rapidly, rapid words and chuckling laughter and stillness. Miriam grasped the bedclothes and lay rigid. Something in her fled out and away, refusing. But from end to end of the world there was no help against this. It was a truth; triumphing over everything. '*I* know,' said a high clear voice. '*I* know . . . I don't deceive myself' . . . rapid low muttering and laughter. . . . It was a conversation. Somewhere within it was the answer. Nowhere else in the world. Forcing herself to be still, she accepted the sounds, pitting herself against the sense of destruction. The sound of violent lurching brought her panic. There was something there that would strike. Hardly knowing what she did, she pretended to wake with a long loud yawn. Her body shivered, bathed in perspiration. 'What a lovely morning,' she said dreamily, 'what a perfect morning.' Not daring to sit up, she reached for her watch. Five o'clock. Three more hours before the day began. The other bed was still. 'It's going to be a magnificent day,' she murmured, pretending to stretch and yawn again. A sigh reached her. The stillness went on and she lay for an hour tense and listening. Something must be done to-day. Someone else must know. . . . At the end of an hour a descending darkness took her suddenly. She woke from it to the sound of violent language, furniture being roughly moved, a swift angry splashing of water . . . something breaking out, breaking through the confinements of this little furniture-filled room . . . the best, gentlest thing she knew in the world, openly despairing at last.

The old homœopathist at the other end of the town talked quietly on . . . the afternoon light shone on his long white hair . . . the principle of health, God-given health, governing life. To be well one must trust in it absolutely. One must practise trusting in God every day. . . . The patient grew calm, quietly listening and accepting everything he said, agreeing again and again. Miriam sat wondering impatiently why they could not stay. Here in this quiet place with this quiet old man, the only place in the world where any one had seemed partly to understand, mother might get better. He could help. He knew what the world was like and that nobody understood. He must know that he ought to keep her. But he did not seem to want to do anything but advise them and send them away. She hated him, his serene, white-haired, pink-faced old age. He told them he was seventy-nine and had never taken a dose in his life. Leaving his patient to sip a glass of water into which he had measured drops of tincture, he took Miriam to look at the greenhouse behind his consulting-room. As soon as they were alone he told her, speaking quickly and without benevolence, and in the voice of a younger man, that she must summon help, a trained attendant. There ought to be someone for night and day. He seemed to know exactly the way in which she had been taxed and spoke of her youth. It is very wrong for you to be alone with her, he added gravely.

Vaguely, burning with shame at the confession, she explained that it could not be afforded. He listened attentively and repeated that it was absolutely necessary. She felt angrily for words to explain the uselessness of attendants. She was sure he must know this and wanted to demand that he should help, then and there, at once, with his quiet house and his knowledge. Her eye covered him. He was only a pious old man, with artificial teeth making him speak with a sort of sibilant woolliness. Perhaps he too knew that in the end even this would fail. He made her promise to write for help and refused a fee. She hesitated helplessly, feeling the burden settle. He indicated that he had said his say and they went back.

On the way home they talked of the old man. 'He is right; but it is too late,' said Mrs Henderson with clear quiet bitterness, 'God has deserted me.' They walked on, tiny figures in a world of huge grey-stone houses. 'He will not let me sleep. He does not want me to sleep. . . . He does not care.'

A thought touched Miriam, touched and flashed. She grasped at it to hold and speak it, but it passed off into the world of grey houses. Her cheeks felt hollow, her feet heavy. She summoned her strength, but her body seemed outside her, empty, pacing forward in a world full of perfect unanswering silence.

The bony old woman held Miriam clasped closely in her arms. 'You must never, as long as you live, blame yourself, my gurl.' She went away. Miriam had not heard her come in. The pressure of her arms and her huge body came from far away. Miriam clasped her hands together. She could not feel them. Perhaps she had dreamed that the old woman had come in and said that. Everything was dream; the world. I shall not have any life. I can never have any life; all my days. There were cold tears running into her mouth. They had no salt. Cold water. They stopped. Moving her body with slow difficulty against the unsupporting air, she looked slowly about. It was so difficult to move. Everything was airy and transparent. Her heavy hot light impalpable body was the only solid thing in the world, weighing tons; and like a lifeless feather. There was a tray of plates of fish and fruit on the table. She looked at it, heaving with sickness and looking at it. I am hungry. Sitting down near it she tried to pull the tray. It would not move. I must eat the food. Go on eating food, till the end of my life. Plates of food like these plates of food. . . . I am in eternity . . . where their worm dieth not and their fire is not quenched.

END OF VOLUME ONE